DEC 0 9 2002

THE
PRINCE
OF
DEADLY
WEAPONS

ALSO BY BOSTON TERAN

Never Count Out the Dead
God Is a Bullet

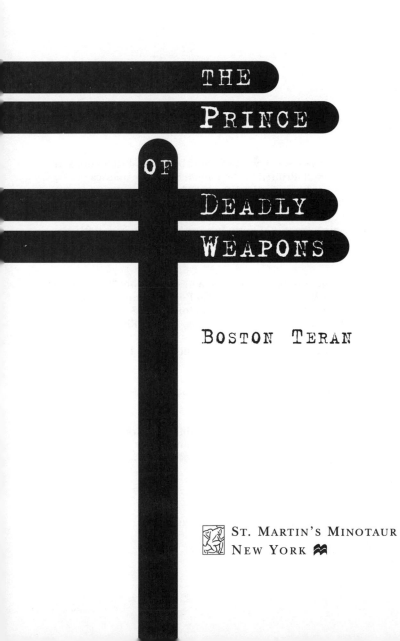

THE
PRINCE
OF
DEADLY
WEAPONS

BOSTON TERAN

ST. MARTIN'S MINOTAUR
NEW YORK

www.minotaurbooks.com

Grateful acknowledgment is made to reprint an excerpt from "Comfortably Numb." Lyrics by Roger Waters. Copyright 2000 Roger Waters Music Overseas Ltd. Warner/Chappell Artemis Music Ltd. London W6 8BS. Reproduced by permission of International Music Publications, Ltd. All Rights Reserved

Library of Congress Cataloging-in-Publication Data

Teran, Boston.
    The prince of deadly weapons : a novel / Boston Teran.—1st ed.
      p. cm.
    ISBN 0-312-27118-2
    1. Cornea—Transplantation—Fiction.   2. California, Northern—Fiction.
3. Money Laundering—Fiction.   4. Diamond Smuggling—Fiction.   I. Title.

PS3570.E674 P74   2002
813'.54—dc21

                                                     2002069839

First Edition: November 2002

10 9 8 7 6 5 4 3 2 1

DEDICATED TO

THE BIG D
For the flight over that labyrinth of a Delta
Don't fly too high – Don't fly too low
–If only–

ACKNOWLEDGMENTS

I want to thank John Cunningham of St. Martin's Minotaur for having faith. Kelley Ragland of St. Martin's Minotaur for keeping it all beautifully in perspective. Mari Evans of MacMillan for being smartly steady. And my agent, David Hale Smith, of DHS Literary, and Seth Robertson of DHS Literary.

On a personal note: as always, to Deirdre Stephanie and the late great Brutarian . . . to Mz El . . . to G.G. and L.S. . . . to Harriett Bara who has made an art form out of cleaning up my act . . . to Janet Wade for her music clearance . . . and to the late Ralph J. Hallman, Chairman, Social Science Department, Pasadena City College, for his richly observed study of alienation and tragedy, *Psychology of Literature*.

It is the Minotaur who conclusively justifies the existence of the labyrinth.

—Jorge Luis Borges

The pilgrim entered the cathedral . . . walked a short distance . . . and found himself at the entrance to a large labyrinth on the floor. Starting from the west, from the direction of the setting sun, the place of death, he walked through the labyrinth's winding pathways. . . .

—Helmut Jaskolski,
*The Labyrinth: Symbol of Fear,
Rebirth, and Liberation*

AFTER THE MURDERS

DANE RUDD APPROACHED Rio Vista out of an unending dusk. The sky was a distant and seething reef of branded reds. With just his battered leather suitcase and a name, Dane Rudd's whole life now rested in a set of eyes borrowed from the dead.

The shadow of earlier times moved across the California landscape. Some believe life should be viewed as a sacred loan, and what we leave behind measures the meaning of our days. With that in mind Dane Rudd continued on through a purpling flat of miles but he also understood that within every act of charity may lie the heart of an executioner.

PAUL CARUSO was on hands and knees in the back of his hangar at the Rio Vista, California, Airport. He should have been fixing the fuel line on his Navion. He should have been at his restaurant helping the old lady with the shift close and serving bar. He should have been doing a lot of things, but what he was doing was trying to get at a six-week-old kitten shacked up inside the wall where a configuration of pipes led through to the outside. He was wearing a leather glove and pleading with the little bastard to "come on out" when a shadow moved across the open hangar door.

He looked up. His gray hair and hammered down Roman nose were streaked with grease. Sunset came red hard through the open hangar door so that the man standing there seemed not much more than a forged silhouette.

"Paul Caruso?"

Caruso stood. The voice was unusually deep and raspy. "Can I help you?" Paul asked.

"I was at the airport restaurant looking for a pilot to take me up to see the Delta, and the woman at the bar . . . your wife, I believe, said I should talk to you."

Caruso came around the Navion to get a better view of the man. It turned out he was young, maybe twenty-five. He wore a faded leather coat and sunglasses with gray-black lenses and what little bit of eye Caruso could see behind them looked almost fluid. The young man glanced at the huge leather glove on Caruso's right hand.

"A goddamn kitten took to living in the wall. I been feedin' her milk, though I don't know why in Christ I'm wastin' the time. She's got this infection in her paw and I was trying to catch her and get her to a vet."

To the young man that glove looked like something more suited for snagging a lion. "It appears you have a real man eater hiding there."

Caruso's heavily pockmarked face spread out in a smile and a set of teeth that had seen way too much bad work on them broke through. "I got a Cessna outside I can take you up in. And I got time tomorrow after—"

"I'd like to go up now, if possible."

"It's almost sunset. We wouldn't have—"

"But that's part of what I want to see. The sunset."

Caruso slid off the glove, walked over to his workbench. He took a rag and got to cleaning away spots of grease that ran up his arm. All the while he watched this young man, who stood waiting with a kind of stoic grace, and never once moved.

"Sunset, hunh?"

"Mr. Caruso, for the last two years I have been legally . . . blind. I got my vision back thanks to a transplant, and that just recently. There's a lot I need to see."

The young man's response left Paul unable to jumpstart the next moment of conversation so he reached for a cigarette. He

4

slipped it into his mouth with a half filthy hand, then said, "What's your name?"

"Rudd . . . Dane Rudd."

Paul found a wooden match in his tool case. He struck it across the underbelly of that workbench and a sparkline of sulfur fell to the floor. "All right, Mr. Dane Rudd . . . let's go on up and chase that sunset."

DANE FOLLOWED Paul Caruso through the unwavering heat that came up from the tarmac. Among the tie-downs was a sea-plane. The Cessna was up on floats with castered nose gear and wheels. Dane looked the plane over. "Takes off from land or water?"

"Either one," said Caruso. "Takeoffs and landings. I do some search and rescue. Mostly boater fuck-ups in the summer. And when the old lady and me need to get away we fly up to the lakes."

As Paul began to undo the tie-down chains connected to the wing spar and tail he told Dane Rudd, "I can't stay up long. There's a memorial tonight I have to attend in Sacramento for a young man who—"

"It wouldn't be the Taylor Greene memorial, would it?"

Caruso just stood there, his expression candid disbelief. "Yeah, it would."

Dane Rudd walked past him, then past the hot red painted letters along the Cessna's nose that read THE BIG D. He slid under the wing and came up beyond it. "I'm here for the same memorial."

JUNE 2000

BEFORE THE MURDERS

CHAPTER ONE

ON THE BUREAU by the window was William Reynolds' wallet and a gun. Life boned down to its tragic simplicity. His features in the motel room window formed a brotherhood of lines and cracks men in their late forties begin to have in common, when all the systematic codes they've built their lives around prove to be irreconcilable with living.

He had always made it his business in these situations not to think about the confusion of sacrifice and family, not to dwell on the tenuous truce between happiness and honor. He closed his mind to the stomach-wrenching memories of a wife and child lost to him and focused instead on that stretch of Route 166 coming toward him out of a rugged California emptiness.

WHEN TOMMY Fenn's Super Cub cleared the Calientes his younger brother Shane worked up a twelve-gauge like some magic wand as if he caused the lights of Cayuma to break about two miles out. Shane yelled over the drone of the Piper's single propeller, "A little magic from the doomslinger!"

Tommy nodded. They followed Route 166 for about another mile as it bore on toward town. Shane got that shotgun good and packed. "I hope this guy's alone."

Tommy's voice was pitched for a fight, "I'll bet I can tell you what the fuck he's hoping."

Shane's mouth moved in agreement. He kept pressing shells

into the chamber then yelled again to his brother, "Maybe we should save one of these for Taylor!"

"That pussy deserves a little taste of moral outrage."

Aσ HEADLIGHTS breached the distance the phantoms of William Reynolds' life disappeared. The vehicle was coming on fast but when it cleared the gas station lights William could see it was a semi hauling cattle.

The metal truck swayed with the crosscut wind and that juggernaut of steel slatting banged and shuttered and the high-set monster eyes satellited past the motel and empty coffee shop and on toward Bakersfield, leaving nothing but a thin wake in the dust that had collected on the road and a growing silence.

The road silence grew around and within him, but he remained on guard close to the corner of the window, peering from the dark into the dark. As time crept on moisture began to collect along the bone line above his eyebrows. It was that age-old testimony that you are never much beyond what might, and could, go wrong.

In the provence of those minutes William found himself reaching for his cellular phone. As it rang he kept vigil over that moonlit run of ground from where this Taylor Greene might come. Then, he heard his voice, he heard himself say, "I called because I needed to talk to someone, but . . . but no one is there. And I just needed to say it . . . I'm more afraid of being alone, than of dying."

Uσing THE lights of the Buckhorn Café and the motel behind it as markers Tommy banked the Piper hard to the south. Cayuma was a desolate patch of frontage that went about a hundred yards back from the highway. Beyond it were sage fields and ravines, then a brace of harshly sloping hills. Beyond the hills there were long stretches of recently furrowed ground and traces of flat hard sand where more than one son of a bitch had made a night landing for fun, or profit . . . or out of sheer desperation.

The first line of scarred hill tips that the Super Cub cleared south of Cayuma killed all ground light and then Tommy began to nose her down. Before them was a long pool of night and earth. They had flown into this valley the day before, scoping out a strip where they might safely land and then get away unnoticed after the killing.

The descent was quick. Their faces mooncolored in the glass as the night and earth took on tones and shapes. Their features showed the perilous bravado of youth as the tires first scored ground that rose too quickly to meet them.

Their buckled down images were a narrative of dire invincibility as the plane shuddered then lipped left as the tail rose and for one instant a sensation went through both brothers that they would tip over. But they held on with an alien intensity until the earth went soft, and the plane came to a quick and violent stop.

WILLIAM BEGAN to tire, and all those physical disagreements when a man has outrun his strength had begun to play havoc with his nervous system.

Maybe the Greene kid wasn't coming. Maybe this was gonna turn out to be a no-show thanks to some mind-smearing second thoughts.

If he could just get a couple of hours alone with him, William knew he could turn that young man into an emotional liquidation sale. He would have him spewing out everything from the monstrous secrets he might have hidden away to the most trivial memories.

Then he was hit by a shotgun thought that made him turn on the light to find his cigarettes. What if someone had found out about the meeting?

TOMMY AND Shane did a ghost crawl under the barbed wire separating Cayuma from the sage backdrop that stretched all the way to the hills. They worked the dark to a lineup of Dumpsters not forty yards from the motel.

It didn't take them long to make out which was Reynolds' cabin. There were only twelve. They were set back from the Buckhorn in three rows of four. His was in the last row, and on the side farthest west. It sat a little away from the others, as if it had at one time been a storage shed or caretaker's room. From there any car coming off the highway, either east or west, and into the Buckhorn lot could be watched.

They had spotted Reynolds when he turned on the light for those few moments it took to find his cigarettes. The light was off now.

The brothers stared at that red clapboard shack the dust and sun had turned to the color of rust. They were both sitting on the same anxious question: What if Reynolds had broken his word to Taylor—and he wasn't alone?

LOOKING OUT the motel window William, for a moment, drifted on what might be called a thought, that had of late unmasked itself. He could see it there in the tired sorrow around the eyes. Could feel its deep bitters in the anonymous reaches of his soul. It was powerful and perplexing and simply this: Given some chance to remanufacture life, would he again stumble into the same mistakes like some—

An explosion of light blew through the glass like a violent passionflower. The right side of his face felt as if it were engulfed in flames. He was rocked back into the stale, dark room. His reflexes became bursts of chaotic overdrive reaching for his weapon which eluded him.

Across some great distance a door was blown open and from the black depths of the room came a shocking jolt that lifted him over a chair and into the bathroom where the cold tiles hit flush against him. He tried to crawl but every terrible burst of gunfire tore him apart until he could move no more, until he was just a piece of naked, raw flesh being destroyed.

And then the firing stopped and he thought he heard boots on wood running, and chalk shrill screams, and voices, weak but human say—say—say what—

Everything about him felt of blood and its terrible meaning began to engulf him in silence. It spread like some great channel of water until all that had been him, all that he could name and feel and see and remember, was gone.

CHAPTER TWO

TAYLOR WAITED IN his little house that overlooked a lazy stretch of Disappointment Slough. Paralyzed by feelings of apprehension he sat at his desk before the living room window. The room was streaked with moonlight reflecting off the water. He stared into the waving shadows that seemed to bend with the slow-moving current.

Taylor found himself again staring at the newspaper, the determination of some will drawing his pallid eyes to that single column in the *Sacramento Bee*:

> CAYUMA, CALIFORNIA—A Federal Reserve officer from the Los Angeles branch was murdered on Monday, shot-gunned to death at a motel just east of town, authorities said.
>
> William Dean Reynolds had just begun a two-week vacation and was on his way to visit friends in Morro Bay. Authorities believe the 51-year-old investigating agent was the victim of an attempted robbery, but are looking into the possibility this homicide may be connected to past or recent investigations—

Taylor couldn't read on. He closed his eyes and prayed Reynolds had kept his word and told no one else about their meeting. Fear held tightly around Taylor's throat. He looked at the near corner of his desk, at the picture of his father, with his dark movie theater looks and faulted powers.

For certain men, taking measure of another is a fixed science. They move through the labyrinthine turns our characters take with a soldier's steady march till they reach the spot where life is compromised. Taylor had always wondered if he was one of those men who could become victim to a threat, who would fall from the cliffs of courage to his death, thanks to a few well-placed words.

How easy it had been for Charles to compromise him. He'd done it right there at the bank, with its silent lovely sunlight and those expensive celebrity guitars that Charles collected, lining the walls of his office like victory shields. Charles was a perfect part of the dream that enemies are made from. As much as Taylor's father was.

Taylor had looked at Essie's picture on the far corner of Charles' desk. That's all Charles really needed. He'd had someone break into the house, probably one of the Fenn Brothers, and steal the photo.

Charles stood, using as backdrop a ground-to-ceiling plateglass window where Taylor could see boats moving up the Sacramento toward the channel ways of the Delta. He stood and the light around his back from the window obscured his face, but not the photo he took from a drawer and placed on the desk in the tide of his rising shadow as he'd said to Taylor: "Any calls for help are made from here."

Taylor told himself he was now unfit for human consumption. He'd left his conscience at the door, like an umbrella or a pair of shoes, to be retrieved as needed. That such a transparent idea should be so humanly popular turned his stomach. *Later*, he should have remembered, always left the party of your life long before you knew it.

Taylor was twenty-six years old. Because of what he'd tried and failed, because he was afraid they would kill Essie, he would be twenty-six forever. His life would be a perfect metaphor to the notion of all that laundered money can buy.

Tall willows on the shore brushed against the windy California sky as a thought climbed out of a small hole in Taylor's consciousness. Could he somehow be born again, in the quiet safety of somewhere else, where the rope of his past did not get to strangle him.

From trickery to truth, and back again, as the magicians say. He could take money, leave and change his name. Travel and change it again. Dissolve and materialize through a succession of beings until he was lost in some dreamy, distant reality.

Then his breathing went stiff as he remembered reading about those people who disappeared only to turn up years later, to be discovered with new names but the same old lives.

What difference? He was now a futile gesture entrusted to a body. He thought about killing himself. From his desk drawer he took a plastic vitamin case. He opened it. There were enough Percodan and Valium to gamble on.

He could hear a boat coming up the slough. The engine had a lazy, smooth cadence but it frightened him nonetheless, until he heard laughing on board and saw the reefy outline of partyers on the lamplit deck of a cabin cruiser moving up the channel toward Bishop's Cut.

He swallowed one Valium and a Percodan. He felt thorny projections behind his eyes and wished his mother was still alive.

He walked out of the house and stood on the scarred wooden dock. He looked out from his small island in Disappointment Slough toward the levee road that ran along the berm of Empire Tract. It was a dry black Delta night. He squatted and searched for his face in the water. He stared into his own eyes. They were dark and more mysterious there in the water.

"Hello, you ghost," he said.

The water made his face seem to nod back at him.

"We have our secrets, don't we."

CHAPTER THREE

ESSIE LAW LAY in bed, but sleep was a struggle. She could still feel Taylor's voice, swamped as it was with pain and despair. She had told him she'd come over, if he wanted, but Taylor was adamant that she stay away.

Her body grumbled something that left her unsettled and made a drink mandatory. She leaned against the balcony railing of her second story walk-up. The Walnut Grove street she lived on was little more than an alley half a block from River Road. Taylor, she knew, was not like most men. He was more prone to hurt himself, rather than others.

DAMON ROMERO and his date were on their fourth drink at the St. Francis Club when he quietly and subtly let a slip of hand take that short run up the back of the lady's neck. It was the perfect blend of feeling, grace and fiction as he said: "Let's go put the top down and ride."

EsSIE GLANCED at the open balcony door. Her phone sat waiting on the desk. Maybe she would try and coax Taylor into letting her come over. She got as far as the threshold before the dreaded hell of a question hit her: Why should she have to coax anyone, someone, Taylor away from despair and pain? Why couldn't someone, anyone, Taylor just want her help, just ask for her help?

She fell back into watching the street, where people talked in flimsily lit doorways. And where from washed-out storefront curtains music softly came. She followed couples as they coursed the shadows heart-deep into themselves and on toward the river. But something in Taylor's voice just wouldn't shake loose.

IT WAS a perfect night to drive with the top down. The water of Disappointment Slough sparkled with small crystal starfires of sky. The woman stretched her head back and let the wind have at her throat and chestbone.

Damon Romero ran his strong flat hand along the woman's leg. Each stroke across the sheer skirt fabric rose a little higher, teased her a little more. Then, when he could sense her muscles ease toward him, he let his hand drift back, becoming almost invisible to feel.

"Why don't we find a place to stop," he said.

She turned to him and one silent eyebrow rose asking what he had in mind.

IN THE twelve miles it took for Essie to travel from her walk-up to Disappointment Slough the fabric of her feelings tore apart and came together endless times.

She wanted to go where she felt she was needed, but she wanted to go back because she felt she was not needed enough to be asked. The simple act of asking meant that much to her, and in some small way she was ashamed.

Life was such an incurable exercise. It wreaked havoc on the heart and turned all the mind's disciplines about how to act into so much infinitesimal drama.

THEY DANCED in the darkness to the car stereo. They danced in the mottled wet shore tide, barefoot and slow. The scents of night were heavy as musk and the long flat distance of Disappointment Slough was spotted by a few lights that seemed to belong to nothing but black space.

The woman was breathing into Damon Romero's chest when a harsh pop rode the water from one berm to another.

He stood back and looked down at her. "Did that sound like a gunshot?"

ESSIE PULLED off the road, drove down toward the landing. Taylor's car was parked in its usual place, on a breach of cleared ground just back of the sloping berm.

She still had misgivings, murky breaks of confidence, as she stepped into the humid quiet of evening. She talked herself through these misgivings. She would not let the mere confusion of need or happiness dictate to her.

Through the trees, she could vaguely make out the lights of his house. And the front door, it seemed to be open. His boat was moored up at the dock. At least, Taylor was home.

She reached for her cellular. She would not settle for pureblind silence even if it meant the calamity she feared most.

His phone rang.

The calamity of being alone. Truth, come dressed as thyself. One of her stepfather's favorite phrases.

Taylor's machine kicked in.

She had not pressed him hard for fear he would—

A rucksack noise brought her head around fast. Through the rushes came a man. Momentarily frightened Essie stepped back toward her car as the man said, "Did you hear a shot?"

Essie saw his pants were rolled up to the knee, his legs wet. A moment more and a woman pushed through the reeds beside him. "What?"

"It sounded like a shot. From there." He pointed into the slough, at Taylor's house and the lights.

The woman started for the edge of the berm. Romero yelled, "Be careful!"

"What are you talking about?" asked Essie.

"We heard a gunshot."

"It sounded like a shot," said the woman. She was squinting at the house. "How well can either of you see?" She waved. "Look. Look here!"

Essie crowded up beside her. So did Romero.

"In the doorway. In the doorway!" yelled the woman.

From the berm Essie now saw a shape awkwardly slumping across the doorway's yellow light. She screamed into the phone. "Taylor, if you're there—" The tape was now just that dead space after the perfunctory greeting. "Please. I'm across at the landing. Taylor!"

Romero kept repeating, "Is that a body?"

"Taylor, goddamn it."

"Maybe we should call—"

Essie felt she was absolutely falling into some kind of death. She forced the phone into Romero's hands. "Call for help. Call the—" She was running down the berm, trying to get her boots off as she went.

The woman followed. "What are you doing?"

Stripping down to bra and panties, Essie charged the water. It hit her chest like cold cement. From the shoreline to the island was almost one hundred yards.

Her arms flung out wildly. Her head snapped at the air for breath. She wasn't halfway when both legs began to bend with cramps.

Essie had to close down to keep going, to separate from the cross weight of pain along her back and the stomach sickening contractions. She shut her eyes.

Her world was now a dark narrow funnel no larger than a candle flame. A piece of pitch dark space that spread throughout her, that filled her, as if it were air and had the power to hold her up. She could feel being outside herself. It was someone else whose arms were knifing at the water, someone else whose breath came in short—

Her head hit the dock. She came out of the water bleeding and groggy. Racing up the slate steps toward the one-story bungalow her wet feet slipped out from under her. When she landed her wrist was caught between her hip and the step railing. The wrist broke.

She carried her forearm in her other hand as she made her way up through a maze of trees toward the front door. And there, lying in the yellow light of that threshold was Taylor, a gun in his left hand. He sat in his own blood. It had leaked its way down through his shirt and pants from a wound just under the heart.

She knelt beside the body, in Taylor's blood. She pressed her hand against his chest to feel if he still had a pulse. His white face didn't move when she called to him. There was nothing in the closed eyes that registered he heard her shivering pleas. But behind the cold, blood smeared shirtcloth there was a pulse.

CHAPTER FOUR

Roy PINTER LAY on his back in bed. There was a powerful scent of pot about the room. His girlfriend, whom he'd nicknamed Flesh, had completely covered his cock with heaps of whipped cream and double double chocolate Häagen-Dazs. She'd even added a little crème de menthe to the festivities. She was going to be a man's perfect fiftieth birthday party.

Flesh was that. Twenty-seven years old, with legs that went all the way from the ground up and into a man's psyche. Her body, and those legs, had gotten her a gig in the Vegas chorus, which helped earn enough money to carry her through law school.

Pinter would tell everyone who'd listen, and he was shamelessly egotistical and shallow in these matters, that Flesh gave the best head of any Assistant D.A. who'd worked under him. And he'd made them all do "the bow," which Flesh, jealous as she was, did not appreciate hearing about.

Flesh started to work her way down that sundae of a man. Roy's beard and ponytail were covered with sweat, the sheets so damp they stuck to the skin. He bent his head ever so just to watch Flesh take him into her mouth.

The liquor of ecstasy. Slave time starring your best bitch. The sense of being completely served was one of life's greatest gratifications.

Roy managed a few breath-ridden words: "I'm probably the . . . only . . . banana split in existence . . . with polio."

Her free hand grabbed at his legs, those thin pieces of bone he had to carry around on metal crutches. Her riband fingers cinched up his ass, then wormed their way inside him.

Electric colors went through his head, then one of life's little perversities got into the play—the phone rang.

He could feel his blood pounding against the cold insides of her mouth.

The answering machine kicked in. "Mr. Pinter, this is Sergeant Farr, out in Tracy. I thought I'd let you know right away 'cause you're friends with Nathan Greene—"

SGT. FARR had just taken Damon Romero's statement when Roy and Flesh approached him in the emergency room hallway. "Mr. Pinter."

"Sergeant, this is Ms. Flescher. She's an Assistant D.A. in the department."

Farr knew who she was from the gossip hot line, but he put on his best pro forma. "Thanks for coming."

"Where's Nathan Greene?" Roy asked.

"Fourth floor," said Farr. "Outside surgery. They're operating on his son now."

"How bad is it?" asked Flesh.

"One bullet just below the heart. The boy had pretty much bled to death by the time we got him here."

"Fill us in," said Roy.

Farr began. He got as far as the man and woman coming from the St. Francis and parking on the Empire Tract side of Disappointment Slough when Roy caught sight of something just over Flesh's shoulder and said, "Essie."

His voice sounded as if all things painful could be found there and Flesh turned to see.

In a small room whose entrance was halved by a curtain, Essie sat. She was wrapped in a blanket. Her legs were bare, her feet bare. Her wet hair had begun to dry in disheveled mats. A doctor was setting her left wrist in a cast while an officer took notes between questions. She had a look of bewildered exhaustion going from face to face.

23

"Excuse me, Sergeant," said Roy. Then, to Flesh, "Why don't you get the Sergeant to fill *us* in while I—"

Her response was acrid, "Fill *us* in. Of course, sir."

FLESH LISTENED but her eyes and emotions were elsewhere.

"She was at the landing, I gather," said Sgt. Farr. "Trying to see if Taylor was home. The two witnesses came along thinking they heard a shot. They saw a body in the doorway and . . . she swam across."

Flesh could imagine what would happen inside of that black garden of a mind when Roy found out she swam the slough to try and save Taylor.

Essie's not even that attractive, thought Flesh. There wasn't one thing about her that stood out, except for the eyes. As dark and deeply green as they were. And also, maybe, the simple fucking fact that she had character. Yeah, Essie was not part of that contingent who was on a collision course with any of the life climbers that might get in her way.

"We're not even sure at this point if the wound wasn't self-inflicted," said Farr.

Flesh turned to him at hearing this ugly possibility. "Accident?"

"Or suicide."

FLESH AND Roy rode in an elevator up to the fourth floor, alone.

"What did Farr say?"

He knew her silence was directly aimed at him. "I was just trying to be—"

"They said the shot could have been self-inflicted. They found Percodan and Valium on his desk."

Roy sagged back against the wall. "It will kill Nathan."

"Just think, if Taylor dies, you might get another shot at her."

A matter of sheer reflex had Roy swinging that metal crutch, ready to come down on Flesh until she warned, "Go ahead. But when I'm done with you there won't be one charitable place in the world where you can go and try to run for public office."

IN A small waiting room near surgery Ivy Buckner searched out her reflection in the window's glassy black. The sacerdotal image of Taylor lying shot and dying haunted her thoughts. She felt as if the world were pressing in on her. As she tried to screen her face to see how it was holding up in these unnerving hours Roy and Flesh passed across her image entering the room.

Ivy turned and started toward them. "You're finally here." The elegant black gown she wore made a soft ruffling sound as she hugged them both.

"Where's Nathan?" Roy asked.

"In the bathroom. He's sick."

Roy turned to Flesh. "I'll go."

She gave him a spare expression that seemed to say, "No, really."

Once the two women were alone Ivy walked back to the window and stared out. Her folded hands made a small white ball. Flesh followed behind her. She saw the nails of one hand digging into the back of the other. Flesh tried to make small talk.

"You look quite lovely tonight, Counselor."

"The Southern Delta Association had one of its formal dinners. I dragged Nathan along." She glanced at the clock.

"You're going to have to explain to me the magic of turning forty and looking as good as you do."

A forced smile. "Small bouts of anorexia. A doctor who knows how to prescribe. And plenty of exercise."

Flesh took cigarettes from her purse. Ivy pointed to the NO SMOKING sign. Flesh lit one anyway, then went and sat beneath that very sign. Again Ivy glanced at the clock.

"He's been in surgery three hours."

"At least he's still alive."

Ivy's voice trailed off. "Yes."

THE BATHROOM was gray, empty and noiseless except for Nathan, in a stall, puking. Roy waited till the heaves slowed before calling, "Nathan?"

A gagging breath. A spit. "Roy . . . that you?"

"Your favorite charitable contribution has arrived."

A toilet flushed. Roy watched as Nathan staggered out of the stall. The surface of his handsome face was drenched with sweat. He wiped the vomit from his mouth using the sleeve of his tuxedo coat.

Nathan put a hand out for Roy to take but pulled it back on the chance it still carried traces of vomit. He bent to the sink and washed his mouth. He tried to wash the sleeve of his coat. As he did heart sounds came up through the deeps of his chest and throat. "My boy," the words seemed to blindly wobble out, "My boy."

One hand, now clean, reached and took hold of Roy's coat. Roy fought to keep his crutches balanced on the tile floor. He found himself helpless. He wanted to take Nathan's hand but couldn't. He did not know how to untie himself and express this level of closeness and affection.

There was a knock at the bathroom door, and Flesh calling to them.

"What?" said Roy.

She came in. Her mouth clipped in tightly at seeing Nathan so ravaged. "The doctor wants to talk to you."

EYES CLOSED, Essie went about the anxious task of praying Taylor wouldn't die. She felt someone move in beside her. She opened her eyes to find it was Flesh.

"Hello, Francie."

Flesh leaned against the wall by the sink. "You're the only one who's never called me Flesh, you know that."

Essie's head moved slightly her way, "I'm not sure you entirely appreciate that name . . . Any word from surgery?"

"Nathan and the doctors were just going to talk when I came down."

Essie knew now, the answer was in.

Flesh saw there were streaks of dried blood down the back of Essie's shoulder. She reached for a paper towel, she wet it in the sink.

"Taylor hadn't been right for days," said Essie. "I sensed something was wrong. I should have followed my instincts and questioned him."

Flesh sat beside Essie. She took her arm and began to wipe at the blood—it was Taylor's blood. "Do you have any idea what was bothering him? Was there trouble?"

Essie did not really hear her. She leaned forward and her gray-green eyes clouded. Nathan—Ivy—a doctor—with Roy steps behind them, were coming up the hallway. Up a long yellow tiled hallway. Their body language said it all.

CHAPTER FIVE

CHARLES GILL WAS a bank president who had been, and still could be, one fuckin' nasty session guitarist. We are talking a string player who lived the sonic addiction but was forced to opt out.

He and some club soldiers from the Sacramento crib were in his private studio built on the family estate. He'd built it right, too. This is where you could get plugged in, plow it on and come out with something the pros would cream over.

Tonight, Charles and his boys were passing all strategic arms limitations for sound. He'd bought a couple of Mesa Rectifiers that were driving two cabs with V-30's. The boys were into nothing but good time running the playbook from Pink Floyd to God-smack.

Charles was doing his renegade version of the first Pink Floyd solo on *The Wall* album when his private phone kicked in.

ROMERO'S VOICE came through in a clipped static. "Charles."

Charles closed the studio door behind him and the music that had been stinging out across the lawn was stilled.

"You on a cellular?"

"Yeah."

"Anything business we need to talk about, I'll see you on the dock."

CHARLES STOOD in the deep shadows of that forty-room mansion the family owned. The white schist stone gave the vast grounds an intensely silent feel. While he'd been talking to Damon a light went on in his bedroom that left an impression on the terraced stone patio below.

The music must have woken Claudia. He stepped out of the grainy darkness to see his wife watching him. Before he could turn away, that bit of light on the patio stone went black.

They say masters can play the game blindfolded. Time would tell.

EMPHYSEMA HAD pretty much devoured the General's lungs, so he and an oxygen tank were now constant companions that had to be chaperoned in a wheelchair.

What Korea could not do, nor Vietnam, nor Laos and Cambodia, nor napalm, nor Agent Orange, Philip Morris had successfully achieved.

Forty years of hard inhaling had turned retired Brigadier General, and former President of the People's Bank of Rio Vista, Merrit Hand, into nothing but lung-choked body slop.

When the stairs of the mansion became a breathing impossibility Merrit had his daughter Claudia and her husband Charles move in as he built himself a one-story guesthouse on a long, sloping lay of grass across the driveway. From his screened-in porch he could see the levee and the landing that led out into Steamboat Slough.

His life was predominantly down to watching his grandchildren, and the cruisers and runabouts that worked their way through a warm river breeze. But tonight the Fates had come calling. His immobile face watched from the screened-in darkness as Charles and one of his carriers talked on the dock.

DAMON WAS running on adrenaline fever as he explained how everything went like some perfect accident of events; first, tweaking his date at the St. Francis with a few well filled cocktails, and conning her into a little romantic starlight at Disappointment

Slough. Then Damon slapped his hands together to mimic the shot.

"No one saw Tommy or Shane, or their boat?"

"They crossed from the far side of the island to Ringe Tract."

"And Taylor's girlfriend was at the landing?"

"Yeah . . . but you know what else . . . when I talked to Tommy . . . he said Greene shot himself when he saw them coming."

THE GENERAL glanced at one particular photo on his wall; one of the many that included congressmen and senators, that showcased presidents gladhanding him, that centerstaged celebrities and authors and heads of foreign state. Out of this self-centered cosmography that one particular photo would become unbearable after tonight. It was taken at Taylor Greene's baptism, where he played godfather to the newborn.

The sound of a motor caught his attention and the General could see the hull of Damon's open-bow Offshore making its way back down Steamboat Slough and leaving a trail of white tide that rose then folded away.

Again, the photo pulled at him, but the General had to avert his eyes. He had allowed the son of the man who had served him in war and peace, who had been a loyal and steadfast friend, to be swept from the earth. This photo would now point out the proximity of disgrace. In his old age, his dying old age, within that deserted edifice his body was becoming, Merrit Hand would be known to himself by the worst four-letter word he could imagine—traitor.

CHARLES ENTERED the guesthouse without knocking. That was a cheap show of power he would not have even attempted on the General three years ago.

"I came to tell you, it's done."

The General did not bother to move his wheelchair around to face Charles. Charles had no intention of wading through the

General's last play at control. And so they remained two milky sketches with only moonlight to tie them.

"Did Taylor come to us when he found out? Did he give us a chance to even cop a plea with him? Or pay him off? No. Mr. Righteous, he knew his old man had to be involved and what did he do? He contacts some investigator with the Federal Reserve. And you can bet he would have turned us all over if it would have helped his old man get immunity."

The General turned his wheelchair toward the bedroom and passed right in front of Charles. He stopped. "You never told me how you found out Taylor contacted an investigator."

"And I'm not going to. I have my alliances, and they won't be jeopardized."

The General stared at this void he called son-in-law. This thirty-seven-year-old piece of cash-pampered deficiency. And to think he had a hand in creating it. A punkshit Frankenstein. Well, the only excuse was, Charles had been what his Claudia wanted.

"If Nathan finds out what you did, he'll—"

"I had this done with your approval," said Charles.

"You did this over my objections."

"If you call silence an objection."

"It should have been good enough."

"Why you Mt. Rushmore–faced obscenity."

CHAPTER SIX

TAYLOR GREENE HAD a bumper sticker on the back of his Volvo that read: DON'T TAKE YOUR ORGANS TO HEAVEN—HEAVEN KNOWS WE NEED THEM HERE.

Immediately upon his death, as was Taylor's wish, organs were removed. Kidney—liver—one lung. These had not been damaged by the bullet. His corneas were removed, along with valuable bone, skin, heart tissue and tendon.

While the doctors went about their precious task Essie watched the streets of Stockton from the back seat of Ivy's Range Rover. Essie's image on the rolled up window was like that of some ill-fated butterfly impressed upon glass.

"Why . . . ?"

To Essie the word sounded almost immaterial as Taylor and his father had voices that were remarkably close. She turned to Nathan, to that sad tale of a face and told him, "Something was troubling Taylor. He was despondent. And secretive. That's what I was going to see him about tonight."

NATHAN STOOD behind a wall of glass and looked out over Discovery Bay Marina. Its size and affluence were untouched by any in that thousand-mile waterway known as the California Delta. From its church and school to a stunning clubhouse Nathan had birthed it, and built it. It was to be his son's legacy.

It all seemed pointless now. The town houses and the condominiums of bleached white stretching on for waterside acres, the yachts and speedboats docked alongside the architecturally undigestible homes. This was all now stark contrast to the catastrophe within him.

He pushed down another glass of scotch and returned to his grand room's wet bar. The eighteen-foot ceilings absorbed each step across the handpainted Spanish tiles. He thought back over the last few weeks. Taylor had been unusually distant, making excuses to avoid a lunch or after-hours drink.

Nathan had thought little of it then, but now, did this signal some sea change in his son's life? Dear God—Nathan was struck with the image of his son discovering who his father really was.

IVY POURED pills from a vial into her hand. They were an extensive potluck of mood altering colors and sizes. Essie sat on the bed in one of Nathan's guest rooms. She wore a robe he'd lent her.

Ivy found the appropriate Valium. "I'm a walking pharmacy." She handed the pill to Essie. "This will cut the edge enough to sleep."

Essie took the pill and started for the hallway bathroom. "It was a good idea me not going home tonight."

"Yes, you wouldn't want to be alone."

Essie stopped at the door, "But I am."

NATHAN WAS behind the bar when Ivy joined him. She sat and rested her hands on the tin and stone bar surface.

"How's Essie?"

"I gave her a Valium."

Nathan held up a bottle of white wine.

"Please," said Ivy.

She watched while he worked out the cork. His jaw kept wincing, as if something were biting at the flesh. She could not bear to see him suffering through this. She turned her attention to that glass wall where a sloop could be seen gliding smoothly from the harbor and up Drake's Bay toward Indian Slough.

"Fuckin' doctors," said Nathan.

Her eyes came around to find him.

"Taylor's not gone two minutes. Not two minutes and those fuckin' ghouls are telling me, 'He's an organ donor and'—"

"It's not the doctors."

"Like I didn't know. Like I was a mental invalid."

"It's not the doctors."

He passed the wine to her. She drank with little or no energy. She looked back at the glass wall trying to see the sloop.

"Roy said the police found pills, vials of pills, on Taylor's desk. He wasn't into pills. What was that about?"

"I gave him some Valium."

When she turned to face him, she saw the roots of confusion spreading across his face.

"When?"

"Two weeks ago."

Confusion turned to anger. "Why didn't you say something?"

"He asked me not to."

"And when he said that, you didn't think to—"

"I respected his privacy as much as I want mine and yours respected."

"Did he say why he wanted the pills?"

She got up and walked to the glass wall. The stress of all this was starting to break her down feature by feature. She searched out that sloop, but it was far up into the bay and all but a bled out shadow.

Nathan rubbed at the dreadful tension in his neck. "My mind's been going round and round about which is worse, suicide or murder?"

She closed her eyes. "You can't allow yourself to think like that."

"I say it, but the mind rebels. I don't believe it was suicide."

A sigh emerged from within her. "Please."

"Do you suppose Charles might have—"

Her eyes opened. "Please, stop."

"What if Taylor found out we—"

"Stop." She'd had enough. She walked across the grand room and opened French doors that led onto one of the terraced grottoes. At the short stone wall overlooking the harbor she put her head back. She let the night breeze have at her chest and throat. Moments later Nathan joined her. She tried in some way to shut down this line of questioning. "The General wouldn't allow the scenario you're considering."

"The General is dying, and Charles has it in him to believe he's a turk."

"Charles won't do anything to ruin his relationship with you. He may be the bank now that the General is not well, but the brokers know it's you who cleans their money and invests it so—"

Through the streaming image of the harbor lights and yacht club restaurant reflected in the half open French doors Ivy made out a form passing on toward the hallway. She ssshhh'd Nathan with a hand, started for the door. Ivy put a finger to her lips and pointed, then went inside.

Leaning into the hallway entrance Ivy caught the back of Nathan's robe pass into the guest room and the door close behind it. She walked back out onto the terrace, her eyebrows pinched with trouble.

Nathan asked, "Do you think she could have heard?"

"I think that silence on this subject makes the best sense."

She eased the French doors shut.

Nathan went to the ledge of the terrace stone wall and sat. He was falling into a deep despondency, a benumbing stasis, knowing there would never be another lifeprint left upon this earth by his taken son.

Ivy joined him. They sat together in silence under the tall potted facias, with the scents of night heavy as musk. Ivy held Nathan. He breathed into her chest and spoke: "Taylor told me when he signed up to be an organ donor . . ." Ivy could feel against her chestbone Nathan's voice shunt ". . . it was his way of passing on a few hopes and dreams to someone who . . . who . . . might need a hope or a dream."

She could feel him start to cry again. "Something good will come from this," she said. "I know to believe that now is hard. But just wait and see. I promise. Wait and see."

CHAPTER SEVEN

THE DAY OF the burial began with rain. The funeral procession made its slow way from the Immaculate Conception Church in Sacramento to All Souls' Cemetery in Vallejo through a slab lit drizzle. Turning onto Redwood Parkway a small pickup skidded the lane and sideswiped the hearse. The whole procession pulled onto the shoulder, and that wagon train of vehicles strung out in the mist waited as license and registrations were exchanged.

"I guess Taylor's telling us he's not ready to go into the ground yet," said Charles.

Claudia glanced at the girls sitting in the back with their grandfather. They had not heard his remark. She now turned to her husband, "Why don't you say something else not fit to be repeated."

THERE WAS no sign of a break-in. No sign it was a robbery in progress."

As Roy lit a thin cigar, Flesh answered him. "Taylor could have heard something outside. Confronted a prowler. A fight ensued."

Roy held that short, thin cigar toward his chest as if it were a gun, "Residue on Taylor's wrist suggests the gun was held like this. Close and consistent with someone shooting himself."

Flesh watched through the windshield as Essie walked that line of cars in the rain. No umbrella, nothing to protect her, alone, leaning in each window trying to assure and reassure the mourners. "His cheek and head were bruised," she said.

"And possibly consistent," answered Roy, "with his body recoiling from the impact of the shot as he hit the doorframe. And we'd know more if Essie had not contaminated the murder site by moving the body."

"Her concern was not the fuckin' contamination of evidence."

"I'm just making a point. We were discussing—"

"I don't like your tone."

STILL, SAD human figures gathered around the casket and were covered by a sovereign white canopy that rose like a wind-rolled shroud above them.

With the come and go of the rain and the priest's final moving words Essie should have been choked up with loss, with memory. But she wasn't.

She could hear the tears in others, but a steady stream of anxiety in her turned the half sentences and distressed, plateglass looks between Nathan and Ivy *that night* into unholy scenarios.

WHERE DID he get the pills?" whispered Roy.

Flesh whispered back, "The Percodan was from his dentist for an abscessed tooth."

They stood at the rear of that small world around the casket.

"They haven't found any prescription for the Valium."

The ground had gone soft from the rain and Roy's crutches began to slip. Flesh braced him by tucking an arm under his. "You sure you don't want to sit?"

A mourner turned, staring them into silence, then the mourner turned away. Roy mouthed "fuck you" to the mourner's back. Flesh leaned over and whispered in his ear. "If there is no Valium prescription, I bet I know where he got them."

NATHAN'S HOUSE was peopled wall to wall. He stood with his arm around Essie and told some of his business friends and their wives about Taylor's infamous "State of the Union" twenty-first birthday party.

"He rented a houseboat and invited exactly fifty friends. Male and female. But there was a catch to the invitation. Everyone had to be on board naked and everyone was issued a state and they had to spray-paint the name of the state down the front of their bodies.

"Well, the party took place just off Bethel Island, and for those who don't know, there's about a dozen marinas there. So it wasn't long before sheriff patrol boats cruised over to find the kids drinking and dancing away.

"There wouldn't have been any arrests. They were gonna just let them go except my son climbed on top of the houseboat and started dancing to"—he forgot the song—"just as a sightseeing boat goes past. Well, he told me later, when I bailed him out, he did it only because he wanted to make sure the tourists got to really see one of California's natural wonders."

THE RAIN had stopped. From the grottoed terrace where Roy and Flesh sat Discovery Bay drifted in and out of a fluid haze.

"What does the sheriff's department think of the witnesses' statements?"

"The man owns Romeo Boat Sales," said Flesh, "and the woman is an accountant with Southwestern Airlines. Neither has any baggage. It was their fourth date. The sheriff's department can't see how their being at the slough could be anything but coincidence."

Roy noticed Nathan approach the General and Charles. A whole conversation lasted about three curt sentences and then Nathan pushed the General's wheelchair toward his private den.

Ivy walked into Roy's view, knocked on the glass wall to get his attention. He motioned for her to come and join him. He turned to Flesh, "Get yourself a drink while I have at her."

IT WAS the first time Nathan and the General had been alone since Taylor's death.

"I know Roy feels it was a suicide, even though he won't come right out and say it."

The General looked away. He wanted a cigarette, the full blow, even though his lungs were a wasteland.

"Was there anything," asked Nathan, "ever, that said to you, Taylor might . . . *kill himself?*"

The General felt like an imposter of the man he had once been. He wheeled over to the couch, where Nathan stood waiting for an answer. He went to speak, but before he did he looked away. "You are going to have to leave yourself open to that possibility. I tell you this as a grandfather, father, and a friend."

It was, to Nathan, a timorous response. He sagged into the couch's deep down cushions. Maybe the General's answer was a corollary of his age and illness. Or maybe death breaks down human walls and feeds distrust; about life, about friends.

Nathan folded his hands, leaned forward to go face to face with the General. He began his best gold-plated pitch, "Merrit, I am at the crossroads of my life. And for everything I have ever done that you asked of me, I come to you with a request."

DID TAYLOR get the Valium from you?"

"From small talk to straight talk in two sentences. Well." Ivy took Roy's cigar. "And who is asking me this? The bereaved friend . . . the prosecutor?"

"Bereaved friend."

"And it goes no further."

"Correct."

She drew in the smoke, then answered, "Yes."

"Why did he want them?"

"If I tell you, you must swear on your life . . . no, on Essie's life . . . you will never mention this to Nathan."

He took the cigar back. "Hit me where I live. Agreed."

Essie was at the bar when Nathan reappeared from the den. She asked Flesh, who was beside her, "Do you think you could know someone for years and be totally wrong about them?"

"Only if you're me." Flesh tasted her double vodka and tonic. She handed it back to the bartender, "You want to give this drink something to be proud of?"

She turned to Essie. "If this is about the possibility Taylor committed suicide, I don't for one minute be—"

Essie's look stopped Flesh cold and before she could clean up her thought Nathan's voice cut across the room. "Ladies and gentlemen, could I please have your attention."

It took a few moments for word to pass through the rooms of people. Nathan caught sight of Essie and called her to his side. Nathan stood between her and the General as the mourners gathered together on the steps, in doorways, around the bar. All except Roy, who hung back on the terrace so he could tell Flesh what he'd found out.

"First," said Nathan, "let me thank you for being here today. For helping Essie and I deal with our sorrow, and for allowing us to help you deal with yours."

Flesh whispered to Roy, "What did Ivy say?"

"She gave him the Valium, and you know what else? Taylor told her he was thinking about going to a psychiatrist. That he felt his life was a failure."

Nathan continued, "As you know, Taylor was an organ donor. He told me once it was his way of passing on a few hopes and dreams to someone who might desperately need a hope and a dream."

"Flesh, I think we might be looking at a suicide."

"Taylor had started taking flying lessons three weeks ago out at Rio Vista," she said. "He had made plans for a trip to Hong Kong."

"Maybe he was desperate," said Roy, "to find something to keep his mind off killing himself."

Nathan pointed to Ivy. "Ivy and I were sitting on the terrace the night Taylor died as we spoke of this very subject. I was looking out across our beautiful marina and was touched by a thought. I'd like to think it was Taylor's spirit that put it there, in those moments when he was moving between our world and the next."

"You know what I think," whispered Flesh. "You want it to be a suicide."

"From this day forward," said Nathan, "I am going to use all my skills and talents, my drive and will, to one end. It will be to build a research center, in this community, to be the finest in America, for organ transplantation. And I am going to build it . . . in my son's name."

There was a run of polite applause.

"Why should I want it to be a suicide?" Roy whispered. Nathan quieted the crowd.

"Because," said Flesh, "maybe it will help break the spell of Taylor and you'll have another shot at her."

Nathan rested a palm on the General's shoulder. "I also want to add that Merrit Hand, my good friend and Taylor's godfather, has promised his and the bank's full support in making this project a reality."

Roy had plenty of filthy things to call Flesh but she was up and gone, joining that crowd of hand clappers. What made him angriest—she was right.

Charles was sitting with his wife and two daughters and there was no shortage of congratulations coming his way for what everyone assumed he knew of and was committed to.

Charles smiled through the backwash of a thought—the old carcass wants me to carry him to heaven on my fuckin' back.

NATHAN LAY in bed and stared up at a black ceiling. Ivy lay beside him.

"The General hasn't been able to look me in the eye since Taylor was killed. I feel he knows, or at least suspects, it was Charles."

Ivy leaned up on one elbow and put a hand over his mouth. "You are going to poison yourself with thoughts like that."

He removed her hand and held it. "I'm gonna build that center and I'm gonna use it as a way to destroy him. I don't know how yet, but I am."

"And how do we keep from being destroyed along the way?"

He let go of her hand and stared up into that sky of a ceiling. "Nathan . . . ?"

A LIGHT cleared away the darkness where Taylor had lay dying. It cleared darkness from the doorway. Across the living room this single wave of light moved leaving a black tide in its wake. The light then found Taylor's desk.

Essie looked upon the scene. It spoke to her with its punctuated meaning: Nathan's picture at one end of the desk, hers at the other. And between, just open empty space.

He had been the connection, a construction that made them close even though she had worked for Nathan almost three years. Now, there was a break in their lives. A distance. A hole that had to be filled. And it wouldn't be filled with eulogies or wakes, not by a research center or memorial. It demanded something living, something that swept over dreamlike and nostalgic memories. It demanded answers.

By moving Taylor's body you contaminated the site—

Facts can be blunt instruments. And that statement of fact was meant to harm, to hurt Essie in some deeply vulnerable reach and reinforce what she already felt—that she had failed him.

Essie let that flashlight again find the room. She saw Taylor's books stacked and open wherever he had last been reading. His CDs, not a one, as usual, in its case. And the one-armed bandit she had given him as a Christmas present. She walked over and

43

ran her hand across its enjoyably tacky facing. The card that came with it was still perched up on top. She reread what she had written that holiday past:

Something for you to play with when I'm not around. Love, Essie.

Her chest clutched. Her breath made traumatic stops and starts, her neck clenched. She wanted to surrender to her emotions. To let herself be devoured by human frailties. To collapse with pain and wanting and loss. To just cry herself away. But she didn't.

What if Taylor found out—

She did not want to believe the worst about Nathan or Ivy. But their faces through the off-lit glass seemed to be a succession of bleak, angry and frightened snapshots into their being.

Don't overreact, Essie thought. Don't blind yourself to other possibilities that it was only something unwise—imprudent—something that would shame but not silence life.

She drifted around the room in confusion. She had to believe, had to make herself believe, dare herself to believe that there was a shapeless, invisible thread that moved through all of this. A measured rope that would guide someone, anyone, her, through a maze of moments to reach a point where truth be known.

She talked to Taylor. She made a promise there in the dark. With the silver of night reflecting off the slough water. She made a promise she would keep at any cost. A promise that his life would not end up like it had today, the subject of graveside gossip. She made her promise, and she would tell no one. No one.

CHAPTER EIGHT

THE BURROW HAD a cheap, rave breakfast. Essie often ate at the Rio Vista Airport restaurant as Taylor had rented a hangar there to store goods he'd imported.

It had been almost three months since his death. Essie was there that morning to continue cleaning up his business affairs.

The night before Roy had taken her and Nathan to dinner in Lodi and given them the news. Essie scanned an article in the newspaper that was, almost verbatim, what Roy had told them— an investigation failed to furnish legitimate evidence that Taylor Greene's death was a homicide.

Essie was disgusted. Taylor had become an official postscript to his own story.

"It's a shame," said Paul Caruso, as he brought Essie breakfast.

She looked up. Sancho Maria, his wife, was right there beside him. "A goddamn fuckin' shame," she said, then leaned down and pulled Essie toward her.

Sancho Maria was dark skinned and sensually padded. Paul Caruso told everyone Sancho Maria reminded him of Liz Taylor . . . "after she'd been knocked around by a few earthquakes."

As the three talked of hard pain Essie noticed the Fenn Brothers walk the tarmac from their hangar to Taylor's. A cell phone began to ring. The man in the booth behind them answered and got into one of those self-indulgent cha-cha business calls, talking loud enough for everyone to hear how important he was.

Through the sunbleached window Essie watched to see what the hell the Fenns were doing around Taylor's hangar as Paul clipped that Hawaiian-shirted yuppie man on the back of his neck. He turned. Caruso pointed to the far wall. Just above a huge painting of the ancient Cretan Labyrinth was a sign that read: TALKING ON A CELLULAR IN THIS RESTAURANT IS A NON-STARTER. CEASE AND DE-SIST.

"I'll just be a minute," was the man's placating response.

"You ain't got a minute, geek, before you go through the glass."

It looked to Essie as if the Fenns were undoing the lock.

The man considered Caruso's nicked-up face, his torque wrench arms, and the Am-Staff stare on that woman beside him. He killed the call.

Essie stood up. The Fenns were opening Taylor's hangar door.

THEY HAD pretty much just gotten into the dark stacks of furniture and boxes when Essie came in asking, "What are you doing here?"

These were punk garage tough boys and they carried themselves accordingly. Tommy held up a key. "Charles Gill got word some piece of furniture he'd ordered was delivered weeks ago. He sent us to get it."

"Where'd he get that key?"

"I guess from Taylor's old man."

"Don't touch anything till I talk to Nathan."

As she turned to go back to the restaurant and make the call Tommy slipped a cellular out of his back pocket. "Call him right now."

She began to dial and Shane mumbled, "Just a little taste of moral outrage from the doomslingers."

Tommy gave his brother a look that said "kill the riff." Shane turned his attention to Essie. "It must be tough having a boyfriend freakin' off himself."

AFTER THE MURDERS

Dane RUDD LOOKED out the window of that Cessna and into the heartland of the Rio de Sacramento and San Joaquin. These two rivers formed the headwaters of the California Delta.

"It stretches forty miles in one direction and fifty in another," said Caruso. "One thousand miles of waterway for fishing, sailing, marinas, anchorages . . ." He stopped. "I sound like some dickless, loser tour guide."

As the plane banked the red horizon fell away to the west and below was a weaving pattern of streams and tributaries, of channels, sloughs and currents that connected and reconnected in an astounding complex of nature.

It was like looking down upon some vast and labyrinthine living body composed of water and earth that spread placidly toward the edges of sight, toward the gates of distance.

"You can see," Caruso said, "there's more than one way in and one way out of those streams."

As Caruso talked he kept trying to sneak a glance in or around the edges of Rudd's sunglasses and get a look at his eyes.

"You can't tell anything," said Dane.

"I don't getcha."

Dane took off his sunglasses. "They transplant the cornea, not the whole eye. It's impossible to see if there was any surgery at all."

Caruso was shamelessly unashamed of a need to stare. So he stared, and stared.

Rudd's eyes were light, light gray. Almost transparent. More tone than true color or set shade. Closer in feel to water than earth.

"I thought that maybe if you'd had blue eyes before and the person who died had, say brown eyes, you'd have—"

"No," said Dane. "The real dramatics are from my side." He slipped back on his sunglasses. "I'm here because of Taylor Greene."

"Taylor was the donor? Does his father know?"

"If you want to thank a donor's family there's a process you go through by sending a letter to the eye bank, they in turn contact the family. It's their option to read the letter, and contact you."

"And Nathan did?"

"He sent me an invitation to the memorial."

More than once Dane had glanced at the dirty T-shirt Caruso was wearing. On the front was printed, in diploma-style script: *"Graduate of the Men's Colony ... Class of '91."*

Caruso caught Dane's half grin. "What?"

Dane pointed to the shirt. "How long did it take you to get your degree? Or should I say, release?"

Caruso came back with his own larcenous grin. "You know what the Men's Colony is."

"I do."

"Most people are so stupid they don't get the joke. They think it's some trade school or college."

"Well, in a way it is, isn't it. Many of our most aggressive, free-thinking citizens have done intense post-graduate work there . . . for their personal advancement, of course."

Caruso grunted through his teeth. He held up a forearm as if it were a rockhard prick. "And the white collar boys are always the ripest."

"It's good to know," said Dane, "the hard measurements of justice."

Caruso again grunted through his teeth.

Dane went back to looking out the window. The last of the sun poured forth like fire across the spreading landscape. The water burned with light and you could follow those blue sparkling lines as they cut deep and far into the life-green land. You could see boats that left frosty wakes as they sped on, and those with sails, fleecy white and tall, moving like gentle landmarks with the current, pulling their shadows toward the bay.

There were old ferries and unused girder bridges. There were windmills and the remains of harbors, tule reeds that stood high as a man against the wind, and poplars that tracked the shore. There was farmland, squared patches so huge you would think they could feed the world.

It was a beautiful trace where the past and present blended almost unnoticeably. Its very distance, and its very silence, made the world below more something of elegy than earth.

"From here," said Dane, "the world is heartbreakingly beautiful."

CHAPTER TEN

AFTER THE FLIGHT Caruso offered to stand Dane a couple of beers.

The Burrow was one part coffee shop, one part bar and booths, and one part tree shaded patio. The building, which looked out over the western runway, anchored a small complex of offices, bathrooms and showers.

The Burrow was also one of the Delta's more well-known eccentricities as the inside walls of the coffee shop and bar were covered with representations of the ancient mythological Labyrinth. There were funky paintings and framed photographs. There were cutouts from magazines and books of famous renditions glued then glazed into a kind of world-tour collage.

As Caruso was back in the kitchen explaining to Sancho Maria what Dane told him, she'd sneak glances through the kitchen door and watch this intensely absorbed young man take in image after image of that famous maze where Theseus and the Minotaur confronted life, and from where Daedalus and his boy escaped toward the sun using wings made from wax.

It was all there for Dane to walk, that journey memorialized on Greek coins and sandstone slabs, on the subterranean walls of Egyptian burial chambers and in the floors and bas-relief of the great cathedrals of Europe.

There were labyrinths designed as prisons and cages and oubliettes. There were those that symbolized the escape through Samsara, and those that spoke of the karmic law and the night sea voyage. From Pompeii to the postmodern ideal, with steps along the way for Brueghel and Picasso and Dürrenmatt and sculptured creations you could walk and those of petty hipster visual maze artists on the rip.

There were labyrinths of the one path and those of the many and those of the seven convolutions. As Dane took in that puzzling pilgrimage of straight and blind paths, he could see that since human life was young enough to think and feel the mystery of that symbol had been with us.

"I'm a fuckin' headcase, right?"

Dane turned to find a beer waiting for him.

They sat in a booth where Caruso had assembled, besides beer, a bottle of tequila, a lemon, a knife and salt. "Let me tell you something, okay," he said, placing these accoutrements on the table for a little extra righteous enjoyment. "From the age of fourteen to the age of forty I was in and out of prison; seven times I was in lockdown—for possession, dealing, burglary, robbery, armed robbery, assault. But the last time in stir, and I was in for nine years, I got lucky on two counts."

Sancho Maria walked past with a tray of beers. "You're not gonna make him sit through the bullshit story of your life?" She winked at Dane, "You can doze off any time you want. Just stretch right out there in the booth and if you need a pillow, give me a holler."

Caruso's lip curled as he waited for her to be gone. Then he started right back in repeating himself. Dane could see this was talk first, drink later, so he reached for the lemon and knife and held them up as if asking would it be all right to start.

"Sure, sure . . ." said Caruso. "Like I was saying. There were two things . . . The first was her." Caruso pointed to Sancho Maria as she passed back on her way to the bar with a tray of empties. "She was a corrections officer at the Men's Colony."

The way Dane's look moved from one to the other caused Caruso to say, "I shit you not. She was a corrections officer and we fell in love." To Sancho Maria, "Right?"

"Pity me," she said. "I liked the way he used to walk the yard."

"You should have seen her when she was wearing a flak jacket and had a riot gun tucked up under her tits."

From fifteen feet away she punctuated his statement with, "It was the riot gun that got him hot."

As Dane sprinkled salt on the back of his hand Caruso leaned in close as if sharing something very, very special. "And the second thing that happened was I got into reading about mythology. Bullfinch . . . Edith Hamiton . . . all that shit blew my mind but you know what story hooked me the most?"

Dane downed a shot of tequila, finished the ritual with lemon. Then, behind those sunglasses his eyes went from wall to wall to wall. "I think I can muscle up at least one serious guess."

"Fuckin' A. I mean, what's a more right-on story if you're in a six-by-twelve lockdown for a decade."

Caruso pointed to the entrance wall. Dane turned to see a framed parchment maybe four feet across and three feet high, the paper cracked with age, of Daedalus and his son flying from that stone entrapment on wings.

"The dude that created the labyrinth got himself imprisoned there. Did you notice what was written on the nose of my Husky?"

"The Big D."

Caruso nodded gruffly. "You're observant, that's good." He licked salt from the back of his filthy hand. "The D was for Daedalus." He couldn't get a shot of tequila down fast enough to get back to his story. His ragged teeth went at the sliver of lemon, and Dane waited.

"Daedalus made these wax wings for him and his kid to blow out of there on. There was the sun above, and water below when they humped it over the walls. The sun burns wax, and the waves and fish can get at you, so he told his kid . . . 'Don't fly too high . . . don't fly too low.' "

Caruso poured another shot of tequila. No time-wasting salt and lemon, just the straight drop. "That statement became my mantra for survival when I was whacked. It meant moderation . . . middle ground . . . and mind my own fuckin' business."

The Fenns swung in from the coffee shop giving off their best all-star vibe as they talked it up with other flyers they knew who ran out of Rio Vista. Shane came over to the table. "Sayyy, Paul."

He held up a cellular to be scrutinized. "Check out my new phone. You think I could get good reception in here?"

With a minimalist's civility Caruso answered, "For about one second."

Tommy told his brother not to fuck around, nodded to Caruso, then cut on over to the bar. Shane leaned across the table and reached for a slice of lemon. Just a little space-invading pleasure trip. He glanced at Dane. "Nice eyecovers."

By the time Shane had swung up onto a bar stool beside his brother, Sancho Maria was at the table telling Paul, "We've got to get ready for the memorial."

The men stood. "You have a place yet?" asked Caruso.

"No."

"There's showers here. We could lend you towels if you want."

WHEN THE three walked out of The Burrow dusk had turned the world a soft blue that lights only began to fill in with detail.

"It must be wonderful having your sight back."

Dane did not answer right away, which surprised Sancho Maria. Instead, he followed a two-prop as it approached out of the last fired edges of the horizon, its engine getting closer and stronger till it landed on the western runway near them. He then said, "It depends on the view you bring. I'm not forgetful I'm standing here because someone I never met died in some accident."

That word *accident* pulled Caruso around toward Dane. "Accident . . . who coated your asshole with that bullshit?"

CHAPTER ELEVEN

THE MEMORIAL FOR Taylor Greene was underway when Dane arrived at the dock in Sacramento. It was taking place on board a cherried paddlewheeler that had traveled the Delta waterways a century ago and was named *Little California*. The boat, moored that night on Wharf F, was lit for all its beauty. A stirring showpiece in the full regalia of whites and red and gold.

Dane stood alone on the dock where the glow of that packet boat fell away at his feet. He wore a black collarless shirt, black jeans and boots, a white vest, and with hands folded behind his back, silently took in the proceedings.

The decks were crowded with people talking and drinking and playing games of chance, the profits of which would go to the center that was to bear Taylor's name. A fullout breeze made the strung lamps along the upper decks sing with movement, and waiters and waitresses and game dealers were dressed in the riverboat style of that bygone era.

It was a vision steeped in memories of Bret Harte and Mark Twain and Herman Melville. An ambience meant to project an epoch when people carried their dreams around with them in knapsacks as they moved along the rivers of our history. When characters like John Oakhurst and Huckleberry Finn and The Confidence Man were there to greet us with legend and lore. When brawls and colorful speech and the clacking roulette wheel ball and Stephen Foster's banjo and bucketboard slapped water and towns with names like Poker Flat and tragic outlaw songs filled our imagination.

How rich and fraudulent rituals are, Dane thought. How the

magic of their accoutrements moves us with exhilarating nostalgia for a moment of time when divinities lived inside us, and we cradled dreams of self-sacrifice and social betterment. When our neighbors were our friends, and our shadows were a helpful compass to set direction and time.

But that selfsame ritual cuts with its poisoned view into the deeper reaches of truth. For even then, when Little California was the Concorde of its day, we as a nation, through selfishness and fear and greed, shut our eyes to a world we created with holsters and cut decks, with scabbards and lies and closed brutal hearts.

Dane approached a long table beside the plankway up to the boat where those invited got their name tags and presents and signed on board. At one end of that burgundy-clothed table was a large photo of Taylor Greene smiling effortlessly. At the other end of that table was the first architect's rendition of what, hopefully, the center might become. Dane saw too, that in the empty space between what had been and what might be was the inevitable truth of how a young man came to find himself twenty-six, forever.

"It was no accident," Caruso said. "Taylor was murdered."

Dane Rudd understood, full well, the power of guilt to determine people's actions. As a cutting tool guilt was finer than any scalpel, or any blade. To effect wellbeing or to destroy, guilt was one of time's most potent and mercurial archangels.

The woman glanced at the young man whose dark fine hair stood up across his high forehead.

"I'm here to sign on board," he said.

CHAPTER TWELVE

NATHAN GREENE WAS on his cellular shredding some poor set of ears that worked for the catering company. The wine delivery had been screwed up and they were about to run short. "No one is going to shit on my son's memorial. So get some fucker down here and deal with it," he shouted, "or I will castrate the lot of you!"

He flipped the cellular shut. Nathan, Ivy, Charles, and the General were in a private room on the lower deck that had at one time been the captain's quarters. The room was done in solid oaks, with mahogany trim and brass hurricane lamps. It was stately and beautiful, but of more importance yet the room held sound well.

Nathan turned to Charles, who sat in a luxurious red leather chair and smoked. "Where is the money? Why haven't the loan papers been addressed?"

Charles looked across the room at the General. Nathan turned to Merrit and waited for what he had to tell him.

"Some of our people . . . have come . . . to the decision . . ." The old man was desperately fatigued . . . "this deal . . . isn't warranted."

Ivy could see all sense of calmness leave Nathan's face.

"I don't hear that when I talk to them."

"Yes, well," said Charles. Now Nathan turned to him. Charles put his cigarette out. He crossed his legs, then let his arms fold across his lap. These became time-consuming movements done for the art of making someone wait. "Our people are sensitive to what you've been through, Nathan. And what you want to achieve.

You've *helped* make them money, but, they don't like the deal."

"I've *helped*—"

"Wait," said Ivy, who was sitting by the General. "It took months for the Delta Association to feel comfortable with this deal."

Charles interrupted, "Which is why—"

"It took a lot of hand holding."

"Which is why—"

"And a lot of promises."

"Which-is-why—"

"And some serious perks."

"Which-is-why we included in the package the development of a mall and town houses first."

"The center is first," demanded Nathan.

"Once there's a revenue stream—"

"You're talking a five-year delay," said Ivy.

"Once there's a revenue stream—"

"What is this 'revenue stream' crap? Suddenly thieves and drug dealers are financial experts. The only revenue streams they understand is what someone else shoots, snorts, swallows or shits. Charles, have you been running me down with these fuckers?"

Charles held a hand out toward the General so he could answer, which he did, with a somewhat defeated nod.

"I won't do it," said Nathan.

"Well, then let me suggest something else," said Charles.

"I won't do it."

"I've been approached by some new contacts with clients in Sierra Leone and Colombia."

"You're talking serious borderland shit now."

"They're interested in the deal, as you want it done."

"There's a war in Sierra Leone and we have agents and soldiers all over Colombia. How well do you know these people?"

"Hardly at all," said Charles, "hardly enough."

"They could have sting operations tracking them," answered Nathan. "They could be on the verge of indictments and trying to pedal their money out quick."

"All that is true," said Charles, "which is why *you* would have to take a much more proactive role in handling this."

"What you mean is I'm going down into the rat hole and get dirty."

"If you want this center done your way, then a change of plans will have to take place. That is called compromise. I'm sure you've heard of it."

Charles' cool contempt forced Nathan to put a choke hold on his anger toward that thin and meatless fraud. And it wasn't just how all this was being turned against him, or how Charles now seemed to rule over the General. He could whitewash his way past all that, but it was knowing, with strained and urgent assurance inside his punished soul, that Charles had had a part in Taylor's death.

"I won't fuckin' do it."

Charles looked up at the ceiling for effect. On the shimmering decks above people talked and listened to music, they drank and happily gambled away their money to be donated to a research center they knew would bear Taylor's name. And, more importantly, they waited for Nathan to announce the date when groundbreaking would begin. "I guess," said Charles, "you'll figure out a way to let those people down . . . easily."

Nathan had had enough. Both Ivy and the General could see his wide, flat, blue-collar hands flex as he started across the room. The General called to Nathan just as Ivy cut him off.

"You two out," said the General.

WHEN THE door closed behind them Charles turned to Ivy and whispered, "If you don't keep him in line you know what it means for both of us."

NATHAN SQUATTED down beside the General's wheelchair. There was a buzzing in Nathan's head from all that running blood and he could barely see.

"Give up on the center your way."

"I won't. And he knows I won't. And you know I won't."

The General closed his eyes and wished everything would fall away in peace.

"Merrit, remember how we used to deal with pricks like Charles. How we'd take them up in a helicopter like we were gonna party and then when we were a nice comfortable five hundred feet or so above the jungle we'd quietly toss their asses out."

All that willful and dogged ferocity that had been Captain Nathan Greene was still there. And what had helped get them to where they were today was now a frightening and self-fulfilling reality the General could not run from.

"I have grandchildren to think of."

"And I used to have a son."

"Give up on having the deal . . ." he sighed, ". . . your way. Or . . . or work with these new people."

"We could be exposed. Everything we built could be destroyed."

"I know you'll watch out . . . for us."

Nathan straightened up a bit. "I'm ashamed to ask you this, but can you control him?"

"I look in people's eyes now . . . and . . ." The General's head slipped a bit to one side. ". . . I see . . . they know I'm dying and they're not afraid of me. Death gets even for everything we have and have not done."

He held up a hand as if swearing on a Bible. The fingers tremored. "I won't let anything happen to you. You are the *only* son I ever had. I can say no more than that."

No more was said. Nathan went to the door and called the others back in. "I'll meet these clients, but we stay in play. No setbacks. You make it happen."

Charles agreed. "I understand the stress you're under. If one of my girls died—"

"Taylor didn't die, okay. He was murdered. And everyone in this room knows it." Nathan's eyes scarred as they took in Charles. "I'll find out who did it. And I will burn them to the fuckin' ground."

There was a knock and, when ordered, a woman led Dane in.

The palpable tension on that quatro of faces was unavoidable.

"Mr. Greene, you said that as soon as this young man arrived he was to be brought down here."

A finger snap commanded the woman out and fast. Nathan turned his anger on Dane. "You want to explain what the fuck is going on with the wine delivery?" Dane was caught off guard but he tried anyway to get a moment in against that full frontal assault. "This is a memorial, not some shitass wine tasting your people can screw up."

"Mr. Greene—"

"I don't need wine in an hour, I don't need it in half an hour."

"Mr. Greene—"

"I don't need it in fifteen minutes."

"I'm not who you think I am, sir."

"Excuse me?"

His tone was dead calm. "I'm Dane Rudd. I wrote you, and you invited me."

Nathan's face went slack. Ivy said, "Oh . . . my."

While Nathan stumbled over his embarrassment and ill-placed anger introductions fell to Ivy. "General . . . Charles, this young man had a corneal transplant and it turns out . . . Taylor was the donor. We invited him here for the memorial."

Nathan walked around a desk and folded into the seat as Dane went from hand to hand, shaking them.

"Nathan," said Ivy, "why don't I take the General and Charles upstairs while you—"

Dane quietly finished her sentence, "Recover." He smiled at her, then at Nathan. "It's all right."

Nathan stared at his hands. Dane watched Nathan. "I'm sorry about your son."

Nathan remained silent, with all those life questions running through his blood. The confusion of anger at Taylor's murder, and what to feel for this young man, this innocent stranger, regret over his own faults and actions, his hate for Charles, his compromised position, his despair, and his human loneliness.

He looked up into those gray eyes with their jet-black core.

There were phantom misgivings as he tried to find his son there. As he hunted that midnight face for someone he loved and laughed with, and in all truth, failed.

"If this is too hard for you, I will leave."

Nathan shook his head. No, he did not want the young man to leave. He closed his eyes and hid them behind his hands. He started to cry. "I'm so sorry," he said, "I'm so sorry. I didn't mean for you to see me like this. It's just, I'm confused and over-whelmed."

Dane came around the desk and put his hand on Nathan's shoulder and left it there. He did it so lightly and slowly the feel of it just seemed to materialize. "Mr. Greene, I want you to know, you're safe with me. Do you understand? You're safe."

CHAPTER THIRTEEN

CHARLES MADE HIS way through the crowd on the VIP deck when a metal crutch crossed his path. Roy was sitting on a backless chair leaning against the upper deck railing. Flesh was there beside him in a pale blue skin fitter that covered about a half-inch of thigh. Both were a few cocktails into the balmy night.

"How would you like to sponsor my run for the state senate?"

Charles was too wrapped up in the moves and counter moves of the last few minutes to give this any serious thought so he hit Roy with some of his more well-known negatives: "You're a pothead, Roy. And you've either banged or tried to bang every cunt who worked in the courthouse. Excuse me, Flesh, for being so blunt."

She corrected Charles on one point, "Roy would prefer they do 'the bow' to banging him."

"Whatever," said Charles, as he watched Nathan cross the deck, leading the young man he had just met toward the stage where a band played some tripe from the Celine Dion songbook.

"I have one of the highest conviction rates of any public servant in the last twenty-three years," said Roy, "in either Sacramento or Contra Costa counties. And I'm a lock on the handicapped vote."

Charles knew that with Nathan those bloodstained death remarks were not just bullshit, not with the kind of atrocities that son of a bitch carried around in his memory bag done at the behest of his *dear* General.

Flesh saw that Roy had gotten nowhere with Charles so she took a turn at him with what might be described as a quiet little vamp on spontaneous declarations. "Ivy and the Delta Association did a great job on setting that land deal for the center. But what happens when the General dies? You and Nathan aren't exactly a tight fit anymore." Charles turned to Flesh. "A state legislator with a legal background who was in your corner, one who was friends with that Nathan and had honest influence over him, might be something worth considering."

Having the cunt put it in his face like that, with her erotic smile and black lipstick, Charles took a moment to search out Essie; he found her near the prow with a small group of people. She was wearing a simple black dress and white pearls and she was laughing with the others at what someone had just said.

"You know, Roy, you were right. Essie looks knockout tonight."

As Charles walked away Roy threw up his hands, "I didn't say that, Flesh."

She was beyond believing or disbelieving. "And I'm here trying to help you." She flung her drink in his lap then went for a refill.

Roy couldn't pull himself up fast enough with one arm to save his crotch from the ice and vodka. But as he swiped at his pants he did manage to get off one good barb: "I'll be here waiting, in case later you want to lick it off."

THE UPPER deck was shaped like an amphitheater. A proscenium stage had been set there for the band. It was on that stage that Nathan would make his tribute speech and announce the date of the ground-breaking ceremony. As he readied the microphone Dane leaned over the railing and looked down onto the lower decks where a streamline of people moved through the shadow-toned lamplight. He spotted Paul and Sancho Maria, got their attention with a whistle, and waved them to come on up and have a drink. Caruso pointed to a security guard at the base of the stairwell dressed as a riverboat gut puller with white puffy sleeves and black armbands. "Can't. We're not VIP."

WHEN NATHAN was ready he had the riverboat lights dimmed to black. Gambling wheels stopped, drinks were no longer served, people gathered to watch and listen. A video camera had been set up far back from the stage and there were monitors on other decks and in small rooms and above the bars for those who could not see or hear firsthand. Nathan whispered to Dane about where he would like him to stand.

Flesh was with Essie when Roy joined them. Flesh rattled her cocktail glass so the ice sounded like the tail of a diamondback and meant—behave. From above the bridge a spot switched on and a white portal of light filled the stage and everyone now saw Nathan was not alone.

Flesh whispered to Essie, "Who is that?"

Essie had no idea who the young man was standing at the edge of that raised platform, with legs together, hands folded behind his back, and head slightly bowed.

As Nathan began, his words reverbed out across a tide of faces, were carried on cables down through deck after deck of that reconstructed river wagon. He spoke with a father's pride of his own son's exuberance for life, his charity, his selflessness, his common decency, his sense of love. Each simple and cadenced phrase, one by one from the heart, silently reinforced within Nathan his own failure in the face of life. As he worked his way through the painful missive he saw, more and more deeply, how choice after choice had left him poorer of soul. And in that he was not alone. That secret was shared by all, in some fashion, as failures of choice play no favorites, they abide by no laws of chance. Failure of choice is one of life's threads that may strangle us, or, if we can understand where it leads, can set us free.

Nathan spoke of how people wished they could recall the past, recast it as the present, have it relived for all futures to see and praise. "And in a way," he said, "a handful of God has touched us with that possibility. Though sorrow cannot be changed, it can be amended."

Nathan glanced upstage. "Ladies and gentlemen, I want you to meet someone who is a living symbol of what the center wants to achieve." He pointed toward Dane. "This young man was on the verge of losing his sight and were it not for my son, in part, being an organ donor, he would be blind."

As Dane's face rose, the camera panned and zoomed, captured a momentary stare of perfect dark calm, and the crowd moved in from the edges of just plain interest toward the pure business of what tomorrow might bring.

"My dear and only son believed organ donation passed a hope and a dream to someone in desperate need of a hope and a dream. I'd like you to meet Dane Rudd. Recipient of a hope and a dream that allows him to look into your faces, to see how your hearts respond. I can't tell you what it means to have him here."

Nathan spoke at length on how the center would be a place for second chances. People heard the words, but it was the sight of that silent, attractive young man given new life that had their attention, that tilted the scales of an idea toward reality. Some it inspired, others yet complained cynically among themselves that Nathan was using the boy as a human souvenir, a token success that would help make the sell.

But the emotion of it reached them all. Charles, sitting with his wife, relived dreams that he allowed his father-in-law to steal from him, as Merrit spit blood into a handkerchief, which only amplified the hostile end that swiftly approached. And Roy, who lived with anger over the judgment of fate against his legs, while Ivy became more and more the closet junkie knowing there was no second chance for what she had done. And then Essie, who promised she would remain their collective memory, alone, to one end.

Taylor Greene was murdered—

And the moment was not lost on Dane either. He, the least of all. As Nathan began his emotional plea for a call to action to end the atrocious ignorance and suffering of the past and make the center a reality in his son's name, Dane looked out into the half-lit expression of nameless hopes and faces, past the cold moon spot and the camera, toward the river and skyline of Sacramento where clear and crystal tidbits of stars stretched on and on into that wandering notebook we know as America. And where his own future hung in the balance.

He heard the words, and others yet unsaid.

Taylor Greene was murdered—

CHAPTER FOURTEEN

WHY DIDN'T YOU tell me about . . . him?" Essie's jaw stuck out toward Dane, who was making his way past the stares and congratulations that followed the tribute.

Nathan apologized, but to Essie it sounded like artificial and expedient lip service. Then he added, "Truth is . . . I was scared."

"Of what?"

"That you wouldn't approve. That you'd see this as an invasion of your feelings for Taylor."

"Having my feelings disregarded was invasion enough. Nathan, do you realize how much you've hurt me by—"

They went silent in mid-sentence as Dane slipped between them. A forced calm followed that he easily picked up on. After a barely managed introduction came a few badly managed minutes, which led Nathan to a polite escape, leaving these two strangers at the mercy of the moment.

"If my being here is uncomfortable for you—"

"Uncomfortable," she said, "is the understatement of understatements."

A waitress came by with drinks, which neither took. Essie noticed, as did Dane, a couple manage one of those nonchalant stares as they opportunely happened past.

"I'm sorry about Taylor," he said. "Since I never met him it feels utterly strange to say his name. And yet, it feels right, since he's had such a profound effect, already, upon my life."

Essie tried not to let what he said reach her.

"I only found out tonight you never saw my letter. That you had no idea I was coming. This isn't exactly the kind of surprise I

69

personally would have planned. I want you to know that."

"You overheard Nathan and I."

"I met some friends of yours, Paul and Maria Caruso."

"You're trying to sneak past my question."

"I would never try to sneak past anyone who was obviously in so much pain."

The muscles of her face held back a sudden surge of loneliness and tired anger. The band began to play again, only now Charles had joined them with a Schechter strapped on and plugged in for the ego ride.

"I understand pain," Dane said. "I wear the marks left for me to remember it by."

He was staring at her when she glanced up. A man in a sharp doublebreasted suit with a pinkie ring and cigar swung past eager for a look-fix of those eyes.

Dane shook his head, his squared cheekbones bared back. "Second time around has me going through some very strange doors." He tried a smile but it was halved by a spell of sadness. "I better remember to bring along ID and maps, so I know who and where I am when I get there."

Her eyes flickered at the recognition of what he meant. But, "I would never have allowed myself to meet you," she said. "Never."

SHE LOOKED hurt," said Ivy. "Very hurt."

Essie hadn't blown Dane off and they seemed to be having something that might approach a conversation. "He's a handsome kid," said Nathan. "He comes across intelligent, presents well. He could be a real asset."

"You're not thinking of using him as a sort of public relations gimmick for the center?"

The music got hotter and more aggressive. Nathan didn't like the idea that Charles was onstage trying to be Mr. Guitar Slinger at *his* son's tribute.

"You haven't answered my question."

THE PRINCE OF DEADLY WEAPONS

"You know what the kid said to me downstairs? You wouldn't believe it. He's got a good heart. He's like . . . Taylor, that way."

INTRODUCE THE players, girl," Flesh said, draping an arm over Dane's shoulder.

While Essie introduced her and Roy, Flesh got right into Dane's back-pedaling stare. She had a cigarette in one hand and a cocktail in the other and carried them like a gunfighter would a brace of pistols. She was being coy and obvious as she spoke. "I read that you can't tell if someone had a cornea transplant. They form fit a few layers of tissue onto the person's eye. It's like grafting on glass.

"Of course, I wouldn't be nearly as tacky as most of the human knockoffs doing shark patrol around your face, just so I could see for myself." Flesh said this, of course, with all her available eye sparkle and mouth pout.

Dane slid from her grip. "If someone ever asks me who's got the perfect nightgown smile I'm gonna have to reach into my memory bank for your name."

"Nightgown smile, hunh." Flesh looked from Essie to Roy, who wasn't happy with her little performance. "Nightgown smile." Flesh's nostrils flared a bit. "Where are you from?"

"California originally . . . Palmdale . . . San Diego . . . San Louie Obispo. We moved a lot."

"And how did you lose your sight?"

"Christ, Flesh." Roy groused around on his crutches. "We're not two minutes into the conversation."

Flesh shrugged, "I'm Queen of the Prelims."

"You an attorney?" Dane asked.

"He's not only good-looking. Am I right, Essie!" Essie held back, tried to keep a polite and reserved distance. To Roy: "He is good-looking, isn't he?"

"Don't forget, Flesh," Roy told her, "ward policy says you have to be back by midnight so they can chain you down."

71

She huffed, "I'm an Assistant D.A. Roy here is a D.A., Sacramento County. Now, how did you lose your sight?"

"I never lost my sight completely." Cold certainty took control of what he was about to say. "I was on a subway platform going from Manhattan to Queens. It was near two in the morning. That's when you get to experience the other side of the other side. I was waiting there thinking how my whole life was ahead of me when an express train changed all that.

Dane took a moment, as if he was reliving the episode. "Some freak with a crossbone trigger flung a glass at me from between two cars of that train as it blew through the station. There were chemicals and ammonia in that glass. A little reminder cocktail from the world's circus. I got hit in the eyes and went down and heard a woman scream above the rattle of those metal wheels and what I heard freaked me: 'His eyes are burning.' "

When Dane finished, all that glib trimmed conversation was gone leaving only the meat of a wound. What followed was clipped facial expressions and silence until Essie broached the one question they all wanted to have answered: "Did they catch the person who did that to you?"

"For all I know they're still riding the subways and toasting their good fortune."

None of them knew quite how to handle his making a dark joke out of such a personal scar. Eye contact became a notable chore, except for Dane.

"It must be very frustrating," said Flesh.

"Frustrating?" As he answered he looked at Essie. "As someone rightly once said, that would be the understatement of understatements."

More silence now which made the party around them turn into an untidy clutter of noises that grew louder and more abrasive. Essie communicated to him silently using her heartshaped and sorrowful mouth to make the words: "I'm sorry."

"Of course you're not strangers to what I feel." Dane turned his attention to Roy and Flesh. "You're Nathan's friends. You were close to Taylor, I heard. You had some control over the investigation. A friend is murdered and no one is prosecuted?"

"Now wait a second," said Flesh. "We could never prove he was murdered."

"But we know he was," said Essie.

Roy's body constricted. "Everything indicated suicide."

Essie came right back, "Taylor would not commit suicide."

"I understand," said Dane, "how tough it is. You can't resolve something, you feel impotent."

"Excuse me," said Roy.

Essie went right on, "Everything wasn't done that could have been."

"Roy and I have this very same argument."

Roy's hand grabbed at his beard. "Show me facts. Give me leads. Give me something. Idiot people shouldn't be out there talking up—"

"Am I one of those idiot people?" Essie demanded to know.

"I didn't mean—"

Essie walked off. She'd had enough. Flesh called to her. Angered, Roy turned on Dane. His mouth was a wall of smoke-stained teeth.

"I was just trying to make a point about how you can feel impotent when things can't be resolved to your satisfaction. When you can't pull it all together."

Flesh knew that for Roy any form of criticism, whether justified or not, any comment that even hinted of criticism, whether real or imagined, was an indictment of his crippled body.

"Everything said suicide."

"Did you go to college?" Flesh asked. It was an embarrassing bridge and well beneath her skill but she worried that Roy would make a fool of himself and a possible politician should not be making a fool of himself in public.

Dane answered civilly, "When I was sixteen I won scholarships to college. I was one of those Harvard to Berkeley–type brainchildren people want to strangle or set on fire, that is, until they discover how much they can make off of them."

"We did everything we could as prosecutors to get to the truth.

And I have one of the best prosecution and conviction rates."

"I certainly didn't mean anything more than I said."

Flesh pressed on, "What are you going to do with your life now?"

"I'm going to try and improve on the old one, and I think I'll take a few steps in that direction right now, and excuse myself."

Dane hadn't cleared a line of heads before Roy went all to hell cursing and commenting and telling Flesh, "Did you hear the little shit?"

She grabbed his arm and dug her nails in and told him to keep his voice down and she kept squeezing and digging so hard he almost tipped over and she said, "Yeah, I heard the little shit, only the little shit is you."

ESSIE WAS on the bow of the lower deck when Dane found her. Alone, at the railing, under a drifting rope of lamplight, she was telling herself what in her heart she already knew. They had moved on. They had their lives and hopes and needs, and they had their evasions and lies and headstrong excuses.

She looked down at the water and watched herself rise and fall on a seiche of tide. It had been six months and what had she discovered that disproved what they said? A few slight unimportances she kept to herself and did not understand.

"I didn't mean for my conversation to upset you."

Essie came about. Dane sat on the railing beside her. "But did you mean to upset them?"

Dane's body turned toward the river with a spartan economy. He took in the night a long time. "Let's just say I'm trying to imagine what Taylor would like me to see, if he could ask."

Dane stood. She was examining him now, studying the letter of his words. There was beauty in her face, he thought, a beauty beyond features, formed in that realm where color and character connect, where the angle of bone and curve of flesh demark tendernesses and dark spots of obstinacy. This was a face you could believe would wear with courage the bruises of the world while

THE PRINCE OF DEADLY WEAPONS

offering you glimpses of gentleness and love and care.

"I saw Disappointment Slough from the sky today. And I'm going out there tomorrow. I'd like it if you would take me."

A hard breeze had blown up from the bay and she turned away from it. "I can't."

"The Carusos offered to let me sleep in a trailer they keep at the airport."

She shook her head. "I can't."

"I'll be leaving from their coffee shop around nine."

As he walked away she told him for the third time, "I can't."

THE CARUSOS lived at the airport. They had a small Airstream parked in their front yard. After they brought Dane sheets and a pillow and said their good nights Dane dialed out on his cellular. He turned off the lights and watched from the darkness to make sure neither Sancho Maria nor Paul returned.

"I'm calling to fill you in," Dane said, when the line at the other end was answered . . . "Yeah, you all are right. Even the fiancée is certain Greene was murdered, and she's not bashful about saying it . . . The kid's father? I can't make him out exactly but he's a pitchman. Has the stroke down. My gut tells me he's a con's con . . . Yeah," said Dane, trying to cover up the bitterness and pain he felt at the accusation . . . "Who better than me to spot a con."

He reached for the cigarette Caruso left. He went to put it in his mouth and light it. He stopped. "If you quit your little litany of warnings long enough I'll give you the good news . . . Nathan Greene wants me to stay on . . . Yeah . . . To be part of his dog-and-pony show. The miracle of modern science he'll troop out to fundraisers . . . I don't think you could have wished for a better situation. It gives me a solid reason to stay here and . . ." Dane's back stiffened. "Right. Be careful what you wish for. I'll try not to forget it."

CHAPTER FIFTEEN

I THOUGHT WHAT you did tonight was incredibly selfish and vain."

Charles would have come at that statement but there was a sensory struggle going on inside him and he could not orient to the feelings. He stood in the bathroom doorway twirling his toothbrush nervously between two fingers.

"The night belonged to Nathan." Claudia slipped into bed. "And Taylor. Not to one of your overheated guitar solos."

"I should never have let your father talk me out of my music career."

To her he seemed almost pathetic. He put the toothbrush down and wiped his mouth on a towel. Why quibble, she thought, with a bank clerk who couldn't carry his own excesses and over-confidence.

"Was it a few drinks too many and Nathan's speech about second chances? Was it because you heard someone's heart and it rattled you? Or was it that handsome kid who is probably everything you aren't?"

Disturbed, he told her, "It was all of that. And more."

"You go through these self-purges every year, but they come to nothing. And I would like to correct your statement about my father. When you were busted for dealing to your music friends, who got the charges dismissed so your record was clean? My father . . . who then offered you a job so you could make a living."

"And you know what that offer meant."

"I know who and what my father is. I know about Nathan. I know they'll both be buried in Arlington Cemetery. I know what you've become. It was not my father who compromised *you.* I watched you take that turn, remember."

"Tell me then."

"I have two daughters I love, and who enrich me. I was deeply into you once upon a time. With your long hair and pretty, pretty smile. I went for the package. I am guilty of youth."

"Tell me why."

"Get yourself a girlfriend, or a boyfriend, or a hobby."

"Say it."

"I own some very tony vibrators and I'll take my vacations."

"Say it."

"And we'll survive the distance."

"Say it."

She shut off the light and pulled herself down under the sheets. He heard the sharp intake of her breath which meant "leave."

BEHIND A lace curtain Sancho Maria watched Dane. He sat on the silver metal steps of a small Airstream the Carusos parked in their front yard. He had bummed a cigarette from Paul and that shirtless, barefoot man-child held the burning tip upright and stared at it. He stared as the red glowing fire ate away paper and tobacco. He stared as the snake charmer would when facing down the snake.

From behind Sancho Maria, Paul whispered to her, "If I hadn't turned out such a mess, we could have a kid like that."

She slid away from the window and got her arms around him to still his heartache. "You are not a mess. And, we really don't know anything about that boy."

"You're talking like a corrections officer now." He gruffly and playfully grabbed her.

She slapped his bare ass on the way to bed. "Lockdown."

ON WEEKENDS The Burrow drew quite a crowd. Word gets around which local airstrips have the best restaurants near a runway where you can fly in, walk to a good meal, then fly out.

Dane was having coffee at the bar. Sancho Maria was serving. Paul was working the coffee shop and they could hear him burn up acres of testosterone anytime someone deigned to activate a cellular.

Dane kept sneaking looks at the wall clock, and just before nine Essie walked in. Standing at the door she looked extremely reticent. He walked over to her. "Thanks for coming."

Her voice, when she spoke next, sounded as if she were trying to get past the privacy of her situation. "I sat up most of the night uncertain and afraid of what would happen to me, how I would feel and act, if I took you there. So . . . I will take you there."

As THEY drove out toward Airport Road they had to pass a last row of hangars. Above one set of doors painted in huge silver and black letters was written: THE ROCKET BOYZ. This is where the Fenns had their plane repair business and kept a crop duster.

Essie noticed the brothers were playing coolios to a group of beer-drinking fly freaks as they showed off a '99 Stationair that had set them back almost three hundred thousand dollars. She had asked Paul where they could have gotten the money and he told her word was Charles spotted the Boyz a loan.

It wasn't sitting right with her. Ever since Taylor's death it seemed Gill and the Fenns had gotten tight. She'd noticed it the first time that day they marched their way into Taylor's hangar on a little errand for Charles.

Music from the Rocket Boyz' hangar banged out across the haze swept tarmac. As Shane came around the Stationair he spotted Essie. His deadeyed raver grin locked on and her insides contorted.

It must be tough having a boyfriend off himself like that—

As they swung away from the hangar Shane bent and squinted to see who was riding shotgun and Dane heard Essie say under her breath, "That's one prick asshole I'd like to run over, and *then* set on fire."

CHAPTER SIXTEEN

Essie's Ford was a '63 Falcon, all cleanly original except for the new four shift on the floor and a heavy duty clutch, which she worked with decisive efficiency. They crossed the Rio Vista Bridge and drove in silence till they reached the Ryer Island Ferry.

The *Real McCoy*, as it's named, was a diesel powered affair with overhanging pilot house and metal railing, port and starboard. It could hold maybe four cars, but this morning, as they crossed Cache Slough to Ryer Island, there was just the Falcon and half a dozen Italians on a cycling tour of the Delta.

As they began the crossing Dane noticed Essie had started to relax. He got out of the car and went to the railing and looked out upon country he had yet to see.

Essie, too, got out of the car, but she remained alone leaning back against the fender. The sleeves of Dane's white T-shirt had been cut off and she noticed a tattoo on his right shoulder she could not, from that distance, quite make out.

Ryer Island was a flat trace of uninterrupted waist-high slender reeds. The sun was only now burning off the last of a dewy ground mist and it seemed the earth was being born through this smoking creation.

Behind those sunglasses Dane's gaze went from point to point until he saw a flock of birds bound up out of a timeless wave of green reeds.

He did not know what the white birds were. But he followed their silent formation as it struck toward the sun. He held them in his sight until their ascent blended into the sky and they were no more.

By this time Essie had walked to the railing and gotten a good look at that tattoo. It was a black and red lightning bolt, two, maybe three inches in length. Both tips were shaped like arrowheads. One pointed upward, the other downward.

"Is there a story attached to that?" she asked.

He saw she meant the tattoo. "After the subway incident, when my eyesight began to go, I decided to bum around the country and really see it, on the chance I would be blind."

His hands slipped into the pockets of his faded jeans. He got one motorcycle boot up on the railing to balance himself as he leaned back. "I refer to this as my Fear and Loathing in Las Vegas period. A fluke hooked me up with a vanload of social radicals."

He shook his head. "They were trying to keep alive an internet mag they'd started called *Twisted Clarity*. Actually, it was more of an anti-mag mag.

"There were five of them. Imagine Tom Paine and the Merry Pranksters. The Beat Generation as dressed by Marilyn Manson."

Memories gave way to something more reflective. His hands slid from his pockets and gripped the railing. He watched those Italian students chat and laugh and pose for snapshots that would mint time and place on the coin of memory.

"Then one day the messenger arrives and strikes you down." Dane paused. A slow wiring moved up through the muscle of arm and shoulder, then into the face. "You listen, you hear. And when that's done, you are no longer you."

He turned to her and smoothed over what there was that edged those feelings. "The lightning bolt represents that reality, the arrowheads a commitment to strike out in new directions. The up and down speaks for itself about the pull of reward and warning."

Silence followed, held together by the wash tide and cable motor turning. An Italian asked Essie in hobbled English if she would play photographer for a group smile. With that done she returned to the railing and Dane said, "What made you so angry back at the airport?"

Without answering she walked to the car and leaned in the open window to get at the glove compartment. She returned with a badly flattened half pack of cigarettes. "I don't smoke much, so these are about three months old. You want one?"

He did. They smoked.

"You always wear those sunglasses?"

"My eyes are light sensitive. If you don't want to talk about—"

"One of my stepfathers grew up in the Delta. He was a mechanic and on Sundays he had a part-time job running this ferry. He would take me along and I'd get to play engineer, which for a ten-year-old was a hoot.

"As a boy he had been an extra in a movie that was shot here called *All the Kings's Men*. This ferry was actually used in the movie. He had it on VHS and would play it all the time. He was more connected to the past than he was to the present; it's the one thing about him I remember most.

"I'm telling you this as a way of explaining something to myself. Reminding myself about how I should not be."

She got quiet after that. He waited as she did. She could feel unsettled niches inside her and then, without beginning, she began. In a stream of words she told him about the Fenns, about that day in Taylor's hangar, their sudden relationship with Charles over recent months, the new plane, the tension between Charles and Nathan since the murder, and when she used the word *murder*, she did so with emphatic assurance.

"Did you tell this to your D.A. friends?"

"I did not."

"Why?"

"I will not let them call me an idiot. And I will not let them know what I am doing."

"What are you doing?"

She waded through the thought of telling him she was trying to unearth evidence, if there was any, in a small collection of details she'd been quietly stitching together without anyone's knowledge. But until her intuition made it a necessity silence was the next best thing.

"Do you think those garage punks were somehow involved?"

"I think it's possible with them," she said. "But I think some things much worse than that. Much, much worse."

CHAPTER SEVENTEEN

SNUG HARBOR IS a marina and RV park under huge ancient willows near the southern tip of Steamboat Slough. They would use Taylor's runabout, which was docked in a covered berth on the cove side of the harbor, so they could get to the island in Disappointment Slough.

The quiet waters and deep green overhanging shade made the docks and dwellings feel like something you'd find in Louisiana rather than California, and as they pulled past the tent camps Dane caught sight of a sign pitching the resort. It was one of those clean American mottoes meant to lure you in with its accursed sweetness: *There are no strangers here . . . only family, old friends, and newly found friends.*

ROY WAS at The Point restaurant in Rio Vista having a Bloody Mary and trying to get the bad taste of last night out of his mind. As Flesh had ordered, he'd invited Nathan to brunch so he could smooth over any problems on the chance word got back about his conversation with Essie and Rudd.

The Point looked out on the Sacramento and from a waterside window Roy killed time watching the white proud yachts and the black gray freighters move between the bay and the city.

Roy hated boats of any kind, and here he was living in the Delta. They made him seasick, his polio turned into a catastrophic humiliation on a rolling deck, and to top it off, he couldn't swim. He couldn't even float.

He was mindlessly watching a barge pass when he caught sight of a runabout. He recognized the boat, and Essie driving. Then he saw who was with her.

Mr. Well Spoken. Mr. "I Didn't Mean Anything More Than What I Said." Mr. Distinct Good Looks, as Flesh kept reminding him on the way home.

His whole body twisted trying to follow the runabout with his eyes. Mr. Well Spoken had been there less than a day and already he had one hand in their lives.

REACHING DISAPPOINTMENT Slough was a meander of sweeps and curves that traced a path through Sevenmile Slough and down the San Joaquin, past Prisoner's Point and the Empire Tract. The way was marked by nested ports done in the river architecture of the twenties and by bascule bridges whose cool shadows touched the day. It was a dockside world of restaurants made from the hulls of steamers and small harbors with clustered sailboats whose masts stood above the trees like the spears of knights would unto the sky. There were the remains of homes the changing tides had taken back, and vast drifts of silence filled with pampas grass and, of course, the overwhelming throaty scent of life on water.

Essie found herself wandering into a thought. Was it she taking Dane somewhere, or was it he taking her? Was there some guiding consciousness in control, or was it just drift? For one short solitary moment she was darkly frightened. She got away from the strong undertow of that idea by asking, "What do you think of the Delta?"

He turned to her. The sun was against his face. "I was taking it all in. The eye-delightful simplicity. And telling myself how easy it would be to imagine living here and being . . . roughly free."

CHAPTER EIGHTEEN

Roy WAS GOING on and on with his self-absorbed expiation concerning last night's argument when Nathan just flagged. "Enough."

While Roy pulled at his ponytail Nathan said, "I heard you were talking to Charles about backing you in a run for Congress."

As if this course change were just an intrusion Roy went on, "Do you know who gave Taylor the pills?"

"Ivy told me it was her. Has Charles offered to back you?"

"Did she tell you why he wanted them?"

"Listen to me on this. Stay away from Charles' money. I'll get you people who will—"

"Did she tell you?"

Roy's fingers kept spidering through his gray hair. Nathan hated that, always, and at this moment even more so. He turned away and sighed. He tried by looking out the window to find something he could concentrate on that would stop the urge to ask, "What did she say?"

"I kept it from the police. Away from the press."

"What did she say?"

"I did this for your sake. For Essie's."

"This is about you, Roy. What did she say?"

"You have to swear not to tell Ivy we spoke of it."

"You know you are going to hurt me."

"I don't want people to think it was murder when it wasn't. At least, we have no proof—"

"But some people believe it *was* murder, Roy, and I'm one of them."

"I'm not trying to hurt you." Of course, Roy knew he was being selfish and hurtful, but if it would make the case for his life being better. "Taylor was thinking about suicide. He told Ivy."

Nathan's eyelids sunk until they shut. "Did he say why?"

"Because he felt . . . his life was a failure, compared to yours."

WHEN THE runabout passed the St. Francis Yacht Club the boundary on Essie's pain tightened. "The two witnesses came from that yacht club bar."

As Dane looked the St. Francis over, the runabout came to port and Disappointment Slough opened out before them.

The river is a road that moves, so says the old adage, but the pull of the tides seemed to have no direct control on the water there.

Up that few mile stretch were thickly treed islands which hid small cabins. There were calm glades and wreaths of hyacinth that drifted on the idle current. It was, to the eye, a continuing series of classically lit camera poses from some easy past.

They tied up at Taylor's dock.

"How did a place as beautiful as this get a name like Disappointment Slough?"

"That is a mystery no one has ever been able to answer."

He looked toward the far berm. "You swam from there?"

Barely above a whisper, "I did."

He followed Essie up the walkway and under shaggy poplars toward a clapboard bungalow with screened-in porch and metal roof. The house was wrapped in a brown-green thistly brush that covered the island's three, possibly four acres. Dane noticed a slight swell of earth forty yards or so from the house, where stood a stone well and a windmill. The windmill was now used as a river beacon which lit up at night.

Essie pointed to a cracked piece of railing. "That's where I fell and broke my wrist." She turned to the front door. "And that is where I found Taylor."

Her mouth stiffened as she tried to maintain a rigid discipline on her emotions. Looking at that door, now under a spell of delicately shaded sunlight, one would never suspect that death had visited so violently.

Her body suddenly shuddered. "I'm not sure I should have come. I feel too many questions, too many hurts."

She started back for the boat but Dane grabbed her by the arm. She jabbed at his grasp with an elbow and got loose. "You don't know. You don't know."

She sounded like something caged. "They say it was part my fault. That because I'd moved the body I'd 'contaminated the site.' Should I have left him there and not checked to see if he was breathing?"

Her body trembled. "Is that what I should have been about?" The full force of the past was having at her. "I still see him lying there and I'm not good at pretending things away. It is part of my mind and my heart. Blood and all.

"Am I the only one who hurts enough to keep caring? Where is Nathan? Where is Ivy? What about Roy? Even if Roy believes it was suicide, why should he rest on that? Taylor was his good friend's son. This isn't a matter of fact.

"I'm not slick or shrewd. I'm not one of those people who can sit around and think sinister with the best of them. But something happened here." She pointed to the doorway. "Something more went on than what they say.

"Fuck!" She screamed so loud the slough echoed with her. "I need to be alone for a few minutes so I can calm down. All right!? All right!?"

She didn't wait for his answer. She walked through the brush on the thinnest thread of a trail up to the windmill, where she sat on the edge of the stone well and lit a cigarette. She seemed to be shivering.

DANE WATCHED her. She was quite something, he thought. All heart and feelings. Compared to her he was—Dane could barely manage a comparison. She was the honest contrast to everything he'd been.

How much more did she know? How useful would it be? He could offer to help her, to make a plea for her trust. But his instincts warned to call in and have that choice cleared, because he had been advised that any decision he made on his own they disagreed with could jeopardize his shot at freedom.

If he did make the call, with everything that had happened, with the possible leaks in security, where would that leave her? What might she become vulnerable to?

He looked at the spot where Taylor had lay dying. I have thrown my life away once, Dane thought . . . and for what?

ESSIE STARED down into the cool hollow of that well and used the trancelike quiet to help her settle out until the telltale signs of fatigue stopped her crying completely.

She smoked and gave everything that plagued her a chance to just ease away, if only for a while, so she could think more clearly, be more in control of her decisions.

She only heard Dane once his shadow moved across the morning sun upon her face. Looking up she said, "I'm sorry."

"No one should be sorry because they are admirable."

She grimaced. Having the physical need to do something she went to stub out the last half of her cigarette on the well stones and Dane said, "I'll finish that."

He paced the brush, thinking privately, hands folded behind his back except for when he took the occasional drag on her cigarette.

He stopped and looked up at the windmill. The metronomic clicking of those dry wooden slats sounded as if it were the very prose of existence stepping out the marks of time, reminding life of its brief seconds over the course of eternity. Without explanation or reason he asked Essie, "Are you familiar with that overly traveled proverb 'Am I my brother's keeper?' "

"I was dragged to religion classes."

"The phrase could probably use a little facelift to get it past the time warp. Am I my sister's keeper . . . my mother's . . ." He watched the tip of that cigarette burn . . . "Am I keeper to someone, anyone, even myself . . . I wonder." He walked back toward her and the briars cracked under his black boots. "Am I keeper to a human being I have never met, but who now holds meaning to my very existence . . . I wonder."

He stopped where the shadow of that windmill wheel fell across the patchy, caked ground. He stared into that slatted mandella where shadow turned to light turned to shadow turned to light. "And if I'm not my brother's keeper, then who could I depend on to be there for me when the time comes I am desperate and alone. Who?" His voice began to trail off considerably toward some intense corner of self. "Who will be there to make ends meet?"

He looked up that windmill where sky and sun bled through the brown lattice framework. He watched the breeze's sudden effect on its wooden cadence. He looked back to Essie.

"I threw my life away once because an idea like 'Am I my brother's keeper' meant nothing to me. And because it meant nothing, I was left with less than nothing. This is my way of telling you—no, asking you, to let me help find out what you want to know. As a means to paying back a personal debt."

It took her a while to get past the fact she was unwilling to field this unexpected offer. And there were hard questions: "What happens if those little pep talks wear off and you get bored and want to move on and make money? What happens if I invest my trust in you and those catchphrases suddenly make better conversation pieces than pieces of reality?"

"If you feel better off alone, be better off," he said. "I will stay and play sales promo for Nathan. But there is one thing I do know. Anyone . . ." He took off his glasses and stared at her. It was a stark look, almost too much so. ". . . Anyone can be standing on a subway platform alone, alone, when the express comes past carrying your worst nightmare."

CHAPTER NINETEEN

THE HOUSE ON Disappointment Slough still belonged to Nathan. Essie hadn't been there for two months, not since Nathan had asked her to box Taylor's clothes and take them to Goodwill.

While they opened doors and windows to clear out the stale odor of mold and dry, dead air, Essie began by telling Dane about those snippets of conversation she'd overheard that night between Nathan and Ivy. That, and the fact that Taylor's death had been immediately considered a suicide, had forced her to question everything.

As they sat in the living room and smoked, Essie went into detail about Nathan and Ivy's relationship. She did the same with Charles and the General, Roy and Francie. She filled Dane in on their interlocking lives, their secrets, their drug use, their petty needs, frailties, backgrounds, dreams. From their strengths right through to the suspect edges of character she wanted him to know as much about them as she did, on the chance he had an insight about the human wilderness she was wandering through.

Since Essie had graduated from junior college she'd been Nathan's secretary, and then his office manager. That was how she'd met Taylor and where she first heard those serpentine nasties people passed around the espresso machine. Those with money have always taken a hit from the trash whispers, and the more money you have, the more venal the ass swiping.

She'd been told Nathan and the General might have been involved in clandestine activities during the Vietnam War, certain high-risk government moves that had made them influential allies, but which had rubbed off on their present lives. Certainly, no one ever said this to Nathan's face, and everything he did was marked by legal contracts and the terse air of the honest man. Taylor used to refer to all that claptrap as "minds that had nothing better to do than go malignant."

But now, she was not so sure.

"You think Taylor might have found out something about his father that made him vulnerable to suicide?"

"Not to suicide," she said defensively. "To something else maybe, but not suicide."

"You don't think his father—"

"Nooo. Not that. He couldn't hurt his son, if that's what you mean. But I don't trust Nathan anymore. I'm not sure who he is and that scares me. It keeps me from confiding in him, or confronting him about what I heard."

She got up and began to pace. One hand worked the other for support. She looked at the empty desk in the bay window alcove where Taylor would sit and make his calls, where he'd lounge with a beer and just watch the Slough. The light coming through the window was beautiful muted shades and Essie suddenly realized she could no longer truly hear Taylor's voice. Not the pitch or tone, not his soft caustic laugh. All that had been Taylor was drifting out to sea on the blind curse of time.

Essie went on to explain how since the funeral she'd been collecting information: letters, documents, contracts, any and all correspondence that passed between Ivy and Nathan, between Nathan and Charles, Nathan and the General. She made copies of Nathan's travel receipts and phone bills. If there was a number she did not recognize she'd call the phone company and have it checked. She logged the names in her computer and alphabetized them. She carried a backup of that list in a briefcase in her car trunk. There were so many boxes of information stored in her garage, she told Dane, the Falcon had taken up permanent residence on the street.

Essie took a long breath, rubbed her lean throat and standing motionless by the desk told Dane how she had begun breaking into Nathan's office computer late at night. How she'd raided his e-mails, drafts of notes, personal correspondence. If he wrote it, she stole it and made copies. She'd done the same with his home computer as Nathan had years ago given her a key to his house and when he was out of town he'd have her check to make sure things there were . . . safe.

She had Dane follow her to the screened-in porch which had been used as a second bedroom during the summers. One wall was lined with boxes stacked three high. Everything in that house the night of Taylor's murder she had photographed then packed away. What was on the desk, what had been in the desk drawer, in the desk trash can, what had been strewn about the living room, was meticulously labeled and numbered with a corresponding master list.

She was staring at the bed while she spoke. What dreams had been created there with the white salt of their sweat and a touch of consuming passion. The need for meaningful physicality that she had been keeping at bay pressed out suddenly against her ribs and into the slender lift of her breasts. She closed the door and walked out of the house and went down to the dock.

Staring at the water she thought of the stiff procession moving toward the grave site in the rain and realized in the dark wire of her feelings the act of filling in the truth about Taylor was her way of separating from the past, it was her stumbling process on the path to getting well.

As Dane joined her on the dock the wooden frame shifted a bit under their weight.

"Remember I told you the Fenns were in Taylor's hangar picking up an antique cabinet Charles ordered?"

"Yes."

"Well, two days after that the man who rented the hangar next to Taylor's called me. He'd seen my confrontation with the Fenns and told me they had trashed the cabinet. That it was in a Dumpster behind his hangar."

"What was that about?"

"I don't know." Her cellular began to ring. "But I took the cabinet out of the trash. It's in my garage with everything else."

As she went to answer the call Dane said, "Good thing we're not in The Burrow."

Her eyes danced a bit. "Yes . . ." Then, "Nathan . . ." Surprised, she looked at Dane. "How did you know?"

"I was with Roy this morning at The Point. He saw you. He was apologizing to you, through me, for his behavior last night."

"I hope you made him do some serious groveling."

"He left quite a long trench across that gravel parking lot, I can promise you."

Nathan did not confide in her about Taylor's conversation with Ivy. He never even considered it. "Listen, Essie. I guess you know Dane is going to be staying here a while, for when I talk to investors and such . . . He doesn't have a place to stay, not really. I was wondering . . ."

She turned away from Dane. She knew what Nathan was going to ask. The awkward blips in his conversation gave it away. "I think it's a good idea."

Caught off guard he said, "What?"

"Letting Dane stay at Taylor's house. That is what you were thinking?"

"Yeah . . . well. It was a thought . . . the house is empty."

"You'll have to get some propane up here, and have the electricity turned back on."

"Could you, would you see to it?"

Her mouth was dry. She had to wet it first before continuing. She smiled, as if that would help her in some way get through what she'd say. "Sure, and you know what else, Nathan, I think you were right bringing him here. It's going to be a good thing all the way around."

"I'm sorry I was afraid to tell you, Essie. It's not like me, but since Taylor's death I don't seem to have the confidence I used to."

"We're gonna get you your confidence back, Nathan. You'll see. We're gonna make that our number one priority."

She clicked off the phone and turned to Dane. "You now have a place to stay."

"Thank you."

"You don't have to do this. You can stop now and forget everything I told you. You can."

"But I can't."

She shook her head. "I feel guilty. Lying to him like that."

"In a way, you've been lying to him since the funeral, haven't you?" He started back for the house. "I'll bring those boxes into the living room so I can look through them."

I'VE GOTTEN a good lead on some information . . . it shows promise. That's all I can tell you . . . Who?" As he talked on his cellular Dane looked at all the boxes stacked up on the kitchen table he'd gone through since Essie left. "That I won't say." Dane reached for a faded section of newspaper he found in one of the boxes. "We're not gonna make this a struggle, are we?" The paper featured an article from the *Sacramento Bee* about the violent murder in Cayuma, California, of a Federal Reserve agent.

"I will not . . . I will not . . . No . . . No . . . Listen to . . . Listen . . . List . . . Greene is dead, and your agent is dead. Someone at this end found out Greene had contacted him, or there is a leak at your end . . . That's right, at your end.

"You need to know if there is a money laundering operation going on here as you suspect. The who, where, what, why, and if, but I won't jeopardize someone . . . That's the word . . . I won't 'jeopardize' . . . 'Cause I know how you guys operate . . . I've seen your loyalty up close."

Dane began to pace the room holding the article in his hand. "Who am I? I'm nothing, remember? Just a set of handcuffs with a body attached who cut a deal to save his ass.

"While you're reading me what's left of my rights let me read you this . . . Yeah . . ." Dane read from the newspaper article he was carrying, "A Federal Reserve agent from the Los Angeles branch was murdered on Monday . . .

"It's an article from the *Sacramento Bee* . . . All Greene's possessions have been saved . . . Everything . . . What was on his desk the night he was murdered was even saved . . . By whom? . . . I'm not going there . . . Now, of all the articles out of all the California newspapers what are the chances he'd save . . . That's a quick one-eighty change of tone . . .

"You pressed me . . . do this or face hard time . . . You had cold-blooded down pat and I'm here 'cause I wasn't in a position to negotiate then . . .

"Then as in *then* . . . If you think I'm trying to cover for someone so I can use them, think it . . ."

CHAPTER TWENTY

DANE WORKED WITH subtle urgency to infiltrate a handful of lives. He needed to show results and keep showing results so he had an edge over his handlers negotiating the narrow limits of their patience. He also had to deal with the knowledge he was eminently expendable.

Time was his enemy but he never let on as he went with Nathan to investor meetings where he was the perfect show and tell, shaking hands, replaying the night when a wraithlike figure on a speeding train flung chemicals in his face. His selfless dedication and story brought an almost metaphysical honesty to the project.

It became apparent Nathan was growing genuinely fond of Dane. They'd meet for lunch and drinks just as he had with Taylor. Even Ivy saw how smoothly comfortable Nathan was becoming with his new life. Dane was filling in the shadow hole of a dead son, and she more than anyone, except possibly Charles, wanted the past firmly, and finally buried.

And while all this played the bulk of the money for the center was being put together during short junkets Nathan took to San Francisco, L.A., and Mexico, meeting with contacts for drug money coming out of Colombia and diamond traders who clandestinely secured jewels stolen from war-torn Sierra Leone.

ESSIE AND Dane were in her garage going through the last of the material she'd boxed and collected. The door was open and music drifted on the night air from Sugar's Bar right across the alley on River Road.

What began with promise had burned down in the process. That maze of papers and photographs they'd been through was still so much paper and photographs. If something there had any value it was, as yet, buried under plain sight.

While Dane was checking the small antique cabinet that had found its way from Taylor's hangar to the airport trash Essie closed up the last box, put it to one side near the garage door, then used it as a place to sit. There was something on her mind she needed to get at.

"I watch you with Nathan and I don't know if you're being genuine or it's just an intelligent lie since we're sneaking around behind his back trying to find out if he's done something wrong."

"It's both," said Dane, without looking up from his scan of that pine sideboard. "And, unless you haven't noticed, I'm acting no differently than you."

Under the trim fronting he felt raw nubs so he tilted the sideboard up on two legs to get a better look, as the garage was lit by a single overhanging bulb.

He noticed small roundish discolorations the size of a quarter under the front trim where his fingers had felt the shrayed wood. These were matched by the same discolorations and splinters along the ridge of the bottom trim. "It looks like something was ripped from here. Dowels maybe, or decorative columns. Did you notice anything like that when you first saw it?"

"No."

"If it arrived damaged Charles would have sent it back and not trashed it, right?"

"Right."

Essie looked into the alleyway. She listened to music from Sugar's and watched the street where headlights flared then disappeared like simple thoughts that come and go. "I see the way Nathan relates to you, the easy joy he has when you're around, it makes me glad and angry at the same time."

Dane looked up.

"The way you can just hang with the Carusos and talk on their terms even better than Taylor ever could makes me glad and angry at the same time."

He set the sideboard down slowly on its legs so as not to disturb her. Essie leaned her head back against the garage wall. "You're stronger than Taylor and more self-assured, I see it. And it seems to me, for better or worse, you're more calculating and resourceful than he could ever be. That makes me glad and angry at the same time."

Dane stood.

"I sense you have more courage, or maybe it's just a kind of audacity that comes with living and suffering. You certainly have lived and suffered more than he ever did, until the night he was murdered. All that makes me glad and angry at the same time."

Dane crossed through that bare throw of light and stood over Essie. She did not look up. She was just being an honest creature feeling and saying what she felt. She leaned her head to one side so she could watch that piece of space where headlights flooded then blacked away on their ride up River Road.

"And the fact that I want and maybe even need your help, and that you have tried to help, makes me glad and angry at the same time."

She finally looked up to let him know she was done. He leaned against the wall near where she sat. His jeans were covered with filth from dragging around that hole of a garage.

"I don't have any neat or clean answers," he said.

She rested her arms on her thighs. "I wish I was twenty-five without all the extra baggage."

"I read that twenty-five and twenty-six are considered the crossroad years in a person's life. When you really begin to become who you will ultimately be."

"I'd rather be twenty-five without all the extra baggage. And I don't want to do all this soul searching in a filthy, dark garage." She put out a hand. "Pull me up, dust me off, and buy me a beer."

———

97

Sugar's was a bastion of working class blues with pool tables. The drinks were cheap and it was notorious for its sway of California music from Spade Cooley and Rose Maddox to the Flying Burrito Brothers, Dwight Yokum and the infamous Bakersfield connection. Dane and Essie were in a back booth and they'd had enough beers to put a little perspective on any bad day.

"My mother was married five times," said Essie. "Twice to my real father, three times to other men. And it seemed to me each had the same dire similarities.

"One night when I was out my mom and me were sitting right there." Essie used an empty bottle as a pointer aiming it at a booth by the bar. "She announced she was about to lock up number five.

"I said, 'Mom, what's with you? Don't you realize you've been marrying the same man over and over again?' And you know what she said to me?"

Essie looked down the throat of that dead Corona as if a genie might appear. "She said, 'Es, honey'—I hate being called honey, even by my own mother—she said, 'Es, honey, don't you understand . . .' "—Essie's voice dropped dramatically—" 'there is only one man.' "

Dane started to laugh. Essie wagged the empty bottle at him and grinned. "My sentiments exactly, until, until, until about five seconds later and I realized"—Essie hit the bottle down on the table as if it were a gavel—"what if she were right? What does it say?"

"She either keeps making the same mistakes over and over again, or she's right, and there is . . . only one man."

"Exactly." Essie tapped her beer bottle against his. With the booth being so small they kept inadvertently brushing against each other and then they'd politely have to reshuffle themselves so the other had a little space.

"What about your life on the home front?"

Dane hesitated. "My father is dead, my mother doesn't realize she isn't. And sometimes I wish I were twenty-five without all the extra baggage."

He drank his beer. She watched his neck muscles tense as he

killed off the bottle. When he set the bottle down Essie asked, "That's a pretty blunt answer. You want to expand on the details? The when, why, where, and how it makes you feel?"

Dane stared into that open room where they played pool under low overhanging lights. He looked as if he were caught in the spell of some deep grievance. "Let's not, and just say we did."

DANE WALKED Essie back to her place in silence. The alley was quiet and they could hear the music coming from Sugar's. It was a ballad of sad romantic charm. A track straight off Tulare Dust. Neither could see Roy's car in the deep shadows across an open lot of weeds.

As Essie unlocked her front door Dane said, "I screwed up my life. I told you that. I just can't talk about it. I'm sorry." He turned to go, then, as an afterthought said, "I wonder if we're all just accidents with the power to think."

PINTER WATCHED Dane get into that funky black Rampage pickup he drove. He'd gotten the plate number earlier that night.

CHAPTER TWENTY-ONE

NATHAN'S OFFICES WERE on the second floor of the Discovery Bay Yacht Club building. Ivy had been put in charge of redecorating and she had done so with a careful eye toward class and pretention. It was old prestige California as seen through the pages of *Architectural Digest.* All the couches had to have the Monterey stamp on them, and every cushion used original fabrics or flawless replications. The rooms swam with the colors of summer and you got to the offices by way of a wide open veranda whose windows looked out on a showcase of docked yachts.

When Nathan asked Ivy why she'd spent so much on originals when copies would have served just as well she said, "If you give them class, they will give you money."

ESSIE HAD just returned from her monthly go round with the company accountant. She scooped up her messages from the switchboard operator who told her, "I left a box on your desk that was delivered here for Nathan. He was in a meeting and told me he didn't want to be disturbed."

Essie was listening with one ear as she read through her messages. "Fine, I'll take care of it."

"Essie, I need to tell you something." What caught Essie's attention was the tone of the girl's voice. "The box," said the switchboard operator, "it has blood in it."

THE BOX was twelve by twelve by twelve. It said on the side PLASMA, along with all the usual cautions and warnings about handling. There was an envelope attached made from fine bonded paper. She did not need to look at the bank's return address to tell her the package was from Charles. She had enough copies of his handwriting in that paper mountain she'd stored away to tell her that much.

She opened the envelope, read the note.

Nathan—
As per Merrit Merton. This is to be delivered to the
Animal Blood Bank in Tehachapi—

THE DOOR to Nathan's office opened and Dane walked out. Essie waved to him, and through the doorway as he passed she could see Ivy on the phone and Nathan as he paced and listened. Occasionally Ivy would ask Nathan a question and he would rifle back an answer that she would relay to the listener. Then he abruptly closed the door.

Dane came to Essie's desk. "It seems my opinion is valued when it comes to deciding whether escargot or scampi would go better with veal."

He noticed the box sign: PLASMA. He turned the box a bit. "Did somebody here order a transfusion? 'Cause I could sure use one after the last hour."

"Taylor did charity work for animal shelters and vets who had those free clinics. If they needed plasma or something Taylor would pay to have it flown or driven there. Paul . . . he always paid Paul to do it."

Essie had been staring at the note the whole time, slapping the bonded edge against her fingers. When she looked up her mouth flexed. She handed Dane the note. "Charles never did anything like this in his whole goddamned life."

As he read the note Essie bent down and from under the desk

brought up her briefcase. "The only charity I could imagine getting him off would be if some rocker on the skids was forced to auction his guitars."

She snapped open the briefcase clips, took out the master list of names she'd been collecting. "I think I recognize this Merton from the list of Nathan's calls 'cause he has the same first name as the General." Essie thumbed through that two-inch stack. She held up a page, "See?"

There were a dozen numbers listed under Merton's name, with the dates calls were made to each number. The area codes covered a wide swath of California and Mexico. One particular international number was notated: SIERRA LEONE. And, as Dane quickly realized, the calls began a few days after the tribute to Taylor.

As he handed her back the list Nathan's office door opened and he quickly strode toward them. Dane slid across the desk in front of Essie trying to give Nathan little or no opportunity of seeing, then questioning, that two-inch dossier she was nervously stuffing back into her briefcase.

CHAPTER TWENTY—TWO

Es, I'M LOOKING for the . . ." He saw the box . . . "That's it."

She handed him the note. It was now back in the envelope. "This came with it. I assume we're helping some shelter or vet?"

Nathan didn't bother to open the note. "An investor friend of Charles is an animal freak and Charles told him what Taylor used to do, so he passed my number along."

"Can I help?" asked Essie.

Nathan snatched up a piece of paper and a pen. He started to write. "You can help with the boys downstairs. I've got to put together a dinner for six or eight, in the private room."

Dane watched Essie lift the box. "Where is it going?"

"Ah . . ." Nathan was forced to take the note from the envelope . . . "Tehachapi."

"How's it going to get there?"

"By plane."

She reached for the phone. "You want me to call Paul to see if he can take it?"

He stopped writing and took the box from her and set it down beside him. "No."

"But Paul always—"

"The Fenns are gonna take care of this."

"The Fenns?"

Nathan's office door opened and Ivy, who was still on the phone, covered the mouthpiece and called to him. He motioned for her to hold still. "Charles talked to the Fenns. They'll handle it."

"Are you sure that's the way to go?"

Ivy called again. Nathan's hand tomahawked at the air for her to be quiet.

"Are you sure?" Essie repeated.

Dane could hear her tone was becoming querulous.

"I'm sure," said Nathan. He went back to writing out his notes.

"You want me to take the box to the airport?" said Essie.

"I'll take it."

"I can do both."

"I know you can," Nathan said. "But you can't."

Ivy called to Nathan again, this time she was adamant. Nathan hurriedly finished his notes then handed them to Essie. "Get all this together, will you, Es?"

As Nathan was about to go Dane put on a goodwill smile. "Nathan, after all that talk of food I could use a little exercise. Why don't I drive it out to the airport. That way you can both get things done."

Nathan slapped Dane on the shoulder. "After all that talk of food, *you* need a little exercise." He aped a grin. "Let me tell you, son, when you get to be my age you just pass a restaurant and you'll gain five pounds. Thanks for the offer, but when I get a few minutes I'll drive it.

"Stop by the dinner tonight, though. About nineish. I want a few people to meet you."

Nathan went back to his office, leaving the box on the desk.

As the office door closed Dane turned to Essie. "He sure didn't act like it was a big deal."

"Then why did you want to drive it to the airport?"

"For the same reason I assume you did."

"I don't trust the Fenns. I don't understand all these little comings and goings."

Dane motioned for her to keep her voice down.

"Maybe I could take the box in the bathroom," she said, "and open it before he comes back." The box was heavily taped with masking and would have to be closed back, right and clean. That would take time and the proper tape. "Maybe it is nothing."

"At least sound like you believe what you're saying."

"I want to know, how's that?"

The light had moved across the window and was now directly in Dane's eyes. He slipped on his sunglasses and stood. He stared down at the box.

"What are you thinking?" asked Essie.

WHEN NATHAN came out of his office Essie was at the window watching Dane's pickup hustle out Marina Road toward Discovery Bay Boulevard.

"Essie?"

She turned abruptly.

"Where's the box?"

She took a breath to calm herself. "Dane said you looked tired, so he thought he'd do you a favor."

IVY WAS just starting to dial Charles when Nathan came back into the office, closed the door and leaned against it.

"Put the phone down."

The way he said it made her put the phone down.

"He took the box. Dane . . ."

The crows' feet at the corners of her eyes went white ever so slightly. "Do you think it'll be all right?"

DANE MADE sure he was well out of Discovery Bay and miles down Marsh Creek Road before he pulled over.

He found a spot of ground along the train tracks hidden from the road by trees. There was debris everywhere. Beer cans and bottles. Discolored mattresses with rusting springs. A rising mound of white toilets and strewn clumps of used food wrappers.

He stared down at the shotgun seat where the box was. Does the act of one person, in some way, profoundly affect us all?

As he reached for the box an Amtrak came racing up from the southeast. The ground shook the truck shocks and the box trembled. Willow branches were sucked into the maelstrom made from those metal bodies that clacked violently as they ran on. The blue and red cars strobed against the sun across his windshield and in the waketide of those disappearing cars trash confetti came spiraling back to earth as Dane began to open the box.

NATHAN WAS hovering over Essie when her phone rang. He was working on the dinner arrangements but his thoughts were decidedly somewhere else.

"Discovery Bay . . . Nathan Hale Greene's office."

"Pandora's Box has been opened," said Dane.

Her eyes slanted nervously up toward Nathan who was a bare foot away. "Mr. Greene prefers all forms of solicitation be made in writing. Letter or e-mail."

Nathan's eyes gleamed onto hers.

"I understand," said Dane. "Just know, it isn't blood in that box."

Essie was frightened. Her adrenaline rushed making the front of her throat just throb. "We look forward to hearing from you."

"Diamonds," said Dane. "That's what's in the box."

She fought off strains of vertigo as she looked at Nathan. "Thank you," she said, and hung up.

CHAPTER TWENTY—THREE

THE ROCKET BOYZ' hangar door was open when Dane pulled up. He stepped out of the truck but intentionally left the box on the shotgun seat.

THE INSIDE of the hangar looked as if the Fenns had ripped off the Paul Caruso school of interior decorating, then done a student body left. The walls were full of movie posters from such cultural masterpieces as Pornogothic, The Girls from H.A.R.D. and Lethal Projection. There were photos that featured oiled-up chickies with fake blood running down their naked flesh while they ate each other to death. There was a collage of Mea Culpa stills in her most pouty, bondaged poses, and magazine centerfolds so far off the path of anyone's food chain it was downright frightening. Some strip and stroke shots set new standards for fetished sleaze and there were bumper stickers interspersed with such classic phrases as "Kill 'Em All And Let God Separate 'Em . . ." and "Blowin' by Jesus."

But the Fenns did show an occasional touch of wit. In one poster they had superimposed Dolly Parton's plastic grin on some sadomaniac in black leather who stood in a dungeon and wielded a whip, while around her boots were hundreds of human skulls Dane could only imagine were staring up at her with ultimate devotion. In another, Michael Jackson's face had been pasted onto the bare caped body of a white hermaphrodite who was impersonating the Wicked Witch of the West.

Shane was bent into the cowling of their Piper Super Cub grinding down the tail of Cherrymax rivets on a doubler he'd made to shore up a crack. Tommy was at his desk computer doing a parts search.

The grinder was putting out 12,000 rpms. Sparks and all, it was loud work. Neither heard nor saw Dane enter, so he watched the Boyz to absorb, if he could, a little more of their world, and who they were.

On a corkboard were snapshots of Tommy when he served in Kuwait. The only snapshots with Shane were of him doing the pussy cling. Dane noted a signed photo of Maurice Richard, the wild-eyed tempest who had been hockey's first real cult hero.

Tommy noticed Dane and stood. He whistled to his brother, who didn't hear him. Dane waited through the grinding screech as Tommy slipped under the wing and hit his brother on the shoulder. Shane must have been putting out some concentration because he came around startled and angry at being startled till he saw it was his brother whose jaw pointed for him to look about.

When Shane saw who it was he shut off the grinder and set it down on top of a MIG welder. His goggles were covered with flecks of metal, as was his white bleached hair. He lifted the goggles. "The dude with the hip eye shades." To his brother, "I told ya, check 'em out. They are strictly."

"What's doin'?" asked Tommy.

Before he answered Dane pointed to that signed photo of Maurice Richard. " 'The Rocket' . . . is that how you got your company name?"

"You into hockey?"

"When I lived in New York and I needed a taste, I'd go see the Rangers or the Islanders. Sometimes we'd trip down to Philly and see the Flyers."

"You don't come across like you'd be interested in hockey."

"No?"

"No. You seem too . . ." Shane took his hand and got it down near his balls and let it tremor slightly . . . "You know what I mean? You know what I mean."

"Sure," said Dane. "You think I'm the type that likes to stay home, jerk off, read Camus, make model airplanes and sing 'Kumbaya' . . . when I'm not cruising the truck stops looking for some humper in a cowboy hat to put his boots up my ass."

Tommy smirked. Shane's lips curled to hold back a laugh. "You gave him a little stage one and he upped you," said Tommy.

"I'm broken, man, I'm broken . . . call the pallbearers." Shane walked over to his workbench and looked back at Dane. " 'Kumbaya' . . . fuck me." He started to wheel a torch cart back toward the plane.

"Why you here, man?"

Dane was checking out the Super Cub. "I got a delivery for you guys." He thumbed a hand toward his pickup.

"What delivery?"

Dane didn't answer Tommy right away. He kept looking the plane over up close and drifted into: "A couple of guys in The Burrow were talking about this type of plane. They said it could land on a matchbook and needed a nothing stretch of ground to lift off. The wet sand on a beach . . . a field . . . a small piece of flat hilltop. Practically anywhere."

Shane and Tommy glanced at each other. The last time they had dropped that Super Cub into a field was a looming and shadowy distance that suddenly and inexplicably hung over them and Shane said to his brother in passing, as a way of almost playing with that night, as if tempting its presence, "Magic from the doomslinger." Then, as he opened the nozzle on the oxygen and acetylene tanks, "And a little taste of moral outrage to go with it."

Dane noted the odd drift of looks between the brothers and the enigmatic phrases and Tommy asked again, "What delivery?"

Dane turned to him now. "The guys were saying this plane was perfect for running drugs and slipping past the law."

Tommy didn't like someone throwing around inferences, but unlike his brother, Tommy used silence to get a point across. He didn't want to make any more of it, but Shane, "We don't know anything about that shit, Officer. Our only drug is Christ the King. We get high on our Lord and Savior."

"Right," said Dane. "And slip me an Ecstasy pacifier, so I don't break out laughing at all that Quo Vadis crap."

This was becoming a turf war of shit talk and Tommy wanted it done. "We don't have all day, guy."

Dane pointed to his truck. "Gill left a box at Nathan's. It's plasma. I guess you guys are gonna take it down to Tehachapi." Dane noted the turn their attention took. "Nathan was backed up with work so I brought it over. You want me to—"

"I'll get it," said Tommy.

As he went to the Dodge Shane got that cutting wand lit. "I heard you had an eye transplant and Taylor was the donor."

"That's right. But it was the cornea, not the whole eye."

"Right. Well, I saw this movie once. A guy gets a transplant and starts seeing shit from the other person's life. It was one of those softcore movies and he starts seeing bits of pussy . . . chicks he fucked . . . chicks who sucked him off."

Shane looked up at Dane. Dane's stare was fixed, his face blank. "You have any of that shit happen to you? Anything?"

Dane kept staring at Shane but said to Tommy who had passed behind him with the box, "When I was carrying that to my truck, a guy in the parking lot bumped into me and knocked it out of my hand. You may want to open it up and make sure everything inside is all right before you fly it to Tehachapi."

Tommy set the box down by his computer. "I'll take care of it later."

"If you do it now, and something *is* wrong, I'll—"

"It's cool, man. Thank Nathan."

"I'd feel better knowing I hadn't fucked up."

Tommy wanted this guy out. Wanted it done. Wanted to get him on his way. He took the box and went to a worktable at the rear of the hangar. He scraped through a toolbox till he found a razor.

When the box was half open Dane started Tommy's way and his brother let that flame just rip. A ten-inch laser of blue-white burning whoosh cut across Dane's path.

Dane stepped back.

"Sorry, man." Shane got the flame down to a harmless idle. "I heard you were on a subway platform in Rockerville when some freak threw chemicals in your face that made you go blind."

Tommy had opened the box. He'd looked inside and with an expression of pure boredom closed it back up.

"I wasn't exactly blind then," said Dane. "But I am sensitive in certain kinds of light."

"I better put this torch over here then," Shane said as he set it down.

"Things are cool," Tommy said. "Thank Nathan."

Dane was turning a thought when Shane nudged him and then pointed the tip of that cutting wand at the poster with Michael Jackson pasted onto the body of a hermaphrodite who was doubling as the Wicked Witch of Oz. "Remember that scene in the movie? When the old bitch gets water flung on her and she starts to melt. All that smoke coming off her and shit. That must have been like what it was for you.

"Of course, what happened to you was a lot worse. I'm sure you wouldn't want to go through that again. I know if it was me, I'd be blown out."

Shane then started to say "I'm melting . . . I'm melting!!"

His voice was complete creep shit and Dane went at him. He rammed Shane into the cowling and grabbed that angle grinder with his free hand. He thumbed the grip switch and that carbonate wheel went up to 12,000 rpms before Tommy could shout, "Don't do—"

The grinder had no protective shield. It was just a pure four-inch pneumatic saw that could undo your skull in less time than it took to blink.

The blade was smoke-heating the flesh that protected Shane's jugular. "I'm not gonna play some jerk-off fool's idea of a joke."

"Put that fuckin' thing down! Now!" Tommy ordered.

"Having something thrown in your face like that can breed demons. It can make you want to drink too much and dress in black. Play Mad Max on The Yellow Brick Road."

"Put it down."

"They say people who have a few demons tucked away inside them usually like to edge up other people's lives. Give them a little taste."

"I'm telling you."

Dane let the blade scar the cowling inches from Shane's throat. It made a blistering squeal and sparks flew everywhere. Shane's body locked.

"*A little magic from the doomslinger.* Was that your phrase? Well," said Dane, "I just came into your crib and took it."

CHAPTER TWENTY—FOUR

Sancho Maria was serving bar to an Edward Hopper placement of characters when Dane came in. He slid onto a stool near the door where he could not only be alone, but watch the Boyz' hangar.

He did his first beer in two swallows, then he looked down at his hands. They were still trembling; thank you anger, thank you rage. There was a twisted irony to the saying, You have the whole world in the palm of your hand, that was not lost on him. So much for second sight.

Sancho Maria brought him another. His lips parted in a brief smile, and they talked. But she had been a corrections officer too long, she had been married to Paul too long, not to feel a person's bad weather coming on like a storm.

Alone again, Dane kept slipping that hangar a look over his shoulder. Things were quiet, but he couldn't see into the shadows.

When Sancho Maria was bringing a tray of drinks to a table she passed behind Dane. She leaned over his left shoulder and tucked a cigarette into his shirt pocket. Then she tapped him on the back. It was done tenderly, with a mother's touch, as if she was somehow, without knowing details, signaling to him, through his body, that things would be all right.

The moment, inconsequential as it may have seemed, brought up a flood of meaning and feelings and Dane tried to get a hand on hers before she pulled away, to let her know that he had heard her.

PAUL WAS at the restaurant counter ranting to a row of hangar rats how the small coffee shops of America were being wiped out by those "ass lickin' Starbuck froufrou phonies, with their lattes and fat-free milk" when Sancho Maria called him to the bar.

OUTSIDE THE restaurant, under a stand of eucalyptus, Paul found Dane sitting at a picnic table. Dane hadn't gotten nearly close enough to even-hearted when he heard, "You drink my beer, you smoke my cigarettes, and not one fuckin' hello . . . well, hello anyway!"

Paul swung onto the picnic table. He sat above and beside Dane. Dane looked up. Paul was cracking his shell-shaped knuckles. "The old lady thinks something is bothering you. And you know what kind of radar cunts have for that shit. Well?"

Dane turned his pitched stare toward the tarmac. A single-engine plane was propping toward the runway. There was a blanket of silence otherwise with Paul watching the boy and the boy's veiled expression concentrated on the Fenns' corrugated hangar.

Paul waited. The kitten he'd found weeks ago was slow-cruising the grass. "Look at her," he said. "You know who's gonna feed you, don't you, you dirty little bastard." The cat leaped onto the picnic table and landed air-light. He scooped her up by her black nape. She hung before his face while he advised, "Don't fly too high, don't fly too low." Dane flicked ashes onto the dead air. "I keep saying it. Hoping somebody will listen, besides me." Paul glanced at Dane again. He seemed more intent on the cloacal shadows of the Boyz' hangar. "Nothing like talking to yourself when you're among friends."

Dane leaned back. "Remember, you asked me once if I had any aphorisms appropriate to my own life?"

The kitten was in Paul's lap. He was tweaking her belly while she playfully bit his fingers. "What the fuck is an aphorism?"

"A saying. Like, 'Don't fly too high . . .' "

"Yeah . . . yeah. I got it."

Dane leaned forward. He smoked. He ran a hand through his

black hair and started. "Speech is silver, but silence is golden." That single prop was coming around to the runway behind them with its propeller growing louder. "I am a slow walker, but I never walk back." The plane took off, cutting the air as it climbed. Dane waited, his forearms resting on his thighs, his boot toes lifting and dropping until the quiet folded in over that wild noise and he could finish. "Strike harder and twist the links, where others' skills have failed, *he* can still invent resource."

Dane sat as he was for a minute or so, his boot toes lifting and falling, taking an occasional drag on his cigarette, flicking ash into the dead air. Paul said nothing, but he recognized the unsettling energy Dane was giving off. It had been, at one time, his own defiant and self-destructive trademark.

"What's the matter?"

Dane looked up. Paul was staring at him like a parent who was trying to read right down into his child's wiring and see if there was a way to shut off all those Cain-flexed emotions.

"I can see," said Dane, "for you, those aphorisms didn't personally 'kick.' "

"You want to talk?"

"I think I have one that will give you a little boost." Before he started Dane glanced at the Fenns' open hangar door. It was just gauzy black space, and no sign of Tommy or Shane.

"Never eat at a restaurant called Mom's . . . Never play cards with a man named Doc . . . And never, ever, ever, ever sleep with anyone whose problems are worse than your own."

Dane looked up to find Caruso grinning. " 'Never sleep with anyone whose problems are worse than your own.' " He held the kitten in one hand while he pointed at The Burrow with the other. "Talk about dead on."

"That would go for Sancho Maria too."

"What do you think I fuckin' meant?"

Tommy showed. He wasn't carrying the box, but slung over one shoulder he did have a gym tote large enough for it.

"What's so interesting about the Rocket Boyz?"

"I had a little slip and slide with them a few minutes ago."

Shane came out of the hangar and started to roll the doors closed. He was talking rapid fire to himself.

"What about?"

" 'Cause I wouldn't sit through their lounge act."

"What were you doing over there anyway?"

"I was doing Nathan a favor."

Shane got the hangar door locked. He and Tommy stood on the tarmac facing each other. Tommy, it seemed, was trying to get his younger brother's anger under control.

"Look at them, Dane. They're screw heads. Strictly bad shit. I know they deal. And they fly across the border into Mexico doing who knows what else. I don't understand why they haven't been busted by now on something."

"Well, the clock's still running."

When the Fenns started across the tarmac Dane stood quickly and the kitten, startled, leapt from the table to the ground and sprinted down the walkway.

"Let me tell you something, Dane. To give you a little hit of what those *Boyz* are about. Their father was a dealer. I did time with him. The cops pulled a bust on a mobile home he was shacked up in where they had one of those nine-seven-six phone sex lines running out of. That stoned fucker had such a lockdown mentality he shot it out. There in the house. And over what? A lousy sex line. The boys were about ten and watched their old man give up the ghost right there on the living room carpet.

"I tell you this so you know what kind of gene pool they come from. They got the same lockdown mentality as the old man. They're gonna get the needle one day, mark my word."

"I guess I better not bring a box lunch if I'm gonna mix it up with them."

"Don't do that."

The Fenns were not walking toward their plane, but instead, were making for a white Bronco that was sitting on jacked-up wheels. "Paul, do you think the human tragedy is the failure to exact change, or is it not trying?"

"I was in stir long enough to know life never gets that fuckin' articulate."

Tommy handed his brother the gym tote, then opened the driver's side door. Dane started down the walkway and Paul followed.

"With all that reading you did in prison, did you ever wonder what was in Theseus' head, why he took that walk through the labyrinth?"

Paul's eyes narrowed. Dane was making toward his pickup.

"What do you think, Paul?"

The Bronco's engine revved, the dual mufflers kicked out bull-horn widths of smoke.

"Where are you going?"

Dane swung the driver's door open and slid down into his pick-up. The Bronco was moving now, Dane turned the engine over.

"You haven't answered my question."

"And you haven't answered mine."

Paul tried to grab the door and keep it from closing but Dane was too quick.

CHAPTER TWENTY-FIVE

ESSIE WAS IN the yacht club kitchen with the chef detailing
Nathan's menu for that night when an important call was trans-
ferred down to her by the receptionist. She took the call in the
manager's office, which was no bigger than a file card with a desk
of stacked invoices.

"Delivered," said Dane. It was a raspy connection but his voice
came through like cool machinery. "And the Boyz are hip to what
they're carrying."

The office had no door. Essie went around the desk to get as
far back in that cubbyhole as possible so she could talk. "How do
you know, and where are you?"

The dishwashers were right against the wall behind her so between the water hose spraying those clacking plates and glasses
and the cooks and waitresses yelling over each other Essie had
to cup her ears to hear Dane as he shorthanded the moments
from when he first walked into that hangar to following the Boyz'
Bronco as it humped its way east on Route 160 out of Rio Vista.

Head bent and turned away from the office door she asked,
"What are you gonna do following them?"

"Get someplace we can talk. Call me on my cellular."

The phone clicked shut on an unanswered question. She stood
and looked out the office doorway through smoke rising off the
stove to another open doorway which framed the private dining
room where she watched Nathan slip a video into the VCR that
sat on a hutch shelf against the far wall.

She made her way across the hot noisy kitchen handing about

her purse for her cellular to call back Dane and then on into the silent, cool dining room where a worker laid out crystal goblets and fine china plates with the Discovery Bay insignia imprinted in gold.

Nathan worked the remote and the video taken of the tribute that night on the riverboat cued up perfectly to the beginning of his speech. That moment now played quite differently.

"Dane called," Essie told Nathan, "to say he delivered your package."

Concentrating on the screen Nathan answered, "It wasn't my package, it was Charles.'"

He seemed preoccupied, as if caught up in the urgency of something else. She moved slightly to get a better look at his face. He was watching his speech, adjusting the sound till it was just so.

Was that a secret face she stared at? Was all this just so much sales pitch and pretense? Or was there a chance he knew nothing about what he had just been part of?

Her hand found the cellular in her purse. "Nathan. I'm feeling a little off . . . would you mind if I took a break?"

COMING OUT of Rio Vista Route 160 rode the eastern bank of the Sacramento. But here the river thinned since it no longer benefitted from the current that flowed south out of Steamboat Slough.

The Bronco was maybe a thousand yards ahead of Dane burning well past the speed limit. He looked at his gas gauge. It was dangerously low and he had no idea how far they were going or where.

Through a slatted grid of old growth and olive trees Dane could just make out a watery light held in place by those high-leveed banks as he told himself, promised himself, swore to himself, that he would not allow himself to be someone things just happen to.

A gray stream of clouds was moving against the sky above Stockton and the Delta. Dane caught a snapshot of himself in the rearview mirror. His features stared back at him angular and taciturn, and for that brief instant he considered what he really was for attempting this.

I'M GONNA turn that skank motherfucker into my bitch."

Shane's shoulders hitched unmercifully while Tommy rode the steering wheel as the highway wound north coming out of Isleton.

"I'm gonna burn a trail all the way up that yuppie prick's asshole."

"You're not gonna do anything," said Tommy. "You understand?" He put a warning hand right in his brother's face. "We got a life now. We got a plane. Money. A future. And I'm not letting you go pull some reckless tribal shit like the old man."

Shane kicked the dashboard, drove a fist into the door, rammed his back against the seat. He did not like being compared to his old man. "When the time is right I'm goin' out to that shack he lives in and—"

While his brother ranted Tommy hit the horn and rode its blowing sound over his brother's hardline bullshit.

"Fuck you!" screamed Shane. He slammed a fist against the glove compartment lock and it jawed open. He manhandled the junk inside looking for a joint.

"Don't you light up, not with what we're carrying."

Shane was beyond obeying. He was riding that vintage Fenn rage. "Then why do we got a joint inside the car anyway?"

When Tommy saw the flame on Shane's lighter he warned one last time, "I shit you not. Don't—"

Shane's stare was straight arm defiant, all flush and fury in a show of no quarter. Shane lit the joint and as he did his brother backhanded him catching the joint in his sweep. Sparks shot outward as Tommy swerved the Bronco right off the road where it skidded on the open gravel shoulder as Shane swore and screamed and tried to get the burning cinders off his skin.

Dane was coming out of a curve just past Tyler Island Road when he saw reeks of smoke and dust on the shoulder where the Bronco's tires had locked up.

The Boyz were a mere hundred yards ahead of Dane and he had no cover on his side of the highway and the only chance he had of not being spotted was to do a wheel-spinning downshift that hooked his pickup over the white line and hard across opposing traffic toward a girder bridge that spanned the Sacramento to Grand Island.

He had barely cleared the shoulder before an oncoming truck horn tore into the air as he steered the Rampage down an angled swale of windblown sedge then up a short rise of eroded earth and onto the bridge.

By the time that pickup had sped over the crisscrossed girder shadows and found a place to stop Tommy was moving around the front of that Bronco carrying a tire iron.

Ivy was in the yacht club lobby putting in a little social time with one of her clients when she saw Essie through glass doors cross the arbored walkway toward the parking lot, an unlit cigarette in one hand, dialing her cellular with the other.

There was something about the way Essie walked and looked that had a feel of panic and tribulation to it.

The tire iron came down on the hood of that Bronco with punishing force. "Get out of the car, you white trash faggot."

Shane was locked in and not moving and the tire iron slammed down just above his head and put a black crease in the roofline.

"You little fag shit. You gutless fag shit."

Shane looked like something frozen behind glass. The hard-ass doomslinger turned shit scared mannequin. When Tommy lost it, when everything inside him went overboard, Shane knew. He was not gonna trade blood with the hallucination that had taken over his brother's body and whipsawed the tire iron right at the car door.

DANE WATCHED the assault persist through twisted shapes of undergrowth that ran the length of a guardrail he hid behind. His cellular began to ring as Tommy whaled that tire iron at the Bronco's flank causing at least one car to slow, the passengers to stare.

Whatever was happening, whatever the cause, the brothers were like two factions of the same warring body until something Shane said or did brought his brother's attack to a halt and Tommy flung the tire iron into the weeds.

Dane ran down the slope to his pickup. He reached into the open window. The cellular was on the front seat. He got hold of it and clicked on. "Yeah."

"I'm outside in the parking lot," said Essie. "We can talk. Where are you now?"

He scrambled back up the hill. "I'm at a bridge on Route 160 just past a town called Isleton."

The brackish clay gave way beneath his feet and he partly slipped back down the hill. Essie could hear his grunts. "What's happening?"

He tried to steady himself. "The Boyz have pulled off the road and are getting into some kind of fight."

Dane got his footing back enough to climb the hill again. When he could, he grabbed hold of the guardrail and pulled, boots crabbing up the last few feet. He stood. Essie could hear his voice snap, "Shit!"

The Bronco was gone.

CHAPTER TWENTY—SIX

Dane's PICKUP SKIDDED back onto the road and swept under the steel towers of that girder bridge and his neck craned into another turn and when he got the wheels straight and gears shifted and was tearing up Isleton Road where it worked its way north he grabbed the cellular.

"Dane . . . Dane?!"

"Yeah."

"Do you see them?"

"No. But if they'd gone back the way they came I would have seen them. I'm sure."

The speedometer on that small black Rampage kept climbing and still no sign of the Bronco.

"Could they have gotten off the main road? Could I have lost them?"

"Where are you now?"

The landscape moved past him like a backdrop that was roto-scoped on the horizon. There was nothing he could anchor a mark on until a green and white road sign rose out of the distance across the river and shot past.

"Ryde."

She tried to think, to see. She knew the country. She had been on that road since she was old enough to see over the dashboard.

"Well?"

But the anxiousness she felt was bleeding out her ability to vi-sualize what she knew by heart.

"Are you there?"

She closed her eyes and focused on the narrow corridor of that road. Somewhere behind her a yacht horn shrieked into her concentration but she pushed it away by focusing down tighter and tighter and suddenly she was aware she was in that same place as the night she swam Disappointment Slough.

"Are you there?!"

"There's no road. None till you get to Walnut Grove, which is a few miles. So keep going. Go!"

Dane's boot had the accelerator tongue flat against the floorboard.

"The gas gauge is starting to lick at empty."

"Maybe I should call the police and tell them—"

He cut her off, shouting, "No!"

SHANE STARED at the gym bag in the backseat. They were carrying a shitload worth of jack and the whole fuckin' day hung over him like some black invocation. It was one thing to play neck for those sons-of-bitches. All right . . . All right . . . But to have to take it when some mouth jockey comes right into your crib and throws his smack at you and you can't get to retrofit him for the box . . .

He looked at his brother. Tommy was grimly agitated as he watched the road just peel away beneath the Bronco. Shane wanted to say "Let's rape 'em. Take the fuckin' bag, load the plane and just sky it. Leave them holding each other's dicks—period."

THROUGH A broken line of trees the deep green flat of orchards and farmland spilled outward under oncoming gray thunderheads. Details were, for Dane, inconsequential blurs. Everything was the road ahead, the road ahead.

Essie stood alone like some castoff by the dockside railing, her breaths short, pensive. "Walnut Grove isn't going to be far now . . . you'll be able to see River Road . . . remember . . . where we went drinking that night down at Sugar's . . . Remember?"

His eyes were fixed on that small core of space where the asphalt cut the horizon; his hands felt hot against the steering wheel.

"Unless they stop there's more than one way to go . . . but they're gonna have to take one of two bridges . . . watch the bridges."

He had to catch them first.

"Watch the bridges," she told him.

"I heard you."

In the wavery distance his eyes marked a shield of light coming off bumper chrome.

"This might be them—"

The road took a hard turn and rose imperceptibly and with it Dane saw the Bronco sitting on its huge tires until it was lost behind a wall of wind rippled undergrowth and palms.

When Dane's pickup took the hard turn he could hear the polished burn of tire tread along the white line and then Walnut Grove was there between the slanting shadow of trees and open spots of sky, like some brush landing that grew out of another century.

Dane had to watch traffic now. A van slid in front of him and he gunned past using the slow lane. A head croaked out the van window cursing and Dane put his fingers to his lips as if to say "Ssssh" and then he spotted the Bronco again strobing through the steel girders of a bridge that crossed the Sacramento.

"They're on the bridge."

"Which bridge?"

"The one to my right. South of River Road."

"Tell me if they turn left or right."

Dane pushed it into the fast lane using traffic for cover. "They're going right," he said as he made the turn that would take him across.

"That's gonna lead them inland, Dane. Walnut Grove Road."

He looked at his gas gauge. "I don't know how far I can make it. I'm living on fumes here."

"Listen to me. They can't be going too far. Not Tehachapi. Not even Stockton. Otherwise they wouldn't have come this way from Rio Vista. It's my guess they're going somewhere close in the Delta."

WALNUT GROVE Road cut an angled line to the southeast across Tyler Island. On his left Dane passed scrub hills that made up the West Thornton Gas Fields. The earth there was the color of parchment and honey. He saw the old levee road which traced Snodgrass Slough as it made its way down toward the North Fork of the Mokelumne River.

A strange circuity struck him that he had not felt even the first time he saw the Delta by air. The way those sloughs and rivers swept in at odd angles then slipped away almost as suddenly, as silently. And the places you came upon looked so much like places you had just been. It was as if this intense, high speed meander he was taking had gone a long distance but not gotten very far. And he wondered if this was the world subtly warning him of its ways.

The Bronco wasn't high stepping anymore, but doing a casual sixty-five and it forced Dane to ease back rather than edge out. He kept wary. "How does it feel," he asked Essie, "to know you were right?"

She opened her eyes and stood looking at the water, water which might well have passed through a channel way exactly where Dane was now. She remembered how it felt having been right once before, or close to right anyway, the night Taylor was taken from the earth.

A collection of emotions seized her. At the center one was more especially true than the others. "It scares me," she said. "It scares me."

"How I wish . . . they're turning off the road."

WHAT IS going on? Where are you now?"

There was a bridge, another slough. The ground ahead was mostly open farmland except for a road just before the bridge which led down to a landing of some kind cut from the berm thicket. The Bronco had turned onto the road which passed two wooden buildings facing the slough then curled around and down further yet to a sand parking lot that backed both buildings.

From his description she knew right away. "Giustis," she said. "You should see a wooden sign—"

Perched above the trees he saw the clapboard calling card. "Yes," he answered. He was maybe a hundred yards back. "If I follow them down that road I'll be found out."

"Cross the slough," she told him. "Cross. There's plenty of trees on the other side."

IT WAS a risk. But so was staying where he was. He had to pass less than fifty yards behind them. If they caught sight of his pickup in their rearview mirror . . .

SHE HEARD the change of sound his tires made as they went from road to bridge to road then swerved left.

She could see it now. The Bronco taking the turn past Giustis. Then Dane gunning it across the bridge. She felt like she had crawled into his head, was there behind his eyes watching.

THE FENNS parked in the lot below the bar. Shane walked quietly behind his brother who carried the gym bag over one shoulder.

Shane knew he didn't have much time to make his case. Romero might already be there waiting for them. "I don't know why we just don't take that bag, load the plane, and go."

Tommy did not respond. He did not turn around. His brother

got nothing but back. An RV pulled into the lot and passed along-side them kicking up dust. They had to continue on Indian file up the driveway.

"Tommy. You hearin' me? They couldn't do shit. Let's just rack 'em."

CHAPTER TWENTY—SEVEN

A ROAD RAN parallel to Giustis across the slough and tucked in behind a hedgerow of bulrushes. From there Dane could talk to Essie and watch the landing without being seen.

"Where are they now?"

Dane saw the Boyz park when he'd crossed the bridge. He now scanned the road that fronted Giustis and a long series of wooden stairs half hidden by trees that led down from the road to the dock. Two boats were tied off, a third was being refueled.

"I don't see them."

"Maybe they were never going to Tehachapi. Maybe they're set to meet someone. This Merton. Maybe him. Maybe there."

THE RESTAURANT was dark and quiet. It took the eyes a little getting used to the lack of light. Tommy and Shane sat at the bar alone. In the far room a few tables were occupied.

"You didn't answer me."

Tommy sipped his beer. "I answered you."

"You said nothing."

"I thought that was enough." Tommy glanced at his watch. "Drink your beer."

IT'S ALL stolen, isn't it?" said Essie.

"Charles sends some bullshit package to Nathan who is to bring it to the Boyz who are going to deliver it to so on and so forth."

Essie looked at the yacht club building. Its mural windows stood out in stark relief against the sleek white stucco lines and reflected in those huge glass panels a tidal darkness that was sweeping away the blue distance. "Maybe the Fenns are using Nathan, and he doesn't know."

"The Fenns have the classic look of Jethros who have reached their high-water mark as bottom feeders."

"The rumors about Nathan and the General that Taylor always blew off as gossip, they must be true then. What I saw and heard that night between Nathan and Ivy, that must be true."

Deflated, she sat on a bench. There were gulls overhead and another shrill air cutting of a yacht's horn. "I don't want it to be true. I don't want to know I believed in the wrong people."

The trees and bulrushes around Dane twisted with the tidal storm that was closing in and he squatted to hold his cover. "There's what you think you see, what you want to see, and what you actually see. If that's too much, there's not seeing at all. I know firsthand."

WE SHOULD punk 'em, Tommy."

Tommy put his beer down. "I got to hear this rant from you every time. Every fuckin' time." Shane was turning into the bad thoughts dreams were made from. "You believe they'd just sleep-walk through a loss like that? They got people carrying these jewels out of a country stuffed up their assholes."

"Let 'em find us."

"You're thinking strictly trailer park. How-much-I-got-in-my-pocket-now shit. We can't go maverick. Look at Nathan and the General. That gig they built for themselves. I served dudes like this in Kuwait. All brass and ass. Any B-felony bullshit they can pull off we can pull off. And Charles, that Gen-X illusion married good otherwise he'd be somebody's bitch in stir for dealing."

Tommy got right in his brother's face, got him in the grip of his stare. "We will learn their business, their contacts. We will do as they ask. We will change their fuckin' diapers if we got to. And don't fuck with Rudd. You hear? Don't go maverick. 'Cause when the time comes we are gonna ask for a little gold leaf. We are gonna ask to be their partners. Serious mainline shit. And if we don't get it, then all bets are off. We will take it to their crib. Show 'em what a serious dose of—"

Tommy stopped short as Damon Romero slid into the darkness beside them. "Sorry I'm late."

Why didn't you want me to call the police?"

It was becoming cool as the sunlight slipping through that great river of rain clouds grew less and less.

"Dane? I could call Roy."

The door to Giustis opened and Dane eased himself up to see over and through the wind-turned bulrushes. "What if the Boyz are gone by then? What if they've managed to hand off that gym bag before they're hit on?"

Romero stepped out into the grainy daylight. The bulrushes were snapping wildly and Dane had to push them away from his face to see who this was.

"Is that the only reason?" Essie asked.

"What other reason would there be?"

"Getting away with a little taste of 'moral outrage' . . . Dane?"

Romero looked over his shoulder and Essie was listening closely now, not just for what Dane said but how he said what he said, and he was listening as he watched and here came the Boyz stepping through the doorway and joining Romero and he could hear the silence at her end loud and steady as the ticking of a clock.

From decency to rage to cunning and the day wasn't over yet. "I won't lie to you," Dane said. "There's a part of me that can relate to the Boyz' roadside approach to life. If that's what you're asking."

The Fenns followed Romero across the road.

"Is this about me, Essie . . . or you?"

Tommy had the gym bag slung over a shoulder.

"Is it because the people you believed in were not worth you?"

The first spots of rain fell on her face and everything she felt she refelt in instant variations. Was this about him . . . or her? Was it because the people she believed in had become suspect and so she felt a need to test him? Did their deceit demand she test her selfhood against them? Was it because the system she put her faith in had failed her? Or did she just plain flat-out hate the Fenns and wanted a reason, any reason, to exact a little "moral outrage" of her own, to be there ringside carrying a skull and crossbones sign when they looked up stunned from their own destruction.

"The Boyz are back," he said. "With a man I've never seen before."

Essie stood. She wiped the drops that wet her cheeks and eyes as Dane described Romero; the strut walk, the lean well-manicured profile, each word marked by a hand movement, his shirt open one button too many, maybe a gold crucifix brandished around his neck, maybe a crucifix.

Where were they going?

Dane lost them for a moment in the trees along the levee side of the road. He ran through the bulrushes pushing open a pathway, his eyes darting from point to point to point until he picked them up in the half shadowed patches of tinted light making their way down that long series of plank steps to the dock.

"The dock," he said. "They're going to the dock."

Romero stepped onto the dock, as did Tommy.

"They're getting on a boat."

Shane was left to release the pile line.

"Is it possible to follow them?"

Essie couldn't see how. Romero stepped into the closed cabin of that daycruiser. He took the helm, sliding down into a pedestal seat. She couldn't envision that rival landscape of channels and waterways fast enough to give him a chance. Shane jumped onboard. She couldn't create a cogent roadmap from memory with the kind of immediacy he would need.

Dane could hear the twin inboards fire as he shunted his way through the trees and rushes shouting into his cellular, "They're taking off! Is there a way to follow them?"

"I don't—" She stopped herself from finishing that sentence of a thought.

The dayboat swung out into the slough. "Essie!"

The rain hit against her eyes and cheeks. A thrust of anger went through her. Anger at being impotent. At being helplessly unable. At being a set of eyes and a mind that stared into the phone voiceless. At being—

"Stay with them as best you can!" she said. "Give me a few minutes. And keep the line open!"

As the dayboat came around Essie raced across the yacht club parking lot toward her Falcon. When the huge inboard Cats kicked out full throttle Dane could hear it across the slough and the cruiser shot forward. It was heading back up the Mokelumne, back the same way the Fenns had come.

CHAPTER TWENTY-EIGHT

Essie CLAWED AT the glove compartment box trying to get inside so fast the cover snapped loose. She found her map of the Delta beneath a stuffing of car insurance forms and compacts. As she shook the map open the sky erupted and left its acetylene mark from heaven to earth. She got the map flat across the rain-spotted engine hood when thunder breached the miles.

Against a green background the map traced in the Delta roads and sloughs, channel depths were numbered, the location of ferries and bridges was placed, whether bridges swung open were raised or stationary was scripted in, as was the clearance of each for boats.

"Dane . . . where are you?!"

He told her he was running Walnut Grove Road west. She finger raced to that spot on the map.

"Listen to me," she said.

Through a rain-spatted windshield he could see the dayboat ahead and to his right. "The slough swings away from the road soon," she said. Tommy was inside the covered cockpit beside Romero. Shane was standing behind them, holding onto the rocket-launching-type rod holders bracketed into the roof's tailing edge. "After that, there's one of two ways to go. They can stay on the river till it turns into Snodgrass Slough or . . . they can take what's called the Cross Delta Canal, which leads back to Walnut Grove and the Sacramento River."

Dane tried to link together those dizzy turns of water. He flipped on his wipers. They did little more than change dust into dirty motes of wet mud.

One glance told Dane Essie was right. The slough would start to pull away from the road in a mere hundred yards. The dayboat leaned starboard and left a surge of white foam. Shane's shirt blew wildly outward.

Through a snapping vignette of open slough where the trees fell away Dane rode the shoulder as best he could and tried to read the name painted on the transom of that cruiser as it cut into the charcoal distance.

Rainspots dotted the map Essie held in place against the wind as she told him, "Walnut Grove Road will turn into Route 13. You take 13 north."

He clipped a look at his gas gauge. The gas tank was not on empty, it was below empty.

"The Locke Bridge crosses over the Canal Cut. If they come that way you'll—"

He cut her off, "And if they go the other way?"

Her voice flatlined. "Then we've lost them."

NATHAN, ARE you all right?"

Watching the tape of that tribute had brought back the gray hours of his life. A dark graph of memories that rose from duty and honor to the vile and unsavory which he shipped through without the least shame.

"My life is a pretty soiled record."

Ivy put an arm around his shoulder and neck to comfort him.

"Tell me I'm not selfish for going on."

"You'd be selfish if you did not."

He tried to get fixed on what he was working toward. Then it occurred to him Essie had been gone over half an hour. "Essie wasn't feeling well. Check on her, would you?"

LIGHTNING AGAIN cut apart the distance as Dane stood on the bridge just below Locke looking down into the heart of the Cross Canal. From tide to sky that cut of water was overlapping shades of overcast that bent and distorted perspective except for a spindle thin thousand-foot television tower that rose like a compass into the rained-out distance.

In the southeast there was thunder. A broad and deepening burst sounded as it moved north over Discovery Bay that Dane could hear through the cellular before it struck the world above him.

He squinted through wet eyes. "If they come this way, all right. But if they don't, there has to be a way to follow them."

She held the soaked map to the hood and forcibly pointed her finger at the impossibleness of it, as if he could see and understand. "A mile up, Snodgrass breaks off into Lost Slough and The Meadows. There's no roads. None. And you can't go where there's no roads."

"Why not?" he said. "People do it all the time."

She explained to him about the land east of Locke which led to the junction of Lost Slough and The Meadows. He looked through the bridge spans to see for himself. The ground was as she had said, an uncharted overgrown spanse. An impractical emptiness of high weeds and brush. Of vined-over trees and marshland, whose only real marker was the elevated track bed of the SPRR.

Yes, he thought, yes. People do this all the time. There's a history of running roads that don't exist. Of running roads that won't, can't take us where we need, want, must go. It's what breeds conjurors and con men. What drives and devours, defines and redefines our being. It puts our flaws on such perfect display and leaves us with miracles and madness. It's what justifies the terrible and the meaningful and brings us closer to death and life, to necessity and loss, in the same breath. The last as first, the first as last.

FROM THE yacht club lobby Ivy looked out into the wet parking lot and spotted the bewildering scenario of Essie leaning over the hood of her Futura and vehemently talking on a cellular while she tried to keep the slanted rain off her face.

RIGHT AS she was repeating, "There's no road th—" he saw the dayboat. It was a faint few seconds with its bow speared upward slightly against the tide.

"They're going the other way."

He looked again through the bridge spans toward that ground east of Locke. Behind him a car kicked out wheels of water as it sped past.

"The tracks go through, don't they?"

"Yes but—"

"They cross the slough?"

"Yes, at the junction of—"

DANE DIDN'T know how far he'd get but he was going to try and find those tracks and follow them if he couldn't drive right up on them.

He sped into Locke, which was not just another bare four blocks of Delta waterside, but the only town in America built by the Chinese. It was a living anachronism, an ongoing monument of western tongue and groove or straightboard construction.

He sped down Levee Road through this haunting piece of rain-shrouded history, past lonely parked cars, past a wet tourist trying to get in a few snapshots of Main Street before he moved on.

The road curved past wooden sidewalks and false fronts with the dim lettering of forgotten lives. At Key Street it curved again past tiny homes with vegetable gardens. The tension rode his stomach like a stone as the asphalt turned to gravel turned to rocky mud, past sagging porches, past dogs that chased him from the far side of wire fences barking wildly, past ratty vacant lots, past dunes of stacked garbage.

He'd been turned around and turned again and he was lost.

Essie told him, she told him to look for that thousand-foot-tall television tower as a point to set his bearing. To keep it just on the back of his right shoulder.

Through the grimy windshield he found the tower against a thinly gray sky. But it was straight ahead. He came to a hard mud-slapping stop. Out the driver's window there appeared to be a field of chest-high weeds that softly rose a half mile out.

There were few trees to block his way. He righted the pickup. As he downshifted the lightning bolt on his shoulder flexed and using that steel spire as a compass needle he took off.

He drove gunsight straight. The weeds bent and folded as he blew through them. His tail end slapped bottom. He braced himself. Shapes appeared and disappeared around him. The ground rose, the ground fell. A wrecked car rusting silently faced out of the oncoming weeds dead ahead like some vicious apparition ready to tear through him and he had to swerve hard.

The ground rose again, it fell again. The truck pitched and tilted like a drunk. He could hear the shocks crying out and his teeth lockjawed.

Essie—"

She pitched around at hearing Ivy's voice behind her. Her face stared out from beneath an umbrella. "What is going on?"

The ground sloped upwards at a sharp angle before Dane's truck and the weeds peeled away leaving sky.

"Essie, why were you yelling like that?"

The engine stalled. Dane floored the gas pedal. The engine kicked over. He pumped and pumped with his boot and tried to press the pickup on using the palm of his hand against the steering wheel but it was flat-out dead.

Essie's heart was pounding as Ivy asked, "Who are you yelling at?" Her tone seemed to demand an answer. Her face was distorted, concerned.

The pickup was out of gas. Signed, sealed and certified DOA in the heart of God's country. It began to slide back down the hill until Dane jammed on the emergency brake.

"I was talking to Dane," said Essie, pointing to her cellular.

He fought his way on foot up through yards of rain slick weeds and shapeless undergrowth.

"He needed directions." Ivy took a firm step forward, her eyes moving from the phone to the map to Essie. "He was lost."

Dane reached the hilltop.

Essie knew she sounded nervous. "That's why the map."

The tracks moved like a fixed line through the marshland before him.

"I'm not questioning you. It's just . . . you sounded so angry, frightened."

He ran the tracks trying to use the ties.

"He just couldn't hear me so well."

His boots caught gravel. His ankle bent. He stumbled.

As Essie spoke into the cellular Ivy took a step closer. "Dane?"

The gray above him again was broken apart by lightning.

"Dane?"

The trees along the tracks were a wild and violent fanfare.

All Essie got was silence.

He could see the bridge now. Its black steel outline a doorway to the horizon.

"I must have lost him."

Dane's lungs grasped for air.

Ivy tucked in alongside Essie now. Face to face, was she being read?

He flashed on what it must have been like for Essie that night.

"Nathan said you weren't feeling well."

Having to swim the dark of Disappointment Slough only to find death.

"I wasn't. I'm not—"

Spent, he sagged into the slick wet steel and held on.

Ivy reached for the map. "You better come in, then call him again."

From the lee side of the bridge he looked out to where the sloughs converged.

Do nothing, Essie thought, to arouse suspicion. Nothing. He'll have to understand.

The junction was a deeply wooded Eden of silence. Of still waters pocked by rain.

Ivy's face was coolly affectionate. "Get under my umbrella."

He listened for a boat as he moved stealthily out across the bridge staying as low as he could.

Side by side they walked back. Essie felt Ivy's arm against her own and it disgusted her.

Thunder rolled in from the distance like a great hood of terror, then he caught sight of something on the water at the entrance to Lost Slough.

Essie looked down at the map now in Ivy's hand. It was a dripping, dangled mass.

The last bits of foam sat like curdled milk on the water's surface. A boat had left its mark but was it their—

THE GROUND beneath him began to shake and as the thunder died away Dane heard it coming out of the distance. Its sheer power hurtling toward him.

He stood. He saw the locomotive. Its black speeding force eating up the shadows. There was no time to get off the bridge. None to even jump. It was all he could do to press back against the steel, grip a truss and hope and when that train surged onto the bridge everything shook in a way he had never imagined possible. He felt it down within the well of him.

The engine horn blew and he was sure his eardrums would be shattered. He went to close his eyes, but didn't. He wanted to see. To see.

The train was just inches from his face. It was a blur of smeared colors and blades of light. It felt like something living whose velocity and power could just pull you in and sweep you from the earth.

The air it drove at him was ferocious cold, he could almost feel its steel on his skin. The train spit gravel and water and filth from its wheels that he could taste. And he could smell the wet heavily tarred ties. His senses were like fine sharp knives.

Do you put the brake on your dreams, he thought, if you dream of anything? Is who you really are what you want to be left with? He thought of all the truths and lies he'd told and heard. What people will do for justice and money, for greatness and greed is no different. The con man and the honest man suffer in the end the same, for they are forever in jeopardy from themselves as well as others.

He needed to remember why he was here.

CHAPTER TWENTY-NINE

I N COURTROOM 412 Flesh watched Roy manhandle a defendant who had been indicted for armed robbery. During the hour-long confrontation Roy stood, his questions coming rapid-fire from memory.

The level of self-punishment for pride that Roy Pinter rose to in making a case never ceased to amaze Flesh. She had seen him stand on those metal crutches till the pits of his arms bled.

There is in the human condition such defiant nobility as well as a troubling absurdity that seem to walk in each other's shadows, and more paradoxically Flesh had begun to feel of late, they were one and the same.

Roy whispered to her during a break. "Meet me in my office. I have something you need to see."

E SSIE HURRIED past Nathan's office, her hair streaked with wet, and then Ivy entered carrying that map which was now a useless mass.

In a bathroom stall Essie listened to Dane's cellular ring busy and she whispered, "Where are you?"

A S FLESH poured coffee Roy said, "Rudd doesn't have a valid California driver's license."

She reached for a wooden stirrer.

"He doesn't now . . . he never did."

She licked the stirrer dry. She turned. "He was living in New York a long time."

"He doesn't have a valid New York driver's license."

She walked to Roy's desk and sat opposite him.

"He doesn't now . . . he never did."

She sipped coffee then said, "Maybe we should run right out and arrest him."

"Maybe there's more."

From just above the brim of that coffee cup she eyed him.

"No Dane Rudd ever graduated from Harvard."

She waited.

"No Dane Rudd was ever registered at Harvard."

And waited.

"He didn't graduate from Berkeley either."

She put the cup down.

"And the only Dane Rudd that was ever registered at Berkeley was back in '68. And that couldn't be him. No matter how clever he is."

She watched Roy begin to play with his ponytail in that way he had when he was anxious and aggressive.

"Just to set the record straight, Roy. Dane never said he went to Harvard or Berkeley."

"He most certainly did."

"Sorry, darling, lover, maniac, you were listening with your ego and not with your ears."

"He said—"

"*He said* he got scholarships to 'Harvard and Berkeley–type schools.' "

"The only people who talk like that are bullshit artists."

"And certain successful prosecutors."

"I think he's pulling some kind of scam."

"I don't like wasting goodwill chasing bad ideas, so if you don't mind I'm going back to my office where a real workload is waiting for me."

She was about to stand when he said, "I have more I want you to hear."

She waited. Sat back. Reluctantly she would give him the benefit of a few more minutes.

He reached down and opened a desk drawer. From it he took a file folder. As he laid it on the desk Flesh wanted to know in no uncertain terms, "What have you been doing?"

He opened the file. "I have been very low-key. I haven't used this office in any official way."

"Roy, you're trying to build a name for yourself to get into politics. We don't need any flagrant fouls right now."

"I say Rudd is pulling some kind of scam."

"Please."

"Trying to anyway."

"No need to check your life contract. I can see the clause dealing with the idiocy of male pride is still in full force and effect."

"This is not about pride . . . well, professional pride maybe." He opened the file. "The truck Rudd's driving—"

"That little black piece of shit."

"It doesn't belong to him."

"In a junk pile is where it belongs with all the toxic waste collecting in your head."

"The truck belongs to a William Singleton, with an address in San Luis Obispo."

"Terrible to have a friend or two."

Roy took a thin sheaf of clipped-together pages and handed them to Flesh. "Mr. Singleton has quite a rap sheet."

Reluctantly she took the pages, reluctantly she began to read. "Disturbing the peace . . . vandalism . . . hollering and shouting . . . curfew laws broken . . . trespassing . . . picketing . . ." Her eyes got needle thin as she looked at Roy. "Picketing . . . ?" He stopped playing with his ponytail. "This is all 415 penal code shit."

She flipped to another page. "There's no jail time . . ." She flipped to another page. "The judges always seem to have given him probation." She held the pages up. "This is a fuckin' social activist's rap sheet, and you know it."

"He broke the law."

"He's not Dane Rudd."

"He's a friend of Rudd's."

"Guilt by association now?"

"Call it whatever you want. But this is about a lawbreaker with a rap sheet. And if you keep reading you'll see there's also a marijuana possession charge."

"Marijuana possession. Well, Happy Birthday. I think the law is at its best, in this case, when it lays low. Don't you?"

"Rudd's got some kind of game going. Otherwise he wouldn't be such a fraud and a liar. All his information wouldn't come out in such vague-faced snippets."

"I don't want to break in on your little rant," she said. "But—"

"Listen, I'm going through all this because I'm concerned about Nathan."

"You're concerned about Roy Pinter. Pinter's personal machismo."

"Mr. Well Spoken is a bullshit artist." Roy scratched his fingers together holding his hand in the air just above his eyes. "This is what he's after."

Flesh mimicked Roy with her most meanspirited stare.

"Here's what I think," he said. "Rudd got into trouble somewhere. This is why he skirts the information about himself. He's got shady friends. Maybe they're druggies besides radicals. He needs money. Wants money. He sees a scam right in front of his eyes. A way to play Nathan, Essie. To endear himself to people with money. Money is why he's hanging around."

"He probably got into trouble?"

"Yeah."

"Like going blind?"

"I haven't made any calls about that yet to the hospital and eye banks."

"Don't even go there. 'Cause if you do and word gets back to Nathan or Rudd you will come across like some vile idiot unfit for any public office. And then, you will have to deal with me."

"I've been low-key."

145

Her meanspirited stare became something so much darker, so much more demanding that he do as she say or else, he backed off. "I'm not gonna fuck us," he said.

She shook her head in fatigued despair. She stared out at the window. The rain spotted the glass and above the rooftops lightning pricked the heavens. It was all just a silent play, a moment of visual music that spoke of eternals. Her mind wandered. Roy's flaws were suddenly not so cute and had to be checked. "What is it, Roy? Really?"

She leaned forward. "Do people like him just infuriate you on some primal level? Is it because Nathan likes him? Essie? Is it because that first night he questioned you on Taylor's murder?"

"Suicide."

"Is it because he's decent? That he's willing to try and give something back for the good that was given him?" Her stare became much more deeply impassioned. "Or is it that you just don't believe people act out of goodness. That they're just not capable of such feelings and can direct their lives accordingly?"

"In one short, blunt, honest, cynical, logical, straightforward word . . . no."

Her long, lean body wilted.

"People are selfish not selfless. People are hidden motives, not honest motives. They do good for one reason, and that reason is themselves. They want power, they want money. They are so greedy they want both. More often than not they will lie, even when the truth sounds better. They will lie because that is who they are and they are afraid they will lose the edge in getting. Dane Rudd is just one more of those."

"Talk is sometimes such air pollution."

"Why has everything Rudd told us about himself turned out to be a couple of shades untrue?"

"I'm getting out of here on the chance that what you feel is like some airborne virus I could catch."

"Because he has an agenda. And if he told the truth about himself, it would get in the way of that—"

She cut him off. "All this says a lot more about Roy Pinter's agenda than it does about Dane Rudd's."

She started for the door.

He began to pull at his ponytail. He wanted to tell her that he intended to prove her wrong and put it up her ass when he did. But he knew better than to say it.

Flesh stopped at the door. Turned. She concocted a mean little smile from her best features. "It's my opinion the cock is the worst enemy the world has ever known."

CHAPTER THIRTY

Essie would not die waiting, so she added one more lie to the day telling Nathan Dane's truck had broken down and she needed to pick him up.

She pushed that Futura hard through a slowing rain toward Locke. She kept speed-dialing Dane's cellular but the line remained eerily busy.

Troubling ghosts were rampant inside her. The speedometer rose at the violence that she imagined had overtaken him. She cared too much to be careless and foolish. The practical thing to do would be to call for help. Call Roy and explain.

She speed-dialed Roy's number but when it came time to press SEND, she could not. She cared too much to be careless, yes ... she cared too much to be foolish, yes ... but even so, at a more secret heartcore level she felt making that call would be an act of betrayal.

Searching slowly Essie rode the streets of Locke to the spot she last talked to Dane. The rain had stopped, the asphalt turned to dirt. She stepped from the Futura and looked up at the television tower she'd told him to use as a guide mark spiring above the distance.

She tried to call him again as she lined up that tower on her right shoulder and looked out into the direction of those acres of untamed brush. A busy signal was all she got for the effort.

She leaned back against her car. She frowned and plotted at the possibility the ugly and unthinkable had happened. And Nathan, by him she felt utterly victimized, utterly vandalized. Was he just a fiction who had pawned her? Were her affections and allegiance and sympathies just so much maid service for his greedy, and in this case, nefarious self-interests?

Had he worked her as only a father could do, as a surrogate of authority, as someone feigning generosity and kindness? And what about Taylor? How had he been used?

A sudden barrage of crows drove skyward from that unkempt field of undergrowth and caught her eye. As she followed their black tracer mark across the high trees she saw Dane.

Bits of sunlight were just starting to break through the gray. He was walking down a rutted pathway toward her carrying a gas can. His rough shape framed by shanty porches and overhanging drenched branches. He was so utterly matter-of-fact in the way he maneuvered pools of slick-faced road mud and waved, so utterly everyday in nodding to her as if nothing at all of consequence had happened.

A moment washed through her of him that night on the deck of the riverboat in the dark world of Nathan's shadow and she knew. She knew as the crows swooped and rose where he walked among their fleeting caws like the cry of angels in the afterglow of some brandished dream. She could not see his clear-cut face, but she knew nonetheless.

They reached each other at the remains of a wooden white roadside fence. "I thought you might be—"

"I ran out of road," he said. "Then I ran out of gas. After that I just plain ran out."

"You're all right, though?" she asked.

"I would have called you but I dropped the phone somewhere. Maybe it's in the truck, I don't know."

"It doesn't matter."

"At the gas station I tried to get you."

"It doesn't matter. You're all right."

In the rise and fall of human emotion, in the bewildering measure of its beauty, the wind shook raindrops from the leaves all about them, and she embraced him.

They stood together like that and he felt her head against his chest and it frightened him, knowing who he was and what he'd agreed to, to save himself from prison.

She could feel his heart as she stared at the ground and watched the great tree shadows around them plume and scatter like the rustling motion of some rousing crowd.

"I caught where they went," he said, "and I saw them come back."

He could have been any boy, in any town, at any time. And she could have been any girl. To her the moment was that clear and simple in its voice to voice silence.

"I was very scared," she said. "Very scared."

He brushed at the wet in her hair with his hand to tell her he understood. And then he thought, he should not even have done that.

"You're bleeding," she said.

He looked down. His T-shirt sleeve had been cut through and without letting him go she pulled the sleeve up and he saw the lightning bolt on his arm had been scored by something rusted and nasty.

AL THE Wop's was a historic saloon and steakhouse on the "street of overhanging porches" in the town of Locke. Of course, thanks to the self-serving national penchant for political correctness, it was now referred to by its more boring proffer—"Al's Place."

The inside walls were lined with antique signs telling you what had been and there were enough gewgaws for even the most trivially driven minds. But the centerpiece of Al's was the twenty-foot ceiling. What really brought in the sightseers was that carpet of dollar bills stuck there. A quarter million George Washingtons, the most recent tally said, looked down on you from behind that wooden stare.

There was also a long, dense mahogany bar and this was where Essie and Dane sat hunched together like conspirators or lovers.

Between their beers Dane mapped out on a napkin in blue pen the railroad tracks he had followed, the bridge over one slough he finally crossed. "The boat," he said, tracing another slough that veered to the northeast, "went there."

"Lost Slough."

"What's in Lost Slough?"

She took the pen for another napkin and started to draw. Just abaft from the bar, steaks were being grilled. There were pockets of laughter and conversation so when she spoke it was in an intense whisper with her mouth up near his cheek and ear. "It's a six-mile loop," she said, "of turns and tule islands . . . and more tule islands and turns. It's narrows that stream off into heavily wooded nothing. Only a small craft, or one with a shallow draw can navigate most of it."

He watched, he thought. He took the pen back. She was practically on his shoulder now. His black hair, still wet, shined. As did his eyes.

"When I finally crossed the bridge, I walked. Maybe twenty minutes later I heard a boat coming. I hid in the reeds." He drew parallel lines extending the slough that ran under the bridge to the northwest. "It was them. Only a fourth man was on the boat now. He wore a suit. Had a moustache. He was short and heavy-set."

"They picked someone up in Lost Slough."

"Yes."

"He wasn't on the boat back at Giustis?"

"Not that I saw." Dane ran an arrow up that slough he had just extended. "That's where they went."

"The Meadows."

"What's that?"

"It's a long channel that veers back toward Locke. The water is as calm as a lake. Great place for boaters. The shore property is private but people tie up there anyway. It's all very easy and free so you'd think you're back in the nineteenth century. But," she took the pen from him and began to extend those twin lines for the slough he'd drawn downwards, then curled them around like the backwards upside-down top of a question mark, "all the way back in, where the channel narrows and ends"—she marked the spot in ink—"the Boyz have a place."

He looked at Essie and in the small bit of half darkness they shared all that talk around them seemed a trivial season long.

"Where do we go from here?" she said.

He did not answer. He eased around her and reached for another napkin.

She watched him as he began to write. Bits of feeling began to take force in her body. When he was done he slid the napkin toward her. In simple capital letters was the word *PLYMOUTH* and balanced appropriately underneath it in fancy script was the word *ROC*.

"What's this?"

"That is what was painted in red on the back of their boat today."

She held the napkin and Dane came around on his barstool with beer in hand. He blotted his shoulder with another napkin where the blood was drying. He leaned back and looked up at that dollar bill sky of a ceiling. "So, that's what the heavens look like." He drank down some beer. Tossed aside the blood spotted napkin. "Think of the power one simple wooden match would have in the right hand."

"How do we deal with all this . . . with Nathan?"

He did not answer, his attention was firmly on that ceiling, and only finally did he say, "Gives one pause to hope, doesn't it?"

CHAPTER THIRTY-ONE

THEY STEPPED OUT into the street where the sunlight reflected up off ground puddles and mud flecked windshields. They walked side by side up that tunnel of overhanging balconies tilting on aged stilts. Their boots clopped and echoed on the plank sidewalk.

"Nathan is a liar," said Essie. There was a profane surety to the tone of her pronouncement. "He's a liar and a money launderer. And no telling how much more of himself he's sold out."

Dane wondered how many people he'd exploited said the very same thing, the very same way about him. "Yes," said Dane, "I believe you have described him very well."

They reached the corner and the sky opened before them on that narrow street. The few clouds left were bits of gray flaw in an altogether overwhelming stretch of blue cloth.

They walked on toward where they had left the cars. On through this narrow streeted and unadorned "Chinese town." They walked in silence through deep stretches of shadow cut with light and past storefront windows that had been painted in to keep out prying eyes.

"How do you feel," Dane asked, "inside? About what's happened."

She stopped and looked at him and as she did she caught sight of herself on the wavering glass of a painted-in storefront window. Hers was a compressed portrait of hate.

"That's how I feel," she said, pointing.

His eyes came around to find her reflected stare looking out from blackness.

"And I feel," she said, "as if my legitimacy as a human being has been defiled."

"Everything of and about you bought and sold, right?"

"Exactly right."

"And the remains divided."

"Exactly."

"And you can understand why people put a brake on their dreams, if they have any dreams at all after the soul-shredders cut a few good decades out of them."

"I can."

"And there's no real virtue in values 'cause the gods come and go like presidents—"

"Faster."

"—and lies abound, and appear so well-packaged, so commercial-proof, as to defy your scrutiny."

"Fuckin' right," she said.

"And you say to yourself, why fight? Why think? Why care? Why try? Why vote? Why complain? Why run? Why be at all?"

She began to tremble.

"So, what are the alternatives left to us?" he asked. "Do we cop out . . . rot out . . . burn out . . . or just die out?"

Her chest held and held as if daring her to breathe. Her stare on painted black bared down back at her with pinched eyelids above wide eyes. This feeling, was it a forewarning or just the fundamental law of the incomprehensible making itself known?

She looked down at the napkin she still held in her hand and on which Dane had written PLYMOUTH *ROC*. A thought slipped through the anger and uncertainties. Am I to become another spiritual tragedy?

"What?" he asked.

It was as if Dane had half heard her thoughts. The sunlight had brought out the tourists with cameras and Essie avoided their glances at all costs.

"What?" he again asked.

She started up the street. He followed as she folded the napkin and found a safe spot for it in her purse. They took an alley be-

tween buildings that fed into a steep plank stairwell. This led to
River Road, which itself was the top of the levee that held back
the big river, the Sacramento.

This is where their cars were parked, and while they smoked
leaning against the hood of his Rampage they looked back silently
at the town of Locke as it descended into a short fall of land below
the level of the river.

"What were you thinking back there," said Dane, "on the street?
I saw something in your face."

She stared at the wooden buildings. They were stained dark
from the rain and now, with the heat of the coming sun, steam
rose from the wet wood so Locke appeared like some smoldering
apparition from the halcyon days of our history.

"I wasn't thinking . . . I was feeling what you said, and it frightened me with its accuracy."

Watching her Dane became painfully aware of a feeling that was
moving against him. He wanted to hold Essie. To somehow, some
way take on what he saw in her face so she would not be frightened. But he held himself back.

In the yards and fields crows picked at the rainsoft western soil,
and when the wind blew they rose in swift flocks to the corrugated
roofs of long-since joss houses and opium dens, of fantan parlors
and pauper hotels where they watched and waited like some telling omen of time.

"The town looks like it still holds mysteries, doesn't it?" said
Dane.

"We know now Taylor was killed. And we know now why."

"Do we?"

"He found out what we found out. And either the fuckin'
Boyz . . . or Charles Gill . . . or that man on the boat . . . the General . . . maybe even Nathan . . . had a hand in what I have said
since the beginning. What I have felt since the beginning. What I
knew since the beginning."

"The town does look like it still holds mysteries."

"Are you listening to me?"

"More than that."

"And I will tell you something else. I know now why Taylor was so unhappy that last week. And I know now why he never opened up to me. He meant to keep me safe. I'm sure of it. That's how he was. He would rather suffer than have you suffer."

That, Dane could clearly understand.

She turned and looked across the hood of that pickup out at the Sacramento. There were boats on the river now and they shone in the sun and the wake from their outboards looked like white spun gold. She turned again as boys with bikes sped past then took the corner of River Road on skidding mud spun tires.

A waking jealousy made her say, "I wish I was twenty-five without all the baggage." She tossed down her cigarette then dug it under her boot heel. "But I'm not, am I?"

"I should have taken the box," he said.

She was not sure she heard him right.

"What could they have done if I just drove away? If I just took the box and simply drove away." He turned to her. "If we just took it."

She had heard him right. And there was not a touch of ambiguity or reticence in his voice, or in his stare.

"It's too late now, of course. But there will be a next time. This is what they do."

"Why are you talking like this?"

"We could be ready. Waiting with a plan."

"Are you trying to tempt me?"

"They used you, right? And they're using me, right?"

"Is that what this is?"

"Maybe I am trying to tempt you. Maybe I am trying to tempt myself. You know, temptation is a good thing. And I should know. I did temptation, and it did me. Yes, temptation is a good thing. It strikes at boundaries. It contrasts priorities. It draws that infamous line in the sand."

He looked down at those corrugated rooftops where the steam rose like some testimony of phantom gestures. Then he turned to Essie, his face an underplayed smile. "Yeah, I may be trying to tempt you. But maybe, I'm just trying to clean up the rough edges on a little personal history."

A wrinkle broke above her eyes. "I wouldn't," she said. "Not ever."

"Good," he said. "Because we have to be sure of who we are. And you shouldn't be surprised now, not now, with all you've seen, how fragile your being 'sure' can be."

"I hear you."

"I'm going to ask for your trust on something, so I have to know what it is you want."

She was going to tell him she wanted to be strong enough to define her own place in the future. But it was more than just that driving her. It was part judgment, part pain. There was rebellion and malfeasance inside her. She knew, she knew.

And so Essie began to explain herself by saying, "I'm standing on a subway platform and the express goes by." Her eyes were quietly possessed. "Someone on that train throws chemicals in my face and I can feel my eyes burning . . . fuck, I want what you want."

Dane found himself suddenly reaching out and putting a hand on Essie's face. His fingers climbed and combed through the hair at the nape of her neck. He pulled her toward him and her face slipped into the turn where his throat and shoulder met. Her breath was warm and gentle. His eyes closed.

For a moment she again felt he was just a boy and she was just a girl and there were no black gardens to walk through where all of life's traps lay hidden.

Cool reflection would have told him this was useless, foolish, dangerous, destructive. But some more deeply collective need was at work and made him disregard those simple decrees.

There is an old adage—you run the con long enough, you run the risk of it running you. Dane wondered, questioned, had he bought into the pitch of a second chance? And not some gamer's description of a second chance.

CHAPTER THIRTY-TWO

DANE HAD ASKED for her trust, and as dangerous as what he had suggested plausibly was, she had said yes.

She stood just inside her open balcony door looking upon the night. Dane would be at the yacht club dinner very soon. Things would change very, very soon. Just above the rooftops the trees sounded like touched strings and all her pretense at calmness had little effect. A drink was mandatory.

She sipped and stared and thought about what he had said back there on River Road. She stared and smoked and then in the window she stood beside the desk light reflected like some soft mirage. In the glassy shadows Taylor's picture caught her eye.

Again the trees sounded like touched strings as she sat at the desk. She put her drink down, her cigarette down. She turned off the light and reached for his picture.

In that darkness she felt a powerful transition going on inside her. We bear our pains like children and it is only by giving birth to them that we free them. And in doing so give voice to the needs of going on.

She told him silently, almost mournfully, she was going on. Essie knew you cannot disregard the future and expect not to be disregarded yourself. She knew you cannot be married to shadows unless you care to exist with fictions signed in blood that do nothing for the living, give nothing to living.

Essie would not allow this to happen to herself. She felt too much honest hunger to let it happen. She took Taylor's picture and kissed it and she cried thinking about all those deeply wished pleasures and deeply felt promises that once had been so alive.

PEOPLE WISH they could recall the past, recast it as the present, and relive it for all futures to see and praise . . ."

With lights dimmed the investors around the dinner table watched the video of Nathan's tribute speech to his dead son that night on the deck of the *Little California.*

"And in a way," Nathan went on, "a handful of God has touched us with that possibility. Ladies and gentlemen, I want you to meet someone who is a living symbol of what the center wants to achieve."

From where he sat at the head of the table Nathan studied the body language of his dinner guests as the lens held on the face of a boy who would have been blind but for the chance of a dream offered through his dead son.

The shadowy discourse of that quiet boy standing reverentially off to one side of the stage said as much as any words. Nathan saw one older couple at the table touch hands. He saw a coarse gray face across from them soften, and the edges of distance on another grapple with something heartfelt. Nathan knew, he had them.

A second chance at immortality is about the finest angle on a sales pitch there is for raising spirits as well as raising money. The tragedy of someone's suffering being of benefit to someone else is one of the most time-honored selling tools in the world. It is almost a religion unto itself.

But something untoward had come over Nathan that caused him to be unable to watch the monitor as he spoke of his son's charity and selflessness, his sense of love and common decency. Each phrase he had worked on to make just right in those days of pain were now again like honest nails driven into the complete sense of denial he had been living with.

These feelings were either fueled or aggravated by the fact that he was succeeding now just as he had in the past, by failing as a human being. By lying. By scamming. By cunning.

Why had he not given himself over completely to finding out

who had killed his son? Was the memorial just a desperate alternative to his personal failures as father, as man? A testament to his own guilt rather than his son's dream? Or was he more concerned with just the plain simple trappings of going on?

He tried to look within himself for that which was unconscionable and selfish for an answer, for that which was beyond love and common decency, when a light from the door opening behind him fell across the table.

A shadow filled that pale rectangle and as he looked up a pair of hands came to rest affectionately on his shoulders and Dane, smiling, said, "I had car trouble, otherwise I'd have been here sooner."

DANE JOINED them at the table. He sat beside Ivy and answered the potential investors' questions like a gentleman. He absorbed their stares and their small talk and their smiles. Nathan saw it was the same each time. The boy was like a cup into which fragments of an investor's countless dreams could be poured. He was the poster child they could use to toast their good deeds.

Nathan drank and watched and listened and as he did an intolerable clarity began to overcome him. There was little to no difference between himself and his dinner guests.

He tried to remain natural and interested in what was going on around him, to return Ivy's silent looks of affection and pride, but at the same time he went through an irrevocable process of trying to qualify and quantify his compromises of character.

He told himself he could have done all this straight. Just him and the boy. No Charles. No General. No numbered-trust-account favors. No laundered money. He could have changed his life and humped out the miles like a soldier.

"What's it like," a woman sitting across from Dane asked, "to get a second chance at seeing? Is the world different? Do you feel different?"

Nathan's stare rose from the rim of his goblet as Dane went around that amphitheater of faces to hold on the woman across from him who looked to have navigated years and sorrow.

"I never took anything too seriously," said Dane. "I was your standard issue twenty-year-old. High on do me, give me, take me. You might say I could only read the writing on the wall after I blindly crashed into it."

Dane's eyes closed a moment, then opened. He played with his napkin a bit, then fidgeted with a knife beside his plate while he took time to think.

"Ma'am, things look different because I feel different." His raspy voice crackled a bit. "I can take a picture of Nathan's son and I can look into the eyes I'm seeing with. That shows you how *heartbreakingly beautiful* the world is. And maybe that's the point of what a new set of eyes is worth. You get to see, really see, what is not only heartbreaking but what is beautiful—because you are a part of both."

He turned to Ivy. "Isn't that right?"

Her muted attractive face tucked in a bit and quietly agreed. Then Dane folded his hands and addressed the table with a boyish sincerity. "That's what your investment is. A statement that because you see differently you feel differently and so will act differently. That you see things which are heartbreaking and you want to help make from that something beautiful."

Dane now turned his attention to Nathan. "Take Nathan . . . it was Taylor's heartbreaking loss and inspiring sentiments that became the groundbreaking idea behind the center. Nathan chose to find beauty at the heart of sorrow. And we can all share in that."

Nathan put the goblet down as the circle of faces at the table closed in on him.

"I want to tell you something else about Nathan," said Dane, "that will give you an insight into the goodwill of his character. It is also a way of making a little confession."

And just like that, with their interest piqued, Dane began telling everyone about the box of plasma delivered earlier that day to Nathan's office. With humble charm he detailed how this charitable undertaking begun by Taylor was now being carried on by the father. You could have filled a book of virtues with the stares and slight nods and smiles of the dinner guests that someone would so go out of their way for such helpless creatures.

Ivy and Nathan, enervated by how close this conversation came to the dark traces of their crime, tried to find solace in each other's stare.

"They'd both been working so hard," said Dane. "I decided to do them a favor and deliver the box." He rested his hand on Ivy's forearm. "And this is where my confession starts . . . I was walking across the parking lot and reaching for my keys when I dropped the box."

Before reactions could settle in, before Nathan could disarm this conversation by saying it was all right Dane just went on. "So, when I got to my truck I opened the box."

Dane could feel Ivy's arm stiffen. "I'm so embarrassed." He let the words hang as he repeated, "I opened the box, Nathan. I looked inside. I felt you needed to know. I looked inside to make sure I hadn't destroyed anything."

CHAPTER THIRTY—THREE

DANE SAW THE struggle on Nathan's face. A momentary failure of self-mastery had exposed him. It was an emotional flaw whose geometry Dane knew all too well. That empty form known as permanence had been ruptured. They could well now be dealing in hazards and extinction. Dane felt his heart flex and fill quickly, then more quickly, more urgently, as he said, "Nothing damaged, nothing lost. Your package got delivered, Nathan, just as you planned it."

WHILE THEY had brandy on the patio that overlooked the yacht club bay Nathan took a moment to pull Ivy aside. He felt her arm, it was clammy and cold. She was, he saw, on the verge of a horrible anxiety attack.

Neither said a word, neither dared until Ivy realized, "He's leaving."

DANE WAS just about down the patio steps when Nathan leaned over the wall and called to him. Dane stopped. With hands in pockets and jacket collar now turned up he came about. His body arced back to look at Nathan. This was all done with a cool essential calm kind of turn.

There were so many dinner guests nearby all Nathan could say was, "I'm going to call you later, all right?"

There was an aqueous light that reflected up from the bay and along the white stairwell walls where Dane looked at Nathan and said, "If you think you need to."

DANE SAT in Essie's darkened living room and placed the cordless phone back down in its cradle. He smoked and leaned forward in the chair. He rested his forearms on his knees and closed his eyes.

Everything that would ever happen in the world was happening here, happening now. Everything that would ever happen to him would happen here, would now happen.

There is no journey too small that would not prove it true. One man who had not gone more than a hundred miles in his own life had shown that.

Every wicked arrangement, every violation would come to pass. Every ploy or plot. From the foolish to the sublime. From the pathetic to the exquisite. Noble, ignoble. Each part of that one paradox—was all this a necessity?

Essie came back into the room and Dane's eyes opened. He looked up and she offered him a drink he did not want, did not take. He pointed to the phone. "Nathan left three messages in the last hour for me to call him tonight."

"Are you going to?"

"Tonight . . . no."

"What will happen now?"

His head moved from side to side as he mused over the possibilities.

"Do you think he will try and hurt you? Do you think he will try something violent?"

Dane stared at his hands. At the smoke that rose from his cigarette. A phantom gesture not unlike today with the steam rising from the rooftops of Locke. And when he spoke it was as if the words were deeply felt and long remembered. "You lay out a premise, you set the tone, then you cap it with a temptation. There's only one thing left after that . . . the close."

"Who taught you that?"

Dane sadly looked up at Essie. "That . . . was my father."

Dane then just sat there. He felt as if he had inherited some-thing horrible. He could only describe it as a dire need to hold together the extremes of excess and deficiency. This feeling seemed to him beyond the appeal of rational law and he knew that it could, could tear him apart.

"Is it all right," he said, "if I tell you there is hardly anything I haven't done wrong at least once. And maybe, I'm no better than any of them, only more so."

She set the drink she had been holding down. She took his cigarette and laid it on the ashtray lip. She put both of his hands in hers and pulled him up.

He watched the shaded outline of her hands as they rose to touch his face. They sloughed their way up the skinline feeling out the bones and flesh until his stare was poised between her palms.

"I made a confession tonight," she whispered.

He could smell the body soap and perfume she wore so beau-tifully and inexactly real.

"And I made a promise."

Her eyes locked him in. There was such future there.

"I told the past—"

She leaned up and kissed his neck.

"—I'm going on."

Her mouth slid along his cheek like wet air.

"I'm going on."

She found his mouth and her kiss felt as if he might have only dreamed it.

"We're going on."

It was a weightless moment.

"Do you hear, we're going on."

They could have been any boy or any girl, in any town at any—

A door buzzer cut the moment. A tinny bleating and their em-braced form marked on the window came apart.

———

WHEN ESSIE opened the door Roy was leaning against the alcove wall. "Sometimes," he said, "I think you moved to the second floor just to make it difficult for me to see you."

She crossed her arms. "That's your vanity talking, Roy."

He nodded. "Probably."

She got her back against the opposite alcove wall. "Why are you here, Roy?"

He braced up on his crutches. "Do you think we could go out for a drink?"

"I won't take any part in hurting Francie."

"I just . . ." He listed anxiously as he reached for her but Essie pulled away just enough to make it impossible. "I only wanted to talk."

"I can't."

He glanced through the partly open door and up that shadowed stairwell to her apartment. Mr. Well Spoken was probably hiding in the dark and getting a fuckin' earful of his little beg session. "Company?"

"Yes."

Roy's upper teeth bit at the edges of his beard along the lower lip. "Why did you stop going out with me?"

"Because I realized you weren't, and could not be, kind."

"I just needed time."

"It wasn't time you needed."

"Let's go have a drink and I'll replead my case."

"I could try and be funny and say 'I'm outside your jurisdiction' but the truth, Roy, kindness is showing compassion, at least sometimes, for someone else's well-being when it comes into conflict with your own. You were terrible at the one and too greedy for the other."

Roy's eyes darted toward the stairwell. "How 'bout Mr. Well Spoken. I bet he comes out of the shower just dripping compassion."

That was the old Roy. The verbal shark attack hiding as a smile. "Good night, Roy. Say hi to Francie for me."

She started back in. Roy bit down hard on his bad feelings. "You know, Essie. You're the kind of person I'd like to be, but can't. And you know why?" She stopped and looked back at him. "Because I hate myself too much. Because I'm bitter too much."

When he stood a long time Roy's breathing got thick, almost muddy. His shoulders sagged so his back pressed out awkwardly. If he had only put half the effort into discovering a sense of compassion as he had into carrying around that broken body.

"Dear Roy, did you ever think that you might be exactly the same kind of person you are *even* if you'd never had polio?"

WHEN SHE returned Essie found Dane sitting in the far corner of the balcony, waiting.

"Did you hear?"

"I came out here not to."

"It was Roy."

Dane looked out into that alley of a street, with its mood piece of balconies and lights.

"He hates you."

"Hate has a way of getting around."

"Dane, we're all entitled to our secrets."

He glanced at Essie. "I gotta go."

"You don't have to be afraid."

"Of what happens?"

"Of me."

IN THE blue silence of evening Dane crossed Disappointment Slough alone. The ironies of how something is compared to how it's called took him along all kinds of moody and significant channel ways from Discovery Bay to the dock of Taylor's house on Disappointment Slough.

In deep thought Dane realized he must now confront certain inevitabilities. No matter what he accomplished here, no matter how he resurrected his life, when he was done he would have to leave. That had been the one part of the bargain when he agreed to it which was the most attractive. A new name, an undisclosed location, and all ties to the past severed.

He pulled up to the dock and tied off. He sat in the boat and looked up into the long channel way of Disappointment Slough, into all that solitude and peace.

He could still feel Essie's face against the line of his throat. Her skin and hair were still in his senses. His mind started to conjure and he could not shut it down. He visualized this imaginary life there with her, and a steady dose of Paul and Sancho Maria and the bar at the airport and maybe, maybe he'd even coax Paul into teaching him how to fly and he could hear all the guttural jabbing he'd have to take during that little scenario. Then he stopped. He had so visualized the moments he actually felt as if they were happening.

And in that quietly rocking boat Dane came to realize how much of his own life he had thrown away, and because of that, how much more he would probably have to lose if ever life meant to be again.

CHAPTER THIRTY-FOUR

WALKING UP THROUGH that grove of trees Dane saw something that caused him to stop. It hung starkly from the porch roof light and left him uneasy. He'd had or did have a visitor.

USING THE shadows as cover he approached the house. The wind ran coolly across his back. The porch was tangents of light amidst the branches until he was close enough to detail a perfectly executed rope noose which held a beer bottle by the neck.

HE KEPT to the dark side of the porch. He stayed attuned to any wisps of sound or movement. The wind continued to run coolly across his back, and as he approached the dangling beer bottle the boards beneath his feet creaked like the hull of some old, old ship breathing.

Curled in the lip of the bottle was a business card which he removed while watching the threaded shapes and opaque night-shades around him. The card belonged to the Rocket Boyz and on the back was a handwritten note from Tommy Fenn.

> *Thought we might have a beer and cool our jets some—*
> *maybe next time.*

As Dane held the noose in the web of his hand the phone inside rang and he felt as if something had reached out and grabbed him. He was sure it was Nathan until the message machine turned over and he heard Paul's voice. "Hey, I'm leaving you a fuckin' message—"

DANE GRABBED the phone. "I'm here, Paul."

"You're not startin' to go native and screen your calls?"

Dane backed into the darkest part of the room so he could watch the bay window and the open front door where that bottle slowly swung like a tethered weight.

"No, Paul. I was just outside with a beer."

"In that case I'm fuckin' relieved."

Dane finger lifted a blind of the window beside him and scanned the muted shadows.

"I could give you some bullshit about why I'm calling, but you know why I'm calling so I won't insult you with bullshit and don't, please, don't bullshit me."

Dane walked the perimeter of the walls. He looked into one bedroom, then the next. "Forget it, Paul."

"What was going on with the wonder boys?"

Dane eased open the swinging kitchen door. It made a creaking sound. A sickly apprehensive creaking sound. Through the window he could see the light from the river beacon on that hilltop windmill shining like a small but perfect moon. It tinted the kitchen with a dreamy stillness except for another empty beer bottle on the table that Dane had not left there.

Taylor would have been so perfectly alone here, Dane thought. And if he was someone vulnerable to all those invisible mindcuts that have at your courage, that sneak up inside your fears until you feel their shapes hunting you out, a game like this, well—

"What am I, fucking wood, here? Are you gonna answer me?"

"No, Paul. I'm not. And I won't bullshit you. I won't because you're honest and sincere. And you've been kind to me. So I will just keep silent."

There was a gruff sigh at Caruso's end of the line. But it had a scratch of anger in it. Anger and frustration.

"Don't fly too high, don't fly too low. That's not some frag-assed slogan. Take it from a man who did an eight-by-ten for the long haul. And it's not something you print on a friggin' T-shirt then forget."

Dane let the kitchen door ease closed until there was only a crease of pale light slipping through. "If they ever bring back the Round Table you should get an honorary seat at it."

"That's pure jive. That's you tryin' to get past me politely."

"Politely is the operative word, Paul."

More silence at Caruso's end as Dane went to the hall closet. From it he took his battered leather suitcase. He knelt down and opened it.

"At least tell me one thing," said Caruso, "and then I'll hang the fuck up."

Dane reached into a corner pocket to see if the sheathed battle knife and short-nosed .38 were still there.

"And I want the truth."

Dane held the revolver up using the porch light coming through the open front door to see if the gun was still loaded. "What?"

"Are you alright, son?"

CARUSO HUNG up the phone and looked at his wife. The bar was closed, they were alone. She smoked and waited, he brooded and drank his beer.

"Is he alright?"

Caruso's pockmarked face creased. He glanced at the wall near where he sat. The first copy of the labyrinth he'd collected hung there. It was the one he'd had in his cell all those years and it showed an unaware Theseus being watched by the Minotaur as he made his way through the maze.

"Is he alright?"

"The boy's got the speak and doublespeak down pat." Caruso snapped his fingers rapid fire as he got up and walked over to the wall.

"Do you think any of this has to do with Taylor?" said Sancho Maria.

Caruso stared at the old print. The sorry thing had been taped and retaped so many times just to hold it together. It had chinks of missing paper that made it look like a target practice poster. Caruso ran his hand over the print and thought out loud, "What's in your head, son? What's in your head?"

DANE LEFT the beer bottle hanging in the noose. He closed the front door and turned off the porch light. He sank into the couch drained and put the .38 next to his wallet on the end table beside him.

He lit a cigarette and stared at the bay window. Taylor's desk there, his chair angled slightly, were backlit by a mist sprinkled night sky. A wave of sorrow overcame him.

"Am I alright, Paul asked," said Dane, talking to the desk. "Is there any way in this world to be alright . . . to be, all-right . . . to be, at all, right?"

Clamped to each corner of the desk were black swinging lamps and against the dark blue vagary of the bay window they looked like arms rising up out of the darkness, scaffold arms that seemed to hold two doomed eyes.

He could imagine Taylor sitting there the night he died with all those stark ambiguities piling up around him. "We have our secrets, don't we." Dane stretched forward. "We just hid them in different ways, hide them in different ways."

He smoked and all that sorrow he felt poured words into his mouth. "You did a heartbreaking thing, and a beautiful thing. Yes, I wouldn't say this to the others, but I could understand taking your own life. Maybe out of fear or desperation. Out of shame or guilt. Out of a need to self-punish. Out of some singular sense of rebellion. I could understand taking your own life out of just plain old-fashioned sorrow."

He reached for the ashtray and the barbed-wire cut across his arm stung the muscles. He put the ashtray on the floor before him and looked down at the deep gash. He flexed his arm and the wound puckered like a fish gill breaking that lightning bolt almost in half.

He grinned at the somewhat sadistic dichotomy of it. Then, he went back to looking at the desk, the window. This solitary imprint of time.

"There is one thing I wish I could ask you. I have this purely terrifying feeling that sweeps over me and I could only describe it as a fearless pleasure at the idea of dying. I felt it today when I got ready to operate on warrior boy's throat. I felt it riding that pickup blind. I felt it on the bridge and that locomotive just inches from my face. It's like a come-and-have-at-me defiance."

He sat there listening to the silence as if answers were awaiting. He smoked, he seemed to himself a stranger. "I wonder," he said, "if what I felt is a form of suicide."

There was a deeply breathed pause. A searched-out personal reflection. He looked again at the desk. "Maybe we are closer to each other than anyone might ever suspect. After all, we share secrets, we share lies. We share the same house"—his face grew unforgivably human—"the same possibility for love."

The phone rang. The message machine kicked in. It was Nathan asking to be called.

A faint breath, the machine beeped off. Then, "I could take them," said Dane. "I could lie my way through them, then pocket the difference that it all makes. I could make them listen and believe what I say. I do make them listen and believe what I say because they are desperate to believe in something . . . as we all are. That is the beauty of the fraud, and the fraud of beauty. Yes, we have our secrets, don't we."

He stared at the black air around his cigarette as it burned and he considered all the essential human qualities which were that easily obliterated, which were each of us as we rebel against the overwhelming.

"I'd like to be twenty-five without all the baggage. But I tried that, and look where it got me."

Dane glanced at the end table, at the gun and wallet lying side by side. Don't fly too high, don't fly too low. Maybe Paul was right. But if he was, then what? Do you just settle down to a steady diet of limitations? What about the voice that keeps on wanting to know where you are in the scheme of things. That wants to know if you can or will test the hard divide. That works the combinations of you like some ghostly burglar till you have been opened up and seen for what and who you are.

"He called me son tonight. It probably didn't mean much to him, but that's one time more than I ever was with even the slightest sense of sincerity for my well-being attached to it."

Dane could not see his own lips go white, nor his jaw lock. He could not see the stoic clinch of his body to keep from crying. But he could hear his voice breaking all the way down to his heart and then some.

When he was done crying Dane went into the bathroom and washed his face. He took a beer from the refrigerator; thankfully Tommy Fenn had not finished them all. He sat at Taylor's desk. He set his cellular down beside the beer. He drank the beer slowly and smoked a cigarette composing himself for the call he had to make.

"I have news," Dane said into the phone. "There is a laundering operation going on here . . . Partly my contact, partly luck . . ."

Without mentioning Essie's name Dane went on to explain how the shipment was being handled, which was exactly the same technique of using boxes of animal plasma that launderer in Los Angeles had been using along with his sons to siphon money to UCLA athletes.

"Only this wasn't cash. It was diamonds . . . No, cut stones. So you'd only have them for nonpayment of taxes . . . About two million dollars' worth . . . See what you can find out about a man named Merrit Merton . . . Who else? . . . The Fenns are involved . . . Charles Gill . . . Nathan, probably. I'll know later."

Dane stood up. "How?" He rubbed at the tension in the back of his neck. He walked to the open front door. He detailed his conversation with Nathan and a room full of dinner guests about his accident and opening the box before he delivered it. There was no mistaking the pause at the other end of the line, or the disturbed breathing.

"Nathan's been trying to call me . . . Yes, I could be jeopardizing your operation. That sure is one way to look at it . . . I did it for a reason . . . knowing the risk."

He looked at the bottle hanging from the porch light by a string. He pushed at the bottle with a finger and it began to sway back and forth.

"I had to because . . . I shorted the delivery. You heard me right. I copped about a hundred thousand worth of diamonds before I delivered them to the Fenns . . . I have them hidden away."

Dane went back to rubbing his neck. He went and took the beer bottle from the desk and held it against the muscles along the side of his throat. The little coolness left to the bottle soothed the pain that was working its way up into his head.

"You can't pull me out of here now . . . that is over . . . Why? Because they might suspect something if I just disappeared, right? And how would they react? Maybe they'd shut down the operation and reorganize. That could set you back months, maybe permanently. Maybe you never find out what happened to Greene or Reynolds. No, you can't pull me out of here . . . Yeah, I guess I've seen to it, right."

"You can forget that threat . . . I'm not into begging . . . But isn't that why you brought me here? 'Cause I don't balk in a fight?"

Dane went to the couch and dumped himself down. He reached for the pack of cigarettes on the end table lying there beside the gun. He took the pack, changed his mind, and tossed it across the room.

"I know the risk . . . but it will flesh them out . . . They're gonna go at each other to find who shorted the load. 'Cause shorting loads puts everyone at risk."

Dane glanced at the open front door, at the bottle Tommy Fenn left there still swaying back and forth from a string.

"And their first stop will be the Fenns. Characters like that always are the first stop." Dane rubbed at his temples with an open palm. "I'm sure they'll get around to me . . . *if* Nathan doesn't have someone put a bullet in my head first.

"Whatever you think, this is my territory now . . . Yeah, you're right . . . I could probably write a textbook on the hustle . . . Maybe I will someday and then you'll have all your trainees reading it . . . And maybe you shouldn't have sent me here in the first place. But it's too late for that, isn't it? . . .

"Yeah . . . you're gonna ride with me all the way, or end up having to shut down my end of the operation. And I don't think you want to have to explain that away with everything I managed to help get you, just so far."

He sat there silent. He listened to their threats and their accusations and their demands and even their questions. But behind all that official positioning he also heard they were trying to work up a little wiggle room amidst all that posturing because they were in no hurry to have to explain blowing off an operation like this that'd been delivering. Not with the mortality rate of government careers.

"You always think I'm working an angle . . . You always get back to that." You lay out a premise, you set the tone, then you cap it with a temptation. There's only one thing left after that . . . Dane looked over at Taylor's desk. At a picture of Essie he had taken from Taylor's personal belongings and placed there. "Well . . . maybe I am working an angle . . . Fuckin' sleep on that."

CHAPTER THIRTY-FIVE

NATHAN SAT AT the bar in his living room. Utterly disconsolate he rested his hands on the counter and closed his eyes. He prayed. He actually heard himself praying that all this could be made right. He was suddenly humiliated by the gesture, but it did not stop him from praying; it actually made the process all the more intense and resolute that God would show mercy and get this resolved so he could go on.

Ivy came into the room and his eyes opened. She was wearing one of his bathrobes. She had taken off her makeup. She was drawn and her beautiful eyes were nearly colorless. "Did he answer?"

"No." He saw she was trying to get a vial of pills open. "What's that?"

"Xanax."

"You already took Valium."

"I took Valium." Her long fingernails literally wrenched the top off. "And now I'm taking Xanax."

She poured red wine from a decanter into a glass to get the pills down.

"You can't keep doing that."

"I'm having a terrible anxiety attack, all right? I can't handle these situations." She emptied the glass of wine. She poured another.

"You can't keep on like that."

"He knows." Her eyes fluttered upward. "He knows."

"He may not."

"Didn't you hear him at dinner?"

Nathan saw Ivy start to hyperventilate. She took deep breaths to calm herself. "I feel like I could have a heart attack." Dizziness set in and she had to bend down to try and get the blood back into her head.

Nathan stood and held her but Ivy's body contorted. "You can't touch me right now; it makes me feel like I'm being tied down."

She started to walk the room as if trying to escape what she felt. One hand gripped around the other, the fingers flexed erratically. She saw her ghastly pale reflection in the glass patio doors that looked out over Discovery Bay.

On the farthest outskirts of the bay she watched boat lights as they moved on into the darkness. It was the night of Taylor's death all over again. The wine and pills were not working near fast enough. She walked back to the bar. "He's testing us."

Her hand was trembling as she reached for the decanter.

"We don't know that."

"He's testing us. He's testing us. He knows. He wants to see—"

She went to pour. Her fingers had a puttyish feel. There was no blood in them, it was all in her heart and chest and lungs and feet.

"If he knew," said Nathan, "if he even thought something was wrong, why didn't he take us aside and say it? Hell, why didn't he just go to the police? Or to Roy—"

The decanter dropped like a stone to the tiles on the word "police." It burst apart and scatter shots of glass and long strands of red wine were spit across Ivy's legs and she literally screamed out.

IVY SAT on the floor of the shower in the dark. The water was scalding hot, the room steamed over. Her legs were pulled up to her chest and with a cloth she wiped them down. There were numerous cuts and wine stains that looked like the tracks of some tiny creature that had skittered insanely across her legs.

The wine and pills were taking effect and that one blow-up had pretty much purged her of any energy she had. The shower door swung open. Her head rocked sideways. Nathan stepped in and the steam engulfed him. He was naked. He squatted then curled around Ivy, easing her forward so he could sit behind her with his back to the wall.

"You calming down?"

"Burning down is more like it."

"Ivy . . . I need to . . . ask you something."

Ivy's head dipped despondently. "Please, nothing now."

"I've been avoiding it—"

"Please."

"You told Roy—"

She tried to pull away. "Don't I mean anything to you?"

Nathan's grasp tightened, she could feel the blood pumping through his forearms.

"I haven't had the courage to ask you this before. But courage or not, I have to know now. You told Roy—"

Her fingers clutched up around her face. She did not want to see, to hear, to speak . . . to remember. "I know what I told Roy."

"Is it true or did you just say it because you felt Taylor might have suspected—"

"I was trying to protect you from pain." Her body convulsed for one cruel moment. "Now try to think of me."

"Taylor didn't say anything to make you—"

Ivy wailed, "I was trying to protect you. Don't you understand? And fuck Roy for breaking a confidence."

CHAPTER THIRTY-SIX

CHARLES GILL WAS at an all-night rave club in Rocklin called Dance Heaven getting his fill of sonic addiction. He loved to come to this jammed-down hole in a strip mall where the bass tore your eardrums apart and fed off the vibe. Let his imagination indulge that all those young scenesters were there waiting for the stud mystery, waiting as the MC yelled into the mike, "Even guitar gods need a little earthly assistance," and then Charles would step into the applause through a pulse of lights and faces.

That sense of being carried away on a youthful fantasy left him bitter because except for the fact that his position and money allowed him a few artistic eccentricities over people who hadn't the slightest interest, Charles would be condemned to a life of unfulfillment.

His beeper went off. He thought it was the old lady trying to invade his privacy with some annoying complaint or demand. But it was Romero.

ON WEEKENDS the General's granddaughters would sleep in the second bedroom of his cottage. Claudia would fix dinner and it gave them all a chance to be together, without Charles.

Claudia was making her father a cocktail when headlights pulled into the long driveway. She bent up the blinds and tried to squint through an approaching spillway of light. The car parked near Charles' studio and as the driver's door opened she recognized it was Damon Romero.

"I love having . . . the girls here overnight," said the General as he wheeled in from the bedroom hallway. "Sometimes, when . . . you've gone back to the house . . . I turn out all the lights and . . . I sit . . . by their door and . . . listen . . . to their breathing. I . . . love the sound. It's so peaceful . . ." He came up alongside his daughter, tired. "I did that . . . with you too."

She looked at her father. The man in the pictures on the wall was gone. He was down to those perverse inches before the finality. His hand weakly gestured toward the window, "Who's out there?"

"Damon Romero. He must be waiting for Charles."

The old man's nostrils flushed. Claudia leaned down and kissed her father on the side of his head. The skin around his temple was like poorly colored plastic and the veins a stonewashed blue.

She handed him his cocktail. He had to hold it with both hands, and even so, the ice kept rattling against the glass. It was heartbreaking enough for her and humiliating, she was sure, for him.

Another set of headlights pooled at the end of the long dark driveway then turned. Claudia peeked through the blinds and asked her father, "The night Taylor died Romero was here. I saw him on the dock with Charles from my bedroom window just hours after. And Charles only meets him in the most discreet circumstances. Do you know how it is he ended up at Disappointment Slough as a witness?"

The General still could not bring himself to look at the dead spot on the wall where Taylor's picture hung.

Claudia felt her father's hesitancy. "I should have listened to you about Charles."

"Rebellion is one of youth's . . . prerogatives."

She turned to her father. "Not just youth, Daddy."

The General saw a flood of light against the cottage wall, then it was gone. His daughter's stare was his stare, only more femininely applied.

Claudia let go of the blinds. "The shit's home," she said. She knelt in front of her father's wheelchair and held his paper-light hands. "I know Charles has gone out of his way to humiliate you since you've been sick. But I have to ask about Taylor, in case I need to protect the girls later."

CHARLES GLANCED down at the cottage as he approached Damon, who was standing beside his car. "What's wrong?"

"Rudd . . . he delivered that box to the Fenns."

Charles stopped and leaned against the hood of his car uneasily. "How did that happen?"

Romero walked over to Charles. "No one knows, he just showed up. But it gets worse." Romero folded his arms and looked down at the ground. "He made the Fenns open the box."

"He made them?"

"The kid said he dropped it and just wanted them to make sure everything was all right."

"And they did it?"

Romero's head cocked sideways. "What else could they do? They said Rudd didn't see anything but . . . he was in the hangar and things got ugly between him and Shane."

The automatic sprinklers went off and they were covered by an expanding swath of droplets so they moved around to the far side of the cars.

They huddled up facing each other. Charles took Romero by the arm. "What do you mean 'got ugly'?"

"I got it all in pieces later." Romero was practically whispering now. "From Shane. You know Tommy is a lockbox."

Charles noticed a pale shift in the darkness down by the cottage. "Hold on."

Romero followed Charles' eyeline. A gray silhouette moved past a footlight that sided the driveway. It was Claudia.

She saw Damon turn away as soon as he noticed it was her. "Maybe I should cover my eyes," she said in passing, "so we don't know we saw each other."

"Go inside," Charles told her.

Claudia, ever so quietly, ever so vindictively, said, "Secrets—secrets—secrets."

CHARLES CAME into the house not long afterward and found Claudia sitting at the top of the stairs. The confrontational pose, the hitch to her body as she began to take off her shoes, told him she was lying in wait.

From the bottom of the stairs he raised his arm and jerked a thumb toward the driveway. "What was all that about?"

"It's a good thing," she said, "I don't have a grand view of the world, and live only in small personal increments. I look to make sure my kids are happy. I look to make sure they are healthy. And I look to make sure they are safe. But you on the other hand—"

"What was that comment about . . . secrets, secrets, secrets?"

From a sitting position she flung her shoes down the long hallway toward her bedroom. "You're not my father and you're not Nathan, but you're arrogant enough to believe you could rule them or replace them, just run right over them. But Charles, you're not strong enough for what's in your head, not smart enough and not nearly brave enough. And the bodies you keep around you like that Cuban boat salesman with the white patent leather shoes are not strong enough, not smart enough and not brave enough to help you."

"Do you know who your father and Nathan are? Do you?"

She stared at him as she undid her shirt's top button, not answering.

"They ran drugs for the army then sleazed their way up from there. They're the Fenns, Claudia. That's who they are. They are Tommy and Shane and the only difference is your father and Nathan had a better education when they started out; they had a little more money and a few up-end connections."

She undid the next button. "And that is all the difference in the world." Then the next button. "You're a minor player in all this, Charles. Remember that and you'll be all right."

"What was that comment outside meant to be?"

"Strictly background. You're that faceless douche who works for the band, not the band."

"Answer me."

She undid the last shirt button and while he stood there holding onto the stairway bannister waiting for her to say something she took off her shirt and flung it down the long hall toward her shoes.

She sat there squared up staring down on him. Her skin was dark and beautiful, her nipples black against the white bra. He knew she was humiliating him.

"Since when did you start wearing a bra around your father?"

The corners of her face pulled back like some dangerous cat's, but before she spoke she let her insides get just calm enough. "When you got busted and my father bailed you out, how do you think you happened to get busted?"

He did not understand why this conversation had started, or where it was going. The whole night was like one aberrant dream crashing into another.

"Your father, right? Is that what you're gonna tell me now?"

"No, it wasn't my father . . . it was me."

Obscene numbness as Charles repeated to himself what he had just heard. "This is a lie to hurt me?"

"I wanted you and I did what I wanted to get what I wanted. Now, here I am. All the poorer for it. A perfect bit of truth, Charles. What I wanted at twenty is useless now. Better I wanted nothing, or better I knew that to begin with."

"This is a lie meant to hurt me."

"It's meant to warn you. To give you pause." She stood. "I live in small personal increments. I have no grand view of the world. I will look out for the girls. I will look out for my health. And I will look out for my security."

184

CHAPTER THIRTY—SEVEN

DANE SAT THROUGH the night and watched the slate dark give way slowly through the bay window. He watched the muted tones of dawn edge into the heavy arch of branches beyond the roofline like some soundless mass until it came to rest upon the desk and chair of a dead son.

Dane walked outside and sat on the stone steps and let the ageless light of the earth rise upon him. This silent invocation, this vision of unknown genius, and the still nightwaters of Disappointment Slough were soon alive with sparkling tones more golden than any golden silence.

And there alone with the cold dew upon his breath Dane could imagine all the rich dreams that had moved along its steady course. The smoke of a thousand fires and prayers that had guided its shores. A continent of men and women who had worn the humble seasons and the hard seasons with faulted but honest human determination only to find they had passed on, had passed away.

And with them all, the flaws and blemishes of evil purpose, the sworn allies of arrogance and greed, the hostile dramas that took an unknowing someone from the back, the sinister motives disguised as a smiling piper, those who worked the shadows of malevolence and murder.

They were all moving upon him, moving around him, within him. The heartbreaking and beautiful contradictions of untamed and invincible forces and he felt shamelessly inadequate trying to impose his will upon events, upon his own life. He stood, and as he often did, folded his hands behind his back. He stared inwardly out upon Disappointment Slough.

How could anything he felt that huge be scaled or mastered? How could anything that vast and high be overcome or escaped? And what truth was hidden beyond its end?

He remained that way a long time, although it was only minutes before the sun streamed across his face. He then walked back to Taylor's cabin to call Nathan.

NATHAN SAT in the drape closed bedroom while Ivy slept. He looked to the clock on the table beside his chair. The Sunday morning shift at the yacht club had arrived by now. Sidewalks were being hosed down, the dining room vacuumed, brunch prepared.

The frightful monotony, those sleepwalking time-in, time-out hours the servile live through suddenly had a great deal more pull when compared to the pollutions of uncertainty he was going through.

In the living room his phone rang and he rose silently to answer.

NATHAN ASKED Dane to meet him in Lathrop, at the property which was ordained to be the medical center. The site was an abandoned 5,800-acre farm that bordered an easy turn in the San Joaquin River at the end of Dos Reis Road. Nathan said he needed to talk and that he would be alone.

NATHAN SAT on the treads of a huge yellow bulldozer that had cut the first crisscross of roads for the trucks to follow. He drank a beer and looked out over this rugged expanse toward the great whale-backed outline of Mount Diablo rising in the eastern distance.

With all that confronted him one thought-plaguing ache stood out. Had Taylor truly felt so much like a failure that it brought him to the brink of suicide? Or could it point more clearly to the

THE PRINCE OF DEADLY WEAPONS

fact he had found out before his death who Nathan Hale Greene was behind the pretense?

Why all last night and all this morning the same thought-plaguing ache without conclusion? Even after Ivy had confessed to him what she knew. And then, he saw why.

IT WAS a brusque, dry wind that kicked up the bone dry dirt along the main road that led to where Nathan sat on the treads of a bulldozer and saw a cavalry line of climbing cake dry earth begin to snake its way cautiously toward him, rising and falling with the broken contours of the land, disappearing behind swales of tall brush only to appear again through brittle acres of thicket, moving toward him slowly, cautiously, finding its way through that maze of pitched and rugged half cut bulldozed pathways and pulling that column of rising dust along through which he could begin to make out the black hood of Dane's Rampage.

Yes, he saw now why all last night, all this morning that thought plaguing ache. Here was another boy who might well have discovered who he really was. For a moment Nathan felt as if his own son's ghost was coming to have the talk that he dreaded would some day surface and he would have to admit who and what he really was.

The day was beautiful and clear. The world wide open and warm. Nathan was a man who had committed atrocities and would again if need be for his survival, no doubt about that he knew, he knew as he watched the pickup come down a short ravine facing and into the open flats where the bulldozer was parked. He knew, yet why at this very moment, why did he feel vulnerable, in need of protection from a force, a feeling, that seemed to be within him?

THE PICKUP came to a stop. Nathan was framed within that filthy windshield. He waved, and held up a beer. He smiled, but Dane could tell it was only a creation.

187

Dane looked all about him to see if they were truly alone. He made sure the gun couldn't be seen in the pocket of his black suede coat, if it got down to that.

Dane waved back, then he stepped out of the truck.

CHAPTER THIRTY-EIGHT

BESIDE NATHAN ON the bulldozer treads was a paper bag that Dane could only see in part. As he approached, Nathan reached either into that bag or toward something out of Dane's view. Dane stopped and his hand went to the pocket with the gun, until Nathan extended an arm. He was holding a can of beer.

"Are we celebrating, or commiserating?"

Nathan breathed a stray huff. "Somewhere in between probably."

Dane's hand moved from the coat pocket and took the beer. As he opened it and drank Nathan looked down a long wash toward the San Joaquin. It was eleven o'clock in the morning. The winter-brown brush and branches on the few standing trees between them and the river flagged with wind.

"What did you want to talk about, Nathan?"

"I was going over the architectural renderings this morning and we are just about on the spot where the main building for the center will be. The hospital suites, recovery rooms." He pointed toward that skin blue roadway of water. "What would you have said if you opened your eyes the first time after surgery and saw that?"

Dane looked to the San Joaquin and beyond, where black fields were being turned by a tractor whose huge wheels created two pillars that moved along in perfect unison then spiraled skyward together.

"I know what I did say." Dane turned to Nathan. "I promised the person who had willed me their eyes that I would try and see the world more clearly and well, from then on."

"Yes," said Nathan, "yes." His tone ached with understanding.

From beyond a swale came the sound of children. Then a boy riding a bike rose in silhouette on the peak of a short ridge maybe a hundred yards from that bulldozer and shouted to unseen friends.

Nathan stared in their direction. If anything violent had been set to happen it was now a simple impossibility and Dane was left to wait.

In his taupe silk sport coat, blue silk shirt, gabardine pants, and simply beautiful shoes which Nathan wore with no socks, contrasted by the poorboy beer and his dusky movie theater looks that stared out from a bulldozer throne and into a landscape of perfect western proportions, it was not hard to imagine Nathan as a portrait of existence from almost any quarter of life. A man capable of defending any conclusion, of capturing any dream, of destroying whatever was inconvenient.

At that moment and in that man Dane saw himself more clearly than he ever had. And he saw Nathan more clearly than he ever had.

The boy on the bike was joined by two smaller silhouettes running. One was a girl, the other a boy holding a kite who began to sprint the length of the weedy ridge top trying to give that paper bird the air it needed to fly.

Nathan glanced at Dane, who sipped his beer. Nathan wanted to read Dane's eyes but he could not as Dane was wearing the sunglasses he usually did to protect them.

"What do you want . . . ?" asked Nathan. Dane did not answer, forcing Nathan into an uncomfortable pause, so he fleshed out the thought a little more with . . . "Out of life, I mean."

"Are you asking what I want my life to be like?"

"Define it any way that's meaningful to you."

Dane stepped into the shadow of that huge monster bull of a ground mover. He leaned against the blade and grinned. "I want to be God," he said, "without all the legwork."

Nathan looked across the short distance between them and he had to cover his eyes to see against the sun that Dane was, in fact, smiling.

"On the chance that choice has been reserved," Dane said, "I'll settle for the chance at a life successfully achieved."

"Could you live here, in this place, make this world, our world, your home?"

On that Dane turned away and followed the fleeting and lithe voice of that small girl on the ridge top with his eyes. She had the kite now and was cheering it skyward as she ran.

She was taller, her legs longer, and she could run faster than the smaller boy. The kite was airborne and the wind stronger now and the red black span of wings kept breaking upward in fluted spurts then would fall back, and the girl tried to run faster and overcome those stays of wind, and the boy on the bike wheeled in and around her and the littler boy had all he could do to keep up.

"Who wouldn't want a place this beautiful to call home?" said Dane. He went to say more, hesitated, drank some beer, watched those kids on the ridge top. And as he did, Nathan saw Dane's mouth and cheeks pull back and crease as if contesting the taste of a thought.

"But I wonder, Nathan, does anyone ever truly feel at home and happy? Even in a place like this?" Dane emptied his beer. Then he squeezed the can till the metal skin crinkled inward. "Or does anything this beautiful leave us homeless in some way? Disappointed in some way? Because we can't measure up to it?"

"What do you mean? There's people here that care for you, that want you to be happy. Essie . . . the Carusos . . . Ivy . . . and don't forget me. I want you to be happy."

Nathan put his head back and killed the last of his beer. He tossed the empty toward the brush. "You're coming off a few hard years." He reached into the bag and pulled out two more beers. "And you're young. And youth is such a fuckin' "—he stuttered the word—"killer."

Dane turned to him. Nathan held out another beer for Dane, which he took. He also saw Nathan had been bitten by his own words.

"I understand, Nathan; it's all right."

191

Nathan tried not to think of his own son. "Yeah . . . yeah." He coated up a bit of a smile. "I'm going to help you. 'Cause I want your life to be successfully achieved."

"You've been helping me in more ways than you know."

"I appreciate your loyalty to me . . . and to Taylor."

"Loyalty is important."

"And I appreciate your honesty."

"Honesty is important. Of course I don't mean to go overboard." On Nathan's uncertain look, "I'm talking about last night."

"Yes . . . last night."

Again Dane turned away. He opened his beer. The boy on the bike now had the kite. With one arm extended skyward, and the other guiding the handlebars he raced down the ridge top and over ground shaped like the swells of a risky sea.

"Is that what you brought me out here to talk about?"

"I brought you out here because a part of this is you. And it could be more of you. I wanted to offer you a chance to reach into all of this and take from it what you're willing to work for. And sacrifice for. To become, ultimately, the right hand of my business."

As if he had not heard anything Nathan said and was solely focused on the cowboy ride of bike, boy and kite toward the river, Dane remarked, "When I was a kid I hated kites. I think maybe because the sky was too remote for me." He drank some more beer. "What about Taylor?" Dane turned to Nathan. "As a kid, was he into kites?"

Nathan's hand came up and covered the lower part of his face as he realized he didn't know or couldn't remember and he told Dane so honestly. Then he looked at his hand as if what had been expressed on his face lay there staring back up at him in an indictment of mercenary understanding.

"I want to see the center completed. After that, whatever happens, happens."

"Self-pity can be a dangerous form of selfishness. And easily seen through."

Nathan's face took on a few trenchant edges. "Was that how it sounded?"

"Yes."

"Well, you see how invaluable you are to me. I need that kind of loyalty."

"And that kind of honesty?"

"Are we going to celebrate or commiserate?"

The boy on the bike made a stretch of dirt road and was speeding wildly to the river with the red and black paper bird high above and chasing him.

"Before we do either, Nathan, I need to tell you that . . . I've lied to you."

Nathan had a rocky feeling. He put his beer down on the bulldozer treads and striking a nonjudgmental pose, waited.

"I was in serious trouble once. It wasn't long after the incident on the subway and I knew I was going to lose my sight. Money was a big issue. I was in college then. And not that 'Berkeley to Harvard' dance which I use to avoid the subject as best I can.

"I was studying law at Princeton. I worked for a criminal attorney part-time and summers. I was sent once to pick up a packet that belonged to a client of his during a request for production. There was information in that packet that if the attorney had in his possession could have led to the discovery of admissible evidence that would have certainly indicted his client."

The smaller boy and girl jackrabbited through the brush to try and catch the bike, but had no chance.

"I was paid by the attorney to make sure the packet went 'undiscovered.' "

The road was a minefield of holes. It was a beautiful wild temptation for that mustang of a boy and bike to swerve and jump.

"Things went bad. The attorney never implicated me, but the school . . . I was very quietly gotten rid of."

The road ran straight into a dry wash with a five-foot drop, and the boy on the bike with whiterimmed teeth and whiterimmed eyes and one hand gripping his handlebars and one holding the rope line went for it.

"So you see, Nathan, I am a perfect accomplice for anyone who has not led a perfect life."

It was a landless moment with the wind rattling through the boy's ears and at the moment he knew the bike could go no farther, no higher, he let go of the rope line.

Nathan said nothing. He rose up and his shadow extended out from the bulldozer and it looked as if this beastly piece of machinery had grown a head and chest.

The bike hit hard and the boy was chucked up from the seat and the wheels made crude herky jerky metallic sounds as they skidded and bounced along the rocky bottom.

Nathan was face to face with Dane now. Nathan was the taller, broader, stronger looking man. "The night of the tribute, when I humiliated myself by coming down hard on you 'cause I thought you were there about the wine delivery, and then when we were alone and seeing you the first time I was just so overcome I started to cry, you said to me, and I never forgot it, you said, 'You're safe with me.' "

The smaller boy and girl reached the edge of that craggy shelving and saw their friend lying on the rocky ground with the bike beside him, its front wheel spinning wildly.

Nathan put his hand on Dane's shoulder. "Well . . . you're safe with me. More than anyone, ever, you are, and will be, safe with me . . . now."

The smaller boy and girl ran to their friend yelling if he were all right but they got no answer until their winded shadows rushed across his face and they saw he was smiling.

"And one more thing, Dane," said Nathan. "I won't ever compromise you. No matter what happens to me. I won't ever. You, at least, will be able to walk away and protect 'all this.' I'll see to it. I swear."

The smaller boy and girl dropped beside their friend who tried to shake the sting from his cut hands, and the girl slapped at him for scaring her but he just kept watching the sky.

WHILE THEY walked toward the cars Dane said, "Nathan, this is hard for me, but—"

Nathan stopped. Dane hesitated.

"Wouldn't you like to know what really happened to your son?"

Those dusky movie theater looks bruised over.

The boy hobbled along leading his bike, the two small friends beside him. The girl still slapped at his back for scaring her as they made their way toward the river to follow that black and red bird's escape.

"Doesn't it eat at you? I'd like to think that I could pay your son back, some day, with that little bit of knowledge."

Nathan said nothing. He turned and walked to his car. His broad shoulders flexed uncomfortably. The wind blew dust through the distance between them and Dane wondered if he had not pushed it that much too far.

Nathan took something from the glove compartment. He stepped away from the car and held out his hand. In it lay a gun. And while Dane stared at the black weapon, on a bench of sand at the shore three children watched a paper bird they had given life to ride the thermals, be carried along on the wind toward forever, or at least until it fell.

"That's how much I want to know," said Nathan, "that's how much. And don't ever forget it."

CHAPTER THIRTY—NINE

How MANY TIMES, Essie thought, have I sat in this very same booth? How many times have I looked out this very same window? There was blood and bone in those memories.

On her table were an open briefcase, notes, a beer, an uneaten lunch. She waited for Dane while brilliant sunlight waterfalled down the glass and she was forced to squint as she stared across the tarmac toward Taylor's hangar.

It was almost empty now, the last few items gathering up darkness until she could sell them off.

Moments remembered are emotions relived. She had been in this very same booth alone, despondent, emotionally beaten, the morning after Roy and Flesh had taken her to dinner in Lodi to break the news before she read it in the papers that "the investigation had failed to furnish any legitimate evidence that Taylor's death was—"

Written on the weights of pain, anger and bitterness, in full measure. Enough to drown you, if you don't swim on. Moments relived are emotions remembered.

". . . The investigation failed to furnish—"

Her gray-green eyes blinked, and blinked again at the pulse of a thought. Then, with camera shutter quickness, simple disconnected details were caught in a breathless clarity.

". . . failed to furnish—"

The Fenns opening Taylor's hangar door—their callous stares looking for an antique bureau—destination Charles Gill—its question mark end in a Dumpster—to the night in her garage Dane found it missing a dowel.

She grabbed her note pad and began to write:

Check invoice to find name of shipper for delivery to
Gill. See if there are any connections between that and

—A voice behind her ear, "Slide over."

Her head jerked sideways.

"Sorry," said Dane.

She swept back her hair and slid toward the window. "Is it all right?"

He slipped down in next to her.

"What happened?"

He took her beer and drank. He was still riding fumes of nervous energy. He saw Paul through the open doorway to the packed coffee shop. He was scooping dirty plates from a table into a bin to keep the turnover moving. Paul nodded and gave Dane a work-tired smile, then he hoisted up that bin and headed for the kitchen.

"Nathan offered me a future."

"What does that mean?"

"He wants me to stay and leave an imprint. He wants my allegiance. My loyalty. A better word would be fealty. He wants to qualify for goodness by having me as a stamp of approval on his businesses. I'm the chip he wants to use to hedge his bet. He wants what he never had in the first place. He wants to imagine someone real." Dane took another drink of beer. He sat the glass down and with spare sadness said, "He wants a son back."

"Did he come right out and tell you what he does? Were the words said? Was there a confrontation about what you saw?"

Dane rested his forearms on the table. He studied the beer glass, the uneaten lunch, the note pads, the briefcase, his hands, as if some inexorable answer lay hidden in those simple still lifes, or that by staring long enough he could get whatever he felt out from inside him.

"It was a beautiful day in Lathrop," he said. "And there were these kids with a kite. They were running along a ridge top. They were just colors moving across the sky and one kid on a bike held the rope line as he rode and the kite tailed high behind him and you could see the river."

Dane looked at Essie. "That night in the garage, you were right. It would be great to be twenty-five without all the baggage."

She extended her hand toward his. "How did you get him to believe you could be trusted?"

Dane leaned his head back. The booth seat was anchored to one wall and he rested his head against it. "I know the right kind of lies to make myself vulnerable to someone. And Nathan wants a chance to . . . play God, without all the legwork."

When her hand touched his, his head dropped down and came to rest on her shoulder.

"We see Nathan for what he's done, for what he is. But I could imagine another Nathan. And another. One not so sad, not so pathetic. One that does not use the lie as a vital character trait. Although I'd be evading the obvious by forgetting what he's capable of."

"Do you think he suspects what we're trying to do?"

"You . . . no. Me . . . yes. I came out and asked him if he ever wanted to know what happened to his son."

Essie leaned forward and Dane's head was forced up from her shoulder. Those gray-green eyes searched for the why behind what he'd done and Dane saw she was not at all sure this had not been a terrible mistake.

"What did he say?"

"He went to his car and showed me a gun."

"Jesus Christ."

"He wants to know, as long as he thinks he's safe."

"What if he starts to think he isn't safe with you?"

"I'm sure that's another reason why he showed me the gun."

CHAPTER FORTY

CARUSO WAS COMING out of the kitchen by way of the bar, wiping his hands on a filthy apron. Sancho Maria was serving drinks and nabbed his attention with a look that pointed her chin in Essie and Dane's direction.

The last booth was a tightly knit silence. Shoulder to shoulder they seemed lost to everyone and everything except themselves.

IT WILL be all right."

Essie heard Dane, but she felt the gap between probability and certitude that something bad could happen had been drastically reduced.

"What is all this?" he said, pointing to her notes.

She suddenly remembered the last few minutes before he sat down. "In my garage. The antique with a missing dowel or front piece. The one sent to Charles that ended up in a Dumpster after the Fenns picked it up." She handed him the note to herself. As he read she kept on, "What if that's how they were shipping something when Taylor found out? What if that caused him to confront Charles or the Fenns? Not even suspecting his own father—"

"Yes . . . yes."

Dane noticed another page from the yellow legal pad. On this she had taped the bar napkin where he had written the name of the boat—*PLYMOUTH ROC*—he'd chased. Beneath it was a series of phone numbers. He held the page out for her to explain.

"Boats," she said, "are registered through the DMV. They have numbers on their bow or stern like license plates. CA and a number . . . AZ and a number . . . NV and a number. For each state. The bad news is they're registered by number and there's no correlation to the name."

"I didn't know," he said. "Otherwise I would have tried—"

"No, listen. I went to the Coast Guard office this morning in Tracy. Boats are also federally documented. It's usually done for larger boats, but this form of registration *is* done by name.

"There's a number in Virginia you call." She pointed to the number she had written down. "You give them the name of the boat and through the Freedom of Information Act they will fax you the name of the owner. The only problem is, more than one boat could have the same name."

Her finger coursed down to where she had noted his description of the boat.

"This may narrow the possibilities, and we might be able to find out who it was the Fenns met. And how all this fits together."

His first reaction was to tell her how smart she had been to piece this out, his second was to write on a new note page a name—William Singleton. To that he added an e-mail address.

She was practically breathing on his arm as he wrote, and when she asked, "Who is this?"

"The old truck I drive belongs to him. He also has that funky website passing for an internet magazine I told you about."

Dane slid the page along the table and between her hands. "One of Singleton's friends . . . had a father . . . who worked with the kinds of government people that would be interested in what is going on here.

"If something were to happen to me, feed him everything. But not so you can ever be connected to me. I have a laptop at the house. Only use that. And never say anything about who you are."

Staring at the torn page of yellow legal paper, at the name, the contact details, there was little need for conjecture on her part. Dane had directly and exactly not said what he meant.

She pushed the page back toward him. "I don't like this." She shook her head. Her mouth kept repeating silently 'I don't like this.'

Dane reached for the beer. "It's not to be liked, it's to be done."

I KNOW my life isn't nearly as exciting as yours." Caruso dropped down into the booth seat across from both of them, "but there is something to be said for the mundane mindless work that fills so much of our lives."

Caruso's Graduate of the Men's Colony T-shirt was appropriately stained. He was wiping his hands on his apron when he asked Dane, "How you doin'? And none of that doublespeak like last night, okay?"

Dane took the page with Singleton's name and information and folded it in half. "I heard you about the Boyz."

"Hearing me, and hearing me are two different things."

Dane folded the paper again and slipped it into Essie's open briefcase. The helpless proximity of the pure truth, she could do little at that moment but watch. Caruso noticed the tension in her face as she did.

Caruso rested his forearms on the table. The tips of his broken thick fingers tapped together. He sat there like some blue-collar inquisitor looking from Dane to Essie, then back to Dane. "The old lady and me would have to be brain dead not to be feelin' the vibe coming off this table. Do you think we don't have any idea what the hell is going on?"

Sancho Maria passed by and placed two beers on the table. Caruso asked his wife, "You talk to 'em?"

The blockish set of the jaw, the deeply blackish guarding eyes, Sancho Maria had the look of someone who would not be hurried along by impulses she would later have to justify or defend. She had withstood too many of life's uncertainties for that.

"They won't listen," she said. "Their minds are set." Her voice trailed off toward a much more intimately felt point. "I just pray it won't take *something else* terrible to change them."

Sancho Maria went about her work and Paul leaned back. He pointed to those collaged walls dedicated to that mythic prison and maze. "What are the magic words? What? What do I always say? Don't fly too—"

From the booth behind him a cellular rang. A big softly shaped man answered and got talking. Everyone in the bar who knew Paul knew what would come next. Caruso swung around and faced a large balding head with wisps of soft blond hair. He tapped the man on the shoulder. The man turned. He was young, puttyish, with glasses.

"You want to kill that call?"

"Excuse me?"

Caruso aimed a finger at the cellular CEASE AND DESIST sign on the far wall. The man told the party at the other end to hold on. He then said to Caruso, "There's no law in California that says you can't talk on a cellular phone in a restaurant."

That was it. He went back to his call. Caruso was already in a black mood at having left no imprint whatsoever on Dane, and now Essie.

Paul's face tightened up. He was mumbling to himself, "No law in California . . . fuckin' pompous wuss . . ."

He reached for Dane's mug of beer. He drank the glass down partway and stood. As he did, Dane noticed Tommy Fenn crossing the tarmac with a couple of scruffy airport regulars. They were coming toward The Burrow.

The big man in the booth saw something right beside him. He looked up. There was Paul with that partly drunk mug of beer. He was all teeth and tight fox eyes. Whatever the big man was thinking or feeling he just looked away and kept on talking.

As he did, Caruso grabbed the phone. For a second the big man stared at his empty hand. Then he looked up again, this time adjusting his glasses. As he did, as he was about to speak, Caruso dropped the phone into the mug of beer.

It made a short kerplunk and hit bottom. Paul hoisted the glass and guzzled down the beer in thick, gruff swallows. And when he was done he let the cellular drop into his mouth and he began to chew on the top end of it like you would that worm at the bottom of a tequila bottle.

Done, Caruso set the glass down. The big man could only stare at the glass, at the badly chewed cellular, at the beer and saliva that trickled down the mug rim. He looked up at Paul, who wore this glint of classless pride.

"You're very sick," said the big man.

"Certifiable," answered Caruso.

The big man got up and squeezed past Paul. He wasn't sure if he was going to be hit next but he just kept repeating "You're sick!"

When he got to the coffee shop doorway Caruso called to him, "Hey, you forgot your phone!"

Paul came around to face Dane and Essie's booth. He had burned off a little bad energy and was ready to try out another dose of reason, but Dane wasn't there.

FENN SLIPPED away from the small clique of pilots when he saw Dane under the archway to The Burrow. Dane moved out onto the grass and Fenn joined him by a huge California oak along the walk path.

"What was that message in a bottle meant to really say?"

"My brother likes to riot. He walks around with rumors in his head about what people have done to him and planning out pay-backs."

Dane went to light a cigarette. The wind was blowing so badly he had to cup his hands around the match to keep the flame alive. Fenn even tried to help by cupping his hands around Dane's.

"We're working to make a life here." Fenn glanced toward The Burrow window where Essie sat watching. "You too."

"Is this your 'Why can't we all get along' speech?"

"It's a good idea. I don't want my brother going predator."

"You show me yours, and I'll show you mine."

Tommy Fenn thought, This is one arrogant prick I would love to bitch down. "I'm trying to work the mood. Take a breath, give it a chance."

One of the men Tommy had crossed the tarmac with called to him. Tommy waved and said, "A minute here." He was waiting on Dane's answer.

"I can do a holding pattern," said Dane.

"Good enough. And I'll keep my brother grounded."

Tommy started away and Dane asked, "Hey, how was your trip down to Tehachapi?"

Tommy said nothing but he knew. The shit was gonna give you a taste. Just enough to try and tempt you.

CHAPTER FORTY-ONE

CARUSO WAS BY the register getting ready to seat the next grouping when Dane reentered The Burrow by way of the coffee shop door. Caruso took hold of Dane and pulled him aside. Referring to that conversation he witnessed with Tommy Fenn, Caruso said, "It's like a drug, ain't it."

"Better," said Dane.

"Fuck." Caruso jammed the menus he was carrying right at and into Dane's chest. "You got a little trace of the *gangsta* in you, hunh."

There was meant to be a heeded intent in the way he emphasized the word "gangsta."

"It's one of my inherent blemishes," said Dane.

WHEN DANE sat back down in the booth Essie handed him her pager.

"A message just came to me, for you."

"Nathan?"

"No."

Dane read the tiny screen as the message scrolled through. It was from Charles Gill. He wanted to meet at the bank tomorrow. First thing.

NATHAN WAS torn between what he knew to be true and what he needed to be true and whether he could work his will on them to be one and the same as he told Ivy, "It will be all right."

She tried to right herself in bed. The room was still dark behind drawn curtains, her voice touched by a groggy uncertainness as she leaned against the stacked pillows and asked, "He knows, and it's all right?"

"He knows, and it's all right."

Her mouth was dry. "How did you manage it?"

He was unsure he entirely had and only answered, "I appealed to his sense of loyalty. And he's hungry as any of us for a life to really work out."

"Money?"

"He's got his own baggage."

"Meaning?"

He explained Dane's response to his offer by detailing for Ivy the pure risk Dane took in desperation after his accident and how it had gotten him thrown out of Princeton.

She listened, her shadowed face too exhausted for any extraordinary expression. She responded, the words cracking against the dry inside of her mouth, "I can see now."

Could she see, or was this just a need to not see? Nathan felt as if Ivy were speaking from a passive stupor where anything he decided was decisive enough for her to believe.

"Nathan, please get me some water."

He rose. In one corner of the bedroom was a freestanding bar. As he handed her the bottle of water, Ivy asked, "Are you certain we're safe with him?"

While she drank he said, "We're safe."

She did not hear his truncated answer. And Nathan, he stood there and considered, was he confronting his own courage by doing this, was he throwing a gauntlet in the face of his own guilt?

Nathan was hungry for some ultimate legacy, something that would carry past the wakes of his life. But he also knew there is, in each of us, a place where resides an eternal antagonist who remains untouched by any virtue.

"I called Charles on my way back from Lathrop."

Ivy stopped drinking. Her eyes blinked fitfully. "Why? You didn't discuss any of this with him, did you?"

DANE HAD no answer for Essie.

"Do you think you should tell Nathan that Charles called?"

"No."

They lay on Essie's couch side by side. Her head was cradled in his arm, on his chest her hand rested. They watched the dusk rise like a slow tide up the wall then across the ceiling. They watched shadows form around details that then merged with darkness. They listened to music from an apartment across that alley of a street. They heard the noises of life through the open balcony doors and a mobile dance out chime songs close by.

Essie thought about what Sancho Maria had said in the bar, but her look, touched as it was by a grave and palpable honesty, had deeply affected her. The world, Essie felt lying there, could threaten her freedom, her life. And she needed more than ever human meaning.

"Have you ever loved someone?" she whispered.

Dane's eyes moved slowly away from her. "No."

"Could you . . . love someone?"

His eyes moved slowly toward her. "I used to feel pity for my mother and father because their relationship had been such a masterpiece of failure. And my father, he was incapable of any real connection, right up until the end. But it wasn't pity I felt."

"Anger . . . was that it?"

"It was fear," he said. "That they . . . he really . . . cast a shadow over who and what I am." Dane paused. To Essie, his face changed, as if some curtain opened, however briefly, and everything shunned or hidden, everything painful or frightening, at the edge of a stage to one's life, had shown through. "They do, you know. At least he does, and in ways I can't speak of, won't speak of. I can only say Nathan pales beside him. And I want you to know that even if I am not completely open with you, I am trying to be honest about what is inside me."

With that he became quiet, with that she slipped her leg across his and cheated a bit by stretching her neck so their faces made one shadow.

"Have you ever been afraid," she asked, "that love could overwhelm you? Truly overwhelm you."

"Why shouldn't it . . . if everything else can."

He knew, as she knew, they would sleep together. That after making love they would cling to each other in naked silence. That they would do as all people do and try to surrender to the truth of the other, to shore up any doubt that existed within themselves.

They also knew in that quiet night-filled room they would try to find safety, even as they defied safety.

CHAPTER FORTY—TWO

DAMON ROMERO TOLD the Fenns by phone to be at their place at ten o'clock Sunday night and not for one fuckin' minute to question or consider otherwise. That was all he said.

THE MEADOWS at that time of the year, at that hour of the night, on that particular night of the week was dead to the world.

Romero boated in. The Fenns had a rudimentary shack which extended back up from the dock in a gypsy fabrication of add-ons and extensions, some clapboard, some cinderblock. The dock squared around two sides of the house. Strewn about the property were all kinds and classes of nautical parts, airplane parts, the wingless hull of a scratch built Wag-Aero. It was the priceless debris of the mechanic and scavenger. All of which cast a keepish tableau of shapes and slants against the moonlight.

The house windows were half open and Romero could see the Fenns in those patches of yellow light and when they heard his boat coming Tommy Fenn crossed the living room and opened the front door.

Romero tied off and came up the dock silently. Tommy's silhouette waited in the doorway smoking a joint. Tommy was worried about what was behind all that bad attitude he'd been given on the phone, and as Romero approached, Tommy put out his hand to shake.

"Get that fuckin' hand away from me," said Romero.

The few other lights on the slough stood out at various desolate angles and heights and were separated by long stands of trees and space so there was little chance of witnessing anything ugly that might happen.

S HANE WAS sitting at the dining room table with a beer and a cigarette. He was working through a snakepile of wire bundles tying them off with cockpit lacing. Romero stopped in the middle of the room. Tommy closed the front door behind them. The place was pure bachelor white trash that had seen a few pay-scale hikes along the way. It smelled of beer and pot. On the dining room table were airplane console wires that Shane had been cutting. There was a CD player going in the living room and a television on in the kitchen.

"What's with the crackdown, Romeo?"

He cut Shane a stare. "You know why I'm here." He did the same to Tommy. "So you better cop to it right off."

The two brothers had nothing to say. Romero went over and hit every button on the CD player to get the damn thing shut off. He walked past Shane to the kitchen and did the same with the television.

Tommy wanted to know, "What is this?"

Romero came around the dining room table and swiped at the tools and wires sending them all over the floor. "We want the jewels back."

He stood where he could see both brothers' faces and the tautology of their astonished stares back and forth between each other only made Romero all the more belligerently enraged.

"Did you think they weren't going to find out? That you could just skim a few off the top and no one would know? That they just filled up a jar and rounded off the number to the closest ten?"

Tommy put a hand up to stop Romero. All traces of calm on Tommy's face were gone. "Damon—"

Romero spewed out phrases in Spanish they couldn't understand. He yanked the dining room table up then dropped it down. Shane grabbed for the spilling beer, his cigarette tumbled out of the ashtray.

"Merton called me tonight. He didn't say anything when he was here making the count 'cause he wasn't certain and he wanted to be sure he had the numbers right before he opened that door. But he called Mexico and got the word. You stupid fuckers, thinking you could pull a scam like that.

"Eight cut diamonds. That's almost a hundred thousand dollars. You guys are gonna have to turn it over. These people Charles deals with, they're not white boy tough. They are into a whole other zone. And they take their empire very seriously." Romero began to pace the room repeating again and again "You have no idea. No idea."

Tommy sat in the cloth chair. He put his hand on the top of an empty beer can and started talking gunfire fast. "Why would we do it? We have it all working here. And we know it could fuck you up. We took that box from the hangar when we got it and we drove right to the bar and you were with us from there on. We never touched the thing. We didn't go near it."

Romero shouted him down. "You went into the box, right! You opened it up, right!"

"We never—"

As if he were repeating a tape, Romero threw back in Tommy's face what Shane had told him about Rudd showing with the box, with them opening it 'cause he said it had fallen, and the confrontation after. "Unless that was all a fantasy," said Romero. He turned to Shane. "Was it a fantasy?"

Shane couldn't, wouldn't dare look at Tommy. And Tommy, he hated his brother at that moment more than anything on the face of the earth. If he could have just walked over there and opened a vein he would have, and let that shit mouth just bleed to death.

"Why blame us?" said Tommy. "Why not blame Merton? Or maybe they fucked up the count. Maybe it was delivered short."

Romero shook his head in abject disgust. "I heard your shit talk in the bar, all right. And I just want to know after you two got to be lead studs where was I, hunh!?"

A silence fell over that small room with its low ceiling. Tommy's mouth clipped open as if it had just been injured.

"That was just trash talk," said Shane.

"No?" Romero shook his head and started for the door.

"We didn't pull a rip. Damon—!" Shane sounded as if he were pleading to be believed.

Romero was standing over Tommy Fenn, Fenn was staring down at his black ankle-high work boots. He looked like a prizefighter who had been pounded right down to his roots. Romero kicked the chair and Tommy's head sprung up.

"Do you realize what could happen if Nathan knew I was connected to you and Charles? Don't you think he might wonder how it was I ended up at Disappointment Slough the night you went to off his kid?"

"The kid shot himself," said Shane.

As Romero crossed the room to leave Tommy stood. "I swear," he said, "I swear we did not pull some rip. I swear to fuckin' God."

"I can hold off till tomorrow telling Charles. After that—"

CHAPTER FORTY—THREE

THE PEOPLE'S BANK of Rio Vista was one of the oldest and longest standing banks in Central California history. And one that was still family owned.

There was a private open mezzanine that Charles used as a waiting room for his guests. And here Dane watched the comings and goings on the bank floor while Charles took a call on his cellular from Damon Romero.

DANE HAD never been in the bank before, but everything about it, the bare redbrick walls and silver Wells Fargo safe, the venerated landscapes of California done in oils and the antique pioneer furnishings gave every ritual the perfect touch of correctness.

Dane leaned against the railing and watched the daily business of small proceedings. Faces approached the teller windows in the secret process of their lives, those that were struggling by inches for personal survival, or confronting the rates of a loan, the inability to get credit, and savings accounts depleted by taxes, school bills and illness.

How easy it is to become a captive to the show. To believe that there is, in what you see, some form of validated idealism. From the bank itself steeped in motifs to draw out your emotions, to the faces themselves. It was all there, in a form that invalidated science and logic.

And as Dane watched these people go about the basics of existence, just beyond their reach the business of centuries was being played out.

CHARLES GILL was in his private office bathroom facing down rank fear. The shifting plates of stomach muscles contracted again and again, each time with multiplied intensity but he held back the vomit. He would not allow his insides to completely turn against him.

He stared at his face in the mirror. The skin cadaverous pale, the eyes watered from the gagging. It was a stark but honest revelation of what he was staring at, both internally and externally.

He turned on the faucet and bathed his face with cold water. He told himself that he would confront and correct this disaster. And not be destroyed by it. He hit himself with every hostile comment Claudia had made. That he was a minor player in his own life, strictly background. That he was not strong enough, smart enough, brave enough. That it had been she herself who had seen to it he was busted all those years ago, as a way of compromising him.

He drank down every insult as if they were warm blood that would give him the strength to see through to his own survival.

I'M SORRY to have kept you waiting."

Dane turned to face a warm clean smile. He and Charles shook hands. Charles' hand was unflatteringly cold.

CHARLES' OFFICE had been the General's until Philip Morris helped clear a way for the next generation. On the office walls now were guitars of famous artists that covered the arc of music from Sun House to Stevie Ray Vaughn. They were enshrined in airtight cases with the names of each pickman scripted onto a gold miniguitar beneath the instrument that had once been theirs.

It was to Dane's thinking, the ego goin' graveyard for support, but he said "It's a collector's dream" as he walked Charles' wall of fame, "but, it might have a touch of the bittersweet, if you felt that part of your life got away."

CHARLES SAT at his desk and swiveled around to face Dane, who stood in front of the floor-to-ceiling picture window taking in a view of Sacramento where the morning sun left troughs of light on the undisturbed river.

"Funny you should phrase it like that," Charles said. "Over the last few days I've been going through quite a revelation on this very subject."

Dane came around the desk. He sat in the same chair and pulled it up to almost the same spot as had Taylor those few days before he died.

Dane was wearing glasses and with the light coming right at his face the lenses darkened so it was impossible for Charles to read his eyes. He had been in the office for more than five minutes and not once had he asked why Charles wanted to see him. He gave off a composed self-confidence that Charles thoroughly distrusted but also understood he himself mindfully needed.

Dane could hear a mordant disgust in Charles' voice. "Have you ever come to realize that your past was bankrupt in ways you never imagined? That you'd been compromised, literally duped, made a fool of, used by people close to you, exploited, and you had no idea? That you put your trust in the wrong people?"

Charles looked at the guitars, glared at them really, as if they had played at his failure. "All that," he said, "was meant to gratify my impulses, like a child. It was a narcissistic way I could pretend I was going back to some place inside me that never was." He kept staring at the wall, at that lineup of instruments. "Maybe it was my drug, my way of feeling safe. Feeling in control?

"I thought about taking them down, but I'm not. I'm going to leave them there as a reminder. A road sign."

Charles stiffened a bit. He didn't really have the kind of face that went with anger. It was too long, too soft, the edges of bone curved rather than cut. The hair was too neat, the eyes lacked true luster. But, of course, Dane knew if history teaches us anything, it is that behind faces like that there can be headlands of despicable possibility.

Charles turned to Dane. "And let me tell you one more thing. When you come to realize that you've been made bankrupt, it brings out a much more belligerent sense of self. It takes you right to the cutting edge."

"All that sounds like some kind of warning."

"Well, I guess it is. More for myself than anyone. But I don't mind you spreading the word."

Dane said nothing. Charles said nothing. Charles sat back. On the river a great boat horn cried out. Charles finally spoke up. "It seems like you've made quite an impression on Nathan."

"We've gotten to be good friends. And I'm happy to help him all I can."

"It was good of you to deliver that package the other day."

Charles wanted to see how Dane would react. He didn't.

"That was just one of those pleasant accidents," said Dane. "Nathan was so overworked, and I was glad to do my part for charity."

"Obviously he feels he can trust you with almost anything."

"You'd have to ask him that."

Charles rose and walked over to an enameled black hutch. "You haven't asked yet why I called to meet."

"I'm game for surprises."

"How about shocks?"

"Shocks are just surprises spiced with a little adrenaline rush."

Charles opened the hutch top drawer. Dane saw him remove a letter-sized leather folder. He returned with it to the desk and sat. He unzipped the folder. He removed papers, what looked to be a deed, a safe deposit box key.

Charles pushed the deed toward Dane. "This is to the house on Disappointment Slough. It belonged to Nathan. He's turned it over to you."

Dane removed his glasses and reached for the deed.

"It's marked where you need to sign. There's a small mortgage on the place. Approximately sixty thousand dollars. An account is being set up by Nathan with time CDs to pay off the mortgage. The account will be in your name, but, for that one purpose."

Dane looked through the documents and thought to himself, You can now follow the path of all that laundered money right to your own front door.

Dane looked up. "Why isn't Nathan here?"

"He's too . . . self-conscious for this kind of thing. He wanted me to handle it. I'm sure you'll talk about it later."

"I don't know what to say. I'm overwhelmed."

"I'm sure," said Charles.

Dane held up the safe deposit box key and the deed. "It's like some new wave feoffment."

Charles' eyebrows pricked a bit. "What?"

"It's an old term. Never mind, no big deal."

"The box key is for downstairs, so you have a place to keep the papers safe. You should get those papers signed now."

"I'll do that."

Dane reached for a pen and began to sign where the pages were flagged by Post-its.

"I guess Nathan feels that you've really earned it."

Dane looked up, he smiled. "Maybe he feels I will earn it."

CHAPTER FORTY—FOUR

WHEN NATHAN ARRIVED at the General's Charles was not yet there. The old man was hooked to his oxygen, taking spare breaths in the sunlight a window afforded.

"Well," said Nathan, "we're in it, aren't we?"

The old man cupped his head with both hands. There once had been a jaguar inside Merrit Hand that could measure out in exact paces the taking down of its prey.

"Merrit, I don't like asking this way. But whatever you have left, I need. I know you have to watch out for your son-in-law. But I'm beyond trusting that flake where my life is concerned."

A reedy length of finger pointed to the bar. "Make us both . . . a drink," the General told Nathan. "The *pussy* will be here soon . . . and I want to know . . . what's going on with you . . . and Rudd."

WHEN CHARLES walked in the room the men grew quiet. It was a tidy silence that clearly said he had arrived at an inopportune moment. Charles slipped his hands into his pants pockets, his suit coat rumpled up. He crossed the room.

Nathan followed him with his eyes. "I'll be going to Mexico tomorrow. With a hundred thousand dollars and some hard answers."

Charles passed both men on his way to the bar.

"What happened with the Fenns?"

As he eased behind the bar Charles tried physically to emphasize his composure. "The Fenns swear up and down what they got, they delivered."

"Wellll . . . ," said Nathan, "that sure deciphers the mystery."

Charles reached for where the bottled water was kept. He would not allow himself to be baited.

"The Fenns took the box from the airport to meet with this Merton. He made the count, called Mexico, then brokered the diamonds. Everything from there on is a paper-and-wire transaction."

"Exactly right," said Charles.

"No one else had access to the box. Just the Fenns, and this Merton?"

"No one else at my end," said Charles.

The General knew Charles was lying. But he'd also had more than one good glimpse into the nightmare of what would happen if Damon Romero should surface in connection with the Fenns, and it was an ultimate he was not yet prepared for.

"The Fenns are your people. And this Merton, who I only know by a handful of phone conversations, which is how you arranged it, is also one of yours." Nathan looked back and forth between Charles and the General. "So there's only two possibilities." He leveled a stare at Charles. "One of yours gamed us." He turned his attention to the General. "Or the delivery was sent short from Mexico, on purpose."

This drew Charles out from behind the bar. "What do you mean 'delivered short'?"

Nathan's attention remained with the General, who conversed with himself silently while he considered. "They'd have shown . . . a good deal of . . . patience . . . waiting this . . . many deliveries."

"I'd like this explained to me."

"We've seen it though," said Nathan.

The old man shook his head remembering.

"Nathan?"

"They could be trying their first push on the terms of the deal."

"I . . . hope not," said the old man.

"Nathan, I don't understand."

Nathan plunked his drink down on the coffee table. "You don't understand. Back when you were Mr. Rock and Roll and the General had to buy off an indictment 'cause you were caught dealing, you mean to tell me you had never cut an ounce, or tricked out a bag to increase your profits?"

Charles took another drink of water. After having to swallow Claudia's savaging on this very subject there was a lot of revisionism going on inside his head regarding the General's actions; past, present and future. "I wasn't in the drug business as long as you *veterans* so I wouldn't have learned all the subtleties."

The General stared at Charles. If there had ever been someone who could be incensed to death, the old man burned with the look of that someone.

"Watch what you say in front of the General, Charles."

Charles took another drink of water. He made what sounded like a bawdy grunt. He'd come around the bar enough so he was just across the coffee table from Nathan. The General sat between both men.

"I won't be intimidated by this father and son head script. You're both not some colossus I have to walk under. You're just two fuckin' money launderers."

"Why you dirty little shit."

"Yes, Nathan, I'm a dirty little shit." Charles set his bottle of water down by Nathan's drink. He forced his hands into his pants pockets. "And I didn't do boot camp. And I didn't do special services. And I was never part of some torture squad."

Nathan's hands locked together. His index fingers and pinkies divined out toward Charles. "Now you understand. I have to face them in Mexico. But *you* have to pay them."

"Me? Even if they're scamming us?"

"You get the money. If they're scamming us, that's one thing. You're clear then. Otherwise, the Fenns have to go. This Merton has to go. After . . . I handle everything. Otherwise, strap on a backpack."

Charles looked at the General. The white tumulus of his bones protruded through the skin. He sat there like some bitter enemy backing Nathan all the way, but Charles knew the old man was too riddled with ghosts to be much more than a compromise waiting for the last rites.

"I'll get the money. But remember, Nathan, this deal was not my idea. I told you the night of the tribute—"

Nathan stood. "Don't go there!"

Charles backed off. Nathan reached for his drink and walked to the bar. Charles followed him with his eyes.

"You haven't asked how it went with Rudd."

Nathan emptied the remains of his glass into the bar sink. "I gathered we would get to it later."

"Why this sudden urge to play benefactor?"

Nathan started up another stronger drink. First came the ice, then the scotch, a stare for Charles while he went along, a sip, and finally—no answer.

"How much does he know?"

Nathan stirred the drink with his middle finger.

"You can't keep this from me. Not this. You don't want me stumbling into a mistake that could cost us all, do you?"

Nathan glanced at the General, who responded with a meager nod.

"He doesn't know everything," said Nathan.

"I thought so. He was just too fuckin' underwhelmed in my office by the whole thing. So perfectly aloof and polite about everything I asked him."

"Maybe that has more to do with you."

"Right, okay. But I guess he's not the portrait of innocence that you've been building up all these months."

Nathan came out from behind the bar and walked up to Charles. "But he does have some allegiance to my dead son, of which I am benefiting. And so you're benefiting. Don't forget it."

Nathan went to sit down, the ice in his glass clacking as he did.

"How did he come to join"—Charles waved his hand despicably—"our little family of man?"

Again Nathan looked to the General; again the General gave a meager nod.

"It was my fault. He delivered the box by accident. He was trying to do me a favor and just took off with it while I was in my office. He dropped it in the parking lot. He opened it to make sure nothing was damaged. He told me later."

Charles stood there silently and compared what he just heard to what he knew. "I think you might be lying to me, Nathan."

Nathan eyed him with a clipped stare. "How am I lying to you?"

"It's odd, but the same week we get ripped, you start playing benefactor. Maybe it was you who opened the box. You had it in your office. Maybe *you* did a little skimming to try to hook me with the blame."

The ice in Nathan's glass stopped clacking. He set the glass down on the coffee table. "You better explain that paranoid chatter so I can understand it."

"All right, okay. I think maybe you and Rudd are working me."

"Are we?"

"Yeah. 'Cause if what you said about Rudd was true, how come he had a completely different story for the Fenns about that box?"

The old man didn't understand. He looked to Nathan for an answer. The palm of Nathan's hand came up and rubbed across his chin as he said, "Go on."

CHAPTER FORTY-FIVE

ESSIE WAS AT the yacht club office waiting on a reply from the Coast Guard documentation service as to whether they could track an owner for the PLYMOUTH *ROC* when Dane returned with news.

Nathan was not at the office but Essie felt vulnerable talking out in the open and took Dane by the hand and led him to a conference room at the end of a long hall.

She closed the door behind them. It was a small and windowless room and before turning on the light they just held each other. They kissed and held each other and stayed that way in the dark, sharing the silence of their intimacy from the night before.

"I have to tell you what happened at the bank."

Conscious of the strange tone in his voice, she leaned past him and turned on the light. He explained about the house on Disappointment Slough, and the small account that had been set up in his name to pay the mortgage.

When she heard, it was as if another part of her had been scored by what she could only describe to herself as a deformed act. "If he loved his son at all, how could he just give up that piece of him?"

"He wants to make sure my compromise is well kept by actually proving that he has compromised me. That he is actually bringing me into the inner circle of his feelings. I know it's that way with him."

"Maybe you shouldn't do it, take it, I mean. The house."

"The more he compromises me, or thinks he compromises me, the more he compromises himself with me."

"But what about *you?*"

The question was like looking into an endless depth of tilted mirrors. Destiny was spinning out pathway after pathway joined at troubling angles and he was not sure which led where now, but he told her, "If I go back and turn Nathan down, what will he assume? What would Charles assume?"

She didn't answer. The enormity of what they confronted lurked inside her. Everything was going through a swift and exigent metamorphosis. Even themselves, who they had been before last night would become someone else today, and someone else tomorrow, and the day after that.

The fax line rang.

"It might be the Coast Guard with news," she said.

IT WAS.

Six pages of boat names and owners came through. A list that read as if someone had scoured the depths of creative banality in their attempts to be clever: *PLYMOUTH ROCK III, THE PLYMOUTHS ROCK, PLYMOUTH ROCK-ON, PLYMOUTH ROCK CHICKS*, but no *PLYMOUTH ROC*.

Essie tore the pages up and flung them at her desk. Dane knelt down and began to pick up the shredded bits of paper, looking out toward the receptionist's desk, then over toward the bookkeeper's office to see if anyone had noticed Essie's outburst.

She was glad Dane had said nothing when he looked up, as there was nothing he could say that fit. At the core of her rage was more than a fact of simple failure. After what Nathan had done, on some submerged and chaotic level, she wondered just how much more awful the world could be.

The phone at her desk rang. The answer to her questions would become clear soon enough.

"Nathan," she said, ". . . yes, he's here. Yes," she said again, with collected politeness, ". . . he's deeply moved by what you did for him. Yes," she said again, ". . . you're right, it will give him a chance to make a life for himself. Taylor would think it a good idea. Yes," she said again, ". . . I know you meant well by it."

Her face looked like death many times over, but her voice was the image of an oblivious servant. When she handed the phone to Dane he pressed the snowy clots of paper into her hand, then squeezed the hand into a fist.

As she listened to Dane go through a composition of brief but "deeply felt" thank yous she tore the crumpled paper angrily into smaller and smaller pieces until each was no bigger than the pupil of an eye.

Finally after a short silence, Dane said to Nathan, "Of course I'll come. How do we get there?"

When Dane hung up Essie noticed he tried to downplay any manner of concern. "Get where?" she asked.

"Mexico. Someplace far down Baja called Punta Final. We leave in a couple of hours."

"How are you getting there?"

"Shane Fenn is gonna fly us."

IVY KNEW as soon as Nathan explained that morning's conflicts at the General's that it wouldn't be long before Charles made his odious presence felt.

The first thing Charles said was, "I have to find out about Rudd from Nathan and not you!"

"Things were happening so fast—"

Charles screamed at her. "I'm not some fuckin' sales pitch you can afford to scam!"

Ivy retreated from her living room to the kitchen as if she would not be assailable there. Charles stepped into the doorway.

"What do you think is gonna happen if Nathan finds out—"

"Stop." She turned away. Everything had become such a complication of disparate stresses. She wished there was a world where no memory existed. Or at least a twilight room where you could disappear and whisper away your misdeeds and no one ever heard and you were never held accountable.

"If you think what would have happened was bad had Taylor

talked with that Federal agent, get a good handle on reality now if Nathan learns the truth."

She wanted a drink of water but her hands were trembling so. She could see Taylor crying, disgusted, not truly believing or wanting to believe what he'd discovered, confronting her for confirmation or denial his father was—

"Taylor might have gotten his old man some form of immunity for rolling over. And the General would be dead by the time an indictment got to him."

If only she could undo the calamity she set in motion.

"But they'd run up the score on you and me and Merton."

"I'm such a coward," said Ivy.

"And good thing you were and came to me instead of going to Nathan."

Trembling hands and all, she reached for water.

"I have to know about Nathan's relationship with that kid. Because there were questions, serious questions, Ivy, that could have an effect on *us*, that Nathan wouldn't answer."

Here we are with Dane, she thought, living out a surreal horror. Life was literally duplicating itself. It was as if some logical mind, some uncanny force was pouring a little fire onto their hubris.

She hesitated. "Go on."

"If Rudd opened that box like Nathan said, why did he make the Fenns open it?"

Ivy sat there like a blank tape. About this, Nathan had not said a word.

I HAVE to fly down to Mexico with Nathan . . . Punta Final . . . Nathan says one thing, but I sense another . . ."

Dane sat on the edge of the well stones on the hill above Taylor's house. Even though the line was staticky he thought he could pick up a sea change in their voices.

"I don't know which airport we'll be stopping at before we cross . . . I'm worried, yeah . . . No, don't have any of your people at the airport . . .'Cause your people look like your people."

THE PRINCE OF DEADLY WEAPONS

Dane intentionally softened his voice when he asked, "I'm not starting to earn your respect, am I? . . . Yeah, maybe under different circumstances we could be friends . . . But we're not, are we? . . . Under different circumstances."

He looked up at the windmill. There was the slightest breeze, it barely moved, the wood clicking off in minutes, rather than seconds. It made the very idea of time seem even more intense, and more powerfully expansive.

"I made all the pitches," said Dane. "I was a Nathan for the next generation. And here I am, face to face with the ultimate sales pitch . . . Do I sound different? Well . . ."

A speedboat rode a crest of white foam coming down the slough. It sent a rippling tide out toward the little island. Dane watched the boat as it rushed toward the sun. The light was so intense it almost burned his eyes.

"Just like anybody, I'm trying to earn this private little dream I'd like to fly away to . . ."

HUNTSVILLE PUBLIC LIBRARY

CHAPTER FORTY—SIX

WHAT THE FUCK is all the way down in Punta Final?" Paul asked.

Nathan sat at The Burrow bar waiting for Dane. He nursed a scotch and tried to short talk Caruso. "Potential investors for the center have a beach house there. Dane and I are gonna go do a dog-and-pony show."

Nathan looked across the tarmac avoiding Caruso's stare.

"And Shane Fenn is gonna fly you?"

"That's right."

Caruso scanned the line of corrugated hangars, one of which was Taylor's. "I don't know why you'd fly anywhere with a piece of shit like that."

It was a testing question that Caruso had no right at all to ask and Nathan answered by acting as if Caruso had no right at all to ask. In the silence that followed Nathan considered the thing that he was. How he'd allowed his son to be used unknowingly as a conduit for every kind of sellable illegality. But the twistings of self he went through to deal with his immediate needs turned a reality that should have made him recoil into a mere matter of record.

That level of coldness he felt was no coincidence. He'd felt it before, in times when he had to reach into the sample case of character traits that helped him survive and excel at what he did. He was, inside, preparing for Punta Final.

"You still do search and rescue, Paul?"

"When they need me."

"So you keep the floats on that Cessna of yours?"

"Yeah."

"Maybe sometime you and the old lady fly up to Trinity Lake.

A guy paid off a debt by giving me the time-share on his cabin."

Caruso knew this was just so much chat to kill a certain line of conversation. "Sure," he said.

Nathan hid behind his drink. Caruso glanced out the window. The Fenns were getting their Skyhawk ready for the trip. The influence of the past months, the little moments either seen or felt, the old rumors about Nathan, the conversations he had with Sancho Maria that a parallel world was being played out right before their eyes caused Paul to tell Nathan, "When you're down in nowhereland, make sure nothing happens to Dane."

Nathan checked the time on his watch. Caruso had been brazenly direct, as if he understood there were unspoken difficulties. "What could happen?" said Nathan.

Nathan's left arm was resting flat on the bar. Caruso draped his hand across Nathan's wrist. The pressure he exerted possessed more than a touch of passing interest. "I mean it, Nathan. I like that boy. Sancho Maria likes that boy. Very fuckin' much."

The bar was relatively quiet. No one noticed the odd and uncomfortably executed moment as Nathan's arm had to bend its way loose of Paul's grasp. Caruso pursued it no further as he saw Dane enter from the coffee shop side.

Dane walked between both men. "Good morning," he said. He seemed to be unaware of what had just taken place. "Sorry I'm a little late, but the outboard wasn't cooperating this morning."

"It's all right," said Nathan.

"Sure," said Paul, keeping a tight stare on Nathan. "It gave a couple of old thieves time to just hang. Isn't that right, Nathan?"

Nathan let the comment pass and stood. "I'm gonna piss, then we'll get out of here." He pointed to a small gray carryall he'd brought that was on the floor by his bar stool. "Grab that will you."

Dane looked down at the carryall, then up at Caruso. Once they were alone Paul asked, "Ready to go sales trippin'?"

About this sudden urgent trip Dane could surmise almost anything as a reason, but he put on a necessary smile for Paul. "Do you think I'm better suited to playing the dog, or the pony?"

Paul shook his head, then waved to a pilot crossing the bar

toward the coffee shop. "I did too much yard time." Caruso looked out the window to where the Fenns were filling up their Skyhawk with gas. He made sure Dane knew where he was looking and who he was looking at. "Be careful, all right. You're goin' down to the forgotten end of the world, and I don't buy this sales trip bullshit, okay. Maybe I'm just a fool, but . . . if there's trouble, you call me. Get your ass clear if you can and call me, all right?"

"All right," said Dane.

"And I don't mean for you to say all right like it's some fuckin' afterthought . . . all right?"

"*All right,*" said Dane again.

All the dints and scars on Caruso's face were highlighted in his tight stare. Dane passed around him. As he did Paul noticed the boy again glance at the carryall, at the bathroom hallway. Then Dane took to looking over one of Caruso's copies of the labyrinth on The Burrow wall. The original seemed to have been etched during the Middle Ages with the dour flair of the European churches from that time.

In the dusty bowels of those stone passages, on the walls which formed its center, there waited a shadowbeast, inexact and shapeless as any dream, and the more fearful for it. "I read once," said Dane, "that certain labyrinths were conceived for the purpose of luring in devils, so that they might never escape."

"You read too fuckin' much, or too fuckin' little." Paul watched the boy as his hands dug down into the back pockets of his black jeans, as the tension in his arms rose to the deep gash across that tattoo flexing at the border of his black shirtsleeve, and the facial features as they prowled private dramas, unspoken difficulties. Paul could track his own youth there in the stormy silence and calm strains.

"Imagine," said Dane, "if there was no monster at the center of that maze. No monster, no beast. How senseless it would all be."

"This is strictly institutional talk, all right. I'm gonna jump past it." Paul glanced at the bathroom hallway. He sat on the bar stool right behind where Dane stood. "Sancho Maria and I know something is going on here. Maybe it has to do with Taylor."

Dane turned to face him. Caruso kicked at the carryall. "I'm trying to watch out for you."

Dane gave him a cursive looking over. "Where's your war glove?"

"What?"

"When we met at your hangar the first day. You were trying to get at that maneater of a kitten hiding in the wall. And you were wearing a huge old leather 'war glove' to protect your hand."

Paul understood. His face belligerently bent to a smile that had secret to it, and sadness. "God shouldn't have made you so smart. It ain't right. As a matter of fact it's worse than ain't right. It's downtown fuckin' dangerous 'cause it makes you believe too much in yourself, and usually when you can least afford to."

Dane stood there silently. Caruso saw Nathan had only half drunk his scotch. Caruso reached for the glass and finished it in one swallow. "I don't want to see you destroyed, son."

Dane nodded. "You know, Paul. The time being around you is gonna be the bread of an awful lot of good memories for me. And I'm not sure how in hell I deserve it."

LATE MORNING shadows fell across the asphalt where Dane followed Nathan. The Fenns were waiting by their four-seater Skyhawk. A doctrine of folded arms and sunglasses. A tentative surveillance.

"Let's get going," Nathan told Shane.

Tommy Fenn suggested, "Why don't I fly you down there instead?"

"You're better off being quiet, boy. Now back away."

Tommy backed away. Nathan bent under the wing and opened the cabin door. He shoved the carryall into the back seat and motioned for Dane to follow suit.

An anxious look passed between the brothers. Their movements were pinched, sullen. Shane walked around to the far side of the plane, Dane to the cabin door where Nathan waited. Nothing more was said, but Dane knew now what the trip to Mexico really meant.

E SSIE HAD promised Dane she would not be at the airport when he left. Concerned as she was, Dane had acted like he believed with certainty things would be all right.

There is no word more hideous for the assurances it arouses than certainty. It is a word whose history of credentials has proven to be miserably limited.

At one end of the Rio Vista Airport was a grove of trees and the leftover sheds of an airplane stripping and painting business. It was from there she watched the Skyhawk come around and start up the runway, from there she watched the blue-white plane climb through gaps in the trees. She watched till all sight and sound of it dissolved in the silent, pale distance.

She walked the pathway between sheds deciding what to do next. She saw the bones and fur of something dead in a weedy patch cluttered with empty paint cans. An irreducible strangeness came over her.

Essie called the yacht club bookkeeper to tell her she was sick and would not be back the rest of the afternoon. She went to her garage. She faced a wall of boxes where she stored the records of Taylor's importing business.

She began the search for an invoice, the one meant for Charles Gill. Invoice after invoice, streaked with dusty light, invoice after invoice, and all the while the irreducible strangeness she had felt seeing that rot of carcass and bone stayed with her.

CHAPTER FORTY-SEVEN

THEY FLEW THE Central Valley south in silence but for the sound of the engines. A dense noise that made the inside of the small cabin all that much more claustrophobic. A storm was moving in from the east they hoped to beat by hours.

Dane, alone in the back with the carryall, watched both men's reflections in the glass and more than once when he could traced the nylon skin with his fingers as if he might discover what it held by touch. At that, he was unsuccessful.

The Delta, and the valley floor, all he saw that first dusk with Paul Caruso seemed to spill on toward the end of the world. From there the earth looked even now to have been groomed by the hand of a painter. Skyborn, even now, it appeared beyond all the manifest destiny of greeds. Something that could never be contrived by human fictions, or portioned with deceit. Something that could never be lavished upon impostors, or given to those who lied their way to truth.

It wasn't long before Nathan leaned around the seat and Dane saw in Nathan's face an intensely drawn harshness he hadn't before leveled right at him. "We're not going to Mexico for a sales pitch. At least not the kind you're used to."

CHARLES TRIED to remain oblivious to his anxiety but there are men whose character is too narrowly built, whose self-deception in these regards is always at the abyss of that wrong decision.

He was working through this little stage of hell waiting for word from Mexico when he saw Claudia crossing the bank lobby. He had no idea why she'd come, as she never did, and then only to bring the girls and she would call beforehand.

"Let's go up to the Rock-and-Roll Museum and talk," she said.

"Is anything wrong with the girls?"

"The girls are fine. But you're in a very bad place, Charles. Very bad."

She scanned his office walls before she spoke.

"In light of our last conversation," said Charles, "these guitars have taken on a new significance."

Of that she was certain. She pointed toward the window. "My father is downstairs."

His eyes followed, as did he. The gray family Mercedes waited in the handicapped parking that fronted the bank. He tried to spot the old man's yellowish skull.

"I don't have a grand view of the world, Charles. I've told you that. I only hope you care for the girls as much as I do."

DANE DID not see the small billy club that Nathan took from his right coat pocket. He did not see anything until Nathan's hand came up and the black fist-size baton struck Shane right across the mouth and jaw.

Shane's head slapped sideways and from his throat came a cracked gasp. The wheel controls he held onto followed the snap and sag of his body. The plane banked hard left, sped up, then began to dive.

The clouds raced toward and over the plane and soon all they saw ahead was earth. The cabin was a chaos of cramped motions and clutter. Dane had been thrown and jammed into the corner of the back seat, the carryall had tumbled down and clipped the side of his head. And when the Skyhawk began to dive Dane was dropped onto the back of Shane's seat and it hit his chest like a shield and drove the air right out of him.

Nathan yelled for him to pry Shane loose from the wheel. To do that Dane had to manage both arms around the seat and lift that half-conscious, groping, fighting weight against the pull of gravity. All Dane could hear was the diving whine of the engine, all he could see was a long hollow of ground in jeweled and muddy colors coming for them.

He grunted and tore at arms that fought back convulsively, autonomically. Nathan used his free hand to reach for a small revolver in his coat pocket and with that hand took hold of the wheel controls in front of his own seat.

As Shane was pried loose Nathan began to right the Skyhawk. The earth stalled then started to roll away, the diving whine straightened into a fleshing soar. Shane's head shook and lolled and there were slaverings of blood from his mouth down his shirt and across Dane's hands.

Shane managed what sounded like a drunken cry. "You dirty fuckin'—"

Nathan answered by hitting him across the chin with that sap. The skin snapped apart. It was a grim and heartless triumph of sure-handed speed.

Shane wailed at the pain and Nathan yelled over the wail, "If I have a fuckin' thief in this plane I'm gonna find out!"

Nathan had the gun in the hand riding the wheel, in the other that black beating stick. His face made a sweep of the tiny cabin. And Dane finally saw—the essence inside the illusion was loose. What could happen to one, could happen to the other. Yeah, it was down to the ragged violent ugly. The white frost stare with the fired eyes that would chase you into any hole, anywhere, anytime. No dreams there. Just a flesh and blood scion of impure truths— Dane saw.

"Somebody," said Nathan, holding that billy toward Dane, "Somebody ripped diamonds from that box you delivered to the Fenns. Somebody! Somebody!"

He waved the black stick across the cabin. Shane's arm came up, whether to protect himself or to fight back, but as fast as it did Nathan struck it down. Then he struck at it again and Shane coiled up in his seat to avoid the blows screaming, "It wasn't us! It wasn't us!"

"I could fly you over the ocean—!"

"It wasn't us."

"I could toss your runny ass from this plane at ten thousand feet—!"

"I swear it wasn't us!"

FOR WHAT he was about to do, the self-hate the old man felt could only be blamed on the dirty thing that had married his daughter and was sitting next to him in the back of the family Mercedes.

"Everything . . . you've done," said the General, ". . . has . . . ended up . . . in one . . . total problem for us . . . all."

"The cause goes back before me," Charles told him. "I know it was your cunt that got me busted. So . . . I'm what you fought for, right!"

A brutish recognition came to the old man looking into a gray sky and he thought to himself, wished really, that all skies all the time should be gray. That's how angry he was, how conscious of death he was, how hateful of death he was, feeling as he did.

The old man put up a steely patina. "If Nathan finds . . . out your . . . connection . . ." The General's hands tried for a demonstrative flourish, ". . . with that Romero . . . and, and . . . there's a chance . . . he will . . . now, you . . . understand."

Charles sat there and acted as if this fact were unreal, or strictly insignificant.

"I want . . . my family . . . intact."

"Your family?"

"So . . . I'm going to . . . give up . . . a man who was closer, closer . . . to me . . . than you could . . . ever—"

"And how do I get fucked over this time?" Charles saw the old man was now looking past him. He turned. Claudia was in the bank doorway watching.

"Claudia wants you . . . out of . . . her life . . . and out . . . of the girls' life . . . for good."

Charles understood how completely this conversation had been preordained. "You Hands are all alike. You're either in someone's pocket, or at their throats."

CHAPTER FORTY—EIGHT

NATHAN LANDED THE Skyhawk at Brown Field, which is just east of San Ysidro and a few miles north of the Mexican border. On rollout, after landing, he said, "You both stay with the plane." Then Nathan went off alone.

At the fueling area Shane sat on the lip of the open cockpit door. The lower part of his jaw had gotten grotesquely swollen and purple. The gash on his chin looked to be in dire need of stitching. Dane stood off from the wing in the sunlight and smoked. Nathan had not thrown Fenn out of the plane, but both were certain this was not the end of it.

Shane sloshed the inside of his mouth with beer as carefully as possible then spit the bloody residue on the asphalt. He stiffly looked up at Dane and daubed at his wounds using a rag that had also been wet down with beer. He winced at the pain. "You enjoyed watchin' it, didn't you?"

Dane stood in certain silence knowing that would make Shane all the more angry.

Nathan returned within half an hour. He was controlled, absorbed. A true hazard come to life. "You're gonna stay with the plane," he told Shane. "If we're not back by morning, leave."

"It wasn't us. I swear it."

Nathan took hold of Shane's shirt and dragged him from the cockpit doorway. Nathan pulled out the carryall. "You can go back to the bars, or the work farm, or the food stamp line. I don't give a crap. But you're done."

Nathan motioned for Dane to follow him. As they walked off Shane flung the wet rag at the ground. "It wasn't us!" he yelled.

"I got a friend," Nathan said to Dane, "who's setting us up with a taildragger I'll fly. He's also gonna soup up some passports for when we cross. 'Cause I have no intention of using the real ones for this."

Dane followed him toward a hangar shed. He did not speak. Nathan stopped, Dane stopped. Nearby a double prop had begun to turn. The rotor sound growling louder with each moment. Nathan stared at Dane as if he were trying to discover something locked away inside the boy.

"Am I still safe with you?" asked Nathan.

"Shouldn't you be?"

Dane could see the turmoil working at Nathan's sudden tailored control, but he rode the line between self-confidence and defiance. "Well, answer me, Nathan. Or aren't I safe with you now?"

Nathan threw back, "Shouldn't you be?"

ESSIE SAT at the edge of the garage where she had that first time with Dane. The door was open. Dust filled the light across the invoice she'd finally found after hours of painstaking page by page by page.

The antique piece had cost twenty-seven hundred dollars. It had been delivered to TG IMPORTING, 1100 Rio Vista Road, California, from ROGERS, OLSON AND CARTER, 80 Plymouth Cove, San Raphael, California.

Why should a twenty-seven-hundred-dollar antique find its way to a Dumpster in back of the airport just days after it was delivered? The sky had darkened since she entered the garage. A light rain fell. The ground dust was spotted with wet droppings. The concrete began to smell of the changes that come with a storm.

She absorbed the image of the page wondering if, how, all things connected.

Words bring with them their own phantoms. They touch us in ways we don't know. They talk to us even as our mind is somewhere else. Then it struck her. Rogers, Olson and Carter. *ROC*. With a Plymouth Cove address.

The rain drove at the Falcon windows, and the passing cars on the freeway kicked out flumes of water that Essie's wipers could hardly handle.

She'd thought about waiting for Dane to return, but waiting would be to deny her own identity. It would acknowledge she felt the unknown or the inconceivable had power over her. She understood, she needed to be able to defend her place in the future or what would be left for her but to complain and brood in dark rooms. To condemn the world from that closed off part of the self. Yet her hands around the steering wheel were white grips and there was a threatful pounding in her head.

On her cellular she again called the number for Rogers, Olson and Carter. Again she listened to a recorded voice say, "This is Mr. Rogers of Rogers, Olson and Carter. No one is here now to take your message—"

She needed to see, to see would tell her something, but what she didn't know. She crossed the San Raphael Bridge in a slipstream of rush-hour cars. Along the bay the water crested in white huffs to the walls of San Quentin on the far shore. And to the south, the barely discernible buildings of San Francisco looked like metallic shields against a warning gray sky.

With all that much world around her she felt smaller and more alone than ever and she cranked open the windows just enough to let in the cold wet air.

Her street map led her from Spinnaker to Catalina to Plymouth Cove. This was the Marin County of decades-old courtyard apartments and summer-style waterside shacks that had survived long enough to reap the glories of gentrification

Plymouth Cove was no different. It was a short thread of a street and the address Essie searched for was the last house on the north side. Small, white stucco, set back behind a throw line of manzanitas, it was eminently unassuming.

Essie parked beside a low stone wall that ended the cove. Beyond it was an enclosed lagoon and beyond that the bay. Lights were already going on in anticipation of nightfall.

There is always a lie to meet your needs, that is one of life's lesser assurances. Essie knocked on the door and waited. Her plan was simple. She was selling off the last antiques from Taylor's importing business and as Rogers, Olson and Carter was in the same business, might they be interested?

Simple enough. But no one answered. She tried looking in the windows, but the shut blinds defeated her. She called on her cellular from the rain-swept porch and again from her car to hear the same voice, the same message.

She watched the house but in her mind saw the plane taking off from Rio Vista for Mexico. She saw that dead thing in the weeds by the shed. She sustained herself through a dark breath and the bondage of small horrors she imagined.

She had to subordinate all that to another thought, one as close as that short stone wall which she jumped to find herself walking alone along the lagoon that paralleled the side of the house.

THE TAILDRAGGER followed the coast down the Sea of Cortes. Both men's faces bled with dusk. The world looked to have been cleaved in half; one side water, one side land.

Nathan had said so little as to mean nothing, and Dane reacted in kind, so both were like chess pieces poised for the play to come.

The towns grew fewer and more meager till they were barely noticeable blots on a barren floodplain or beside a scorched crag of coastal rock. Under a fired sunset the world looked like some atavistic vision formed from brimstone and sand holding back a vaster wash of flat blue that was as beautiful as it was hostile, each and together.

"I lied back in Mexicali to the Aduana," said Nathan. "We're not going to Punta Final."

Dane did not try to speak over the sound of the propeller. "Where are we going?"

"To Puerto Calamajue."

The plane climbed to clear a wall of rock and the sound of the engine pull grew louder. Below in a long valley were volcanos, great black dormant holes deep with ash that looked to have been at one time fire pits for the gods.

"And what is there?" asked Dane.

"Nothing," said Nathan, "but some road, and the sea."

ROY PINTER requested a tour of the Serendipity Tissue Bank in Alameda, California, under the auspices of wanting to become a public voice on the importance of tissue donation. He told the managing director he had been inspired by his friendship with Taylor Greene, then meeting and getting to know Dane Rudd.

For Roy the tour itself was hateful. There was no science that would change the simple fact that he would be forever destined to crawl if it were not for his crutches, that his lungs would always be a stooped quagmire of phlegm because his body sagged under the struggle to be upright, and that his only alternative was a wheelchair which he considered "a shopping cart for weaklings."

Of course, all this hate he kept to himself as he listened outwardly thoughtful to the managing director's dissertation on tissue and organs that bored Roy shitless. Roy shared everything from metaphysics to personal memories as a friendly way of making oblique references to Rudd, trying to elicit information on his background that the managing director might unwittingly discuss.

The managing director was at all times polite, even deferential, but he was not forthcoming until the end of the tour when he said, "Before I did this work, I was a funeral director. And being a funeral director is not unlike being a prosecutor . . . Now, don't laugh, it's true, in that we both have to ask subtle questions to get an answer we need, or want. Now, what is it you really want, Mr. Pinter, because as you know everything here is confidential, unless you've come with a court order."

CHAPTER FORTY-NINE

IN A SWALE by the gray lagoon was a stand of trees shaped like an upturned fist. From there Essie watched shivering in the rain, protected only by a black oilskin slicker with a hood as night closed in upon the house, until the house was darkness within darkness. She could hear the breakwater behind her and see the bleak shape of San Quentin Prison's walls under the distant patrolling searchlights.

There was an alley behind the house and an access gate between the garage and the property line fence. An easy climb. Like a thief ghost she jumped the gate and the labor it took to scale was all emotional, just free-falling fear.

Crouched low she slithered up the concrete walkway, along the garage wall, seeing with her hands as much as her eyes, past garbage cans where the rain hammered out steel drum sounds until she could steal a view of the house.

It had an untaken-care-of feel. The same could be said for the yard which was mostly pools of mud. The rear of the house was U-shaped around an arbored patio that led to two french doors. The dense branches across the arbor were bare and could easily be mistaken in the darkness for a destroyed heap of iron palings from where sporadic rain dropped onto the brick below.

She called up the number; the dark house stood undisturbed as the voice machine answered. That same impulse more profound than reason found Essie again and she moved across the backyard as if watching herself in a dream, as if each step she saw herself take had been foreshadowed by some mysterious force before the thought of it had been made. The ground was soggy and her boots squeashed and the light from the adjoining properties was kept back by the trees.

By the time she reached the patio she knew she was going to break in. She didn't know what, if anything, she would learn or find. But she was going to break in.

The french doors were old and had screens on them, inlaid screens that covered smaller sections of door and opened like windows during the summer decades ago to capture the breeze.

She took out her keys and found the sharpest, longest one, and stabbed the mesh until it punctured. She dragged the key downward in a gutting motion, forcing it and watching, pushing it and listening so she could get at the glass inside and the latch behind it.

Who am I doing this, she thought. Who am I—

She pulled her hand back inside the slicker until it was a deformed fist.

Break the glass—

Her eyes closed. Not to see and to see.

Break the glass and run—

It all felt like some obscene infection she needed to get out of her system.

Run, wait and see if the neighbors hear, or an alarm goes off and security shows—

Ruled by some outraged discipline her hand obeyed. It jabbed like a prizefighter's and in the slice of an instant the glass shattered and she had jumped another wall.

GUARDIAN ANGEL Island was a smoke gray reef they flew over well after dusk. Over Roca Vela thousands of birds ran before their engines. Punta Final with its spartan lights was there, then gone. They flew on now into the blind pitch with only the instrument panel to light their way.

The sea, sky and earth became a mingle of one vast shadow and Nathan said, "You won't see it, the road, till it's right there."

They began the descent. Nathan guided the taildragger with

smooth, precise judgments. An old war hand working a long, slow bank and then the ground began to enfold them.

A black parapet of asphalt appeared. How many times, Dane wondered, had Nathan landed in places like this for just this. He could feel the tires set down and the landing lights offered pathetic little so that at any moment if something unseen arose, or the road fell away, they would be destroyed. And in the black space of that windshield Dane watched their faces reflected side by side and what it made him feel was almost ghostly.

The plane was walking now. The road crossed a long shelf that eased to the sea. Nathan taxied off the asphalt and onto hardpatch desert.

Both men stepped out into the night. The silence and darkness settled in. It was noticeably warm and Dane saw that across the road the ground began to rise quickly to low scrub hills where a dirt truck path led in and he could pick out decaying shacks and oddly fitted runs of pipe and what looked to be a small refinery tank on a hilltop.

"What is all that?"

Nathan was coming around the plane. "The Mexican Interior had a storage depot here. It shut down."

Dane turned and saw Nathan had the carryall in one hand, the gun in the other. Nathan pointed the gun toward the sea. "That way."

NO ONE heard the glass break, the police did not show. Essie managed the latch on the inset door easily. She brought a rag this time to insure against anything she touched.

The french doors led to a tiny dining room, it was empty. To the left was a kitchen, to the right a door to a rear hallway. The living room was ahead through another set of french doors. Essie pulled the slicker hood back. Water streaked down her face she brushed at with the rag. Half breathless she stared at the dark, another broken law to her credit.

She glanced in the kitchen and down the back hallway, which

led to a bedroom in each direction. There was no furniture any-where, the walls were barren. Not one personal or human touch to be found. The house echoed with a vacant empty silence.

Through the french doors she could make out bits of the living room where a bend or crack in the blinds let thin blades of street light slip through along with the distant whispering of night sounds. The room looked empty. The doors gave way without a creak or sigh. There were built-in bookshelves and cabinets on the near wall. They were empty. The room was empty, until she got far enough in to see along the back wall.

There was a desk, a chair, a multiline phone, and a fax machine. The barest accoutrements of an office. A rolling sheet of rain drenched the roof and sent a stark reminder about where she was, what she was doing. She remained frozen within herself. She lis-tened harder, watched harder, paranoid now that someone could be approaching under the cover of that rising storm as she herself had.

She tried to think what she could take from this, if anything. She could feel the seconds running through her body as if it were an hourglass.

The desk had no drawer. She looked in a closet by the front door. It was empty. There were no files, no filing cabinets. She ran her hand up into the mail slot. It was a cold empty hole.

She stood there sweating inside that oilskin slicker, her shirt stuck to her clammy skin. She stared at the desk and chair, at the fax machine and phone with pinched down eyes and a sense of panic.

There had to be something. There had to be a place all those missing pieces went. There had to be. But it wasn't what she saw that finally struck her, it was what she didn't see.

The answering machine. She'd heard it outside when she called. Where was it? She checked the phone on the desk, it didn't have one built in. Neither did the fax. She looked on the floor around the desk. Nothing.

But she heard it. She reached in her coat. She took out her cellular, pressed send and waited. A line on the desk phone lit as it began to ring. Something clicked, then from the black face of that room behind her came a voice—

She clipped around, not at first even realizing.

"This is Mr. Rogers of Rogers, Olson—"

She followed the voice to the bottom cabinet shelf on the far wall and there it was, the answering machine—along with three other answering machines.

She bent down closer as the first machine went through its mundane ritual. A red light said four messages were saved. When the phone clicked off the red light registered a fifth. She pulled the machine toward her using the rag. She pressed the playback. Listened. Each call was a hang-up.

The wooden floor hurt her knees but she stayed there staring into that shelf space. Each of the other machines was hooked up and working. None had saved messages. But why all the machines?

She reached for the second and pulled it toward her as best she could using the rag, making sure she left no prints, the sweat now coming off her forehead to burn her eyes.

She fought the dark searching for how to start the greeting check. When she found the button she pressed.

"Hello, this is Mr. Carter of Rogers, Olson and—"

Another machine, another name, but the same voice as the first.

She grabbed the next machine, found the greeting check.

"Hello, this is Mr. Olson of—"

The same voice again.

She grabbed the next machine and while voices beside her pup-petlike repeated she pressed the greeting check.

"Hello—"

The same voice again only—

"—if you're calling about the boat for sale, you can see it at the Big Break Marina. The number is—"

CHAPTER FIFTY

Yᴏᴜ ʟɪᴇᴅ ᴛᴏ me," said Nathan.

They had reached the last of the asphalt road. From there a rubbled outwash fell away to the Sea of Cortes.

"Which lie are you talking about?"

The older man stood facing the younger. "Not even 'what lie'?"

"You either lie, Nathan, or you don't. You assume I've lied, so I might as well be honest and say 'which lie' rather than be dishonest and say 'what lie'."

"That's fourteen-karat crap."

"I'm only as good as what I work with. Now, which lie are we talking about?"

"You had the Fenns open that box you delivered."

"I sure did."

"If you knew what was inside . . . why then?"

"For all I knew they were exploiting you, like your son might have been exploited. But we know better in your case, don't we, Nathan?"

Even gripped by suspicions there was no getting away from the strange injury Nathan felt at what Dane had said.

"Why didn't you tell me?"

"I guess you've forgotten what a perfectly honest shill is supposed to act like. The golden rule is silence . . . right?"

Dane looked at the carryall, at the gun, then ended his visual tour by staring right at and into Nathan's eyes. "Can't see your son there, can you?"

Nathan made a bitter try at saying something.

"You think it might have been me that ripped you off," said

Dane. "Right . . . no answer? No answer . . . now who's lying, Nathan? Now who's playing the silent card 'cause they don't want to step up . . . who? You think I ripped you off. Then do what you want and I'll show you I'm at least as tough as the shits you put your trust in."

It was an intolerable moment Nathan walked away from. He started down to the sea, as if expecting Dane to silently know and follow him. Dane called out "Nathan," but he kept walking. Dane called again and this time more harshly, more adamantly and Nathan did stop, or tried to anyway but lost his footing on all that gravel and sand. When he righted himself he was a hulking labored outline breathing hard.

"I want you to know, Nathan, if you had thrown that dirty little shit out of the plane, the least I would have done was shut the cabin door behind him."

ROUTE 4 was running deep with rain and every time Essie tried to speed up or change lanes the Futura hydroplaned. The number she had stolen off the answering machine was for Romeo Boat Sales at the Big Break Marina in Oakley, California. Oakley was on the southern berm of the San Joaquin where it fed into Dutch Slough at Jersey Island. This meant Essie was driving back to the heart of the Delta.

Essie tried to think her way through this confusion of disparate fragments, but it was like trying to follow the blue flow of the sloughs. Oncoming headlights glistened off the drenched windshield in brilliant bursts of starfire and she wiped at her face and eyes constantly as if this could clear her mind to meet the task.

In Oakley the rain fell through a damp mist. At the Big Break Marina the boats appeared as cutouts rocking hypnotically on the black depthless currents of the San Joaquin.

The parking lot was empty but for an old man walking sluggishly away from the docks. In the window of the Romeo Boat Sales shop were photos of the different craft you could buy—from modest sailboats to a pre-owned Sunseeker. She went from photo to photo, but none were of the PLYMOUTH *ROC.*

In the boat shop window Essie saw her pale bundle of a face, the drained eyes, the stringy soaked hair. And that day in Locke with Dane when she caught sight of herself in a blacked-out storefront glass came back in all its prophecy. "I'm going to ask you for your trust," he'd said, "so I have to know what it is you want."

She walked those fogged-in dock berths going from boat to boat on a chance, bent inside that oilskin slicker like the reaper herself, reliving that day, as on that day she discovered another woman inside her she never knew, one closer to rebellion and malfeasance when she'd answered Dane, "I'm standing on a subway platform and a speeding train goes by—"

It was all right there. You'd have to be blind to miss it—the PLYMOUTH *ROC.*

Thirty-three feet of tweaked out daycruiser, she stared at. She could see it probably had a down galley and room enough for at least one stateroom. The fog drifted past her face. Do I call out in case someone is on board, do I walk away, or do I—

Laws were falling as she felt the boat beneath her drift ever so slightly. She stepped inside the covered cockpit. It had a heavy-duty sound system, autopilot, plotter. This was strictly turnkey.

If anyone had been below they would have heard, or felt her come on board. She approached the galley door. It was not bolted or locked. She slid the door open with a finger touch, inches at a time. Cold darkness awaited.

Was the galley door left open because someone didn't care, wanted to appear as if they didn't care, or were they just careless? Would there be anything they didn't want found or seen left on board? She kept hearing that voice on the answering machine, bland as the back of a playing card, going from name to name as she slipped down into the galley. That would be where, if something were to be found.

She could smell the stale odor of men as she felt about in the dark for anything, anything at all. That's when she heard steps on the wooden plankway. Angular steps getting louder. She came about and got the galley door closed. She waited, but those angular steps didn't pass, they stopped.

She listened now like some creature cornered. A rope line was flung on board. She could hear it hit the deck. Then a clopping sound as the boat moved slightly. She reached out into the dark for something to hold herself upright. The clopping moved into the cockpit. She bent back, feeling, feeling behind her frantically, pathetically. The jangle of keys and the first muffled cries of twin cats kicking over and her whole insides went cold—cold, empty, frightened, shivering.

And then the boat began to move.

FROM THE beach Nathan watched the black sea for any sign of the boat as Dane went about the task of collecting driftwood and dried sage. When he was done stacking these for a fire Dane went back up the road to the gas storage ruins. He brought with him rags taken from the plane he'd torn into long strips. He found a heavy stone, one he could hold in a fist, and began hammering at a corroded section of pipe that fed from the storage bin until its casement cracked.

There was a faint hiss of air, the pungent bitters of rot, and gas began to trickle forth. Gas and filth. He doused the rags and walked back to the beach. He wedged the wet strips into the chest high pyre. He lit them with a match and pulled his hand away quickly from the whooshing burst. The cut sheets curled like flaming snakes, the driftwood and sage began to crackle harshly.

Nathan, who had been watching for the boat, now turned to Dane. "I did think it might have been you. That's what I'm capable of."

Dane stared at a heart of burning red rag and wood.

"I'm sorry I brought you," said Nathan, "but I'm glad you're here. I'm glad I brought you, but I'm sorry you're here. That . . . is how fucked I am."

From the cord fist of that blaze, Dane followed pathways of wood with his eyes as they darkened, smoked and then ignited into a small heaven of white starbursts. He heard Nathan ask, "Does Essie know about any of this?"

Nathan was his craft. Every emotion, Dane thought, was guided by an altered emotion. Every version of what he felt was protected by an altered version or screened off by an altered version, guarded by an altered version.

Nathan was the kind of man who if nature had permitted, would walk in two directions at the same time. And that he, Dane, should see it so well, could feel the enticements of and at knowing, what did it say about what was behind all that he felt?

"Essie knows . . ." Dane waited as Nathan's face feared up and tightened, he said then . . . "only what you've told her."

The face loosened. "Yes, it's best that way. Best all around. She's a good girl."

Dane prodded the flame with a loose piece of driftwood. "What . . . did Taylor know?"

Nathan stared across the fire. It was gathering up force now, smoke rose in kitestrings from those burning wood threads to be collected into a vaster pall. The air smelled of sage. The moment was prescient with the shape of other times. From Abraham and Isaac, through the ravagings of Joan of Arc, to the napalm crosses of our valence there has always been fire, and those with aims looking across that fire.

"He knew nothing about who or what I am. As a father . . ." Nathan's voice fell into a horrid honesty as he altered what Dane had earlier said, ". . . I was the perfect shill for honesty."

Nathan made an undefined gesture with his hand. "Go back to the plane. Get out of here." When he saw Dane did not listen he made the same undefined gesture. "Walk to Punta Final. Walk to the fuckin' border. I don't care. Just don't stay."

The fire now burned well as high as the men. Dane made a fist with his left hand and hit himself right at the heart. "Greed and goodness . . . there's only one spot they cross."

"Go on!" shouted Nathan.

Dane hit his heart again with a fist but he did not go. The flames yawed and bent violently with the wind.

"Why fuckin' stay and take the risk?!"

Dane hit his heart again. "Greed and goodness." He hit his heart again. "Understand. I want what you offered me back at Dos Reis. That's why I'm here." He hit his heart again. "I'll take the risk." He hit his heart again. "And I also want to pay your son back." He hit his heart again. "And you know how I want to pay him back."

The wind took the smoke and engulfed both men. Their eyes burned, their throats choked dry. But neither moved.

"What happened to Taylor will happen to you," said Dane, "if what happened to Taylor is because of you. And we both know the answer to that. We're living it now. Aren't we?"

What Nathan saw there across the fire, in the smoky reaches where the flames jumped and burned in black space then disappeared as if some invisible hand had stolen them away, what he saw there was himself. As he was, as he is.

"Charles . . . the General . . . the Fenns. At least one of them had a hand in putting Taylor down." Dane drove his fist toward the ground in a stabbing motion. "Like a fuckin' pig or a dog." He drove his fist again toward the ground. "Get a good mental picture of him lying there in his own blood." Dane drove his fist again toward the ground. "Or maybe you need the coroner's pictures to get you hard." He drove his fist at the ground again. "And part of it is your fuckin' fault, and you know it." He drove his fist again at the ground. "How does it feel hearing it like that?"

Somewhere out on the black sea came the sounds of an outboard motor.

"It's like having cum spit in your face," said Nathan.

The outboard motor grew louder, closer.

"When they come after you, I intend to be there. That's how I'm gonna pay your son back. That's where the sheer greed and the little bit of goodness that is me . . . meet."

"If you're gonna leave," said Nathan, "you better go now. They're coming."

252

CHAPTER FIFTY-ONE

ESSIE STARED AT the cabin door, flesh white, twisted down into a corner as if drugged with fear. Her hands searched the black space around her like huge insects, crawling the walls, fingering cubbyholes and crevices for anything that could be turned into a weapon.

The lone sound of a barge horn and the hard press starboard had told her right off they were moving up the San Joaquin and deeper into the delta of sloughs and channel ways.

The daycruiser was making knots. The deep V hull rose and slapped down as it fought the swollen waters. Essie tried to control the unlocked horror of her sheer defenselessness by staying focused on where the boat was going. She tried to mindfeel the surges port and starboard like a chart plotter for some unknown waypoint. But when her hands came up empty and she was left with those huge inboard cats reverbing through the hull as they drove on toward some destination a claustrophobic certainty set in that she would be discovered and killed.

The inboards cut, and panic twisted around her diaphragm. A slight gasp came up out of her throat. She closed her eyes on the chance she had been heard.

She could feel the daycruiser slow. It was, she knew, easing into a dock. She heard footsteps cross the deck and a voice she could not understand against the rain. The boat was being tied off. There was another voice; both began to slide away only to be met by another voice.

Essie did not know how many chances she might have to get off this boat. She didn't even know if this were one but she would not let herself suffocate in fear.

From where she held up to the cabin door was a mere four feet of forever. In a crease of slow-motion inches the cabin door opened like a sidewise eyelid to reveal a treatment of bare rain against a sky touched by lights.

She used the bridge as best she could for cover. The dark slag shapes she first saw were dock pylons. And then through the raining gloom a square of burning window framed the cropped blond back of a man shouting angrily to someone unseen—

It was Tommy Fenn, and she was in The Meadows.

DANE AND Nathan were taken out onto the sea in a sleek tender. It was just they and a helmsman who sat on a raised seat and said to them not one word. About a mile out the helmsman got on the radio. He was a swarthy young man who spoke French and Lebanese.

"They're from Senegal," whispered Nathan.

It was not long after that a searchlight bore out from the distance. The helmsman motored toward the light which grew larger and higher. It took another mile or so on increasing swells before Dane could see the flooding light was atop a yacht.

They had approached from the starboard bow so it was impossible to make out the boat's size and beauty. But as they came about midships Dane could see the hull was probably one hundred and twenty feet and built along the fast ferry design so elegantly popular in Europe.

There was a raised pilothouse that had been pushed forward as far as possible and a submarine-like conning tower just aft of midships. It was from there the cyclopean light kept them at its mercy and burned their eyes.

It was only when they had neared the stern and slipped under the flooding white beam that Dane caught a glimpse of the yacht's name printed into the sleek gray exterior—*The Hunter Gracchus.*

The helmsman led them to a salon past a glass-encased zen garden. Dane looked about as the helmsman dimmed the fiber optic lights. The floor was polished gray sandstone to match the yacht's exterior, the walls were done in bands of satin mahogany held in place by nickel screws. The helmsman had them follow him to a dining room which itself was round, the walls being steam bent slats of satin mahogany. They were told to sit at the table, the glass of which rested on a polished gray sandstone pedestal that was also round. The seats themselves were gray on silver. It was all that wealth could buy of minimalist perfections.

"Unless you're directly spoken to," Nathan told Dane, "say nothing. And even then, say nothing."

They waited. At the far end of the salon a man entered. He looked to be well-fed with steroids and he stood gentlemanly by a low banquette with hands crossed. Through the bent mahogany slats Dane noticed the latticed shadow of another man who had taken up a spot by the door from which they'd entered the salon.

Everything had been done with silence. They had not been checked for weapons, the carryall had not been searched. It was, as far as Dane thought, confidence expressed at its most minimal as a show of control.

THERE WAS an argument going on inside the house that Essie could see only in rain-soaked bits. A man, thickly padded and older, with a thin moustache and black balding hair paced through the window frame while Tommy Fenn's arm moved like a swearing tongue.

To get away Essie need only slip over the far side of the day-cruiser and into the darkness of The Meadows. But, if she wanted to know more about what was behind all those poisoned theatrics she either had to *walk the dock* past the windows, which was at best an inescapable disaster, or chance a swim under the dock and surface where the wooden planking worked its way up the shoreline that bordered the house.

Her body wormed its way down into the water where she could feel the deathly cold wrap around her. Her mouth blew open for air, the black oilskin slicker encumbered every movement. She paddled around the boat, spitting water, and pulled her way into

255

the abatis of pylons holding up the dock. She could see between the shriveled planks thin lattice fills of window where rain spilled down into her eyes in dripping lines and each few inches brought her closer to words she could understand.

"He tried to kill my fuckin' brother, right there in the plane!"

Essie clutched at wet handfuls of splintered beam, at a nub of posting. She stretched to hear better, to see better, to know—Was Dane alright?

Framed through a long slit in the wood planking she could see the short man rub his thick face. He was a worn sixty if he was a day. "I told Charles . . . Charles said he would call. Then we'll deal with it. Your brother is all right."

As soon as she heard the bland voice—

"Is this the talk down, Merrit?"

—she knew.

"Is it?"

It was the man on the answering machines.

"I've been trying to keep this together," said Tommy. "I even told Shane to stay away from Rudd. Start nothing. But if Nathan thinks he and that white bread are gonna do my brother, and I'll just sit here in a coma—"

Her body was growing numb. The men moved past and through the window. From the way they kept looking toward some point in the room when they talked she was certain someone else was there. She bent up toward the planking, it scraped her face, she could just make out another window farther back from the shore. The light from a table lamp shaped out a shadow on the wall, it looked to be a man's.

She groped her way over and between the cross stanchions. The oilskin slicker felt as if it were made of stone. The shoreline was soft beneath her feet. It rose and fell in awkward shifts and once where she put her weight it evaporated like so much air. Her body sagged down into the water. She grasped at a pylon and a rusted nail staff scored into her hand.

She dropped down into the water as a third voice said, "We wouldn't be here now, if one of you hadn't tried a rip on that delivery." Her bloody hand got hold of another post and Essie pulled herself up. Her body could not stay in the water much longer.

Tommy was yelling, "We didn't fuckin' steal anything! How many times do I have to say it? Wouldn't Shane cop to it to keep from being thrown out of the plane?!"

"I have no idea with you guys."

She managed to reach a scuppered warp between the footboards where she could twist around and see that farther window as the short man, this Merrit, maybe it was the Merrit Merton she had in her notes on Nathan, stood beside Tommy defending himself. "I've been in this business for thirty years. And I never shorted a delivery. How long do you think I'd last if I did?"

Essie could see the wall shadow begin to move toward the window where it dissolved into the flatly lit face of a man who said, "Well, one of you is a liar."

And there in the creaking reaches with runoff spilling down through the cracks onto her face, into her mouth and eyes, Essie recognized him. She forgot his name, but it was him all right. The one with the date on the berm that night Taylor was killed. The witness who heard the shot.

Merton's cellular rang. He answered it. All the indiscriminate threads of this were starting to connect.

She crawled out from beneath the pylons and into the tule reeds along the berm. All she had to do was reach that maze of junk and machinery the Fenns stored and the darkness beyond was simple, Locke was but a long exhausting walk in the rain.

She grubbed up the bank as Merton told the others, "We're going to Mexico. Tonight." From a crouch she took off but before she made it into that pathway of stacked heaps a sensor light along the roof line flooded down on her and Damon Romero caught the wraithlike back of an oilskin slicker running into that raining blackness.

She heard them yelling as they spread out. She wasn't sure if they were chasing after her, or chasing away some phantom trespasser. But when a shotgun went off in a cyclopean moment of blue thunder tearing apart the trees far behind she felt as if her heart had burst right up into her mouth and she rushed headlong through a world of remote shapes like a halfmad figure as another blast charred out of the night, and she could have sworn, even over the sound of the rain and her jabbing cuts at the brittle undergrowth, that somewhere above her branches had been sheared away.

CHAPTER FIFTY—TWO

A BROKERED SILENCE could not be as complete as the one Dane and Nathan waited through. Not even the sea's tidal pull seemed able to touch them. The minutes passed in profound discomfort.

Two other men entered the salon. One was slightly older than Nathan. He was clearly African, but with agate eyes and glittering light brown skin. The younger man looked to be related.

They did not speak. No names were given, no introductions exchanged. All forms of polite diplomacy were carried on with the physical nomenclature of slight nods and subtle hand gestures. The two men sat together facing Nathan and Dane.

Nathan took the carryall from the floor and stood. He set the carryall on the glass table and opened it. He began to remove packets of money which he neatly stacked in rows. As he did this the older man glanced past the money to Dane. He held the older man's gaze. It was a moment of sameness and difference. A moment where each face calculates what is behind the face they are seeing, what exists there. The world as we know it is expressed in these tiny gestures, as filled with fraud as they are.

When Nathan was done the older man spoke to the younger man in French, who then asked Nathan, "We know it isn't much, but we cannot allow ourselves to be stolen from. You know, then, who did this?"

Nathan shook his head he did not. He sat. He slid the carryall from the table. He folded his hands and looked from the older man to the younger man to the older man as he said, "Ask the gentleman something for me. I ask with all deference. Sometimes

259

partners change the terms of their deal. Sometimes deliveries are—"

The younger man stopped him. He explained what was said to the older man in language that was terse and hardly positive. The older man's richly colored skin took on a certain tumult and there was no masking what those agate eyes said.

Nathan returned the stare unflinching. The older man made one decisive gesture and it was Dane who saw the well-fed body of steroids cross the salon. A black stun gun had slipped down into its hand.

Before Dane could even say, "Nathan," it was over. Two hundred thousand volts had been jammed into the base of Nathan's skull.

Dane could hear the coarse staccato as the current ravaged right through his body. Nathan lifted out of the seat in shocked contortions. He hit against the steam-bent mahogany slats and by the time he collapsed onto the cold sandstone floor he was convulsing horridly.

The stun gun bared down on Dane's face and held there as if tempting him to act. He did not. He heard the older man say "Cauchemar," and then in French he said, "Empty the meat locker."

ESSIE RAN till there was no more need for running, but she kept running anyway and only when she'd looked back enough times to answer the stark terror she felt, did she stop.

Somewhere in that mile of black wetland between The Meadows and the town of Locke she stood in the dark, soaked and shivering. Her flesh was ice-cold red. She looked down and saw one shoe missing, how or where it had come off was a mystery. From the wound in the palm of her hand blood rivered down her fingers. She had barely escaped drowning in a private doom, and she knew it.

A low bleary cry from her soul broke through in all its human frailty. She was disoriented and fending off collapse. What happened on the way to Mexico? Why were the others leaving? She needed to get to Locke—

She called out Dane's name. "We'll be all right," she said. "We'll be all right."

For support she struggled through the underbrush toward a tree that rose starkly in the rain. She leaned into the bark and held on.

The man . . . the one in the window . . . who was at Disappointment Slough the night of the murder . . . what was his name . . . he'd given testimony at the hospital . . . he'd been so fuckin' kind . . . what was his name . . . ?

Was the world unraveling around her, or was she just unraveling in the face of the world? To open a door to a crime, any crime, is to open a door into one's self.

She stared at a black chamber of thickets and baize-skinned shrubs. Of sloping wetland and marsh with its wind twisted trees. She stared, all filthy and soaked, listening to the rain, trying to calm herself and reach into the living darkness around her as if some animistic power hid there that she could draw out and use to help pull the parts of her together that were fast coming apart.

She was holding on, but she was lost. She didn't know which way was Locke. She had been running blind. Her head moved like a groggy prizefighter looking for some direction, some sign, something—

Then she saw the television tower. Even through all that drizzled mist she could make out the spare trail of lights that climbed its spindle thin construction. And what she'd explained to Dane, she did. She anchored those tower lights rising into the sky like the needle of a compass, pulled her bleeding hand up against her chest, tucked her head down into the hood of her slicker, and started.

DANE WAS taken down a circular stairway. Below, a forward stateroom had been turned into a lazaret of sorts for wine and liquor. There were also two large freezers, both silver. One was shaped remarkably like a coffin. This was being emptied. The contents strewn on the gray stone floor.

The older man looked at Dane, first to see if the boy understood what was about to happen, and if he did, how it was affecting him.

Dane tried to shut out the bare dead sound every time something frozen, and with weight, hit the stone floor. But fear was in play. It was beginning to move against the walls of armor we all wear to defend ourselves against the notion of our ultimate annihilation.

Dane felt pale. He tried to blank his face, to give them nothing to feed on. Inside a trembling and sickness had begun.

The older man asked Dane through the younger man why he had been brought here. Dane pointed to his eyes, and just as he did every time he made a sales pitch he told his story. From the subway platform to this very moment, with every stop in between. Every errant and mordant detail that was either true, or a lie he'd already told. Before he was done the locker had been emptied and Nathan was half-dragged, half-carried into the lazaret.

The light was cool gray. The older man said to Dane through the younger man how his daughter, the younger man's sister, had a liver transplant because of cancer. She'd had it done in London. Then, for the first time the older man spoke in English. "The miracles," he said, "the miracles."

The older man pointed to Dane's eyes and the younger man translated. "What good are those if you couldn't foresee this?"

Everything after that happened swiftly. Nathan, half-conscious as he was, was easily forced down into the freezer. The well-fed body on steroids pressed the stun against Dane's neck as a threat and eased him back, eased him toward the freezer, then took his huge flat hand and rammed Dane's chest. He was driven back over the lip of the freezer and hit the upturned lid.

He grit against the panic. At the flood of hands that shoved his face, his chest, his arms, his legs. All hope for any denial about what this was, was over.

It had taken only seconds. The cool gray light was gone and everything now was freezing blackness and a heart that felt as if it was about to burst up out of its throat.

CHAPTER FIFTY—THREE

SANCHO MARIA AND Paul were at Al The Wop's cozying up in a booth with a couple of cocktails and trying to kill off a long and troubling day when they caught sight of a waifish creature in an oilskin slicker crossing the dimly lit bar toward the ladies' room. More than a few heads turned as the soaking, hooded transient disappeared down the back hallway. Even the bartender leaned out from the bar to get a better look at what in the hell had just gone past.

Sancho Maria turned to Paul. "I think that was Essie."

He was staring down the barrel of his scotch glass, rattling the ice like they were runes, and wondering if Dane was alright. "No fuckin' way," he said.

IN THE ladies' room there were two stalls. One was occupied, the room was otherwise empty. Sancho Maria could see the oilskin slicker lying on the tile just inside the closed stall door, from where she could also hear sounds, something akin to a mangled choke or shiver.

Sancho Maria leaned toward the door reluctantly, she went to knock, to call out, but found herself listening to that garbled voice-sound and trying to peek through the crack in the doorway, but she could not and finally Sancho Maria whispered, "Essie. Essie . . . it's Maria."

Something that resembled a voice answered and the metal latch on the stall door snapped back. Sancho Maria cautiously leaned in with her head to find a pale, pale child thing sitting on the floor of that cramped gray and white stall; she was soaked and shivering and trying to dry herself with wads of toilet paper.

SANCHO MARIA leaned down over the booth seat and quietly said to Paul, "Pay the bill and let's go."

Caruso's upper body and face went through the chapter and verse of physical gestures asking, "What in Christ's name is going on?"

"Pay the fuckin' bill," she said. "And let's go."

WE DIDN'T short the delivery. How many times," said Tommy, "do I have to—"

"Probably until somebody buys your act," Merton told him. "Or until proven otherwise."

Merrit Merton did not like flying in small planes. He had too much need for self-control. But there he was with Tommy Fenn, traveling to Mexico in bare minimum visibility with long trails of rain across the cockpit window on the chance that Nathan had not already been killed.

Tommy hit the steering column with his hands. "It could have been anyone." His look was not sparing.

The plane was loud, it was small. It impaled on downdrafts then jumped like something struck with electricity. And it stunk of pot.

"I have thirty years' credibility," said Merton, "to answer for me."

"Credibility is shit."

Merton could feel the raw cold through the plane's thin hull. "You and I are here because our credibility has been compromised. So—"

"All right."

"—Damon's credibility has been compromised—"

"All right."

"—so Charles' credibility has been compromised—"

"I fuckin' under—"

"—and so on and so forth."

Merton glanced out the window. The mist was like streaming ghosts that rushed past the cabin and light from the earth below looked helplessly far away. "Your plane stinks of pot."

"I guess I'm just shit in every sense of the word."

Merton stared at Tommy. "I've survived thirty years in this business. Blind trusts . . . hot money accounts . . . offshore bullshit . . . carrying gold to Vietnam for American banks. Everything in life succeeds on one simple principle—listen to me now. It succeeds because everyone in that system agrees to lie equally. No system can survive unless everyone agrees equally to some lie. Religion . . . politics . . . business . . . history, it's all the same. History is the best example. Read any book. It all holds together until someone gets scared or greedy, caves or decides to break. Till someone rebels. Then it's over. I don't care what the play is, or is about."

The plane bounced, Merton held on. His mouth flinched. "To survive is to agree equally to a lie. Any lie. Otherwise—" Merton shook his head bleakly. "Understand, 'cause you could get us all killed the way you've acted, if you haven't already."

Tommy dropped the plane. He nosed it five hundred feet just so the blood would go to all those little dark rooms holed up inside Mr. Merton. He pulled up and while Merton piped out a few torn gasps Tommy told him, "I don't fly without a fuckin' flashlight."

THEY WERE driving back to Rio Vista in Caruso's van. Heat blasted through the vents, the windows were closed up tight. The interior of that van was stifling. Essie lay across the backseat, her head rested on Sancho Maria's lap. Essie had already stripped down. Her clothes were a waterlogged heap on the van floor. She was wrapped up in one of the sleeping bags the Carusos kept stored behind the backseat. Her hand was bound up with toilet paper. Paul had taken off his shirt and this Sancho Maria used to stroke Essie's hair dry.

The only sound was the heat blowing through vent fans and

the occasional car whooshing by on the road in a flare of oncoming lights.

"You were right today," said Essie.

It was the first she had spoken, and at that, barely audible.

"In the coffee shop, this morning. About Taylor."

Caruso looked into the rearview mirror at Maria.

"We know things."

Essie's eyes lifted slightly.

"Dane and I."

Sancho Maria kept stroking her head slowly.

"I found out more tonight. Up in The Meadows. Much more."

Essie put her hand up against the vent and held it there feeling the warmth, needing the warmth.

"What about Dane?" asked Paul.

She shook her head. "There was some kind of fight in Mexico. I overheard it at the Fenns'."

Caruso pulled off the road quickly and onto the rocky shoulder. He put the van in park, then leaned around the seat. As he was shirtless, Essie saw the chest scars he'd earned in prison were like white threads his blood didn't touch.

"What kind of fight? Is he—"

"Shane got beat up pretty bad by Nathan. The others are heading down there tonight."

"What the hell do you mean, the others?"

His tone was fearful and blunt. Both faces stared down at her through half shadows. "If I tell you, you've got to swear to me you'll say nothing to anyone. You have to swear."

Sancho Maria stopped stroking Essie's hair. "Jesus Christ, girl, what do you think you're trying to do?"

CHAPTER FIFTY-FOUR

THE OLDER MAN pointed to his watch, then to the freezer. It was tipped over by three other men, as a fourth lifted up the lid. Dane and Nathan tumbled out onto the stone floor.

So bent from the cold, their bodies looked like hieroglyphics of improper jointing. They shook hopelessly, their faces spare grimaces of vein blue and bone marrow white.

Water was thrown on them, warm water. Their bodies began to reflex and recoil. Wrecked sounds kindled from their lungs as sensations told them they were free of death's light, for now.

Nathan began to bang his fist on the polished sandstone floor like a brute beast, as much out of rage and the relief of being free, as if trying to beat the blood back through his body.

Dane fought to stand, but his arms shook so terribly, his body tremored so miserably, it was a lost cause getting hold of anything for support.

More warm water was flung on them. It hit their flesh like bricks. Dane focused on the floor, on the shoes of the men around him, on their legs, using them as an axis his head could follow to know he was moving in the right direction.

Both men were soon pulled to their feet. Each to have his life roughed back into him, shook back into him, slapped back into him, struck back into him.

The older man spoke to Nathan, the younger man translated. "You live by the deals you set." The older man grabbed Nathan's face. "Or you don't."

As Nathan was taken out the older man turned to Dane. He

looked into that no-man's land of a stare, with its dark liquid piercings so huge in that place.

The older man pointed to the freezer and spoke, the younger man translated. "You've had a taste." The older man's arms crossed his chest in the pantomime of a corpse. "It will never be the same. You will never be the same."

He looked at Dane from across the years. It was a leveling stare filled with the surety that nothing he could do mattered. What he got back from the boy resonated with everything he did not say.

But the older man understood these child angels, with all their silent mutinies and enough drive to feed on any curse. He had seen them all, and they all died. He pointed to Dane's eyes. "Now, let us hope, you will truly see with those new eyes. And make sure *they* obey."

C ARUSO SAT at his dining room table in the semidark gravely staring at the phone. Sancho Maria passed through coming from the kitchen. She carried a steaming mug of coffee spiked with whiskey. She stopped. Caruso looked up at her for advice, counsel. She told him, "We'll agree to say nothing."

He nodded. Both went together down a back hallway to a small bedroom. It could barely hold a bed, chair and bureau. Essie sat in the chair, in the dark. She wore one of Sancho Maria's T-shirts and a heavy cloth robe that had deeply worn patches. Her hand had been bandaged.

The Carusos left off the light. As Sancho Maria handed her the mug, she told Essie, "What you say here, we keep between us."

Essie looked to Paul. With the dim hallway for a backdrop he was a mere outline leaning against the doorjamb. He nodded solemnly. "Until you tell us otherwise." He was going to add, or until something happens to you or Dane, but he wisely thought the better of it.

Sancho Maria sat on the bed beside the chair. The box springs squeaked as she handed Essie the mug. The first sips burned

Essie's throat, heat filled her stomach. Then, she spoke. "Charles and Nathan are money launderers."

This bluntly told fact neither shocked nor surprised Paul and Sancho Maria.

"What were you doing up in The Meadows? Who are these 'others'?"

Essie sipped from the mug. Her whole body grew tense. "The night Taylor was killed two witnesses happened to be at the slough. One was a man; handsome, Latin. He gave testimony at the hospital. Do you remember?"

Sancho Maria glanced at her husband. Neither recalled.

"He was at the Fenns'." She looked from one to the other. "A witness at the slough that night and he works with the Fenns. They all work for Charles. Do you see where that leads?"

They listened without speaking, without moving.

"There was another man. I think his name is Merrit Merton. He has different businesses, or seems to. One is exports and imports. I also think he sells the diamonds."

Sancho Maria took a heavy, slow breath. Again the box springs squeaked. "What are you talking about . . . diamonds?"

Essie held the mug in one hand and pointed to Paul with the other. "You sometimes delivered those packages of blood for Taylor . . . the one the Fenns delivered . . . we found out 'cause . . . we thought . . . we suspected something was wrong . . . they used Taylor . . . we . . . Dane opened the box and—"

They heard a plane overhead. They quieted, their eyes quicked up to the ceiling. The sound was still small against the distance, but it was a plane. And it was approaching.

Paul listened hard for the plane's engine. His body tightened away from the doorjamb. "It could be them. Sit here. I'll go see."

Paul pulled back the curtain that covered the dining room window. That window looked out onto the front yard and the small Airstream trailer parked there toward the runway. The rain had slowed; the mist had lightened. The plane, he could hear, was on its descending approach. Those few moments were a dark long time. Then he saw the white fuselage of a Cirrus he recognized.

He called out loud enough to be heard in the back bedroom, "It's not him."

Paul stood there in the harbored warmth of his home. He looked out at the Airstream trailer sitting in the ratty brush of his front yard. He saw Dane that first night, when he slept there. He'd watched from this very window. Dane sat on those silver steps, smoking. That bundle of intense boy with all of life and his secrets walking down the paths of him.

"What if there were no Minotaur, what if there was nothing at the end of the labyrinth?" he'd asked.

But Paul knew better. He'd even known soon enough. In the front yard that cat was nightcrawling for bounty. And it was a perfect yard for bounty. Unkempt and wild, the grass and weeds grown so long up and through the long-since painted broken pickets of a fence. She was sleeking along as natural as can be. Going about the business of her species. Unaware of what ends bring.

Paul rested his forehead against the window. "Fuckin' kid. With that fuckin' remark about the glove."

Sancho Maria touched his shoulder. Paul's face came away from the glass. All the feelings and concern he had for that boy sat there on his face for her to see.

"I could fly down to Mexico."

"No."

"I don't know if I'd find them but—"

"No."

He pointed out toward the world. "If something happens to that—" He lowered his voice. "—If something happens to that boy the promises I make to anyone won't mean a rat's ass."

She took him by the shoulders, she shook hard. He understood, he did not want to, but he understood.

THE LIGHT from back up the hallway just touched one bedroom wall. Essie could make out the tiny cloud motifs in the wallpaper. Small as this room was, it would have been perfect for the child that Paul and Maria never had.

Sancho Maria returned; the box springs squeaked as she sat.

Essie saw Maria was getting ready to say something. "I've always felt overwhelmed around you," said Essie. "The men at the coffee shop, they are. I guess that's because they know you're stronger. I guess that's how I feel. That you're stronger, and could endure anything."

Sancho Maria made the slightest ripple of a sigh.

"But whatever it is you might say to me, I won't do it. If it's what I think you're going to say."

"It's better," said Sancho Maria, "to be given honest bad news, rather than dishonest good news."

"All right."

"The deeper you get into any kind of situation, even foolish ones, the more you start to personalize it. The more it becomes about you. Just consider, you and Dane both, consider, that you've given enough. Say what you know, and be done with it."

Essie sat there resisting. She put the coffee cup down on the floor. Her hand ached. "There's something I want to ask you. Need to, really."

"All right."

"When do you know you've given enough?" Essie slapped the back of her bandaged hand into the palm of the other. "When do you know? Is it usually right before you give up . . . or just after?"

Sancho Maria gave no answer. She got up to the sound of a creaking bedspring and leaning over kissed Essie on the head.

Sancho Maria walked out of the room and closed the door. The short wash of light that fell across the wall was now gone. The wallpaper with its tiny clouds just blackness. Essie sat alone; she closed her eyes.

"If you can hear me," she whispered, "you'll be all right."

"If you can hear me," she whispered, "we'll be all right."

CHAPTER FIFTY-FIVE

THEY WERE BROUGHT back by the tender to the beach. They slogged through the short waves. They were wrapped in blankets, a token of their little visit.

Nathan collapsed in the darkness. Dane looked up and down the shoreline for any remains of the fire. There was none that he could see. Nathan began to retch. Dane walked until he found a rock that he could sit and lean against. When the retching stopped Nathan began to spit, and when the spitting stopped Nathan said, "I won't forget this."

Dane could not tell from his exhausted tone if Nathan meant to revenge what happened, or just surviving that horror was its own devastating penalty.

Dane felt a wave of trembling begin, and it was not from the cold. He stared out at the darkling sea, and the slow easy swells of tide that spread and smoothed their way up onto the shore. It was essentially so beautiful, so absolute, and just beyond it, past what he could see, was the boat.

"You stood it," said Nathan. The voice had gathered back up a little of its gruff anger. "Fuck . . . you stood it." Nathan spit. "We can survive. Dane, do you hear me?" He spit again. "We can survive anything together."

PUNTA FINAL had a graded runway that led to a few dozen beachfront homes. These ran from the barely livable to the taste-less and not so quite baronial. Merrit Merton sat on a crate box, his back against the remains of a cinderblock wall. Tommy Fenn stood off in the darkness beside the plane smoking while his brother walked the tie-downs looking for any sign of the taildragger Nathan had flown out of Brown's Field.

Shane returned bewildered and angry. "They're not here."

"You sure?" asked Tommy.

Even darkness could not cover up the hideously bulging, cut face. Shane had a can of beer, and he was too loaded already to be of any real use. "They're—not—*fuckin'*—here!"

"He probably never stopped here at all," said Merton.

The brothers turned.

"Nathan isn't stupid. He's not gonna be as easy to kill as his son . . . or that *Federal Reserve agent.*"

It took less than a moment before Shane flung the beer at Merton. It hit the cinderblock wall just above his head. He got covered with a rake line of wet. Tommy walked to the plane while Merton just sat there. Tommy reached into the open cabin door. He came out carrying a flashlight. He turned, put the light right to Merton's face. He followed that white mark till he was standing over Merton who squinted, but did not move, did not look away.

"Is that the flashlight you said you travel with? If it is, it isn't much."

"Greene offed himself."

"And you never shorted a delivery." Merton shoved the light away but Tommy brought it right back.

"And what is this about some Federal Reserve agent?"

Shane stalked the darkness behind his brother.

"You think Romero isn't going to be frank with me? We know each other a long time. We do a lot of business together. We are friends." Merton slapped the light away again. "So don't go fuckin' around with the plane, understand?"

Merton stood. He brushed at the wet stains down his coat and pants. This was done more as contemptible show than anything else. "Let's go back." He started for the plane. He walked right past Shane, staring at all that battered manhood. "Even if Nathan were here, look at this place. Who'd be stupid enough but *you* to try something."

D ANE AND Nathan had flown to Mexico under a sun's closing; they flew back with a sun rising. The rim of the earth grew palish pink and blue and the sun, Dane thought, did not so much rise as sublimely come to be.

He and Nathan had said little to each other since the beach, they were so battered from the night before. As Dane watched the sky flower with light one thought image from that devastating hour on the *Hunter Gracchus* had at him. One—it was of that black-marketeer saying "the miracles" as he talked about his daughter and the transplant that saved her life knowing, knowing as he did, that it was paid for by some courier who had smuggled diamonds packed up their filthy asshole out of a wartorn country—what better spoke to the manifest contradiction that is man.

Nathan began to speak in a tired voice. "They used to practice shit like that Senegalese did on us in special ops. In case we got captured. They'd put us in coffins with snakes, they'd tie us up and toss us into tanks of water to see if we'd crack. To see if we could hold our tongues and our shit at the same time. That's what the General used to say. That's how we came to know each other."

"The miracles," Dane said quietly.

"What?"

Nathan was not sure he had heard Dane right. Dane explained what the Senegalese had told him about his daughter while they were bringing Nathan down to the lazaret. "He'd asked," said Dane, "why I was brought there."

"And you told him."

"I told him everything, on the chance it would keep us from being killed."

Nathan moved sluggishly in his seat. "Yeah." His head nodded. "That's part of why the Senegalese got into this deal. His daughter. She's why he's letting us clean up so much of his money. He's trying to buy himself—"

Dane's pointed stare and the realization of hearing what he was about to say directly said about him, and the terrible hole of emptiness that was Nathan Hale Greene opened right up.

Dane saw it. He saw Nathan's face wedge up in disgust, then try to hide behind the slow coming together of a stoic, controlled pose. Dane saw it, and he saw a piece of himself there too. All wrapped up in the corresponding reality of how he got here in the first place.

Silence settled in once more. Dane went back to watching the sky. He watched as the light kept coming up over the earth, like a stage curtain rising at the hand of ghosts.

CHAPTER FIFTY—SIX

PAUL AND SANCHO Maria were about a half hour away from The Burrow opening when Essie entered the kitchen through the alley door. Sancho Maria was ordering the help in rapid-fire Spanish and Paul, he was in the coffee shop handling set-up. Essie could hear him cursing through the walls about the wiring, which as all the airport rats knew, was a mess of inefficiency notoriously prone to blink.

"I checked my messages," said Essie. "I heard from Dane."

Sancho Maria waved off a question from the cook in dragon-snapped Spanish, took Essie by the arm to where they wouldn't get hit by a tray of passing cups or a pair of arms carrying moletas of steaming coffee.

"He's in San Diego, with Nathan. They'll be back tonight."

Paul was shouting through the wall for Maria to hear, "We ought to burn this fuckin' place to the ground and collect on the insurance!" The kitchen door from the bar swung open, and Paul came through right behind it. "You paid up our insurance, right—"

Sancho Maria pointed at Essie. "Dane called."

Paul stopped talking.

"He said everything was okay."

" 'Okay' . . . What kind of fuckin' answer is . . . 'okay'?"

"Quiet," said Sancho Maria. To Essie, "How did he sound?"

"He sounded anything but okay."

THE GENERAL was still in his pajamas, sitting at the edge of the bed being attended to by his morning nurse when Charles arrived.

Charles sat in a chair by the door. He had to wait impatiently through a shot, the swallowing of medication, and the nurse's innocuous chatter. As she was leaving Charles told her, "Close the door."

The General sat stooped, hooked up to a small portable oxygen tank that could be dollied on wheels.

"They couldn't find him in Mexico."

The General struggled to stand. Charles got up and crossed the room. He offered help. The General looked the hand away and started for a chair the nurse had set up by the window.

Getting to the light was a harder distance to cover each day. Charles watched the old man with that manufactured umbilicus, his lifeline to a tank full of air he pulled along on little black wheels in slow, slow shuffling steps. And to sit, every move and bend of the body was done with painful, cautious deliberation. It was a pageant of the pathetic.

The General sat for a long time; ten minutes, maybe fifteen before he spoke. Charles had paced and sat and paced some more.

"Nathan's friend . . . ," said the General, ". . . the cripple."

"Was his friend. They seem to have had a falling out."

"He . . . approached you to . . . raise money."

FLESH WAS sweating up her first serious Q and A for a felonious assault robbery case when someone tapped on the glass that separated her cubbyhole from the hallway.

She looked up—it was Essie. Flesh waved her in, stood and came around the desk with arms open.

"Hello, Francie. I hope you don't mind my stopping by like this."

"Mind? Finally a human being enters my office. And by human being I mean someone who does not practice the law." They hugged. "How do you like my office? It's a perfect mind fuck for a claustrophobic."

Flesh kicked the door closed, had Essie sit. During a few minutes of catchup talk Essie lied away the reason for her bandaged hand. Then Flesh got around to Dane. "I hear Dane is now Nathan's official protege."

Even knowing what Flesh only meant, it was for Essie an acid moment reflected in a look.

"Intense . . . hunh," said Flesh. "In a good way, I hope."

"Yes, Francie. In a good way, we hope."

"Do you think Nathan and Roy will ever talk again? Though I can't really blame Nathan. It's Roy. Men. If they can't use their dicks one way, they've got to use them in another. And usually to the detriment of your average sized, decent hardworking civilization."

Flesh picked up a pair of scissors. She began to snip at the air as if it were your average sized, decent hardworking penis.

"I don't understand, Francie."

"Nathan didn't tell you?"

"Nathan stopped calling Roy. Roy stopped calling. I didn't ask. That's all I know."

Flesh sat there holding the scissors in the air. She'd had no idea. "Francie?"

"Roy told Nathan, in what was supposed to be a private conversation with Ivy, Taylor admitted to her a few weeks before his 'death' he might go to a psychiatrist. It seems he felt 'suicidal' since he was not a success like his father. According to Ivy."

Another uninvited small doom clutched at Essie's throat. "Are you sure that's what Ivy said?"

"To be honest with you, yes. As Roy told me. I won't ask if Taylor ever said anything like that to you."

"And Roy told Nathan. Was any of this because of Roy's relationship to me?"

Flesh held the scissors out like a gun. "They've got dicks. If they can't hurt you with them, they find someone else to hurt in your place."

Essie found herself staring at the scissors and thinking, how much free time people have to spend on their petty grievances.

"We ought to go out drinking one night," said Flesh. "We can have a nice dinner then get down to trading malicious gossip and rumors. Be catty. Say nasty things about people we usually have to be nice to. No . . . wait a minute . . . that's what we do around here for a living."

Essie glanced from the scissors to Flesh's smile.

"I was making a joke. Seriously, I would like to go out one night."

Essie nodded. "Could you do me a favor?"

"Haven't you heard? Around here I'm called 'The Queen of Favors.' "

"I bumped into a man the other day. He had been at the slough the night Taylor was *killed*. I had forgotten his name and was too embarrassed to ask. He said a lot of nice things about Taylor and, well . . . I wanted to send him a note. You wouldn't still have his name in a file somewhere?"

"I might." Flesh looked at Essie. It was an affable but decidedly professional stare that Essie weathered innocently. Without saying anything more Flesh got up.

One wall was stacked with files, in some places three, almost four feet high. Taylor's file was sadly close to the bottom of one stack. While Flesh knelt there tugging it loose so as not to topple the others, the office door opened and Roy's head peeked in.

"Hello, Essie . . . Flesh."

Essie turned. "Hello, Roy."

Flesh pulled the file, stood and set it on her desk.

"I was walking by and I saw you."

Flesh began to go through the file watching Roy with one eye as she did.

"You here to see Flesh?"

"I'm here to see Francie."

Flesh found the name. She wrote it down on a scrap of paper, with a phone number and address. She handed this to Essie.

DAMON ROMERO—even seeing the name made no real impact. But Romero and Romeo—

"I guess you were going to come and see me before you left. To say hello."

Essie folded up the paper. "No, Roy, I wasn't." She slipped it into her purse. "Thanks, Francie." She stepped around Roy and stopped at the door. "Call me, Francie. We'll go out. Maybe we can even trade a few rumors."

As Essie left the office Flesh waved. Roy looked at the file. He used his crutch to move it around to read which file it was, though in his heart he knew. He eyed Flesh. "What was that all about?"

"I was doing her a favor."

Roy's head bent around to watch Essie through the open doorway walk toward the elevator. "What kind of favor?"

Flesh stepped around him and kicked the door shut, killing the view. "I was doing my best to make her hate you a little more than she already does."

Flesh went back to her desk and sat. Staring at Taylor's file she asked, "What do you want, Roy?"

"Charles Gill called."

Flesh kept staring at the file while her mind did curious little turns. "What did he want?"

"He wants to have lunch with me tomorrow."

On this Flesh looked up. Roy crossed his fingers. "I see a state senator in your future," he said.

"Elected . . . or convicted?" she asked.

CHAPTER FIFTY-SEVEN

Essie sat at Taylor's desk with the sunset all about her, waiting on Dane to return. An evening harvest of colors was being carried on the waters of Disappointment Slough toward some indigoed distance. She had seen that very same dusk before carried by the slough from this very same desk as she waited for two different men.

That this too might not come to be, found her. It swept through her heart with a fearful cruelty, a fearful certainty. That did not surprise her. She had been battered by that before. But what did surprise her was something else she discovered in that wave of loss.

It was tiny as a creek would be when compared to the arc of a universe, but it was there. She could sense it, smell it, feel it, not really see it, but it was moving through her body toward her very being.

She could endure. She had in fact, endured. She looked at her wounded, bandaged hand. Even with what she had been through up to now, she had endured. And just as water always finds its way, this apparitional creek of a feeling would find its way. It would seek her out. It would lead somewhere, lead her somewhere.

And she wanted with her heart to believe it would make as deep and indelible a mark upon her as Disappointment Slough did moving toward that indigoed distance and carrying on its back, for her to see, the sunset and sunrise of centuries.

———

WELL AFTER dark Essie saw headlights through the high bulrushes on the opposite shore where the road came down from King Island.

When the car pulled off the road Essie reached for binoculars sitting on the desk. Where the car had stopped dust filled the air and she couldn't see anything in the black space above that halogen set of eyes, until the shotgun door opened and the interior lit.

AS DANE stood back from the dust and rocks kicked up by Nathan's tires he heard an outboard crossing the slough.

He walked to the dock. He watched where the river beacon on the windmill above the house sent a shimmering tunnel of light along the water.

It was only an instant, the boat passed through that incandescent breath of white, and she waved. He waved back, but was certain he could not be seen.

The darkness, the sound of the boat's motor, the water, the beacon of light. It was the alchemic opposite of the night before.

SHE PUT out her good hand and he pulled her up to the dock in one sweep.

Maybe it was because of the darkness or the stark way the water reflected the night sky up through that warped lattice of dockboards. Maybe it was because he was tired and unshaven, or that she herself had been through so much in the last day and night, but she saw now what was there in his face, and beyond.

The raw youth of before looked more cut with finitudes. As if it had been at war with something and neither side had won, but neither side was finished.

She touched his face and he kissed her. They crowded against each other in the narrows of that moment with all the unnameables of time and emotion moving through and around them. And then before she could ask if he were all right, before she spoke at all he saw her bandaged hand. He took it in his and he asked, "What happened? Are you all right?"

And with that she clutched his shirt with both hands and broke down crying, not just because he was safe, not just because she had gotten through her own nightmare, but because he had a human concern for someone else that overrode his own, when he probably needed it more.

AS THEY walked up the stone pathway toward the house, Essie stopped where she had fallen that night into the railing and broken her wrist. Dane turned to see why she'd stopped.

The front door was open and its light fell across the spot she'd found Taylor dying, then on through the low bowers to where Essie stood staring in silence.

"What?" said Dane.

"I'm sure of at least one person who had to be involved in the murder."

NATHAN SAT in the steam shower on the tile floor with a bottle of whiskey and a glass beside him. "I'm nothing," he said. "Nothing."

He reached for the bottle but knocked it over. He was drunk that fast. Ivy grabbed the bottle as the liquor spilled out into a stream of water heading toward the drain. She could barely see his face.

Nathan was trying to deal with the utter fear that he was going to die inside that box and how deathly afraid he was of being dead. And what desperate things he would do to avoid it. "I'm getting old," he said. "Fuckin' old."

Ivy wanted to ask him why he had lied to her about Dane but didn't know how to get to that without opening a door to Charles. She asked only, "Is Dane all right?"

"Dane." Nathan said the name with pointed jealousy. "That fuckin' kid can hack it."

"What happened in Mexico?"

"We paid. Everything is back to status quo."

"That's all?"

"That's enough."

She had seen this part of him to know there was more. He started to rock, very slightly. Back and forth, with his legs crossed, like some primitive chief, or a child. Then he said, "We should have a baby. Maybe . . . we could even adopt one."

He couldn't see her face. He slid across the tiles till he was by her. "I know you heard me."

With every fault and failure, even knowing how Nathan treated one son, the idea of it aroused every little unfulfilled need she had, it touched every womanly temptation, until it reached the part of her that was most guilty of all.

DAMON ROMERO . . ."

Dane leaned back against the kitchen sink and stared at the slip of paper. "From the way you describe him, he could be the one on the boat."

"You can see for yourself. He runs Romeo Boat Sales."

Dane reached for his bottle of beer on the counter. He drank with tired doggedness.

Essie sat at the kitchen table amidst beer bottles and an ashtray with two burning cigarettes. "It means the murder was planned."

When he finished the beer Dane walked over to the kitchen table for his cigarette.

"Charles . . . The Fenns . . . Romero . . . this, Merton."

Dane smoked. "Romero could say he knows the Fenns 'cause they were interested in a boat, so he showed the one that belonged to this Merton."

"They went after you in Mexico."

"We never saw them in Mexico. And it was Nathan who did the going after."

285

Essie undid the top to another bottle of beer and handed it to Dane. "We should have kept the diamonds." She hunched over the table smoking while she stared and thought. "We should have kept some anyway—for proof."

Dane turned away while saying, "Just wait, diamonds will show up." He walked over to the kitchen door. "The worst always does, when you need it."

He leaned against the doorjamb and looked up the hill where the river beacon shone down from the top of that windmill.

"I believe if Nathan thought he could have gotten away with killing Rocket Boy he would have airmailed the doomslinger right out of the plane."

Essie bent around and draped her arms over the chair back. Smoke from her cigarette drifted up toward the ceiling. She stared at Dane. "Maria told me last night we'd given enough. We should tell what we know and be done with it."

He kept watching the windmill where its wooden slats went round and round in a warmish wind, strobing the light within it. "And what did you tell her?"

"I said, 'How do you know when you've given enough? Is it right before you give up, or right after?'"

"You're both right."

She came around and put the cigarette out. Dane heard her bare feet cross the linoleum, then felt her beside him. "You haven't said a word about what happened in Mexico."

He swigged down his beer. She saw something harbored in his eyes, something she did not understand. She put her hand out, the bandaged hand, and touched his arm.

His throat felt no bigger than a string. He was not sure if he was at a loss for words, or words were at a loss for him. But he began the sentences knife short. They started at that burning fire on the beach and he walked her every step of the way to when the freezer lid slammed shut.

"At first," he said, "it was sheer panic. Nathan and I trying to kick our way out. As if by kicking hard enough we could get out of that coffin.

"I read once," he said, "that sometimes the best resistance against an ultimate power is to remain completely still. I tried, I did."

He could feel time walking on that warm wind that turned the windmill wheel. He could feel it walking. "I concentrated on the cold. My breath, I slowed it. Slowed it, slowed it. Closed off from everything. The fear, the fear. It began to leave. To dissipate. But as it did, as it did—"

His voice had risen, he hesitated. "Something more terrifying filled in the quiet, something more terrifying took its place."

"What?"

His cheekbones pulled back hard. He went to smoke, but didn't.

"What?"

"That it would be a pleasure to die. A pleasure. And all the fragments known as me would find rest."

CHAPTER FIFTY—EIGHT

He LEFT HER standing in the doorway and walked that thin footpath up the hill. He stood beneath the windmill with its river beacon of a moon. He set his beer down on the stone ledge of the well. The wind had those wooden slats turning with an easy, steady cadence.

He watched the wooden slats cut the light with their quiet clack, clack, clack when Essie came walking up behind him.

He turned. Standing in the light's soft edge she said, "Know that I will stand by you."

To feel such bare honest affection hurt. To know that such bare honest affection was even felt for him hurt. It brought to bear every bit of shame and guilt that was inside his most lonely being. And he wondered how he could even deserve such affection.

Essie watched as he stepped over to the well. He took his beer and drank. He set it down carefully on the stone ledge. All this was done to the creaking homily of those windmill slats.

The ground on the ridge top was soft and it clung to his boots as he moved about silently with his hands behind his back, until he saw how those wooden blades cut through the light that made his shadow. There and gone, there and gone, there and gone.

He stood looking down upon that moving portrait of dark and light and just began talking. "As much as I know, I don't. I am capable of honesty, but I am a more capable liar. I want to be proud of myself, but when I look inside my own heart and see what I feel there, no such possibility is in sight."

He turned and tried to valiantly make himself understood. "I not only could be the person on that subway platform, I could just as easily be the monster riding that express ready to fling a heartful of chemicals. I feel for what happened to Taylor, but I feel Nathan more deeply. I am one part Paul Caruso and two parts Fenn.

"I want love, but I am certain I will fail it. I don't want to hurt you or Paul or Maria but I am convinced that I will. That the true will of me will make that happen."

He held his hands up and out together. "I just can't seem to—" He began to try and shape this invisible piece of space with his palms and fingers. "Take all the disparate and desperate parts of me and make one human being—fit."

He saw, on the ground, the shadow of his hands made by the river beacon. They appeared to be holding an amorphous world of light. From its shape it could have been a cloud, or a stone, or a skull. He saw too that if he tried to enfold it into his hands, it would be gone. That if he tried to reshape it, it would dissolve through his fingers into the vaster throw of light. And so he stood there.

"I don't want to see and feel all this," he said, hushed. "I just want to—"

She took his hands in hers. "Be twenty-five without all the baggage . . . forever."

"How many times does a human being have to die emotionally before they get it right?"

Essie saw then what she thought she had seen on the dock harbored in Dane's face.

"You have strength of character," said Dane. "You are someone to be proud of." He then went on introspectively, and with a certain degree of shame, "While I am quite something else."

She kissed his hands and held them tightly. Very, very tightly. She wanted him to feel the strength there, coming from her heart, through her fingers and into his hands. "That first day," she said. "Right here. You asked to help. Remember? You gave your word. Right here. Remember?"

"I do," he said.

"Yeah . . . you are quite something else. And I can tell you this and swear it's true. I'm the better for it."

She would, he knew, shore up any hole in heaven, if she could reach that high.

SHE LED him by the hands. His boots followed her bare feet through the flood of beacon light to where it touched the softly arching slope of the hill. She turned her face so that it bore the darkness and began to take off his shirt with a slow and obscene honesty of feeling.

The shadow of those windmill slats scythed across their naked bodies where they lay on the ground like the first two human thieves. She dug her heels into the moist earth and lifted her pelvis bone hard against his own. There were dire cries, filled with dreams. She raised her hips almost daring him to come in further, push further, drive further as a way of getting beyond the terror of their sins, their pasts, their conflicts, their fears, their agonies, their uncertainties, their lies, if that were at all possible.

She could see beyond the flesh of his cheek and her hands along his shoulders that moon of a river beacon light and the fanwheel black there turning, cutting the light in sections, an ever moving of white and dark. There then gone, there then gone, there then gone.

She never once asked him to love her. She never once said she loved him. She only wanted to show him what she was, what she would give. And that it was all right to be a helpless creature in so vast a world. That what you feel should not condemn you to be alone, to despair. That there were no perfect strengths, no perfect assurances. That there was only the heartbreaking and the beautiful, and that they were ever changing, ever moving, ever touching us there then gone, there then gone, there then gone. Like those strips of white and dark where the windmill wheel passed across that river beacon moon.

And as she held him in her arms she wanted him to know, to

feel it from the way she breathed into his body, that if they could not be of one flesh, they could at least be of one spirit. She wanted this at least as much for him, as she wanted it for herself.

THEY RESTED beneath the creaking homily of that fanwheel. The clack, clack, clack.

He lay with his head across her stomach looking up the white path of her flesh toward her face. He listened to her heart. "I could imagine," he said, "that when Sancho Maria was young, she was you."

CHAPTER FIFTY-NINE

IT COULDN'T EVEN pass for a seduction, not with all of Roy's unsettled, slavish needs. Lunch had been set at the Empire Grill on 13th and K Street in Sacramento. The Empire was an eyeline away from the capitol.

The restaurant was a state-of-the-art steakhouse with terrazzo floors and an open kitchen lined in copper where diners could watch chefs dressed in neat white scuttle about visually lavishing their passionate talents on each order. And with the legislature in session, assemblymen and senators were drawing down a lot of tables that day. Reservations were hard to come by.

Charles made Roy wade through one martini's worth of pointless conversation, all the while letting Roy take an earful of all that politics going on at the tables around them. When they brought the second round of martinis Charles opened his briefcase and took out a file.

He was securely matter-of-fact. "I've gone to the Republican Party and established a Committee to Elect. I filed all the necessary forms. I've put in thirty thousand dollars of my own money and I've gotten a commitment from half a dozen other businesspeople who will take a flyer with me and donate—to see—if we can get you nominated for a state senate seat in some district."

Roy thumbed through the papers with a look of naked want.

"Once you decide, and you sign your papers, we'll put together the exploratory committee to see which district to run in, and if you've got the meat at all to get nominated."

Before Roy could ask any questions, Charles went on assuming critical answers. "I want to be involved in politics, but I don't want to be in politics. I'll learn my way through you, and if all goes well. Well—"

"Every politician has business advisors from the community. People who think through important decisions." The waitress came by with a litany of specials only to have Charles give her a politely silent "not now" stroke of the arm. "I don't know if we can get you nominated, let alone elected. But if you want this opportunity I'd have Flesh recommend a good hair stylist and someone who knows how to fit a real suit. And you *know* what else has to be cleaned up."

Charles dipped the olive into his martini using the toothpick. He then worked it like a tiny pointer. "That dick under the desk shit is out. And don't ever smell like you've been hiding in your trunk smoking a joint. Nobody's gonna elect Jerry Garcia to the assembly or senate in Central California unless he's Jerry Garcia, and Jerry Garcia is dead."

Charles slid the olive off the toothpick using his teeth. There was not one moment of flimsy pretense as he went on. "I've seen you in court doing that ego thing standing on your crutches examining witnesses. That's worth coverage. You've got a pretty good prosecutorial record, though you can be an annoying acid tongued unlikable son-of-a-bitch."

"You know what you make me sound like," said Roy.

"Yeah, exactly who you are."

"Jesus Christ. That's just what Flesh would say."

"Flesh isn't stupid. Those fuckin' legs lead up to a brain, use it. Look around here, you've got to impress people. Make people feel they're important. Make people see you're important by making them feel they're important."

"I dragged this body from an iron lung to law school to the prosecutor's office to a courtroom. I can drag it to that fuckin' legislature."

Nothing more needed to be said. Charles watched as Roy signed forms. After lunch had been ordered and a third round of martinis set down Charles went to work.

"I hear," he said, "you and Nathan have had a falling out."

Roy caught himself studying a set of pantyhose that sleeked up to an ass making its way past their table. "Nathan is upset over this little dose of truth I gave him."

"About what?"

Roy's fingers picked at his beard. "I was explaining to Nathan particular details about Taylor which made me feel certain that he had committed suicide."

"That must have been difficult for Nathan."

"I'm a prosecutor, not a fuckin' therapist." Roy's tone had turned unpleasant and severely bitter. He was also keenly aware that he was altering the truth to fit his personal needs. "The truth is the truth. I'm a good prosecutor, but I'm not a fuckin' therapist."

"The truth is the truth," reiterated Charles.

Roy bundled up right there at the table. He kept picking at his beard. It was, thought Charles, a grossly unappealing character trait. Roy's head sunk down into his neck. The deep thinker in that first moment of a private meltdown.

"Nathan hates me . . . *Essie* hates me."

"Well, if it's any consolation, Nathan has been acting very oddly toward me."

Roy went from staring at his drink to staring at the papers he had just signed. This was a chance, a real chance, he thought, to finally, finally justify his own existence.

"As a matter of fact," continued Charles, "I've been uncomfortable with the way Nathan has been doing business. Very uncomfortable."

Roy's face lifted slightly.

"I thought at first it was because of Taylor's death, but now . . . what's your impression of this Rudd kid?"

"Don't bring his name up when Flesh is around." Roy's hand came up like a traffic cop's. "The last time I did you'd have thought we were gonna have to have a fuckin' exorcism she was so mad."

Charles, of course, already knew Roy's impression of Dane Rudd. "Well, Flesh isn't here, and you are."

Charles watched the body twist as it rose in its seat. Roy had to take a drink before he started venting. "I think Rudd is totally, unquestionably full of shit. He's a phony from his tongue right down to his dick. He's a gamer, a liar; probably a con artist."

Charles listened, he nodded. When Roy had run out of adjectives Charles sat there intensely introspective. And then, after carefully letting some time elapse, Charles said, "I'm going to risk telling you something, all right. But you've got to keep it private."

Dane sat in the kitchen in the dark. He needed it dark for what he wanted to say. He had been drinking, but not so much they'd know. Inside him there was this unchained ghost rattling the depths of his secret desires.

He told them what went down in Mexico on the *Hunter Gracchus*. He added the name Damon Romero to their list. He asked about Merrit Merton, but as far as they knew he was a no exist. Dane gave them the address to the house on Plymouth Cove and that maze of names Merton used.

"Do I sound bad?" Dane said. "Well, being devoured will do it."

He let them sit with that. Then, "I want . . . need to ask you something." Even with it dark he closed his eyes to concentrate on how they'd say what they'd say. "I want to stay here . . . here, here, is what I'm talking about. After . . ."

The tone of their voices sounded like they were trying to circumvent what he had asked. The night was warm. He was sweating with stress. He was afraid in that deeply vulnerable way one gets afraid that one's most urgent prayers won't be answered. "I've been trying to earn my way back, right? You can see that . . . yes, I know how these things work.

"I have given it all; you see that, right? . . . There's people here that care for me. As hard as it may be for you all to imagine. But it's true. Here I've managed to become . . . There's people here I care for. Don't take that from me . . . please. I'm asking, no, begging. Can you hear it in my voice? Can you?"

He had to stand up to breathe, to speak, not feel imprisoned.

"No façades, no fakery. This is just your basic issue begging."

He listened and listened and listened and what he heard hurt, and it hurt more, and more, and more.

"Even fate forgives and forgets, sometimes," Dane said. "It does. Just try to imagine you're me and what I asked, you asked . . . Yeah . . . Yeah, that's the little dream I've been trying to fly up to."

CHAPTER SIXTY

THE GENERAL HAD Nathan lock the guesthouse door. He had Nathan keep watch too so that if anyone came down from the main house or the road they would be seen long before they could overhear what the General was about to tell him.

"You . . . must promise . . . to ask . . . nothing. Listen . . . only . . . Until, I'm sure."

The days were growing dim about the General but on this day, in this room, at this moment he was about as close to being the stone-faced martinet of his past as he had been in years.

Nathan looked down at the old man. He did not want to promise. He felt something awful leaning into the pit of his stomach. "It's about Taylor, isn't it?"

The old man's hands clung to each other in his lap. The fingertips of one began to bite into the back of the other. Bite and dig. "Information has come . . . to me. But . . . until . . . I'm absolutely sure . . ."

"When will you be sure?"

"Less than days."

Nathan now stared up at the main house. The nanny was loading Charles' two small daughters into the family wagon. He turned away from any sorrow that he might feel.

"If it is Charles—?"

The General reached out and took Nathan's hands as a way of reaching back into their friendship, into all the abandoned and solitary bits of history they lived together. As a way of resurrecting all memories and emotions. He clung to Nathan's hands as he would cling to life on earth, or to a precious dream, as a way of assuring him. "I . . . won't fail you."

Essie WAS at her desk working when Ivy pulled up a chair and sat. Ivy had not been drinking; she wasn't carrying on through a cloud of antidepressants.

"Do you think I'd make a good mother?"

The question was so exquisitely ill-timed, so oddly out of the ordinary, so especially disgusting.

"What do you think?"

While keeping all she felt hidden Essie said, "Can you imagine any reason why you wouldn't?"

Ivy glanced at Nathan's picture on the wall along with all the other pictures of the people who had made Discovery Bay their home, who had been his friends, servicemen who had gotten their first taste of home ownership right there.

"We could adopt. It would make Nathan happy. And in some small way help him to get past Taylor's . . ."

Even to say Taylor's name in connection with her grasping dream was inconceivable. And yet, in some small way the sad-eyed black and blue of Ivy's soul wondered if she could earn off the guilt.

"I want to ask you something," said Essie. "Did you tell Roy that a few weeks before Taylor died he confessed, if confess is the right word, that he considered killing himself?"

Ivy looked to be entangled in a series of speechless answers. Essie's look was stark, measured, painful, hurt and angry.

We're so close to getting past all this, Ivy thought, so close. And even now I've got to cut and eviscerate someone till I myself am bleeding. "Yes," she said.

Essie was the incarnate of that night Taylor was taken down. Nathan was coming up the stairs, he stopped at the receptionist's desk.

"Goddamn Roy. That was supposed to be a private conversation between he and I." Ivy took hold of Essie's hand. "Please don't bring this up to Nathan. It was bad enough Roy did. It will only cause him more hurt. And I don't want to set him off."

Essie would have pressed her with more questions but Nathan was coming right toward them.

"Promise me you won't." Ivy was pleading.

Essie slipped her hand out from under Ivy's. "I won't say a word."

"Get Dane," Nathan told Essie, walking to his office as if neither woman existed.

CARUSO WAS cashing out the bar register when he heard, "Where's *your* boy?"

He turned. It was Shane Fenn, in the bar for the first time since his beating. There was so much swelling around the mouth he spoke through a slur. "Beer . . . and you haven't answered me. Where's *your* boy?"

Caruso took a bottle from the cooler. Sancho Maria came out of the kitchen having seen Fenn through the door window. Caruso undid the cap and set the beer and a glass down on the bar.

"You're the only one," he said to Paul, "who hasn't asked me what happened. That's 'cause *your* boy told you, right?"

Sancho Maria passed behind her husband. Shane bent around on the bar stool to watch his brother taxi down the runway then take off. He came about even angrier.

"Where's *your* boy? Him and his yuppie bitch got too much happenin'?"

Sancho Maria saw that Paul looked to about have had it. She put a hand on his back. He felt the sign. She came around the bar. A few heads had turned as Shane's voice had gotten loud and disruptive.

She was wearing a brown corduroy shirt with cut sleeves. The shirt was tucked into her jeans. Her leather belt had a silver buckle on it big enough to serve drinks from. She sat next to Shane and quietly explained, "You'll come in one morning and have breakfast. Then you'll go back to your hangar, put on the stereo or your porno tapes and pretty soon after that you'll start to feel sick. You may get to the hospital but it won't matter. When they do the autopsy they'll discover rat poison accidentally got into your food.

"They'll probably shut us down for a few weeks, but we have insurance." She looked at Paul. "We do, don't we?"

"All paid up, darlin'."

That deeply lined Aztec face looked right down into Shane Fenn. Right down into the gut of him.

Shane got it; he got up. He took the beer. "*I* never did time in prison." He pointed the bottle right at Caruso. "And I never will."

CHAPTER SIXTY—ONE

DANE SAT ON the couch staring at Taylor's desk having just talked to Nathan. If what Nathan said was true, then this long narrative of disgraces was fast running to an end, whether they knew it or not.

Dane had begun to dial Essie when he heard a plane engine descending hard toward the house and then all that propeller and power skimmed the roof and the tree branches outside the windows and doors were snapped into a whooshing funnel of air.

At the door Dane saw the *Big D* start to bank. Paul intended to land that Cessna right on Disappointment Slough. Dane reached the dock just as the fluted bottom of those floats touched water and kicked out two long kitetails of white foam.

At dockside Paul came out of the cabin carrying a twelve-pack of beer. And while he negotiated the struts and the wet flat top of the float trying to reach Dane's outstretched hand he began, "Never eat at a restaurant called Mom's . . ."

As Dane pulled him up he filled in with, ". . . Never play cards with a man named Doc . . ."

Paul handed him the twelve-pack and pointed toward the house and as they made their way up through the trees on that stone path they chorused together, ". . . And never, ever sleep with anyone whose problems are worse than your own."

"You know," said Paul, putting his hand on Dane's shoulder, "I was thinking last night in bed. Your initials are D and R. Like in doctor. You ain't the 'Doc' they're talking about, are you?"

"Paul, it's silence that's golden."

WHILE DANE was in the kitchen pouring beers Paul walked the living room. "I think Shane Fenn is about ready to implode." He passed the slot machine Taylor had gotten from Essie. He gave the arm a tug. Nothing. "He was in the bar today, doing a fine impersonation of a total head case."

Paul passed the alcove desk. It was a curious sight. "And Tommy Fenn flew Charles Gill somewhere." There were open boxes around the desk. Some were filled with papers, clothes; some with plastic bags that looked to be trash.

On the desk were writing paper and envelopes. There was also an open plastic bag that *was* filled with trash, some of which was scattered about. "You hearing me?"

"I'm hearing you," said Dane.

By the writing paper was a half-folded and browning copy of the *Sacramento Bee*. A small article had been highlighted in yellow marker. Paul bent down to read:

> CAYUMA, CALIFORNIA—A Federal Reserve officer from the Los Angeles branch was murdered on Monday, shot-gunned to death at a motel just east of town, authorities said.
>
> William Dean Reynolds had just begun a two-week vacation and was on his way to visit friends in Morro Bay. Authorities believe the 51-year-old investigating agent was the victim of an attempted robbery, but are looking into the possibility this homicide may be connected to past or recent investigations—

Dane returned with two mugs of beer. Caruso stood, Dane handed him a mug. "Sorry," Dane said, "no extra cell phones around here to make a true Paul Caruso boilermaker."

Caruso grinned mischievously at the memory. He held out his glass. "To yuppie pricks you can fuck with."

"You like it, don't you?" said Dane.

"It's one of my inherent blemishes."

They touched mugs and drank. Dane went and sat on the couch. Caruso saw the boy was acutely preoccupied, that the smile only just touched the face.

"The other day in the bar," said Caruso, "when you pointed at the picture and asked me, 'What if there was nothing at the end of the maze?' I knew where you were going."

"I know you did."

"I'm not stupid."

Dane was staring at his glass from a long ways off. "No Paul, you're anything but."

"Looking inside too much is as bad as not looking at all."

"You're right," said Dane.

"No slick sidewise answers."

"No, Paul."

Dane drank, Paul drank. Paul stepped back to the desk and pointed. "What is all this?"

"Essie kept everything of Taylor's on the chance there might be an answer hidden in all that as to how or why he died."

Paul held up the newspaper. "What about this, what does it mean?"

Dane put the mug down on the end table. He reached for a pack of cigarettes beside his wallet.

"Why do I always feel that you know a lot more than you're saying?"

Dane lit the cigarette, he blew out the match. "Because I do. And that's not meant to be some smart sidewise answer."

Dane inhaled. Paul pushed the coffee table out of the way with his foot. He dragged the desk chair over until it was right in front of Dane. He sat.

"I don't understand all of you, but part of you I've got inside me. It was the part that landed me in prison. I'm sure it's landed people in all kinds of other places. From a page in some history book to a landfill with a bullet in their head. Those fuckers are not worth the effort. They'll do themselves in with time."

Dane put the cigarette down in an ashtray on the end table. He leaned forward. Both men's faces were inches apart. "I know I'm the wrong person to say this, Paul. But what about the rest in the meanwhile? Do they stitch the body years of sorrow around their breaking hearts till they drown under the weight of all those deep down deaths? Is it only the coming attractions or the aftermaths that ever get anyone's real attention? Christ, I am the wrong person. Coming from me, it must sound—"

Dane just sat there, on the cusp of an unfinished thought. Paul took a breath, he drank his beer mug empty. "In prison I had prostate cancer. Very severe. I was thirty-five. If the little blue pill hadn't come along, the old Caruso hammer would never have worked again. Sancho Maria loved me anyway. We wanted kids. No one knows this but her, and now you."

Paul wiped his mouth. "I tell you so you'll understand. We all live with the aftermath of something."

"I'm sorry, Paul."

"For what?"

"For everything . . . inside me, I'm just sorry."

Dane sounded so deeply hurt, wounded even, Paul clasped the boy's forearms. "I want you to know that every broken-down inch of life is worth it. I want you not to lose sight of that."

Lose sight of it, thought Dane. "You know Paul, you and Sancho Maria are the kind of people people like me dream about, while we still *have* dreams."

"I don't want something to happen to you." Paul's hands bore down on Dane's forearms. "Do you understand, son?"

CHAPTER SIXTY—TWO

Roy DRAGGED HIS naked body across the living room carpet. His stone was tweaked with just enough blow. He crabbed along on his elbows staring at that gaping piece of beauty between Flesh's legs as she slid back and away from him in a playful act of torrid depravity.

"Come on, Assemblyman."

He tried to keep his hard on from being bent awkwardly when he reached the dining room linoleum. "State senator . . . you bitch!" He laughed uncontrollably.

"Come on, Assemblyman." She lifted her ass and held that perfectly shaved V of pubic hair with its diamond teaser at the pierced tip of her vaginal opening. "I'm leaving you a trail, baby."

He tried to grab her foot. Her black painted toenails curled as she jumped back and beat his hand down with one of his crutches. She was drunk; she flung a dining room chair down on his head.

He cried out. "You fuckin' bitch lawyer cunt, cunt!"

"We know when to shred 'em, and we know when to spread 'em!"

Like some deformed worm he lunged again. She beat his hand down with the crutch. She kept sliding back with her legs spread, through the far kitchen door, into the hallway, then back around to the living room. It was a dizzying path and Roy huffed gruffly trying to—

"Assemblyman!"

It was pure loaded pleasure. A coyly insulting lead-in to a little hard, nasty sex. She dropped another chair down on his head, she threw a magazine from his coffee table at him, she tossed his pants at him, she flung his sport coat over his head.

He kept on like some hooded maniac laughing and groping and crawling, his bone-thin legs helpless. She reached back to the coffee table again.

"Fuck!" she screamed.

Like a child he tried to pull the coat from his head. She stood above him in anger. "You fool shit liar. What did I tell you?"

She was holding up a brochure from the organ bank. She flung it at him as she shot past on her way to the back bedroom. She was a screaming harridan who scooped up her clothes. He bent and twisted and curled himself upright. He leaned against the wall.

"It must be some sort of senseless cock vanity that makes you—"

As she jumped past his outstretched arms he managed to catch her foot. She stumbled and kicked at the wall as she fell. Grasping he got one goddamn handful of leg. "At least listen to what I was told—"

IVY WAS right at my desk, looking at me with a face like some kind of window dressing and she just said it." Essie sat in her living room chair with the standing lamp beside it, which alone lit the room. "In my heart I don't believe Taylor told her that. He wouldn't open himself up like that to her and not to me. That isn't possible. That was not Taylor."

Dane was sitting on the edge of the wooden coffee table, arms resting on his thighs, listening.

"If that's selfish or unfair, the belief that he didn't come to me, then I'm selfish and unfair. If I'm being immature or unwise, all right. I accept it. I just can't accept—"

Dane saw something come over Essie.

"What's wrong?"

Essie spoke low, in an unsettled way. "Maybe . . . Taylor opened a package like we did. Maybe . . . something was delivered to his company like that antique in your garage. Ivy bought a lot of furniture for Nathan's office, for his house, even for the bank. There are invoices in the garage. All those calls to Merton's number. Maybe—"

Essie shot up. As she did she knocked over the lamp. The bulb exploded, the room went black.

Dane went to her. She just stood there, not moving, immersed in a cold-blooded thought, with only a few swimming lines of light across her face where the moon had slipped through the blinds to catch her.

Dane put his arm around her.

"Would she do something that terrible," asked Essie, "to protect Nathan?"

"Herself . . ."

Somewhere in the dark Essie saw Ivy's face while she talked about having a baby and saying, "Maybe in some small way it would—"

NOTHING MORE was said. They lay down and slept. Essie awoke to find the bed empty. Dane was in the living room shepherding the dark. He sat on the couch, the balcony doors were open. Essie was wrapped in a blanket. She curled up beside Dane and enclosed him also in the blanket.

Across the alley, above the rooftops, the moon was white and full against a matte of soft black. And the buildings, those flesh-colored buildings with their oddly- shaped rooftops looked almost like towers framing that lunar mystery. The neighbor's glass mobile harped lightly.

They sat like that, as if in some small way they were there to watch out for the world. Dane had not told Essie why Nathan had called. And he was uncertain how, and when, he would.

CHAPTER SIXTY-THREE

A PHONE RINGING woke Ivy. She could hear Nathan's voice say, "I thought it might be you."

There was silence after that, then Nathan saying, "Yes." More silence was followed by another "Yes."

It went on like this; silence—"Yes"—silence. And each "Yes" grew more disturbed, as if the body had to wrestle out the word. Ivy rolled over.

Nathan was sitting at his desk by the window. The light around him had blackened in his outline. He again said, "Yes." His voice now sounded as if it were being drawn to some distant point, as if it were slowly being removed from the body which was saying it. As he listened he wrote down something on a notepad.

When the phone call was over the phone seemed to slip from his fingers and back into the cradle as he was putting it down. He remained just so, like some heavily breathing cloud against the white curtains.

"I'm to meet a man tonight, who, I'm told, has information on how Taylor died."

WHILE HE was in the shower Ivy went and looked at what he'd written down. When she saw the name, with the light streaming across it, she could have drowned in her own terror.

———

SHE COULD hear Nathan in the shower crying, sobbing, and the pain of it went through her as if there were fissures in her flesh that led to places it is better not to know existed.

Through the wall she could feel him hitting the shower tiles with his fist, like some great machine pounding out its breaths, with a slow brutal economy.

THIS DOESN'T feel right," Ivy said. She had to tinker with her voice. "I can't explain it." She was imploring him. "It just doesn't seem—"

Nathan sat naked on the edge of the tub and those dusky, movie theater looks said nothing would stay what he was going to do.

THE NANNY finished loading suitcases into the family wagon. Charles strapped the girls into their car seats, telling them all the fun things they'd see and do. The day was sunny and beautiful, a perfect backdrop for starting a little vacation.

Claudia came from the house checking through her purse. She gave Charles a cursory, "We'll be back in a few days."

"Yes," he answered.

Claudia got behind the wheel, the nanny climbed in front. As the engine turned over the nanny said, "Wave good-bye to Daddy."

The nanny waved, the girls waved. Their heads bent to see their father as the car pulled off. They looked to be almost floating there in the back, like two small angels. And Charles thought, how unaware they are that now would never be again.

A BROAD sweep of daylight cut across the garage. It left its duty trail of light where Essie sat with the door open like she had so many times before. She went through the stacks of invoices again, with the virtued meticulousness of an executioner.

There were deliveries to Taylor's company for Discovery Bay, the bank, Nathan. Many signed by Ivy. At least three she found were from companies with different names but the same Plymouth Cove address. Two, just weeks before Taylor's death. Both were signed by Ivy.

"Essie."

It was Flesh. Essie scooped up the invoices around her and got them stuffed into a file folder as Flesh stepped into the light of the open garage door.

"What are you doing here?"

"Your neighbors said . . ." Flesh's eyes wandered that filled to overflowing space with things she knew, she'd seen . . . "Those were Taylor's."

"Everything in here was Taylor's."

Essie set the folder down and stood. She brushed herself off. She looked like some phantom in the half dark, half light. A little nervous to have been come upon. "I kept everything."

Flesh glanced over that stacked world. "I heard some terrible things last night through Roy I want to ask you about."

"Through Roy?"

"He said Dane had been studying law at Princeton and had been thrown out. That he had been working for an attorney and he made sure certain evidence in a criminal case never made discovery. And now he and Nathan were involved in—"

"This came *through* Roy."

"Through Roy, from Charles Gill. I am going to call Princeton, but first I wanted to ask you—"

"Through Roy, from Charles Gill. That's quite a character sweep."

Essie left the folder where it was and walked out of the garage forcing Flesh to follow.

"Talk to me. This is Francie. Remember, the night in the emergency room."

Essie pulled the garage door down.

"I cleaned the blood from your arm."

It slammed shut.

"You give me some rap about needing the name of a witness

THE PRINCE OF DEADLY WEAPONS

in Taylor's murder, which sounded totally bogus. And not five minutes after Charles is backing Roy for a political run he's pouring out dirt about Nathan and—"

As Essie locked the garage door, "Roy took money from Charles?"

Each examined the other. Flesh threw out her arms. "Something is going on here. Essie? What do you know?"

"Tell Roy, if he doesn't want to get flushed down some drain, to *stay away* from Charles."

Roy, BE prudent who you speak to about this," said Charles. "If Nathan or Rudd found out—"

Flesh knocked on Roy's office door. She could see he was on the phone.

"I understand," said Roy. "I will see you tonight."

Roy waved her in as he hung up.

"I'm waiting on a call back from the Dean of Princeton Law School," said Flesh. "I should have it before the day is over."

"Good."

He reached for his crutches.

"I talked to Essie," said Flesh.

"As a prosecutorial matter, do you think that was wise?"

"I think there's a lot going on here that neither you nor I understand."

"Exactly my point."

Roy hitched himself upright.

"Essie said to stay away from Charles Gill."

He labored toward the door. "We have questions about one man Essie works for, another who she's fucking. What do you expect her to say about Charles?"

Flesh opened the door for Roy. "You mean who you're fucking or who you work for determines who you are?"

On his way out he answered, "If it didn't you'd be doing your tour of duty down in traffic."

Flesh slammed the door at his back.

CHARLES CUT Ivy off before she had hardly begun about the meeting that had been set for Nathan. His utter calm was more terrifying than the note itself. She foundered a moment before she said, "But the General—"

"Ivy, get off the phone, pour yourself some wine, then go think long and hard about the conversation we had in your kitchen."

I'LL BE picked up by boat here, at around nine o'clock, and taken to meet the third party."

"Are you sure about this?" asked Dane.

"Sure? There is sure," said Nathan, "and there is sure. The General is sure."

They leaned against the walkway railing which led down to the guest docks. Dane noticed deep welts and bruises on the back of Nathan's hands and knuckles. They watched the boat traffic move through the glaring sunlight. And even in the shadow of the Antioch Bridge they could see freighters on the Sacramento River, huge against that flat California landscape.

"You don't have to come with me on this. But if you decide, here's where I'll be."

Nathan walked away, his hand hitting down on the railing every few feet. Dane remained. He stood watching the water. He could see clouds in the water that day.

I NEED an answer," said Dane.

Alone on the bank of the Sacramento River, with his hand cupped to one ear so he could hear better on the phone, he confronted his handlers. "I know I'm a material witness now . . . I know the kind of retaliation I could face being out in the open . . . I know the problems with security . . . I know this was part of the deal to beat an indictment . . . I know your rules . . . But I'll take all the risk . . . I just, just want to be able to come back here . . .

It's the first thing in my life I've ever really needed and wanted. Do you understand?"

He walked farther down to the water as he knew he might start shouting and he didn't want to chance anyone overhearing him. "You're between a rock and a hard place? Well, excuse the analogy but I'm chained to that goddamn rock . . . I want your commitment I can stay . . . And I want it on paper. Nice bond government stationery. And I have to have it by seven o'clock tonight . . . I'll tell you at seven.

"It's the con artist in me . . . yeah . . . Describe me any way it works, but call by seven."

CHAPTER SIXTY—FOUR

As SUNSET REACHED out across the landscape Dane Rudd sat at Taylor's desk to write Essie a letter. On the desk was that faded section of the *Sacramento Bee*, on the chance this night did not go well. Beside it, wrapped in a bauble of aluminum foil, were the missing diamonds.

The sky was a seething reef of branded reds. An unending dusk not unlike the one that had colored his approach to Rio Vista the day he first walked into Paul Caruso's hangar. As it cast its burning shine across the writing paper, Dane beared down on the exact truth of who he was. He printed everything he had done, everything he had never told her, so if he were not there at the end, at least she would know the truth. Of him, from him.

THE NOVELIST Owen Wister once called the eye of man "the prince of deadly weapons." Dane now understood the more sublime inference inside that idea. To experience the difference between the life he'd led and the one he would probably be forced to leave behind was devastating. And in light of that fact, the enigmatic truth was Taylor Greene had seen to it, however indirectly, however ironically, and for whatever it might bring, that a hope and a dream had passed to someone in desperate need of a hope and a dream.

Dane put all that in his letter and then went on to tell Essie how much he felt for her, and for Paul and Sancho Maria and the world there, and no matter what, if they forcibly took him into hiding he would find a way to get back.

But he also told her that if after reading everything he'd done, she didn't want him, he understood.

I'm sorry for keeping you all in the dark, he wrote, but I saw no other way. Forgive me.

Dane was staring at the letter when the call came. He let it ring a few times not to seem so desperate, though he certainly felt that way.

"Yes . . ." He listened to a long uncomfortable monologue of inconclusivity. "You can't answer till this is all done, that's the answer?"

Dane took the letter and folded it in half. He slipped the letter into the envelope. "The General is setting a meeting for Nathan. I'm to be there . . . It seems someone with information about Taylor's death is willing to come forward. I told you taking the diamonds would open them up."

Dane slipped his safety deposit box key into the envelope along with notarized instructions giving the house on Disappointment Slough to Essie. He licked the envelope shut. "The day after tomorrow, no sooner . . . Send your people down here, it's your call . . . Anywhere they want to meet. As long as it's outside the Delta. I don't want anybody to chance the connection . . . They should contact me just like you do." Dane listened to the way their voices played on, as if they were a proxy for God's own judgment.

"I know you wish it could be different . . . I won't do anything to compromise myself . . . What do I *think?*"

Dane closed his eyes for an illimitably long time, then in a tone they would not understand till later he said, "I think you should always be careful what you wish for."

Conversation over, Dane got up and walked to the kitchen. He took a mug from the dish rack. He took a beer from the refrigerator. He filled the mug two-thirds of the way with beer and then he let the cell phone drop like a depth charge into the brew.

He lifted the mug and drank. He drank till the cell phone dropped into his mouth and he chewed on the top and spit it back into the mug, then set the mug down on the counter.

"Try and get to me now."

There is no pain you are receding
A distant ship, smoke on the horizon

Charles sat in his studio with headphones on, blasting himself with sound.

You are only coming through in waves
Your lips move, but I can't hear what you're saying

Was this what he had been riffing with his guitar boys the night Taylor died?

I caught a fleeting glimpse
Out of the corner of my eye

They controlled you once, they control you now. Charles was, he knew now with hateful certitude, a boy walking around lost inside a man's body.

The child is gone
The dream is gone

The wall clock told him Roy would soon be leaving work.

DANE PRINTED Essie's name on the back of the envelope. He lay the letter atop the newspaper, resting it against the diamonds.

He lit a cigarette and sat on the front door steps. He watched as that firebrand horizon burned away. Everything in the unmarked voyage of life that he'd thought and felt on those doorway steps came back to him.

The here and now constantly tries to decide the now and forever. It is a limited plan at best. But one, it goes without saying, that shall be with us forever. At its most heartbreaking, and most beautiful.

A GARAGE attendant in the building where Roy worked had been crippled in an auto accident. Roy knew the boy's family and was instrumental in forcing the building management into hiring him.

Occasionally, walking to Roy's car, they would fence, turning crutches into rapiers. It was their self-determined way of venging a little showy black humor on the healthy who watched.

The boy attendant, thrusting his crutch at Roy's passing car window, would be the last known person to see Roy Pinter alive.

DANE SLID the double-bladed knife down into his boot. He worked his black jeans down over the leather top. With scissors he cut the jeans from the heel all the way up till his hand could easily grasp the knife handle.

He checked the gun to see it worked properly. He fired one shot from the kitchen door into the vine-strangled wilderness behind the house. The shot echoed across that frieze of shadows.

He went and put on his old leather coat. He realized he was dressed as he was that first day he walked into Paul Caruso's hangar. It was, he thought, a perfectly befitting accident. If you believe that in life there is such a thing as accidents.

The phone rang. The message machine answered. "Where are you?" Essie asked, "Are you all right? Call me. I'm . . . I'm me."

WHEN CHARLES Gill walked into The Point he asked the bartender right off if Roy Pinter had gotten there yet. As this was one of Roy's regular haunts it took less than a cursory look to see he hadn't.

Charles sat at the bar and ordered a drink. He looked out onto the vast sweep of the lower Sacramento. The dotting of lights had begun and the first hints of fog could be seen drifting across the tops of the office buildings.

He nursed his cocktail and picked from a cup of peanuts the bartender had put down. He tried to maintain an air of casual calm knowing full well the resolve tonight would demand.

DANE CROSSED the blue waters of evening and looked back at the house on Disappointment Slough hidden there among the trees. The river beacon had just gone on. The light was soft and misty above a world still not dark enough.

With the wind the trees along the slough islands bristled like the chatting tongues of crickets, like the wooden sticks of men, like the whispering breath of gods. The air was filled with the scent of water and freshly turned earth.

It was quiet where he sat in the boat, in all directions, and he could see headlights flitter far, far away. Tiny as lanterns moving through the darkening grottoes of that countryside.

From that place of undiscovered self he felt a sudden surge of loss and he was not yet even gone from there. As much as it hurt, as much as it tore at all those puzzled pieces of the human provenance, it wrote something beautiful and heartbreaking on the paper of his days that could never be forgotten, even after he was no longer.

CHAPTER SIXTY-FIVE

I'M WALKIN' AROUND in the fuckin' blind here."

The Burrow fuse box was in a storage closet off the kitchen. Paul was trying to feel his way up and down the fuses when he heard the alley door open. "Maria, I'm at the fuse box."

"It's not Maria."

Caruso came from the storage closet and crossed the darkened kitchen to where Dane was feeling his way toward him. In Paul's hand was a flashlight. He shook it. "Batteries are dead, the power is out. You know how many flashlights I bought for this place that end up missing? People must be putting them up their assholes. Let's wait in the bar for the old lady. I'm tired of bumping into shit back here."

A pale shore of moonlight through the windows fought back the dark, and all those paintings and prints on The Burrow walls made it look like some cavern where the dream pictures of the ancients were kept for all of memory to see.

"Get us a couple of beers," said Paul, "while I sit my ass right down here at the bar and wait for a flashlight that fuckin' works."

Caruso clunked the flashlight down on the bar. Dane brought one beer from the cooler and served his friend. All this had been done without a word and Paul realized—

"There's trouble," said Dane.

Caruso had not even gotten to his first sip. "Why doesn't that surprise me?"

Dane laid out for him what he'd been told was to happen tonight and the why of it. Paul listened grimly, without drinking, and when Dane had finished all Paul said was "Jesus Christ."

"Nathan is supposed to know tonight, so will I. I intend to turn everything over tomorrow. Finished. Otherwise, whatever else may happen, I'm telling you, like I'm telling Essie. You're free to tell what you know. Everything."

Caruso had covered too much world not to know what was about to come. He stood up. He followed the hard pitch of his face, taking in the bar and what was beyond the windows. He leaned with his back against the wall.

"We love this place very much," he said. "Maria and I know we are not ever gonna be rich. That we are overworked and over-looked. And it's perfectly all right. Sometimes, after the close, we sit at a booth in the dark, like this now, and . . . take in the silence.

"We feel safe here, protected here. Even if it's only in our heads. It's a good way to live."

"We leave from Antioch in about two hours," said Dane.

Caruso moved back to the bar. He sat. "When Gill flew back in yesterday he and the Rocket Boyz spent some pretty hard hours at their hangar."

"I don't know if we'll be taken back into the Delta, or out to sea."

Through the open door to the kitchen there was a shift in the darkness Paul noticed. If it was Maria, listening, how much of this had she heard?

"Somebody could get killed tonight."

"Yes," said Dane.

"How can you begin to protect yourself?"

Dane slid the gun from his coat pocket and held it in his palm for Paul to see.

"Put that fuckin' thing away, right now. Right now, I say."

Dane did as he was asked.

"You know, Paul, you're the most honest man I ever met. You don't hedge your bet, you don't hide your feelings. You don't fake yourself. You even wear what you came from on a T-shirt for any-one with eyes to see."

Paul stared at the coat pocket with the gun.

"I'm going to ask you something terrible, Paul."

Caruso's arms, which rested on the bar, made two fists.

"If things go bad in the Delta, we'd be near or on land, I might have a chance in the dark. But in a small boat, at sea . . ."

Caruso's head bowed and his fists came up and he pressed them into the bones above his eyes. "Why," he pleaded, "why?"

Dane placed his hands on the bar. His eyes drifted painfully, searching for how to say what to say. Those pictures on the wall were but glyphs of color and tone, black and white shadow moments that talked with a frightening accuracy. To walk every step of why was to take the unmarked voyage toward that terrifying mystery imprisoned in our stony past. And where, in the end, there waits a god, or a beast, or that vast human reservoir for good and ill that bears and fills our name.

"Just being in the world doesn't make it better, Paul. Not for the world, not for yourself. I know this from having been the Fenns, and Charles Gill and Nathan and so on and so forth."

Dane put his hand around Paul's fist and told him in a voice naked and hushed, "I'm sorry if I hurt you by asking. I'm sorry. I just don't seem to do living well."

Dane turned to leave. Maria was at the kitchen door. He stopped when he saw her. Caruso's head rose as Maria stepped forward. She switched on a flashlight and stood it upright on the bar so its powdery beam underscored their faces.

"You heard," said Paul.

"I heard," said Sancho Maria.

She looked at the boy, her eyes under all that shadow. They were large, and black as a locomotive. She said nothing. She went and sat in a booth by the window. She folded her hands while she wrestled with her thoughts. Paul and Dane remained as they were, with that run of light moving up toward the ceiling between them.

Everything that was this woman could be felt when she spoke. "You hope and you hope . . . and you hope some more. Then, when it's all done, you must let all that hope go on to someone else." Staring at what was before her, Sancho Maria told her husband, "Help him."

CHAPTER SIXTY-SIX

CHARLES MADE A real show of looking at his watch when the bartender brought him a second drink. The Point was packing up and Charles had to speak above the noise. "Roy Pinter was supposed to be here half an hour ago. I don't understand."

The bartender shrugged, moving on to the next order of business. Charles took out his cellular phone, flipped it open, and dialed Roy's office working a mood of deep concern.

WHEN THE phone rang Essie jumped to answer it. "Where are you? Did you get my messages?"

"Yes," said Dane. "I . . . listen, there's something you need to see. Out at the house. It's on the desk."

"Sure. Where are you?"

He didn't answer.

"Dane, are you in your truck?"

The phone blurred, it scratched. She walked out onto her balcony. A damp mist was coming. "Dane?"

"Yes."

"Where are you?"

"I'm . . . on my way to Antioch."

Antioch was not far from Oakley and the Big Break Marina, she knew. "What's in Antioch? Dane . . . what's in Antioch?"

"Nathan."

You get to know someone by their silences, their breathing. It is that other language, what they mean to tell you no matter what they say. It is the liquid contact we have with each other. How we talked before we talked, in a time when life was less well known but better understood.

She had taken him into her very self, with all his fire and sleep, his tenderness and lightwire mind, his honesty and lies, his loneliness.

He wanted to be asked no more, she knew. That small creek of strength she'd felt in the dusk of the slough she had to call upon, she knew.

"All right," Essie said. "I'll go there now."

She touched the phone wanting him to sense, feel, know, if all that had been between them was slight as a kitestring it would be strong enough to bind the universe.

A whispering came through the phone line. "I heard you the other night."

"I felt you did," she whispered back.

DANE HAD crossed the Sacramento and was driving south through Sherman Island. When he reached the tip of Mayberry Slough he pulled off the road and got out of the car.

A pitch dark ran for flat miles and the only thing rising up out of that bending tule grass, maybe fifty yards from the road, was the rotting hull of a huge paddlewheeler grounded there over a half century before.

Dane listened for the plane. There was only the faint wind. He reached into his pocket for the airband transceiver Caruso had given him. When he got the small handheld device working he asked, "Paul, can you hear me?"

Dane listened, he waited. He looked up at the sky. There was silence and the forsaken creakings where the wind moved through that black dried coffin of history.

Dane saw too a mist was coming. Pale, dim wisps of it were finding their way across the marsh, finding their way through the gapings of rot from the hurricane deck of that riverboat right down to its hull.

And for a few seconds there in the pitch dark, alone, watching

323

those trails of dim gray cross the empty shrouded decks it looked to Dane as if that ghostly artifact rent with time had begun to move, as if some blind will of the past had taken hold of that labored old wheel and given it life.

"Can you hear me . . . Dane?"

It was a weak and grainy signal. Dane pressed the monitor button on the keypad to keep the squelch down.

"Paul—"

"Dane, can you—"

"Paul, it's rough but—"

"Where are you?"

The static got worse, the signal wavered.

"At the wreck along—"

"Where are you?"

"At the wreck along Mayberry Slough."

Dane began to hear the plane coming out of the edges of the horizon.

"I pulled over to see how this works!"

"What—"

Dane shouted, "To see how this works!"

"This is it. If you can get on board with—"

"Yeah—"

Paul's voice couldn't get through the static.

"What?"

"A fog. You can probably fuckin' see it. Not good, not good."

ESSIE SAW the letter right off as the only light in the house was the desk lamp shining down on it. Out of breath and taut-eyed her long fingers tore at the envelope and when it didn't come apart fast enough she cursed the paper.

NATHAN WAITED by the dock railing where he had met Dane earlier that day. He felt as if the dark eyes of the world were upon him. The backs of his hands hurt, his coat collar was up against the chill.

Dane came up beside him smoking. "Another night, another boat," he said.

Nathan answered with an unspoken nod.

CHAPTER SIXTY-SEVEN

NATHAN WAS ALONE when he saw a man in a blue wind-breaker and baseball cap approach along the shoreline walk. He was heavyset and when he passed a strolling couple he kept his eyes to the ground. As he came alongside Nathan he said, "Mr. Greene. Nathan Greene?"

Nathan turned. "Mr. Carter."

"Yes."

Mr. Carter put out his hand to shake, but the motion had a spurious feel to it. As they shook Nathan waved Dane over. Mr. Carter turned to see Dane rise from a bench and approach them.

"This is a friend of mine," said Nathan. "He'll be coming along."

Mr. Carter looked the boy over, concerned. "It was my understanding that I was bringing you."

"I don't know if I can handle this emotionally," Nathan answered.

Mr. Carter took off his baseball cap and scratched his narrow balding skull. It was nothing more than a time-consuming gesture. Dane heard a prop engine somewhere out above the San Joaquin. It was flying low and seemed, from what Dane heard, to be maneuvering a long, slow arc. Dane did his best not to look.

"He's just here for support, Mr. Carter."

"Yes, I'm sure."

"See it from my perspective, Mr. Carter. How difficult this is going to be for me."

Mr. Carter put on an understanding expression as he looked from man to man. His thin moustache had been dyed black in an attempt to downplay his age and he had the empty smile of a lifelong pitchman. It could be him, thought Dane. The man on the boat that first day with Damon Romero and Shane Fenn. It could be the man Essie saw at the Boyz.' Merton, it might be Merton.

"I don't want any trouble," said Mr. Carter.

"You'll take us to meet the gentleman," said Nathan. "We'll listen, we'll leave. And my friend"—this was said with deferential seriousness—"will take care of all the details."

Mr. Carter reiterated, "I just don't want any trouble."

"You want to strip-search us?" said Nathan.

"Jesus Christ." Mr. Carter appeared stunned by the suggestion. Nervously he looked around to see if there had been anyone nearby enough to have heard. "I just don't want any trouble."

THEY FOLLOWED Mr. Carter back down the shoreline walk. They could hear music coming through the open door of one of the bars; alongside a berthed trawler men were laughing and drinking beer. Every time they passed someone Mr. Carter averted his eyes.

The boat had been docked by Humphrey's Restaurant, which was on pylons out over the river. You could see from the lights strung along the outdoor patio that the wind was starting to gust inland.

When they reached the daycruiser, Dane knew. Painted on the transom it read—*THE PLYMOUTH ROC.*

BEFORE ESSIE'S Futura had gotten from the dock site up that gravel incline to the road she was on her cellular. The hand that held the steering wheel also held the diamonds. As the phone rang her eyes wouldn't let go of the rearview mirror as the little island and house on Disappointment Slough disappeared into darkness but for the beacon light and that obelisk of a windmill. But when that was gone, she felt a piece of her heart just tear.

WHEN CHARLES' cell phone rang it surprised him. He looked at his watch. Could it all have happened this fast? The bar was two deep with drinking traffic when he answered.

"Mr. Gill?"

"Who is this?"

"It's Essie."

"Essie. . . . didn't recognize your voice." People were leaning over his shoulder trying to get the bartender's attention. "I'm surprised to get a call from you on my cellular. Is everything all right?" He waited for an answer that did not come. "Essie? Can you hear me?" Again no answer.

He looked at the phone's screen, the line was still open. Confused, he got up and excused his way through the drinking and bar talk till he found a vacant crease of wall space. "Essie? Is everything all right? Has something happened to Nathan?"

He wondered if she might think it odd later that he so quickly asked if something—

"We know what you've done," she said.

Charles' expression changed slightly, as if he had stumbled upon some oddity of behavior he did not quite understand. "Essie?"

"You are a money launderer and a murderer." Essie had made her voice emotionally merciless. "And we can prove it and I'm going to expose you right now. You're fucking finished! Do you hear me!?"

THE DAYCRUISER powered its way up Broad Slough. Mr. Carter was at the helm, Nathan sat across from him at the tiny dinette. Dane stood just outside the open cabin holding onto the ladder that led up to the flying bridge. He was listening for the plane, and watching the sky.

The wind was carrying the mist inland more quickly now, and

from Birds Landing to the graveyard of Collinsville the sky had all but disappeared.

Where Broad Slough met the Sacramento Mr. Carter took the port engine out of gear and that boat started to turn downriver. They were moving away from the Delta and toward the bays or the ocean beyond.

CHAPTER SIXTY—EIGHT

THE BOAT KEPT making headway west through Suisun Bay. Off their port side Dane could just see bits of ebonied shore and the flickering dome lights of an Amtrak as it sped through the low misty hills of Contra Costa. Flashpoints of light were there then gone, there then gone, there then gone.

Nathan looked back at Dane, his stare reflected some conflict. When he turned away Dane took a chance and eased the transceiver from his coat pocket and turning sideways to use his body as a shield managed to set it on the cabin roof where it was only inches from his face.

He yelled to Mr. Carter, "How much farther?"

IT WAS the first thing Paul had managed to pick up on his headset since Dane had pulled off the road back on Sherman Island.

The crackling was terrible. Caruso held down the squelch button on his keypad. He heard the boy again. The voice was distant and rough, but he heard him say "How much farther?"

"Jesus, shit." Paul was still circling above Antioch. He hadn't even known they'd left the marina.

THE WIND was making steering difficult and Mr. Carter had not answered Dane. Nathan got up and leaned over his shoulder and more bluntly and loudly asked the same question.

"Just a few more miles," said Mr. Carter. "On a houseboat."

Nathan sat back down. He was growing more and more anxious.

Mr. Carter had been following the channel markers when off the starboard bow Roe Island appeared as a shadowy nightflat expanse whose trees looked like burnt hands of bone reaching up out of the marshland.

Waves of mist coming in from the coast almost completely obscured Preston Point and it was here Mr. Carter ruddered that daycruiser north and Nathan now knew they were powering toward an isolated stretch of Grizzly Bay. For the first time in his life Nathan questioned the General.

The weather had worsened quickly forcing the boat to slow and it was only moments later that Dane first saw them off the port beam. There at the edges of a deepening fog, their steel monolithic bows looked to be something more of legend or dream.

Stark and faceless they were, one, then another, and another, and another. There could well have been hundreds moored there.

The daycruiser had to pass along and beneath these freighter hulls which rose up and disappeared into dead gray clouds. They were like some marvelous and terrible giants from the origins of time. Watching, waiting. The sound emanating from those silent and empty hulls one could imagine coming from the heart of the world.

CARUSO WAS flying at just over a thousand feet following the Sacramento into the Delta. He tried to close out all the engine noise as he listened on that headset, looking down between the mist, threading his way back and forth over the river, when through a tunnel of sparks he heard Dane's voice. "What . . . all . . .'ose . . . moored . . . fri . . ."

Static killed it. He pressed the squelch button on the keypad. There was someone else talking but it was just voice gravel. He banked the plane hoping to clear a little reception.

Dane again. Still through a tunnel of sparks. Slightly clearer,

but just. Paul pressed the headset against his ear. "Th're . . .
must . . . be . . .'undreds . . . of . . . freight . . . moored . . . here . . ."

The mothball fleet at Benecia. It had to be, it better be. They
were at the entrance to Grizzly Bay. Caruso scowled in panic. He
had guessed wrong.

CHAPTER SIXTY-NINE

Ivy HAD JUST opened her car door when she saw Essie's Falcon speeding toward the driveway. She waved and then realized the Falcon wasn't stopping. Ivy jumped backwards and the Falcon hit the door head-on tearing it from the chassis.

Ivy had managed to get around the front end of her car in time. Her face turned away, her eyes closed, her mouth shunted upwards as Essie's Falcon braked and she came staggering out right for Ivy. Ivy had no idea until—

"You helped kill Taylor, didn't you!"

Essie was panting for breath.

" 'Cause he found out you were a fucking money launderer!!"

Essie shouted at the top of her voice. Before Ivy could react Essie hit her across the face. Ivy lost her balance trying to keep from being hit again and fell back against the garage door.

"We know everything," Essie screamed as she kicked and hit and hit and kicked at Ivy. "We know about you . . . and Charles . . . and Nathan . . . and the Fenns . . ."

A neighbor of Ivy's and his college-age son who lived in the next town house came running across the lawn after hearing the accident and screaming.

"We know about Damon Romero . . . and Merrit Merton . . ."

The neighbors grabbed Essie who fought violently and Ivy got loose and ran back up the walkway to her front door.

"We know you helped kill Taylor . . ." Essie shouted loud enough for the people in the complex to hear her . . . "We know you're a money launderer . . . Listen to me . . . Everyone!"

The men were trying to control Essie but she broke away and

Ivy shut the front door behind her. She could hear Essie screaming. Ivy's eyesight warped and her body panicked and she couldn't
find a breath anywhere.

Essie turned to the men who were spreading their arms like
riot-control cops to keep her from Ivy's door. But Essie ran back
to her car instead shouting, "You're protecting a murderer . . . and
a money launderer . . . and who knows what else—"

The men raced after her, but Essie managed to get into her car
and lock the door, and as they grabbed at the handle and tried
to get in the half-open driver's door window Essie gassed the Falcon out of the driveway swerving across the lawn, her hand pressed
to the car horn and still shouting, "She helped to murder someone . . . The police will be coming! Do you hear me . . . the police
will be coming for you!"

WHEN THEY passed Garrett Point at the northwest tip of Ryer
Island Mr. Carter said, "I'm gonna radio we're coming."

As he stretched toward the radio Dane said, "Don't do that."

Mr. Carter turned around in the helmsman's seat. Dane had
slipped the transceiver back into his coat pocket and was stepping
into the cabin, his hair and shoulders wet with nightmist.

"It's no big deal," said Mr. Carter. As his hand flattened across
the console Dane smashed the back of Mr. Carter's fingers with
the butt of his gun.

Mr. Carter cupped his hand against his chest. "What is going
on here?" Nervously he looked to Nathan for an answer but Nathan was staring at the gun in Dane's hand, caught even more off
guard than Mr. Carter.

"Let the boat idle," said Dane.

"She'll drift," said Mr. Carter.

"Put it in idle and hold on."

Carter did as he was told. Dane stepped back. The boat had
begun to rock slightly and Dane grabbed the open cabin doorframe for balance. "Ask Mr. Carter if he also uses the name Merton, Merrit Merton?" Nathan's look shifted to Mr. Carter. "Ask him

334

if he knows Damon Romero, the witness at the berm the night your son was killed." The lines down Nathan's face deepened. "Ask him if he and Tommy Fenn didn't fly to Mexico to find us and kill us." Nathan's eyes became like black flues. "Ask him if tonight is what he said it is."

Nathan did not have to ask, the answer was Mr. Carter's shocked and ashen expression. Nathan rose up, squeezing from the tiny dinette seat. He stood over Mr. Carter, holding onto the back of the helmsman's chair for balance. Mr. Carter recoiled slightly, unsure of what Nathan was going to do.

"Take off your clothes," said Nathan. "Stand up and take them all off."

"The boat will drift," said Mr. Carter in a low and frightened voice.

"Then let it fuckin' drift."

Mr. Carter stood. While he removed his hat and windbreaker Nathan walked up to Dane. Mr. Carter removed his shoes, one took a sock with it. Nathan had hold of the opposite cabin doorframe to keep his balance. "How did you find out all this?" he asked Dane.

Both men swayed with the slight pitching of the boat. Each man a mind unto itself, a force unto itself. Nathan screamed, "Fuckin' answer me," and his voice echoed out from the boat and across the damp and sourceless dark.

Mr. Carter stood with his pants open and half down his hips trembling, watching.

"I wasn't afraid when you had a gun," said Dane. "So what makes you think I'd be afraid now?"

Nathan stepped out of the cabin. He looked back at Mr. Carter who was holding his open pants up by the belt. "Get undressed."

Nathan walked to the stern and sat. The wind swept the current against the topsides. From far, far down the channel came the throated cry of a foghorn. Why have I allowed this to be done to me, thought Nathan. How have I done this?

Mr. Carter waited now in his underwear and one sock. "The rest," Nathan said.

335

Mr. Carter removed the sock. His skin was the color of raw milk and pimpled with cold and then like some ashamed Adam he slid off his shorts. He dropped them on the cabin floor.

Dane stood silently in the doorway between both men.

"We come into this world naked," said Nathan. "And we go out—"

"Please," Mr. Carter begged, "how can I fix this?"

FLESH WAS in her kitchen morosely staring at a health conscious nuked something, a two-day-old half of a tuna sandwich and a glass of chardonnay, otherwise known as the overworked single's excuse for a dinner, when headlights washed over the living room wall.

On reaching the living room Flesh saw Essie scurry from the porch after having rung the bell. Flesh chased after the Falcon as it backed out of the driveway burning gravel and taking a part of the ill-watered lawn with it.

As the car backspun into the empty street Essie pointed to the house and yelled, "On your porch," then sped away and Flesh was left standing at the sidewalk's edge in a sweatshirt and men's pajama bottoms, completely baffled.

It wasn't until she'd stepped back up on the porch that she noticed a manila envelope sticking out of the mail slot.

She pushed her meal aside and spilled the envelope's contents out on the kitchen table. There was a note from Essie with a list of names that looked to be written in the clumsy script of someone driving. There was a folded section of discoloring newspaper, and when her long burgundy fingernails peeled apart the aluminum foil, there were the diamonds.

HOW LONG do you think you'd last in that water tonight?"

Mr. Carter did not need to look far to know. "I wouldn't," he said.

Nathan scooped up the clothes around that naked man's feet.

He left the cabin and flung them overboard, then he returned.

He pushed Mr. Carter down into the helmsman's seat. His flesh folded like putty around the waist. "Keep this boat from drifting. Now, what's to happen out there?"

"At the houseboat Damon Romero will tie off. You'll go over to talk. I'll stay here. The Fenns are waiting."

"I'm to be killed on that houseboat."

"Not there I think."

"And all this is Charles?"

"From Charles . . . There's more." Mr. Carter was shivering miserably, pathetically. He could barely hold the wheel. "That prosecutor, the one with polio. He was taken tonight."

Nathan's face covered the mouth of his dusky movie theater face. "Why?" he asked.

Dane thought Mr. Carter must not have heard because he kept watching ahead, working the wheel. Nathan kicked him in the hip. Mr. Carter's whole body locked up under the blow.

"Why?" Nathan demanded.

"Charles had set the meeting." Mr. Carter was breathing like a man on the verge of a heart attack. "He waited where there would be witnesses." His dyed moustache puffed on each exhalation mimicking the gills of a fish. "Charles will make a show of how the prosecutor never—"

Dane watched from the cabin door as Nathan kicked Mr. Carter again. The fat around the man's ribs and stomach shook violently.

"What was the meeting about?" Dane asked.

"About him." Mr. Carter's eyes went to Nathan.

Nathan squeezed back down in the dinette seat.

"The General must have lied to you," Dane said.

The moment, if true, was devastating in its completeness. Nathan had served the old man like a son and to think he'd been destroyed like . . . a son.

"And Ivy lied to you. She knows this man. I'm sure of it."

Nathan looked at Mr. Carter. "Do you know her?" he asked.

Mr. Carter nodded imperceptibly.

"Does she know of this?"

Mr. Carter shrugged.

The depth to which Nathan's choices were being made for him was a mirror of true despair and tragedy. He knew to go back and leave this undone he could well be undone by it. To go on, to see it done, meant more had to be done after that, and more after that, and more again. He saw now with an awful clarity that he was no better than the fool king who had to push the rock up that hill every day only to have it slip back down against his will, leaving him to fail at a futile task over and over and over until the universe itself had become forgotten. He asked Dane, "Why didn't you tell me this *before* we got on the boat?"

"Because I wanted you to get on the boat."

Nathan slammed his fist down on the dinette table.

"Do you know how to use a gun?"

"Do you mean will I use a gun?" said Dane.

Nathan again slammed his fist down on the dinette table thinking himself manhandled and manipulated.

"Am I safe with you . . . is what I want to know."

Dane's look was distant as the stars. "I'm all there is. Don't you understand that yet? *I'm* all there is."

CHAPTER SEVENTY

CARUSO WAS CHASING static and it unsettled him. He had the Cessna flying west over Contra Costa till he reached the toll bridge that crossed the straights from Martinez to Benecia. He knew they could not have traveled this far, this fast by boat. If they were still on a boat. So, he began the backtrack.

He was maxed to any sound coming through the headset. He had been flying at only eighteen hundred feet. The lights along the river, and the buildings and roads that spread into the landscape, were touched with the illusory and to spot a boat, to make it out especially if it were running down the center of the channel, would be negligible, if not impossible. So he dropped down till he was flying dangerously low.

He saw his face in the dull cockpit glass with its darkened angles of concern. He was only minutes from the mothball fleet and that isolated inlet known as Grizzly Bay but there wasn't even voice gravel he could cling to for hope.

NATHAN SHUT off the cabin light and in the darkness leaned down and told Mr. Carter very quietly to "Radio them."

Mr. Carter was shivering so badly it was left to Dane to reach for the radio mike and hand it to him.

Nathan's eyes never left Mr. Carter. "We're here."

Moments later Damon Romero answered, "I heard the motor. I can't see your cabin lights."

"They went out," whispered Nathan. "Tell him."

"They glitched," said Mr. Carter.

Dane watched through the cabin window with Nathan just behind his shoulder. There were no night sounds but those inboard cats turning their way through water that looked like blue black ice. They watched the gloom as it smoked and seeped its way across the water. Sometimes the wind would open tunnels of darkness and as it did one time Dane saw the boat and pointed. It was there for brief seconds, then gone.

It was maybe seventy yards away. It sat darkened in that empty bay save for a single square of burning light from a small curtained window in the salon. The houseboat looked to be a ninety-footer with radar arches fore and aft on the upper sundeck, which was partly covered with a canvas roof.

Dane turned to Nathan. "What are you going to do when you tie off?"

Nathan asked Mr. Carter, "Do you have any weapons on board?"

"None." Mr. Carter saw that Nathan didn't believe him. "Look for yourself."

That short fat body was shaking with cold so bad it could hardly keep at the helm.

"Cold, isn't it?" said Nathan, as he went and squeezed down into the dinette seat. It would be only minutes now. Nathan stared at the back of his bruised and swollen hands. When he looked up Dane stood across the dinette table watching him. Without a word Dane took his gun, set it on the table then slid it toward Nathan. Nathan's hand clamped down on it.

"What do you have to protect yourself?"

"Just a good set of eyes," said Dane.

The statement went through Nathan like an acid. "Fuck you right to hell," he said.

ESSIE SPED across the tarmac. The planes and hangars were draped in silence. She was driving so fast Sancho Maria saw the Falcon hit the curb outside The Burrow. As Essie was running to the bar, she saw a flashlight beam moving across its darkened interior to meet her.

At the door, out of breath, frantic, Essie begged of Maria, "Where's Paul?"

Sancho Maria pointed that flashlight beam to the sky.

As THEY drew closer the houseboat materialized out of a breached mist. It *was* a ninety-footer, all white. The canvas sundeck roof and railing covers were deep, deep burgundy. There was a satellite dish on the forward radar arch, plastic chairs and potted plants decorated the double-plated bow deck. There were fore and aft stairwells and the art graphics painted on the hull between them in burgundy and deep blue read: FOREVER BOATS. It was perfectly suited for the awaiting deception.

Mr. Carter had eased back on the throttle and reversed the propellers. The daycruiser began to slow. Nathan was just outside the cabin door. Dane was inside the cabin squatting almost to one knee so he could watch out the portside windows and beat any possibility at being seen.

The curtain covering that small square of light on the houseboat pulled aside. A man's silhouette watching shook its hand in the slightest gesture of a wave.

"Is that Romero?" asked Nathan.

"Yes," said Mr. Carter.

Nathan waved back to let Romero know he saw, nodded to let him know he was coming aboard.

Flesh WAS in the bedroom tugging on a boot and talking into her cellular, urgent and rudely fast. "Go fuckin' knock on Roy's door right now. Get dressed." Her cordless phone rang. "He could be getting the best blow job in the world, but he answers when I beep. Now do it!"

She grabbed at the cordless on the bed stand. Her tone edged back to an urgent politeness. "Hello, Sergeant." She tried to stomp her foot down into that unwilling boot. "Thanks for calling back so fast." She hurried to the kitchen, hobbling with a half-on boot.

341

"You handled the Taylor Greene investigation last summer."

She grabbed her car keys off the table where her dinner sat uneaten. "Well I've just received some very disturbing information from a trustworthy source about the case. Very disturbing and I believe it demands immediate action. Yes . . . do you have a fax?"

She put the car keys in her mouth. Her hand swept across the kitchen counter looking for something to write with and whatever was in its path ended up on the floor. When she was done, when she got that goddamn boot on, she ran to the front door cursing, "Fuck you, Roy . . . I *was* right."

THE DAYCRUISER and the houseboat were practically parallel. Damon Romero had come out on the bow deck. Nathan had gone forward to throw him a spring line so they could tie off. Few words were spoken. Dane heard Romero say something like "Thank you for coming" and "I know this isn't easy."

Dane had kept low in the cabin only shifting his position back so he was right behind Mr. Carter. He put his hand on Mr. Carter's spine at the base of his skull. The man's flesh was like ice, but even shivering as it was, the muscles completely jammed when they felt Dane's hand.

"I have a weapon," Dane whispered.

"What do I need to do not to be hurt?"

"Could you make the shore here by swimming?"

The voice stumbled, "I . . . no. It's cold. Too—"

With the first line tied off Nathan took the after spring line and tossed it to Romero so he could pull the daycruiser up against the houseboat fenders to allow for boarding.

"The prosecutor," Dane asked, "would he be over there?"

He could feel Mr. Carter swallow. "He might be."

"Alive?"

"I don't know. I just don't know."

Nathan came back to the stern. Dane saw him look toward the cabin interior as if to make contact before he crossed. The darkness left that an impossibility.

Am I my brother's keeper . . . I wonder.

As Romero pulled in the line, as Nathan waited for the line to be tied off, as Dane waited for Nathan to cross, from the sky came the muffled sound of a propeller.

Nathan crossed. From the PLYMOUTH *ROC* to that FOREVER was one short step. The men shook hands. Small talk followed. A head dipped solemnly. They walked side by side to the sliding glass doors. Dane saw Nathan's hand slip into the pocket where he had the gun. Mr. Carter begged, "What can I do to be let go?"

As the men disappeared into the salon Dane told him, "There's no answer for that one."

They were faced with the sound of the water and the dull yellow light from that curtained window. There were streaming shadows where the glow reflected up off the water against each hull. Dane's hand could feel Mr. Carter's body begin to edge, lean, press away from the seat as if it might revolt. His free hand went down to the knife in his boot and in the time that took, in the short space of a few breaths he heard Shane Fenn yell. There was a shot, and a voice hobbled with pain, a shotgun blast; they were all part of the same wave of ferocious seconds that had Mr. Carter trying to escape from his seat.

One of the shots must have hit a propane tank in the salon galley because that dull yellow window exploded into an inferno of colors.

The air was drenched with shards of glass and shanks of aluminum siding. A body was flung onto and over the bow deck like a broken puppet. The patio chairs and potted plants were catapulted into the bay and the daycruiser was ravaged by a swell of debris that tore through the windows in one concussive swell lifting it right up out of the water.

FAR UP the bay Caruso saw a dragon tongue of flame burst through the cloud cover all scarlet and yellow that the wind threw into a thousand burning match tips. It was silent to the eye, but in that headset Paul thought his eardrums had been shattered.

Then the bay went black again, just as fast.

CHAPTER SEVENTY—ONE

IN A SMOKING haze Dane tried to stagger to his feet but he might as well have been climbing uphill. There was fire, he could see it. There was the noxious odor of melting fiberglass and carpet. The cabin of the daycruiser was a ruined listing oblique. He tried to clear away the disorder and stand using the dinette table for leverage.

Through the blown-out cabin window Dane saw the daycruiser was half up on the houseboat's bow deck trying to mount it, surging and sliding back, its flare being scored apart.

As his head turned groggily sideways he saw Mr. Carter was draped over the throttles. Dane pitched toward the helmsman's seat, got hold of it, got hold of Carter's shoulder, grappled over the lifeless weight of fat, and pulled. The arms and legs glided back like a dancer's taking the head with it. The turtled body sagged. Dane pulled down the throttles and the daycruiser's waterline ground its way back into the bay with a broken propeller shaft that sounded like steel hammers slamming together.

Dane made his way to the stern wobbling under the boat's sway. His mind tried to pull together all the pieces of that destroyed frieze he looked at. He yanked the transceiver loose from his pocket as the daycruiser began to sink.

"Paul—"

Caruso's voice came back crackling. "I saw the fire. What—"

Dane held onto a portside cleat for support. "We're tied to a houseboat in Grizzly Ba—"

"Can you hear me?! I saw the fire."

The houseboat had a blistered hole aft of the helm where flames spit and dotted and smoke poured forth from the galley and the canvas roof on the sundeck rippled with fire.

"Dane, can you—"

"I have to see if everyone on the boat is dead."

The Cessna swept down into the cloud cover. Streaks of gray blew past the windows.

"Paul, can you hear me? Your engines are close—"

Caruso could see just the black cold dark of that knifing current.

"You're close—"

The clouds cleared and as Paul scanned the cabin windows in desperation he saw off his right wing in the snapshot night a two-boat tangle of carnage. "Holy shit!" He throttled skyward and banked. "Do you still have the strobe I gave you?"

"I have to get on that houseboat."

"What?"

"The Fenns took Roy Pinter tonight."

"It's you I'm concerned about. Not that—"

Caruso could hear the boy's voice was rocky. "He might be on that boat alive."

"That houseboat is sitting on two hundred gallons of gasoline."

"I've got to—"

"Put the strobe on. And I'll come down and try to—"

"I'm crossing over, Paul."

An ENGINEER for the Southern Pacific was taking a train across the railway bridge when he saw a disturbing flash of light far up Grizzly Bay. The harbormaster for the Suisun City Marina saw the same flash of light as he was driving home down Grizzly Island Road. At Pelican Point a Department of Fish and Game worker was walking her dogs in a swale just back from the shoreline when she heard what could not be mistaken for anything but an explosion.

It was 12:01 when the first calls came in to the Coast Guard station at Port Charles. They would reach Grizzly Bay at 12:14 and bear witness to the final moments of a tragedy.

FROM A listing PLYMOUTH *ROC* to the deck of that burning FOREVER was just one hard leap of faith. And Dane took it.

When he hit his legs almost buckled. The bow was strewn with broken glass and twisted remnants of metallic doorframe, with chunks of torn-out fiberglass. The salon entrance was now an open mouth of smoke and fire licks.

Dane did the best he could covering his face as he measured his way into that reek of carnage and burning plastic. He choked his way through the detritus of a living room. A couch had been flung into the bar, there were sparks overhead from ravaged wiring. The first of the dead he saw was Damon Romero. He lay bent oddly under an overturned chair with a piece of metal tanking through the back of his skull.

Dane turned, gasping for bits of air. The transceiver was still in his pocket and he could hear Paul calling to him. Dane's eyes blinked and watered. The sparks overhead hissed and when another wire burst the ceiling looked as if it were a sky of summer lightning. He needed to make the bedrooms, which were aft. They were the only places Roy could be if he were on board at all. Then Dane saw Nathan.

He was sitting on the floor with his back against the wall where the explosion had thrown him across the sixty foot salon. The eyes were open and those untouched dusky movie theater looks had an expression of staring off into the quiet. Nathan's pants at the thigh were torn and charred. Edges along the rip were still on fire and there was a pungent stench from the burning flesh beneath.

Dane found himself kneeling down and using his hand to stamp out the fire as if all pain were enough now that Nathan were dead. When Dane stood he had to find his way to a window. He took the transceiver from his pocket and hammered the glass to have at some air. He put his mouth to that pigeonhole of sharp edges and breathed. He could feel the cold damp cleanly fill his lungs. And he could hear Caruso shouting desperately into that hand-held radio. "Are you all right? Talk to me!"

CHAPTER SEVENTY—TWO

ONE OF THE airport managers was a fixed-base operator. There was a scanner in his office and Sancho Maria had a key to that office.

Essie stood in the open doorway while Sancho Maria, who knew the frequency Paul used on his transceivers, tried to hone in. Essie leaned against the door with her arms crossed. She stared at the sky as if married to something in its shadows. She told Dane silently, almost as a plead, "If you can hear me, we'll be all right. If you can hear me, we'll be all right."

Sancho Maria was having trouble hooking into the signal because of a run of cross traffic that had begun about an explosion and a boat on fire up in Grizzly Bay.

Essie quicked it back into the tiny office, pulling up a chair and sitting close beside Sancho Maria. In the dead center of the night they listened to those faraway voices all wrapped in static both knowing Grizzly Bay was only miles from Antioch.

AS DANE started toward the bedroom hall he told Caruso, "Everyone is dead here."

"Get-out-of-that-boat. So I can—"

Dane yelled back through a cough. "I have to see—"

There was another burst of wiring that sent blue white sparklers of filament across the room. Another set of curtains ignited. The wind was drafting the smoke in endless directions. The empty corridor going aft seemed to be floating in murk. As Dane put the transceiver back in his coat pocket he could hear the engine propeller practically strafing the upper deck as it passed over.

He took the safety strobe he'd clipped onto the back of his belt that Paul had made him bring and aimed it down the hallway. He turned it on. It burned white and all the broken glass and mirror pieces in the carpet and along the walls reflected back a thousand eyes of light that guided him.

The Fenns. He'd seen one body lifted overboard. But the other—

When he reached a bedroom he sent the beacon in first. It made a cautionary sweep of the quarters and in that slash of light he saw an unmade bed, a pile of filthy clothes and closed drapes. The next room the beam ran was a cuddy of mirrored walls with a treadmill, a stationary bike, a television and a body wrapped in a plastic tarp.

It lay there as if it were just another casual addition to the room. Behind the strobe and into that hazy cuddy Dane moved through endless light blazing mirrored corridors toward an endless line of corpses while Caruso's voice squawked from that transceiver in his pocket. "Get out of that fuckin' houseboat so I can try and get you off of there. Do you hear me?"

Dane knelt. The daycruiser had begun to keel and its twin propellers turned into blades that sent metallic grinding shivers through the houseboat's hull and it echoed and shook as if fiends and furies were trying to score their way free to have at him.

Dane pulled back the plastic tarp which crackled as it went. Roy Pinter was already turning color. His eyes were closed, his tongue protruded slightly from between tightened lips. The look he wore for eternity was suffering and sadly foolish.

If it wasn't for the strobe Dane would not have seen what he could not hear above the screeching madness against the hull. As he turned to stand and go the light caught an endless line of lunging bloody Shanes who wielded a shotgun barrel like a scythe.

Dane hunched and leapt away. He fell as that mirrored wall took an awful blow from the stock head on. An endless line of Danes clawed and crabbed over a tarped corpse skimming corners and twisting sideways to elude the madness of the dying and disordered coiled driving arms that hammered and whipped and bludgeoned that broken shotgun down at where the fragments of a form had been.

The treadmill arm was severed. The television screen burst on impact and toppled over. The stock sheared and clipped but kept smashing those walls of mirror with every follow-through. The endless line of bodies warped and tore with each new crack and shattered hole of glass. In that darting confusion forms conceived and reconceived themselves in a labyrinth of blazing half black shapes. The funnels of light bent and moved, they hitched and jarred, they arced and fell like wild comets in a chaos.

Driven into a corner of desperate seconds Dane managed to unsheath the knife from his boot as the shotgun swept down on him. An endless line of hands rose to meet the blow. The forearm bone shattered and the strobe flew loose. Dane could feel the crack all the way into his skull and an endless line of double-bladed knives retaliated upwards.

He could hear the flesh under Shane's sternum tear like cloth. As Dane juked backwards he could see Shane's hands try to find the knife. They couldn't. Endless bodies dropped in an avalanche to their knees. Air sucked through that open slough of a wound. Shane's face held on to darker curses as it toppled over, trying to stanch the blood.

Dane used his good arm to lift the broken one and get it against his chest. He used the good arm to reach the strobe and wrap its fingers around the strap. He leaned forward and lifted himself toward Shane against the shrill coarse echo of propeller blades.

Endless beams of light moved with him in to catch both faces and Dane whispered, "Hey, doomslinger, I'm going to watch you die through the eyes of a boy you've killed."

And Dane did. But all that was left of Shane Fenn was a mortal wound where the past leaked out. The eyes gradually rolled down into the darkened cell of the skull, like a boat or a body as it sank beneath the waves.

CHAPTER SEVENTY—THREE

THERE WAS NO way back to the bow deck through the salon. Too much smoke, too much fire. Too much in pain. Dane held his broken arm and labored aft to the exterior stairway where he intended to go up to the sundeck and cross it to reach the forward bow. If he could.

Paul was in another descent when that strobe just appeared burning a hole in the fog like the tip of a candle. Bright and separate from the flames. Moving.

ESSIE'S CELLULAR rang. She scrambled for her purse. It was Flesh. "Where are you?"

"Rio Vista Airport."

Flesh was in her office faxing Sergeant Farr at the Tracy headquarters. "When you asked about Damon Romero, I knew then something—"

SUDDENLY PAUL'S voice came through on the scanner scratchy and shouting, "I can see you. I can see you. Are you all right?"

Sancho Maria slapped her hand on the desk to get Essie's attention. "I have them!"

"Flesh," said Essie, "Hold on!"

351

THE FINGERS of that broken arm were laced through the strobe's braided strap. In the other hand Dane held the transceiver. He crossed the upper deck hunched to one side and fighting off the first waves of shock. The canvas roof that covered part of the upper deck was a burning effigy of cloth streamers that singed the air around him. The satellite dish hung from the radar arch by wires that sparked and burned his cheek.

"I'm trying to reach the forward bow. Can you hear me, Paul?"

"Are you all right?"

ESSIE WAS on the line with Flesh. "They're up in Grizzly Bay. We can hear them on the scanner."

With all its currents of cross traffic and shifting frequencies the pain came through when Dane answered, "My arm's broken . . . Paul. Can you hear?"

"We've got to get you off that boat."

Essie kept talking to Flesh while she listened at the scanner, then Dane said, "Paul . . . Roy Pinter is dead. I saw him on the houseboat."

Essie covered the phone with her hand as if to protect Flesh, at least for the moment. She looked at Sancho Maria to make sure she had heard right.

FLESH WAS pressing the elevator button talking right over Essie's sudden silence.

"I'm going to the Coast Guard station."

"Francie—"

"I've got some calls to make."

"Francie—"

"But leave your line clear, all right." Again Flesh thumbed the elevator button hard. "I still haven't gotten hold of—"

"Francie. Listen to me. I think something terrible has happened."

Flesh stood in the dark and listened. She heard the words, but tried to rearrange the unfathomable brutal fact of them.

A janitor mopping his way slowly through the graveyard shift heard a woman's cry flood the silent corridors, saying only, "How?"

ONE OF the daycruiser's inboards blew. It sent a rip of flames across the water from its keeling hull. The houseboat shook. Dane was thrown against the forward stairwell railing. His broken arm hit the metal bannister full force and the strobe dropped and tumbled down the steps.

He could hear Paul yelling into the transceiver as he fell to his knees on the bow deck. He pulled the strobe toward him using the hand with the transceiver, scraping it along over all that broken glass and pieces of shorn metal. "I'm here," he said. "On the bow deck."

He waved the strobe, then slipped the fingers of his broken arm through the strap.

SKIMMING THE bay Caruso saw that matchlight beam arc then arc again in the illusion of a wave. "I'm coming down," he said. "I'll land on the water. Get close as I can." He pulled back on the column and that Cessna began to climb so he could right himself for an approach.

"Hold on," he told Dane, "I'll get you home."

Dane was on his hands and knees. He looked around him. One boat was sinking in the cold inlet, the other was burning itself away into the sky. The emptiness about both was a world awash in wreckage and what looked to be the head and shoulder of a man.

Dane set the transceiver and strobe on the deck. He slid off his coat, bending his back as best he could so as not to move that bad arm. He picked through the debris for a piece of metal to use as a splint. He ripped loose the lining of his coat and began the excruciatingly painful turns of cloth it took to tighten the metal rod against that bleeding stretch of broken bone.

Dane fought back the cold, the shock. He clenched the strap

around that beam, forcing his fingers to concentrate through the pain. To keep himself from passing out. He used the battered railing to stand.

The sky was filled with ash. Dane's eyes burned from smoke and chemical grime. He pinned them to that inclement bay of fog and distance from where the Cessna's engines came.

And there at the margins of a gaze, where all memory gathers, where no precautions avail you, where you wait naked for the unseen, he had met the world and found himself.

All the universe is fought out within the few feet of flesh we each wear. All that comes against us, comes from that alone. It is the labyrinth within a labyrinth within a labyrinth.

"If I failed," he said. "I'm sorry. I, tried—"

"Talk to me," said Paul. "Why aren't you answering?"

Dane looked down at the transceiver. He thought he had been. "Talk to me."

Dane moved the beam toward the sound of those propellers. "I'm still here," he said.

"I hear you now. You can't pass out, understand? You've got to get to the plane. So talk to me."

Dane tried to hold himself and that beam straight as a needle. "Speech is silver," he said, "but silence is golden."

The Cessna dropped down into that cloud cover.

The bow deck was growing hot from the fire. "I am a slow walker, but I never walk back."

Paul could see the water just beneath him. A cold and wrinkling black. He was current judging quick as he could. "Keep talking."

"Strike harder and twist the links—"

The strobe and the flames intensified. Details pieced together out of that dissolving mist. Caruso saw the wreckage all engulfed in smoke. He saw the strobe all engulfed in smoke. "Keep talking!"

"Where others' skills have failed. He can still invent—"

The Cessna was coming out of the gray, Dane saw it. Those fluted bottoms touched the water. The plane skimmed along kicking out great fumaroles of white froth. It was rushing to him against time.

The engine was pulling back, the nose rose slightly. A wave of air and spray blew over the wreckage driving back the smoke and fire. One of the floats shouldered the bow of that sinking day-cruiser. The Cessna lifted then hit back down on the water just yards from the burning houseboat.

Paul pulled off the headset and screamed out, leaning toward the cabin door, "Come on!"

Dane leapt into the water. The cold burst up through his body. Everything went black, then he was mouth-grabbing for air. The floats were just feet away. He paddled with one arm and his legs. Paul was watching the fire to make sure it didn't get to the wing. He couldn't see Dane but he could see the strobe's light clipping its way toward him.

The float rose with the current and Dane managed one lunge with his good arm but missed. As it dropped with the current he lunged again, but missed. As it rose Dane tried again and this time when the float lifted so did he.

It rolled back down and Dane pulled himself onto the float's flat top. He wormed around enough as it rose again to get hold of a strut. His head bent back. The cabin door was swinging loosely open a grasp away.

Then just as Paul screamed, "Come on!" the other inboard on that daycruiser blew.

THE EXPLOSION was the last thing Essie and Sancho Maria heard over the scanner. And no amount of body English Maria could work on those dials was going to get it back.

IT WAS 12:13 when the Coast Guard cruiser saw an explosion of sparks ray out through the mist. In that few seconds of pure burn they spotted the Cessna taking off.

It was moving, rising quickly. Above the fire, above the smoke. A hundred feet, two hundred feet. It was banking. It hit the cloud cover and then all they could see was a matchtip of light. A strobe tracer to mark its climb.

There was another explosion. Two hundred gallons' worth of gasoline in an aluminum and fiberglass houseboat of a drum. They could feel the shock on the Coast Guard cruiser and pieces of houseboat were flung across the bay as if propelled by lightning.

Everything lit, everything burned, everything went black. Then they saw that matchtip of light. It was falling, turning and tumbling down out of the blackness and into the sea. Until it was no more.

CHAPTER SEVENTY—FOUR

There is no pain you are receding
A distant ship, smoke on the horizon

Charles sat in the same studio, with the same music and the same clock on the wall as he had hours earlier. But now—

You are only coming through in waves
Your lips move but I can't hear what you're saying

There had been numerous messages on his answering machine from Essie, each one repeating the same awful mantra.

I caught a fleeting glimpse
Out of the corner of my eye

They had destroyed you once, they have destroyed you again.

This child is gone
The dream is gone

Roy's DEPARTMENTAL chief and her assistant arrived at the courthouse building by 1:00 A.M. Word of the disaster at Grizzly Bay had begun to filter out. A KRLK news truck was setting up on the shore road along Suisun Slough for the first on-site report. A KCAL news chopper was flying in from Oakland.

Flesh was in Roy's office manning the phones, trying to keep herself together. Any and all attempts to relieve her were met with angry and tearful outbursts of resistance.

She called their contact at Justice, as the diamonds in her possession were cut. The IRS and DEA were contacted, as there were possible issues of tax evasion. An attorney with whom Roy first worked and who'd joined the INS to become part of an HIDA team that handled domestic and international money laundering cases was celebrating his tenth wedding anniversary when the call came.

Within hours of this tragedy doors around it would open. Some would lead to answers. But others—

FIGHTING BACK her panic Ivy finally got hold of Charles; by the time she got off the phone her panic had become an abject and horrified numbness. She peeked through the blinds from a darkened room and watched her neighbors. The man and his college-age son were on their front lawn talking to a collection of other neighbors and pointing toward the garage where Ivy's car still sat in the driveway with its torn-off door just lying there.

The man and his son were reliving the fight with hand gestures and Ivy could hear them in her mind saying, "The girl was screaming, 'You're a murderer . . . and a money launderer . . . and the police will be coming.' "

Ivy closed the blinds, then went and collected every pill in the house. She put them in an ashtray. She ran a bath and set the ashtray down on the tub ledge. She took a decanter from the top of the wine rack and smashed it in the kitchen sink. She picked through the breakings for the right piece to slit her wrists.

A BLACK-AND-WHITE sent from Tracy raced past the golf course along Airport Road. Essie and Sancho Maria had picked up the first Coast Guard reports of wreckage and bodies in Grizzly Bay and a small unidentified plane that had managed a takeoff from the site just before the final explosion.

THE PRINCE OF DEADLY WEAPONS

Sancho Maria tried over and over to contact Paul by radio but something must have been damaged as it wasn't operative. She tried to get his frequency back on the scanner, but that was a frustrating failure. After all the hope she'd handed over earlier that night she needed a godly palmful of it right now for a safe return.

Essie saw the black-and-white coming up through the tie-downs. The officers had been sent by Sergeant Farr to begin the questioning of what Essie knew and if there were other evidence she may have in her possession.

They quickly discovered that the "unidentified plane in question" belonged to Paul Caruso. While they were passing this along to the Coast Guard a single prop began its approach toward the runway from over Liberty Island Road. It was 1:10 A.M.

As the Cessna landed they could see one wing was badly scarred from fire. After landing the women raced toward the plane as it rolled out. One of the officers held them back. The plane was now evidence in what was being viewed as a kidnapping and conspiracy murder case.

The second officer waited by the wing. His tie blew across his shoulder until the propeller spun itself still. One cabin door opened and Paul Caruso half climbed, half stumbled to the tarmac. It was left to the officer to keep him upright.

Sancho Maria tried to reach her husband but the first officer held her back. She explained to him in no uncertain terms her rights and his and when the other cabin door did not open Essie shouted, "Where's Dane?"

Caruso tried to get to his wife and Essie, to talk to them first, but the officer wouldn't allow it. "Did you pick someone up off one of the boats?"

"I did. Yes," he said.

"Where is he?"

Again he tried to get to the women, again he was prevented. Sancho Maria launched into a fiercer tirade about what she knew to be his rights.

"Where is he?" the officer repeated.

359

Paul looked at Maria, at Essie. He was trying to talk to them past the officer with his eyes, to explain with fragments of expression. "His arm was broken. We had to take off. I was trying to pull him into the plane . . . there was another explosion as we climbed."

He paused. The long, long night was overwhelming him, but he tried with the barest nod and breath to speak to Essie as he said, "He slipped through my hands . . . and fell."

CHAPTER SEVENTY—FIVE

As THE MORNING sun in all its cathedraled beauty touched the slips and berths along the channel at Benecia an idle pair of eyes saw drifting on the current what looked to be an arm taken from its rightful owner.

CLAUDIA WAS watching the news from her ocean-front suite in Coronado, California. The first thumbnail sequences glued together with video footage of the search and recovery operation in Grizzly Bay portrayed a vision of money laundering and recriminations. Of possible kidnapping and conspiracy. Of destruction and tragedy etched in sordid half-fact and surmise.

Claudia saw her husband being brought in for questioning and when the girls, who were in a connected suite, heard their father's name they came rushing in.

Claudia had turned off the television. One asked, "Was that Daddy they were talking about?"

"No," said Claudia.

AFTER ONE hour of nonresponse investigators entered Ivy's town house under probable cause. They saw her purse and car keys on the dining room table. They called her name, but got no answer. They found the broken decanter in the sink.

They began a search of that five-bedroom two-story showplace. In the master bath they came upon a tub filled with water, long since gone cold. An ashtray worth of pills waited on the ledge along with an untouched glass of wine.

It was not much longer before Ivy was discovered in a guest bedroom closet. She had been curled up there under a knot of clothes through so much of the night she had urinated on herself.

INVESTIGATORS CORDONED off the Fenns' house in The Meadows. The same had been done with Nathan's house and his offices at Discovery Bay. The house at Plymouth Cove, the one that allegedly belonged to Merrit Merton, was about to fall to the same fate.

Essie's garage drew a crowd of onlookers at the end of the block and from the apartments above and across the alley where neighbors drank their morning coffee and watched in shocked bewilderment as boxes were tagged and loaded into a police van.

WHEN FLESH reached the Rio Vista Airport investigators were working the Fenns' hangar. Representatives of the FBI were part of a small contingent in The Burrow coffee shop interrogating Paul Caruso who was, at this point, the only known survivor or witness to the previous night's tragedy.

Flesh had worked through the night and all that morning. She had not showered. A coworker had stopped at her house and returned with a change of clothes. Her hair was pulled back in a plain knot, she wore no makeup. Her eyes were red and swollen from bouts of crying.

Everyone who knew her or Roy stopped and offered a few words of condolence, or a supportive embrace. To their astonishment this neophyte prosecutor nicknamed Flesh, this sometimes ridiculed prosecutor because of her special treatment by Roy Pinter, was holding it together with a painful and professional maturity.

Paul Caruso sat in a booth and answered one exhausting question after another while Sancho Maria stood beside him with a hand resting on his shoulder that from time to time he reached up and held.

When Flesh entered the coffee shop Caruso was explaining how Dane had told him he was going back onto the houseboat to see if Roy Pinter was alive and could be rescued.

Flesh stood just off from this circle of questioners listening and occasionally an investigator who knew of Roy and her relationship would steal a glance, but when her eyes met theirs they would look away absently.

Flesh took Sergeant Farr by the arm, eased him back from that cadre of questioners and told him quietly that she needed to talk with him.

Near the front door she put her briefcase and extensive file down on the counter. "There's something I need to go over with you," she said.

"All right."

She opened her file. Sergeant Farr noticed faxed pages dense with notes and Post-its.

"The Coast Guard report says they reached the site at 12:13. Rudd fell from the plane maybe, what . . . a minute or two later."

"That has to be pretty close to right."

"Caruso landed here at 1:10 A.M."

"Give or take a few minutes."

"From Grizzly Bay to here, I am told, even at the slowest cruising speeds would take all of fifteen minutes."

"All right."

"So Caruso was up in the air for almost forty-five minutes after Rudd fell from the plane."

"Okay."

"There's a few questions my office would appreciate you asking Mr. Caruso."

PAUL." CARUSO turned to Sergeant Farr. "I want to review something with you, if I may." Paul nodded. "You said that Cessna radio was inoperable."

363

The cat Caruso had taken from the wall of his hangar and which had been on the booth seat beside him decided to leap on the table and have a few licks from Paul's coffee cup. Caruso told the investigators around him, "The little shit is a caffeine freak."

"Paul?"

Caruso watched the cat, stroked the cat as he spoke to Sergeant Farr. "It was damaged in one of the explosions."

Caruso lifted the cat away from the cup.

"But your handheld transceiver was working?"

He stared at the cat, felt the warmth of the sun on his hands in flooded bits of memory as Dane walked into the hangar that dusk.

"Paul?"

"It was working. Yes."

He was a man's voice and a boy's face and those sunglasses to protect the eyes.

"You were over the bay almost forty-five minutes . . . searching?"

"All right, Dane Rudd," Paul had said. "Let's you and I go up and chase that sunset." If he could only have that moment back, he thought, if he could only relive—

"Yes," said Caruso.

"How come you didn't use the transceiver to at least try and call in a Mayday?"

Paul Caruso held the cat against his chest and began to cry. His crying sounded like rainworn water over stones. Sancho Maria leaned down and whispered something unheard by those around them.

"I thought it wasn't working," Paul's voice shuddered. "I just screwed up, I guess. Maybe I panicked."

It was a moment pursued no further by anyone, at least not at the moment. Flesh walked past the table carrying her briefcase and file. She did not believe Mr. Caruso.

Paul wiped his eyes. Sancho Maria understood her husband was not crying because of what had been said. He was crying because he might have lost the son he could never have.

———

FLESH PASSED through the empty bar. Stopping, she glanced at all those cracked and stained portraits of mythology as The Burrow was one of the Delta's more well known eccentricities.

The television above the bar was on, but the sound had been muted. The station was turned to the news where divers slipped down into the shallows of Grizzly Bay looking for remains.

She felt a clammy dizziness come over her. The inside of her mouth turned to paste. She set her briefcase and file down on the bartop and held on for time to collect herself.

Sergeant Farr had followed her in. He put a hand on her back. "Would a drink help? I know I shouldn't be suggesting it, but—"

She shook her head refusing his offer. She turned away from the television and collected herself. "Paul Caruso," she said with quiet explicitness, "landed a plane on water, at night, in a mist, alongside two boats going up in flames. Does that sound like a man who'd 'screw up' or 'panic'? He did nine years in the Men's Colony, for Christ sake. He is one very-tough-fuck."

Sergeant Farr thought a moment, he glanced through the archway that led to the coffee shop where Paul Caruso continued to wipe his eyes.

"I believe he might have thought that since the radio wasn't working, the transceiver wasn't working. He might have. So much was happening so fast."

Flesh took her briefcase and file. On the wall beside the door she noticed a faded print where a father and son flew out of a stony prison on wings made from wax.

"What are you trying to get at?" Sergeant Farr asked.

"I don't believe," said Flesh, "Dane Rudd fell from that plane anymore than you or I."

CHAPTER SEVENTY—SIX

WHEN FLESH ARRIVED at Disappointment Slough there was a news chopper circling overhead all dark blue and black against the sky. The landing and dock site to the island had been cordoned off by a police barricade and Flesh had to ID herself to get through.

Just beyond the barricade people had pulled off the road and were stretched out along the berm in singles or small gaping clusters. Some had binoculars, some Instamatics. Others relied on their eyes.

As she was escorted to the island Flesh saw one civilian on a small daycruiser about fifty yards downstream. The man was videotaping her boat while he was being ordered back and Flesh regarded him with raw disgust, staring, hoping that he would zoom in on her up close so he could see her praying silently and viciously that some day it would be one of his lying dead in full view of a carrion curiosity.

THE INSIDE of the house was a hive of investigators. Flesh approached a lieutenant who was in charge of itemizing the forty to fifty other boxes that Essie had filled over time. These were to be brought from the island with everything else as possible evidence.

Flesh introduced herself then asked for Essie, as she had been told Essie was here to guide them in these issues. The lieutenant led Flesh to the kitchen and pointed through the open back door. "You'll see her up the hill. We gave her a little break."

Flesh put her briefcase and file down on the table, but before going out she just watched boxes be carried from the back bedroom and was struck by how much clandestine time and effort Essie had put into collecting all this for nearly half a year.

ESSIE WAS sitting against the stone well ledge smoking as Flesh made her way up through the thin briared footpath. The day was clear, the horizon so artistically marbled with clouds it had almost no right to be.

The two women embraced, they kissed. Flesh leaned back against the well ledge beside Essie. She rested her head on Essie's shoulder, Essie rested her head on Flesh's in a moment of shared human need and exhaustion. Of the telling acknowledgment about what they had been through.

The news chopper circled above, its propeller blades cutting the sky apart with noise. After a time Flesh said, "They haven't recovered the body yet."

"Roy," said Essie. She spoke with the sadness of a distant friend.

"Roy," said Flesh. And when the chopper moved into the far radius of its arc, Flesh added, "You know a lot more than you've admitted to, Essie."

Flesh stirred when Essie did not answer. Her head rose up. She leveled a gaze at the woman beside her she thought she knew so well.

"Not even remotely surprised by the question?" Flesh did not wait for a response she was certain she would not get. "I talked to the Dean of Princeton Law. He adamantly denies any knowledge of the incident Roy told me about that got Dane 'removed' from the university. Though he would acknowledge a D. Rudd studied law there for two years and left for unknown reasons. When I asked for his records I am told they no longer exist . . . the managing director at the eye bank gave me the complete stonewall and when I said I'd subpoena Dane's records he said, 'Contact the Justice Department.' "

Essie trimmed the lip of her cigarette on the well ledge. Flesh watched her friend's face for any sign of surprise.

"Do you remember William Hyde?" asked Flesh.

"He worked with Roy once. I think he joined the IRS."

"He's part of an HIDA task force now. He's been on the phones for me since last night. And you know what he told me about two hours ago? 'There are things going on here I can not, and will not discuss.' Does any of this come as a surprise . . . or shock?"

If unemotional silence to such a question was an answer, Flesh had been answered.

"You know, Essie, the FBI and the DEA will take someone facing an indictment and offer him, or her, a plea, immunity, the witness-protection program if they think they can use them in an investigation. And if this he, or she, has certain skills, or background, they'll press hard to get what they want . . . I feel it's possible when Dane Rudd arrived in Rio Vista that first day he was no innocent.

"If in fact that was his first day in Rio Vista. That he should just appear at the airport and strike up an acquaintance with the Carusos, who were not only good friends of Taylor's, but of yours, now seems highly suspect. And when I think back to his conversation the night of the tribute, it appears too incredibly pointed."

Essie handled Flesh's leveled stare and everything she said with a fixed and infuriating silence.

"I thought I knew you pretty well, Essie. But you surprise me. Keeping all those files. Secretly amassing information. Not knowing if or when it would be of any value. Even breaking into Nathan's computer at home. Never opening up to anyone . . . except him." Flesh cocked her head sideways and got her face close to Essie's. "Know what I think . . . I think you and Dane Rudd are a lot more alike than anyone would have ever expected. Would ever have guessed. The two of you could probably share one shadow, and I mean all that as a compliment. I swear I do."

Essie took one last hit off the cigarette, ground the stub into the stone ledge, then flicked it down into the well. "You're right, you know," she said. "Dane and I are a lot alike."

"You *are* . . . present tense. As in . . . ?"

Essie looked away, she took to watching the news chopper in its noisy circle above the slough.

"What else am I right about? Am I right about the possibility that Dane is still alive? That Paul Caruso landed him somewhere?"

The sun had moved across their faces and the muscles around Essie's eyes tightened in what looked to Flesh to be a graph of emotions from the dramatic to the introspective. "Roy would be proud of you, Francie. You make a very good prosecutor."

Flesh was taken aback. The statement drew down on her in half a dozen ways, telescoping into every inch of her personal and professional life, and now tragedy. She stood. She started to cry but she fought back the tears shaking her head, denying their existence. Essie grabbed her by the hand and held on. "I meant that as a compliment, you know. As a way of—"

Flesh shook her head, she knew. "I promised myself I would not cry until this was done. Then . . ." She wrung her loose hand as if she could shake the torment out through the fingertips. She daubed at the corners of her eyes with a crooked finger. "What else am I right about? Essie?"

From the kitchen door the lieutenant called up to the women letting them know he wanted Essie back down in the house. Flesh pointed to her watch and flashed her fingers for five more minutes.

"The newspaper you gave me," said Flesh. "I called the ex-wife of that agent killed less than two weeks before Taylor died. I asked her if she knew Dane Rudd. And you know what she said to me? Not, 'I never heard of him,' not 'I know him.' She said, 'That is not something I can, or will discuss.'

"It sounds to me, doesn't it, Essie, that she might have known him. Or at least what was going on here."

The chopper must have had enough footage for a little flash and carry for it started back across the Empire Tract. Soon, its noisy blades were no more.

"Maybe," said Essie, "he was just someone standing on a train platform when the express went by and chemicals were thrown in his face and he was left for blind. And who wanted what I want, what you want, what most everyone wants. And with a borrowed set of eyes, he tried—"

369

For the first time since they started talking Flesh saw Essie's lower jaw begin to tremor, her lips moved to speak but stopped short of words. From somewhere within Essie, all she knew and felt were finding their way, were leaving their mark, were making themselves known. She was now a living moment in the paper of their days.

Flesh knew to stop, she knew. "Inside of me, I feel . . . part of this is my fault. I worked Charles to back Roy and he used it. He used it."

"You can't expect to be able to hold it all there in your hands to see. You can't, Francie. No one can." Essie, when she told Flesh this, was thinking of Dane standing within the river beacon's light.

"If you get the chance," said Flesh, "before I do. Thank him for going back onto that houseboat and trying to find Roy." Flesh's voice broke down. "If I'm right, if you get the chance."

Essie was gazing down at the house and the slough beyond. Her voice drifted, sorrowfully, Flesh thought. "I'll do that." Essie looked back up at Flesh cupping a hand over her eyes to shield the sun. "If you don't mind, I'd like to be alone for a few minutes?"

"I'll see you at the house."

ESSIE WATCHED Flesh negotiate that woeful meander of a path down through the weeds and briars. Alone, the chopper gone, all that was left to fill in the quiet was that windmill wheel slowly moving on with the day.

She looked at the bare open slope, crepe soft in the light. She tried to fold back into the hours they lay there. To drift along the river of those emotions as they went from one port of heart to another.

It would be a matter of days, at most, before the truth were known, she knew. She was surprised the video of Taylor's tribute taken on the riverboat that first night had not fallen into some reporter's hands and made its way onto the six o'clock news. That alone would be enough. That too she knew would happen.

From her back jeans pocket Essie took Dane's letter and began to tear and retear it slowly into tiny pieces. She did not need it, she knew it by heart even before she'd ever read it.

The few missing details of anyone's life only touch upon the idea of who they are, or were. The doubt and dreams carved into their face say much more. What someone feels and thinks and does is what should be inscribed in lightning.

We are mere pauses, and like the windmill wheel moving across the eye of the sun in a blink we are there then gone, there then gone, there then gone. We count our miseries more easily than we do our blessings. We examine everything except ourselves. And we cannot acknowledge that we last not much longer than the average breeze.

Essie sat with the warmth on her face and watched Disappointment Slough carrying the sunlight on its back toward an outstretched country as it had done for centuries. We should all be as simple as water and as strong, but we are not. What we are is everything heartbreaking, and everything beautiful.

She then leaned around and took those bits of letter and dropped them into the well where they fell like flakes of light, tumbling and turning down into that dark stony portal until they were no more.

He would always be with them, she knew. The video alone would ensure it. He would be an image remembered, standing at the far corner of a darkened stage, with his head slightly bowed in a moment of mourning, his hands folded behind his back, waiting at the shadow of their lives. That, he had earned.

With all she wanted to give, with all she felt and wanted to say she but whispered into that well, "If you can hear me . . . we'll be all right."

Then she leaned back around the other way and looked up at that windmill wheel moving fanwise across the eye of the sun. She watched for timeless seconds and then in a voice light as ether told him again, "If you can hear me . . . we'll be all right."